ACKNOWLEDGMENTS

To my sisters: you have suffered through countless (and often scatterbrained) one-sided conversations in which I have spouted dozens of different ideas and narratives, yet you listened patiently and gave me your full attention and support. Each of you has, in your own way, given Lia a part of her character and strength, and I wouldn't have had a story if not for you.

To Nina and Mema: your opinions and feedback have been invaluable. Thank you for not only taking the time to read this story, but for discussing it with such excitement and energy.

To my husband: thank you for the late, sleepless nights you gave to help me through my creative process.

To Bethany, Camlyn, and Aunt Mary: your energy and encouragement have meant so much to me. Thank you for being such wonderful people!

To my friends and family (especially my beautiful daughter): I wish I could name each and every one of you. Thank you, from the bottom of my heart. I couldn't have done it without you.

And, last but definitely not least, I thank God for giving me what little talent I have. I hope I've truly done my best.

For Nathan and Nate:
I'll never forget you.

AUGUST SHADOW

BY
CHRISTINA J. THOMPSON

To GLENDAL

Safe & Happy
Travels!

Christine J. Thompson

PROLOGUE

LIA GREY WATCHED AS HER mother, Rachel, filled the last pie crust with sugared berries. She glanced out the window, tapping her foot impatiently. There was to be a party in town that night, and Lia had been kept home to help her mother bake pies for the celebration. It wasn't often that she was permitted to take a day off from working in the fields with her father, even a day spent working at home, and she was hopeful that she would have some time to herself before the evening's festivities. She reached into her apron pocket, feeling the cool surface of the silver half-token nestled there, and she thought of the candy she wanted to buy.

She glanced out the window again. It was already midafternoon. Rachel placed the pastry in the oven, then turned to look at Lia.

"Are we done?" Lia asked hopefully. Her mother nodded, and Lia bolted for the front door.

"Where are you going?" Rachel wanted to know.

"To town!" Lia answered, throwing the door open and running outside.

"Be back in time to get ready for the party!" Rachel called after her. "Don't be late!"

Lia clutched the small sack of molasses taffy she had bought, chewing slowly on a piece as she walked down the cobblestone street. The July sun was blistering hot, and she could just imagine how nice a swim would feel. She had a few hours left before she had to be home to get ready for the party, and she picked up her pace.

"If it isn't Lia!" a boy called out mockingly. Lia looked up to see a small group of boys standing near the blacksmith's shop. She scowled.

"Aren't you going to talk to us, Lia?" another boy called, snickering. "Come, now, we need something to entertain us!"

"Your ears aren't funny enough, Joseph?" Lia snapped, glaring at him. Joseph had massive ears, a feature that often made him the brunt of jokes. His smile froze on his face, and the other boys pointed at him and dissolved into cackles.

"You need to learn your place!" Joseph spat, muttering a curse. "A woman is to respect a man!"

"Let me know when you become a man," Lia laughed, rolling her eyes. "Then I'll show you what I think of your idea of respect!" His face turned red with anger at his friends' howls of glee.

"You're just a stupid wench!" he shouted. "Everyone knows it! Why don't you go take your place in the whore's alley with the rest of the worthless trash!"

"Say that again, dog!" Lia hissed, her blood growing hot. "I'll beat your face in!" Joseph laughed, nudging one of the boys.

"You see, Mark?" he crowed triumphantly. "I told you I'd get her going!" Mark smiled, his eyes bright as he watched Lia's face darken.

"Coward!" she screamed, dropping her sack of candy and stepping towards the boys. "I could whip you any day!" Joseph's face grew serious, and his eyes narrowed.

"I'd like to see you try!" he challenged, making a fist. "You're nothing but a weak little girl!"

"I'll show you weak!" Lia cried, lunging forward. In the blink of an eye, she snatched hold of Joseph's hair and swung her fist at his face.

"Now, hold on!" Mark yelled, grabbing Joseph and pulling him back. "You can't fight a girl!"

"Why not?" Joseph protested. "She's asking for it!"

"You can't *fight* her," Mark repeated, stressing his words. There was a mischievous look on his face. "So we'll just have to think of something else, won't we?"

"Like a contest?" Joseph asked. Mark nodded. Breathing hard as she glared at the boys, Lia laughed sarcastically.

"Just name it!" she scoffed. "I'll beat any one of you!" Mark looked around, still thinking, then his eyes brightened.

"A race!" he exclaimed. Lia grinned. She knew she was faster than Joseph.

"Where to?" Joseph demanded. Mark pointed.

"To the roof of the cobbler's shop!" he said. Lia glanced at where he was pointing.

The cobbler's shop was a small building, but its thatched roof was tall and steep, and she tried to hide her surprise and dismay. She didn't mind heights, but she knew it would be difficult to scale the slick, straw thatch, and falling would most definitely hurt. She swallowed hard. Joseph was portly and slow, and she was almost certain she could beat him.

"Fine!" Lia agreed, kicking her shoes off. Joseph looked nervous for a moment as he stared up at the roof, then he suddenly grinned.

"Aren't you forgetting?" he asked innocently. "You said you could beat any one of us!" Lia paused, cocking her head.

"So what if I did?" she snapped, confused.

"Well," Joseph began, looking away. "I twisted my ankle yesterday, so it wouldn't be fair if I ran. It was Mark's idea, so he's the one who should race." He smirked. "Unless, of course, you want to back out," he quickly added. Lia pursed her lips.

Mark was nineteen, four full years older than her. She felt a pang of nervous worry as she eyed him, sizing him up. He looked fast.

"You're stalling, Lia," Joseph prodded, taunting her. "Yes or no?" She stamped her foot.

"I don't care which one of you I beat!" she retorted. "Let's go!" The boys cheered, then pulled Mark into a huddle. After a few moments of hushed whispers, they broke apart, and Mark nodded that he was ready.

A starting line was quickly set, and Lia took her place beside Mark. They exchanged a glance.

"You won't win," he told her confidently. She sneered.

"We'll see about that!" she replied. She crouched down, readying herself as her heart began to pound with anticipation.

"On the count of five," Joseph called out, and Lia took a deep breath, concentrating as she listened for his voice.

"One...two...FIVE!"

Mark bolted towards the cobbler's shop. Confused for a moment, Lia didn't move, then, realizing what had happened, she screamed a curse and launched herself forward.

She reached the cobbler's shop only a moment after Mark, jumping to catch the edge of the roof with her hands. She frantically searched for a handhold, then, finding one, she pulled herself up. She wasn't strong enough; she could feel her arms begin to burn almost instantly as they threatened to give way, and she clenched her teeth, commanding her muscles to work. She managed to get her knee over the edge just enough to give her the leverage she needed, then she glanced at Mark. He was having trouble, and she grinned with wild-eyed excitement. He was going to lose, she just knew it!

Clawing and thrashing, Lia climbed up the steep slope on her hands and knees. She was almost there, and she let out a cry of determination as she pushed herself the last few feet.

With a shout of triumph, Lia reached the roof's peak a split second before Mark.

"I won!" she crowed, her eyes dancing. She could hear the disappointed calls of the other boys, but she ignored them, grinning broadly at Mark. "You cheated and I still won!"

"I suppose so," he admitted after catching his breath. "Congratulations, you won fair and square." He gave her a half-hearted smile, extending his hand.

"You better believe I did!" she laughed smugly, shaking his hand. "I told you I could!"

"Stupid wench!" Joseph's voice called from the ground. "Push her off, Mark!"

"Yeah, push her off!" the other boys yelled in agreement. "Push her off!"

Her heart stopped in her chest, and her eyes locked with Mark's. Her skin flushed with fear. The roof was high, too high. He was still shaking her hand, and she felt his grip tighten as he smirked slightly.

Lia wrenched away, yanking out of his grasp. Her hand came free too easily; he wasn't holding her as tightly as she had thought. The force of her movement caused her to lose her balance, and her stomach dropped as her arms spun in a wild circle, trying, desperately, to catch herself. But it was too late.

The world went silent. Lia held her breath, feeling her muscles tense with anticipation, and she grasped at the air, searching for something, anything, to slow her fall. Her fingers ripped at the straw thatch, sending bits and pieces raining down with her, but there was nothing to grab hold of. She closed her eyes.

Her face exploded with a blinding, nauseating pain. Every bit of breath was knocked from her lungs, and her body felt as though it had been smashed apart. She wanted to scream, but she couldn't move a single muscle.

Finally, she let out a rasping cough as she sucked in a breath, then another, and she tried to focus. Rolling onto her side, she groaned with pain, forcing herself to sit up. She ran her hands over her body, checking to make sure she was still in one piece, then she reached up to touch her face.

Sticky, warm liquid gushed from her nose, and she couldn't help letting out a quiet whimper. She was lucky; her bleeding nose seemed to be the most severe injury caused by the fall.

She heard a thump beside her, and she looked up with watering eyes to see Mark's concerned face.

"Are you all right?" he gasped worriedly, reaching out to touch her. Lia forgot her pain in an instant.

"You bastard!" she hissed, struggling to her feet.

"You pulled away," Mark stammered in protest, standing with her. "I wasn't going to do it, I swear!"

"Liar!" Lia screamed. She swung at him and missed.

"I'm sorry!" he exclaimed, moving out of her reach. "I wasn't going to!"

"What's going on?" a man's voice demanded, and Lia spun around to see Ben Samuels, Mark's father. Joseph and the other boys had started to move in for a closer look, but they scattered at the sight of Ben.

"He threw me from the roof!" Lia shrieked, cursing as she charged at Mark again. He turned to run, and, infuriated, she picked up a rock.

"Bastard!" she screamed, throwing the rock at Mark. It narrowly missed him, and she reached for another, bigger one. He glanced behind him, and his eyes grew wide at the sight of her. He froze mid-stride, a stunned look on his face.

Summoning all her strength, Lia hurled the rock, watching as it sailed through the air. A loud crack rang out as it connected with Mark's head, followed by a howl of pain as he doubled over, clutching at his ear. She could see blood leaking through his fingers and running down his neck, and she smiled with satisfaction. She bent down to take hold of another rock, but she felt Ben Samuel's hand on her arm, stopping her.

Ben pointed at Mark and gave him a stern look.

"Go home, boy!" he commanded. Mark instantly obeyed, wincing as he tried to staunch the blood gushing from his ear. Ben turned to Lia.

"Are you all right?" he asked, his voice gentle. She nodded quickly.

"I'm fine now," she snapped, seething as she watched Mark leave. Ben shook his head.

"I'll walk you home," he said. "Just to make sure."

"I already told you, I'm fine!" she insisted, backing away. "I'm fine! Just leave me alone!"

Ignoring Ben's concerned face, Lia retrieved her bag of candy from where she had dropped it and started for home.

• • •

CHAPTER ONE

SUNLIGHT SPILLED OVER HER as the early morning mist began to dissipate. She hovered between waking and sleep, listening to the cheerful singing of the trickling creek. The grass around her was wet with dew, and the folds of her dress were still cool from the night's passing. The reeds moved slowly in the morning breeze, and various insects were already beginning to hum. Sickly sweet and thick, the fragrance of June flowers filled the air, mingling with the fishy odor of the water. Lia loved the peace of the cool of the morning, and she wished she could stay there forever.

There had been a summer celebration in town the night before, and she had escaped the festivities the moment the opportunity had arisen. Lighthearted with her stolen freedom and running as fast as her legs could carry her, she had made her way to the creek. The creek was her haven, her place of refuge, and Lia had fallen asleep to the whisper of reeds and the croaking of frogs.

The sound of rustling footsteps drifted towards her, and she snapped awake. Rubbing the last dwindling moments of sleep from her eyes, she searched the creek's bank for the source of the sound, her heart beginning to race.

"Did you get a good look, whoever you are?" Lia called out defiantly, searching the folds of her dress for her dagger.

Her fingers found the smooth handle of her weapon and she leaped to her feet, brandishing the small knife. Her heart jumped into her throat as a figure stepped out of the tall weeds a few yards away, then she rolled her eyes when she recognized him. It was Mark Samuels, her betrothed. She should have known.

"Good morning," Mark greeted her cheerfully. He smiled, an innocent look on his tanned face, and Lia felt her lips curl with scorn.

"What do you want, Mark?" she asked flatly. He shrugged.

"I didn't see you last night," he said, walking towards her. "At the party."

"I wasn't there," Lia snapped, glaring at him. "How did you find me?"

Mark was close now, and she could clearly see him. He was tall, and his blue eyes were striking in contrast to his dark hair. His body was toned and thickly muscled from working at his father's blacksmith shop, and the other girls in town found him very handsome. Not Lia, though. She couldn't stand him.

"I just looked for you," he answered simply, shrugging again. He chuckled, smiling wider. "Will you put the knife down, Lia? You look ridiculous, you know. Your hair!"

He pointed, and her girlish vanity took over for a moment as she reached up and felt the wayward strands of her chestnut tresses. Her tightly wrapped hair had fallen into a tangled mess, and she knew she must look terrible.

Lia tucked her knife back into her dress and crossed her arms.

"Maybe I didn't want you to look for me, Mark! Did you ever consider that?" She scoffed. Of course he hadn't, why on earth would he consider what *she* wanted? "I have to go, I'm late for work." She turned and briskly walked away.

"Lia, wait!" Mark ran to her side and reached for her hand. Catching it, he pulled her to a stop. "Can't we talk for a bit?"

"What makes you think I want to talk to you?" Lia spat, trying to pull free of his grasp. "Just leave me alone!"

"But I *need* to talk to you," Mark insisted, his voice low. "I've been thinking about what to say to you for quite some time. I want to tell you…." His voice trailed off, and she looked up at his face. He was nervous, the side of his neck pulsing with each quick beat of his heart. Lia tensed.

"Mark, I have to go," she repeated. "Really, I'm late!" Jerking away, her hand suddenly came free, and she stumbled back. Mark reached for her, and her flailing hands instinctively grabbed hold of his. The weight of her fall was too much, and she and Mark landed in a heap in the tall grass.

Lia could feel his body against hers as they lay there, stunned by the fall. She opened her tightly clenched eyes to see his slate-blue gaze looking down at her. He seemed frozen in place, and she realized that he was holding his breath.

"Get off me!" she gasped, kicking at him. "Get off!" Mark didn't move, and she kicked again. He stared down at her, a dazed expression on his face.

Freeing her hand from where it was pinned by her side, she brought it hard against his cheek, breaking his gaze.

"Are you okay?" he asked, recovering quickly. He leaped to his feet and grasped her hand to help her up. Lia stood and brushed at her long, grass-stained skirts.

"I am now that you're not crushing me!" she huffed. Spinning around, she began walking again.

She glanced back after a few moments, and she was relieved to see that Mark wasn't following. He just stood there, watching her leave. She sighed and made a face.

Mark had lived in Brunbury for as long as Lia could remember, and they had played together as children. Then, when he turned twelve, his father began teaching him the trade of blacksmithing. She had gone on to work in her family's fields, and she had all but forgotten about him until almost a year ago, on the day he had pushed her from the roof of the cobbler's shop.

He had bloodied her face, and she had chased him, pelting him with rocks, until one throw split his ear open. Mark would forever carry the scar, a constant reminder of what he had done to her. On that day, she had vowed to hate him, and she would not easily forget that she had been forced to attend a party in town that same night wearing the cuts and bruises he had caused.

To her utter horror and dismay, Mark had arrived at her father's door only a few days later to ask for her hand. Her father had readily agreed to the marriage, thrilled that his daughter had managed to catch the eye of the blacksmith's son, but Lia was far from happy. She couldn't understand why Mark had so suddenly and inexplicably taken an interest in her, and his proposal did little more than strengthen her hatred for him.

There was nothing she could do to escape the arranged marriage, though. The townspeople believed that infidelity was the only reason for withdrawing a marriage oath, even if they were told otherwise, and the gossip that would result from such an event would undoubtedly send a woman into the streets to make her living as a whore. Whores were of less worth than dogs; they were forbidden from being seen in the town during the day, forced to earn their bread by selling themselves in the whore's alley each night.

Lia despised the townspeople and their ridiculous opinions, and she was known for disregarding many of their ideas regarding the proper behavior of a woman. She gave no thought to doing outside chores in her nightdress, nor did she consider it wrong to go swimming by herself. She wandered alone in the hills, and she had a quick tongue and fiery wit that she used often. These offenses had earned her a questionable reputation with the townspeople, but the thought of being labeled a whore was enough to scare even her. She knew she was trapped, and as the year had passed she had spitefully come to accept that she would have to marry Mark when the time came.

As if the knowledge that she would be forced to marry him wasn't enough, the past year had been made even worse by Mark's suffocating presence. He followed Lia everywhere; he was a shadow she couldn't shake no matter how hard she tried, and her refusal of his attempts to spend time with her or talk to her had done little to keep him away. She couldn't even escape him at her creek, the one place she had managed to keep secret from him up until now. Cursing under her breath, she climbed the last hill that stood between her and her home.

Lia crested the hill and looked down upon the town of Brunbury. Located on a busy travelling road, the town was always abuzz with people passing through. The town itself was small, only a handful of buildings and shops to speak of, but it was growing slowly and steadily as those who stopped for a rest decided to settle there. Her parents had done the same thing before she was born, and it was the only place she had ever known.

From where she stood, she could see the dark, thatched roof of the Laughing Vixen Tavern and Inn where she worked, which was close to the outskirts of town, and a glance to the north revealed a tall plume of gray smoke wisping from the chimney of her home. She was dirty and barefoot, and a shielded glance at the sun confirmed that she was, indeed, very late. She knew her employer, Jem, would be livid.

The morning was already uncomfortably warm, and as Lia began to sweat under the heat of the sun she thought of her father, John Grey, whom she knew had been working their family's plot of land since sunrise. If not for her job at the tavern she would be working alongside him in the fields, and she started running.

• • •

CHAPTER TWO

_____

LIA AND HER PARENTS lived just outside of town, as did all the farmers. Their home was small, with only a living area, kitchen, and a single bedroom, and a loft which was Lia's room. The thatched roof leaked often, and the weathered, gray wood of the home was old and musty smelling. Large pieces of chinking had long since cracked and fallen out of the gaps between the boards of the walls, and during the winter months every snowy morning would bring miniature snow drifts lined up neatly on the floor where the wind had blown the icy, white powder in. It was Lia's home, though, and the rotting mess of a building was still comfort to her.

Lia burst through the front door. Her mother was kneading dough for the day's bread on the rough-hewn kitchen table, and she gave Lia a hard look.

"Where were you all night?" Rachel demanded, sweat beading off of her forehead as she pummeled the dough with her strong hands. "And what did you do to yourself? Why are you so filthy?"

Lia didn't answer, and she rushed up the ladder to her room to get dressed for work. She caught of glimpse of herself in her mirror, and was surprised at how disheveled she was. Mark had been right to call her hair ridiculous.

Her dress was still damp, and the grass had left green streaks on the fabric. She slipped out of the stained skirts, pulled her work dress on and laced up the bindings, then ran her comb through her hair in an attempt to tame the mess it had become. She glanced at the mirror a second time.

She knew most people found her attractive, and she was proud of the fact that when she walked into a room she drew the attention of all the menfolk that might be present. They admired her looks, which had added to her poor reputation with the townspeople. But while she was fully aware of how men viewed her, and she was not above batting her eyes to get what she wanted, she didn't think much of her appearance outside of the attention it brought. Now, as she gazed at her reflection, Lia wondered if she really was beautiful. She touched her cheek.

To her mind, her appearance was not altogether unappealing, but she had never considered herself beautiful. Her hair was long and straight, and the dark brown shone a fiery auburn in the sun. Her deep, brown eyes were always alight with emotion, even now. She had a full figure for someone her age; she was only about five months shy of seventeen, yet she held the appearance of a grown woman. Her body was soft and full, the result of the light work she did at the tavern and the ready access to the meals she prepared there. Her hands were strong and smooth; the old calluses caused by the field work she'd done before taking her job at the tavern had since healed and disappeared. She was neither tall nor short, an average height for a woman. She stared at herself, trying to find a word to describe what she saw.

"I'm beautiful," she whispered, then shook her head. No, that wasn't right. She smiled mockingly at her reflection, and her smooth, perfect teeth shone white between her soft, pink lips.

Lia moved towards her bedroom window and threw open the shutters. There was a small, cast-iron bluebird sitting on her windowsill, its head tilted back and its beak open in song, and she made a face. Almost every day for the past year, Mark had been using any spare time he had at work to make little charms and figurines for her, and he left them on her windowsill each morning for her to find. The knowledge that she couldn't even escape him in the safety of her own bedroom made him that much more intolerable, and she had come into the habit of tossing the useless gifts into the ditch next to the road on her way to work each morning.

"LIA!"

She jumped at her mother's call.

"Coming, Mum!" Lia answered. She turned and clambered down the ladder. "I'm going to work," she said as she ran past her mother, who was shaping the last of the bread dough into loaves. Rachel paused to pinch Lia's cheek.

"You're late, Lia," she chastised. "You must beg Jem not to fire you! You're late too often, child!" Lia ran through the door and onto the dusty road, wiping away the smudge of flour she knew her mother had left on her cheek and turning towards the tavern.

The Laughing Vixen did not live up to its lighthearted name. It was a dismal place, a dark, aged, wooden building that stank of ale and urine and stale visitors. A tall monstrosity of a structure, the owner, Jem, had crafted the upper level into a vile maze of tiny, misshapen rooms that were rented by drunk patrons and tired travelers each night. He offered the cheapest rooms in town, which resulted in every type of miscreant and assorted passers-through flocking in droves to stay there.

A night's board would guarantee a patron just enough floor space to sleep, but nothing more. One might fare better sleeping on the streets; many a soul was found the morning after a drunken stupor with his throat cut and his valuables, whatever he may have had, stolen. Because of the tavern's reputation, Jem only offered rooms to men, as was prominently stated on a sign in front of the building. This did not deter business, however, and the tavern always had more customers than it could ever want.

Upon entering the tavern, Lia was met with Jem's angry roar.

"You useless whore!" he bellowed, thundering towards her. "I went without my bread this morning!"

"You can stand to miss a meal, you old fool!" Lia quipped, laughing as she backed away.

Jem was a fat man, always red-faced, and his rat-like eyes shone like polished, black buttons when he was angry or excited. She did not make a habit of being late, but in the year she had been working for him she had come to know what to expect when she angered him. He would pant after her, laboriously breathing as his whole body jiggled and shook with rage. He would tire quickly, then catch his breath while drinking the mug of ale she would bring to him before she went about doing her work.

"Filthy wench!" Jem howled, his heavy frame rocking from side to side as he moved. "I'll beat you till you bleed!" Lia laughed as she darted away, nimbly pouring a mug of ale and setting it on the table separating her from the red-faced giant. Jem snatched the mug, glaring at her as he drank, and Lia chuckled triumphantly as she made her way to the kitchen to start the day's work.

She enjoyed cooking, and she was good at it, which was a rare talent. The tavern's kitchen was large and spacious, the only area of the tavern that could be called clean. Shelves of spices, vegetables, and other pantry supplies lined the walls, and every day Lia would buy a large portion of meat from the butcher. Jem had gone himself that morning, no doubt cursing the entire way as he waddled to the butcher's shop, and he had left a bloody shank of paper-wrapped goat on her worktable. Laughing quietly at the image of Jem's angry and exhausted face, she quickly busied herself carving and cutting the necessities for a pot of stew and kneading dough for loaves upon loaves of fresh bread.

Only a handful of men trickled into the tavern during the day, most preferring to save their coins for a hearty dinner rather than a simple lunch. Unlike the evening meal, which Lia would personally serve, for lunch she would set out a heaping tray of bread and cheese along with a pitcher of ale. The customers would serve themselves while Lia hid in the kitchen, working quickly to make ready for the large crowd and empty stomachs the night would bring.

She loved working at the tavern, and she was comfortable in the company of the strange men that filled it every night. She was lucky to have gotten the job in the first place; women didn't go near the tavern as it was considered inappropriate, but Lia's excuse was that the tavern must have a cook, and it seemed that her reasoning was a sufficient explanation to avoid most reproach. Her evenings were full of stories of violence and heartbreak as the men's tongues, loose with drink, spouted off their most painful and wretched memories: the spurn of women, the comfort of whores, the agony of their life's wanderings. She would scurry from table to table with her pitcher of ale, happily drinking in every word.

More importantly, though, working there provided a welcome relief from the disapproving eyes and constantly wagging tongues of the townspeople. The men liked her, and Lia knew they wouldn't speak of her playful antics outside the walls of the tavern and risk getting her in trouble. She would dance and joke with the men without a second thought; she was safe there, free to behave however she liked without fear of the townspeople's gossip.

As the sun set, the tavern filled with its usual crowd of customers, and Lia was kept busy serving the various patrons. The room was sweltering with the combined body heat of the men, and the yellow lanternlight appeared hazy as the air thickened with vapor rising from the sweat that poured from every brow. Lia, too, was drenched from the heat, but the men often said it was her sweat that perfumed the place, making them forget their own stink. She would laugh at their comments, then retort that it was the ale that made them forget their odor, because she was not drunk and could smell them perfectly well.

Lia stepped into the kitchen to refill her pitcher of ale. She hadn't been gone more than a few moments when she heard a rousting cry come from the drunk men, all of them calling for the 'ale-wench', as she had been fondly nicknamed. She grinned and walked out of the kitchen, wondering what the men were up to.

As she passed through the doorway, she found herself scooped up onto the shoulders of several burly men, her pitcher disappearing, and the room filled with a loud cheer. Her face was bright with excitement, and her laugh, mingling with the calls of the men, carried into the streets.

"Dance for us, Ale-Wench!" someone yelled, and the others took up the call. She was set down, and she raised her hands for silence. The room quieted to a dull roar.

"How am I to dance without music?" Lia asked playfully, hands on her hips. They laughed, slapping their knees, then the men began to clap and stomp out a rhythm. They started singing, their voices as steady as their intoxicated steps.

Lost in the uproarious sound, the men began to dance, holding onto each other's shoulders for support. Lia laughed, tapping her feet and holding her skirts high as she jumped into the fray. She threw her head back in delight as she spun and stomped, the ale mugs sitting empty and forgotten as she danced.

The men tried to dance with her, draping themselves over her and trying to keep up with her movements. One man took tight hold of her hand, and, after managing a wobbly bow, began to move about with her, his feet matching time with hers. She gave a slight curtsy as she pranced, and he spun her about with gusto.

Lia's eyes were wild with excitement when she caught a glimpse of Mark, who was sitting quietly in the corner of the tavern. He watched her with piercing eyes, and she met his gaze defiantly as she romped. She didn't care if he saw her cavorting with the men; he had seen her dancing many times in the past, and she knew that he, like the other men, would never speak of anything she did that might be considered questionable. Mark didn't look away, and when the dance finally ended Lia went back to making the rounds with her pitcher of ale. When she looked again, he was gone.

As usual, the upstairs rooms were filled by night's end, and, after counting the day's earnings, Lia bid good night to Jem.

"Don't be late again, girl," Jem sang in a gruff, ale-tainted voice as he pulled her close. Lia kissed his cheek and turned to leave.

"I won't, for fear you may starve to death, fat beast!" she retorted as the door closed behind her.

Lia frowned disdainfully, hearing the slow footsteps behind her as she walked home.

"You can come out, Mark," she called spitefully. The footsteps quickened, and Mark was soon at her side.

"Are you still mad at me?" he asked uneasily. "From this morning?" Lia rolled her eyes.

"I'm always mad at you," she answered. "You just don't seem to understand that." Mark appeared to relax.

"I understand," he told her matter-of-factly. "I just don't care." Lia scoffed.

"Then why did you even bother to ask?"

"Well, when you're really angry you throw things at me." Mark's words were cautious, and he eyed her, cringing as he spoke.

"As if that would make any difference!" Lia cried. "You still follow me no matter what I do! If you must walk with me, can you at least do it without talking?" Mark didn't answer.

Crickets chirped in the tall grasses lining the road, and the tiny flashing lights of fireflies filled the night. The wet smell of soggy weeds hung thick in the air, the result of stagnant water from the last rain gathering in the overgrown ditches. They walked in silence for a while before Mark spoke again.

"I saw you dancing tonight," he informed her, his voice even.

"I know you did," Lia snapped. "You see everything I do." She walked faster, not wanting to talk, but Mark didn't take her hint.

"You don't mind dancing with the men," Mark began pointedly. "But you won't even talk to me. Why?" Lia glared at him.

"You know why!" she shot back, anger rising in her voice. "I can't stand you! How many times do I have to tell you that?"

"But if you'd only listen, Lia," Mark gently reasoned. "I've been wanting to tell to you why I –"

"I'm home now, Mark," Lia interrupted, pointing at her house. They were nearly there, thankfully. "I have to go."

Mark's nervous explanation was cut short at her words, and he stood there a moment, speechless. A good-natured smile quickly lit up his face, and he waved her to go on.

"I'll talk to you tomorrow," he told her.

"Of course you will," Lia responded mockingly. "I have no doubt." She went into the house without another word.

• • •

CHAPTER THREE

THE NEXT DAY FOUND LIA alone in the hills. She didn't have to work, as Jem was kind enough to let her have one day a week for herself.

"I'm tired, Jem," she had said to him after working for two months without a single day of rest. "I must have a break!" Jem had shaken his head.

"Your cooking makes me too much money, girl!" he had told her. Lia stamped her foot.

"You old goat! I don't give a damn about your money!" she had hollered, making his face turn a deeper shade of red. "I am asking you for rest, and I will have it!" She stood on her toes, waving her finger in his face. Jem, of the mind that it would be better to freely give rather than to have something taken, quickly agreed, and Lia was permitted to keep every seventh day to herself.

Lia wandered the hills that surrounded the town, rolling in the fragrant grasses of the meadows and reclining to stare up at the clouds. She loved being outside, she loved the freedom of being alone. She breathed deeply of the scent of the flowers she crushed as she lay, and she closed her eyes against the sun as it brightly peeked out from behind a quickly moving cloud. The pink and orange sunlight that glowed through her closed eyelids faded as another cloud moved into place, and she opened her eyes. It was not a cloud.

"Mark!" Lia screeched, the quick thrill of fear from her surprise at seeing him dissipating. "What are you doing here!" It was not a question; it was a statement marked with her clear annoyance and anger at his presence. "Is there nowhere I can go to be rid of you?" The last part was more of a wail, a groan of exasperation.

Mark didn't answer, stepping back and offering his hand to help her stand to her feet. She refused to take it, standing unassisted, but Mark wasn't paying attention. He looked absent, deep in thought, and Lia waited impatiently for him to respond.

"Well?" she prodded. "Aren't you even going to apologize? You scared me to death!" Mark swallowed hard.

"I'm sorry," he said quickly.

"You're not forgiven!" she told him angrily. "Go away!"

"I need to talk to you, Lia," he answered, his voice quiet but firm. She put her hands on her hips, sighing in frustration.

"What could possibly be so important?" she asked. "Just leave me alone, Mark, that's all I want!"

"Please," Mark said, his face set with determination. "I'll leave, but only after you listen." She thought a moment, then stiffly waved him on.

"Lia, we've been engaged for a while now," he began, his words sticky and dry with nervousness. "And this whole time I've been trying to find a way to tell you why I love you." He paused, taking a deep breath. "Do you remember the day you fell from the roof of the cobbler's shop?"

Her eyes grew wide, her blood instantly boiling.

"How could I forget?" she snarled. Of all the things for him to bring up, *this* is what he chose?

"I remember the way you looked standing there, the rage on your face–"

"You mean blood?" she interjected. Mark ignored her, refusing to be discouraged.

"There was something about how proud you were, standing there throwing rocks at me," he continued. He paused again, searching for the words to say, and Lia impatiently gestured for him to hurry.

"I've loved you ever since," he finally said. "Your fire....your spirit....." His voice tapered off, and he looked at her expectantly.

"That's it?" she asked mockingly. "You've had all this time to think of what to say, and *that's* all you come up with?" Mark's face turned red. She pursed her lips. He had said he wanted to talk, and talk was what she would give him.

"Not that you care, but I stopped wondering why I was cursed with your so-called *love* a long time ago," Lia told him, her eyes flashing with anger. "It doesn't matter what the reasons were. Nothing you say or do will change the fact that I'm engaged to you, unless you want to do me a favor and die! I have only a few months of freedom left, and all I care about is spending that time without *you* bothering me!"

"I'm not trying to upset you, Lia." Mark tried to calm her, but she would not be calmed.

"Well, you have!" she shouted, and the trees rustled with the sound of startled birds taking flight at her voice. "You talk about that day with fondness? You actually think that what happened that day was a good thing?"

"I didn't say that!" he protested, but she silenced him with a look.

"I'll tell you what I remember from that day, Mark! I remember my father beating me because of my blood-soaked dress! I remember being forced to go to that damn party even though I could barely see out of the two black eyes *you* gave me! I remember hearing everyone whispering and laughing at me! The only good memory I have of that day is the sound of your scream when that rock hit you in the head!" Lia grinned at the thought, picturing the blood gushing from the side of Mark's head, then she scowled.

"I can't stand you!" she cried. "But no matter what I do I can't seem to convince you to leave me alone!" She fumed, her hands clenched. Mark was silent, staring at his feet, then his eyes lifted to meet hers.

"So all of your scorn is because of that day?" he asked, his face smoldering in disbelief. "That was so long ago, Lia! Can you really hate me that much over something as petty and insignificant as a bloodied nose?"

"Insignificant!" Lia's eyes bulged, and her face contorted with rage. "I was mortified, you bastard! Then you, the last boy I wanted attention from, had the *gall* to lay claim to me only a few days later? I've not had a moment to myself ever since! Not a single day goes by without you trailing me!"

Her shoulders heaved. It took every ounce of her strength to contain herself, to keep herself from ripping his face apart. Stomping her foot, she spat a curse and spun on her heel to leave.

"Stop, Lia," Mark said, and she felt his hands take hold of her. He turned her around to face him. "I'm sorry. Please, can't you understand? I just–!"

"Let me go, Mark!" Lia hissed dangerously, her eyes narrowing as she glared at him. "I don't want to hear it! Just be happy knowing that no matter what I want I'll still have to marry you!" His face fell.

"But I don't want–"

"I don't care what you want!" she screamed. "Let me GO!"

She wrenched away, trying to free herself from his grasp, and when he wouldn't release her she withdrew her dagger from her skirts. She swung at him and missed, then swung again. Mark dodged, losing his grip on her, and she pushed him away with all her might. Holding her knife at arm's length, Lia cautioned him.

"I'll not be handled that way!" she warned fiercely. Mark's face softened, and he smiled wryly.

"See, Lia?" he said quietly, gesturing. "See? This is why I love you. This is why I will never stop loving you." Lia couldn't believe what she was hearing.

"What are you talking about, you lunatic?" she snapped. "You're completely insane! How can you love me because I threaten you? How can you love me because I hate you?" Mark just stood there, his eyes bright.

"Don't you understand, Lia?" he asked. "I love you because of who you are. You're beautiful to me." She shook her head in disbelief, but something in his tone struck her.

Beautiful.

She was beautiful to him, and he meant it wholeheartedly.

"You're crazy!" she shouted, backing away. "You're crazy, that's what you are!" She turned and ran.

• • •

CHAPTER FOUR

THE NEXT FEW WEEKS passed quickly, and the sweltering heat of mid-August burned throughout the day only to spill over into wretchedly warm nights. Lia tried to lose herself in her work, but she couldn't help brooding on Mark and what he had said about his reasons for loving her. Everyone in the town, even her own parents, had always been so critical of her. Mark, however, not only thought of her as beautiful, but the very things other people found fault with he professed to love about her.

She couldn't make sense of Mark's logic, and as the days passed she became even more intolerant of him. She refused to speak even a single word to him, and when he walked her home each night she forced him to walk on the opposite side of the road in complete silence. He pretended not to notice, and her increased efforts to convince him to leave her alone were, unsurprisingly, ignored.

Just like every year, Brunbury saw even more travelers in the late summer. The tavern was likewise especially busy each night, and so was Lia. Her spirits were high as she went about her work, moving from table to table to serve the men, glad that when she was at the tavern she could relax and enjoy herself. But no matter the lightheartedness she felt there, her momentary happiness was always dampened when she caught a glimpse of Mark's ever-present figure lurking in a dusty, shadowed corner of the tavern. He came and went each night, making himself a quiet part of the tavern's woodwork as he hid behind the drunken men and chaotic bustle of the place, watching her with unwavering, awestruck eyes. She did her best to pretend he wasn't there.

When Lia had first started working at the tavern, she had been shocked and dismayed to find that many of the men thought highly of trying to steal a kiss or a pinch of her backside as she passed by them with her heavy, round serving tray laden with food. But as time passed, and she grew accustomed to the tavern's atmosphere, she realized that the men were just being playful in their drunkenness. Although she still protested the customers' pinches, she had come into the habit of offering a smile and a peck on the cheek to any man willing to toss her a silver half-token, money that Jem let her keep in addition to her weekly pay.

Most of the patrons realized immediately that she was not for sale like the street whores, but on some nights there would be a gentleman or two who wanted more than a kiss for his coin. One uncharacteristically cool evening was such a night, and as she passed a table she felt strong hands around her waist.

"Come to me, pretty one!" a rough, drunken voice sang. She found herself sitting on the lap of a burly, red-bearded man, his dark eyes shining at her from a pock-marked face crowned by a greasy shock of hair. "And what will my token buy tonight? Just a kiss?" He leaned towards her, his breath rank with ale, waving a token pinched between his fingers in front of her face. She smiled good-naturedly while holding her breath.

"You let me go, friend," she said, trying to stand. "I'll not have any of that nonsense." His hands held her tight, and she could feel him searching her skirts. She tried to pull away.

"There are women in the streets, drunken lout!" she told him, slapping at his hands. "Go visit one of them, they'll have your token and give you your wants!" The man ignored her, growing impatient, and he yanked Lia's skirt up over her knee to get to her skin.

Without a moment's hesitation, Lia took hold of his ale mug and swiftly brought it down upon his head with a loud crack, and when he released her to clamp his hands to his bleeding skull she hopped off of his lap, his dropped token clutched in her hand. Howling with agony, the man stood, holding his head in both hands while jumping up and down in pain.

"You teasing whore!" the man screamed, reaching for her. "I'll beat the hide from your back! Give me my coin!" She dodged around the table, her eyes alight with fire.

"I'll not have that, you ugly beast!" Lia exclaimed, reaching out to take the mug someone at another table gleefully offered her. "You leave me to myself and go visit the whores in the streets! I'll keep your token for the trouble!" The tavern's patrons, amused by the antics, burst into laughter.

Enraged, the bleeding man paused to think, realizing immediately that he was the brunt of the laughter ringing in his hot, purple ears. Seeming to accept his defeat, the man sat, blood dripping down his dirt-smeared face, and called for a refill of his mug. The other men, disappointed to see that the excitement was over, turned back to their meals.

"Come here, girl," crowed a tall, toothless man. "I'll just have the kiss, if you'll give it!" Lia laughed heartily and leaned in, pecking the old man's grizzled cheek. Her eyes shone brightly as the bloodied, redheaded brute watched her.

"And you can keep your coin, sir!" she said, refusing to take the half-token the old man offered her. "A gentleman, you are!" She spun on her heel, laughing, but in an instant her voice caught in her throat.

Mark was standing near the door, and her smile faded from her lips when she saw him. His face was drawn, and she could see the muscles in his jaw and neck flexing even from where she stood. His intensity shocked her, and her heart raced for a moment as her cheeks flushed. He turned to leave, his fists tightly clenched, and the door slammed behind him with such force she could hear it even above the din of the tavern.

Lia sneered, her bitterness rising up in her again. She imagined that Mark had envisioned himself her rescuer, ready to save her from the now-bleeding bruin and thereby winning her heart and admiration forever.

Well, I didn't need your help, now did I! she thought to herself proudly, making her way about the tavern to collect the used dishes. *That bastard's head won't soon forget me!*

The evening passed without further incident, and Lia couldn't help smiling to herself every time she saw the red-bearded man glaring at her. She cleaned up as the tavern slowly emptied, and before long she had finished her duties, waved farewell to Jem, and started for home.

The air outside was cool, a stark contrast to the warmth of the day and the heat of the tavern, and Lia could almost see the vapor of her breath. She looked around, the light of the full moon illuminating the road. She shivered, an odd feeling creeping up her spine. Shaking her head, she began to walk.

"A lovely night," Lia said aloud. She picked up her pace, walking briskly towards her home. She passed the blacksmith's shop, and she could see the red embers that remained from the forge's fire glowing in the dark. Lia's teeth clenched, again thinking of Mark, then she smiled. Her spirits danced as she remembered Mark's expression. He was jealous of her antics, she knew.

A stone skittered away in the darkness. Lia paused and listened for a moment, straining her ears to hear over the sound of the gentle, August breeze that swept through the streets. She shivered again, folding her arms across her chest as an unknown dread filled her heart.

She caught a glimpse of something move, and she whipped her head around. A black shape flashed towards her out of the darkness, and she instinctively threw her hands up in front of her face. A massive shadow enveloped her before she could avoid its attack, and her breath was knocked from her lungs as her flailing body was whisked into the alley between the blacksmith's shop and the cobbler's stand. She was confused, and for a moment she forgot how to breathe.

Rough hands pried at her dress as she tried, desperately, to gather her senses, and she could hear and feel the cloth tearing under the shadow's claws. Adrenaline coursed through her as her heart beat loudly in her ears. Then she snapped alert, suddenly and acutely aware of what was happening.

Her body was on fire with the razor-sharp terror surging through her veins, and utter panic filled her as she quickly realized that she was helpless. She breathed deep to scream, but a hand painfully clamped itself over her mouth.

"I'll get my coin's worth, wench!" a hoarse, rough whisper rattled in her ear. "You'll not take my money without earning it!"

Lia breathed again, this time her nose filling with the putrid smell of sweat and sour liquor. In the shadowed light of the alley, she could see the silhouette of the red-bearded man from the tavern, and her fear was absolute.

"No!" she pleaded, her voice muffled by his hand. "No!"

He laughed quietly as he tore at her bare skin. She felt the weight of his body shift on top of her as he struggled with his own clothing, and she closed her eyes against her tears.

She felt him under her skirt, searching for the right place, and every inch of her body convulsed in repulsion. This man was going to take her, and an overwhelming anger gripped her. She wished her hands were free so she could take hold of her dagger and slice his throat. She envisioned her blade entering his neck; he would bleed out, gurgling and choking as his life drained into his stomach and lungs, and she would gleefully watch his last, writhing moments. She could see it in her mind, and she willed it to become real despite fully knowing that she could do nothing to stop what was coming.

He had found his goal, and with clumsy fingers he aligned to thrust. His coarse beard scratched her face, reeking of curdled bits of food, and spittle from his gasp of pleasure flew from his mouth. Lia's eyes squeezed tight, her feet kicking helplessly.

Then, in an instant, reality faded away. She suddenly felt weightless, her ears growing deaf to the sound of huffing and grunting. Floating as though trapped in a dream, a stupor of white haze and nothingness blanketed her. She relaxed for a moment, remembering Mark. He was following her, he would save her. Where was he?

The man was done quickly, but Lia was unaware of him, still locked in the depths of her mind.

"Now," the man said, breathing hard in her face as he began to sit up. "I think you've earned–"

He did not finish his sentence. An odd sound gurgled from between his rotting teeth and swollen, scabbed lips, and his head snapped back to face the night sky. He fell forward onto her, again crushing her under his weight. Lia was still confused, opening her eyes and trying to focus.

Is it over? she wondered. Her mind was struggling to free itself from the mist that had settled there, and she could not make sense of where she was and what had happened.

He lay on top of her, motionless, and the hand that was covering her mouth was lifeless. Lia turned her face to breathe, gathering her wits and preparing to cry out, when the massive bulk of the man suddenly disappeared from on top of her. She felt the cool air on her skin, and her lungs, no longer constricted under the heavy frame, took in several breaths. She closed her eyes for a moment, then began to sit up.

A hand was outstretched before her, and she instinctively pulled at her shredded dress to cover her nakedness.

"Mark?" Lia whispered into the darkness, her words sounding distant and hollow in her ears.

"I won't look," Mark's voice answered, and Lia's stomach dropped. She took his hand and he pulled her to her feet. He immediately turned his back towards her, facing away. "Are you hurt, Lia?" he asked, his voice barely audible. Lia shook, her words gone from her throat. She gave a slight cough and swallowed hard.

"I'm fine," she answered. "I'm not hurt." She tried to cover her breasts with the pieces of her bodice, but she couldn't; the fabric was shredded beyond recognition. "I....I'm not...decent."

Mark, his eyes still averted, quickly removed his shirt, handing it back to her. His muscles rippled under his bare skin as he moved, illuminated by the moonlight, and even in her waning trance of shock and confusion she could see him trying to contain the emotions coursing through his being. He held the shirt at arm's length, waiting for her to take it from him.

"Lia?" he prompted quietly through clenched teeth, startling her. His voice was gentle and calm, mingling strangely with the rough sound of his grinding jaw. She snatched the shirt from him and pulled it on, clasping it tightly around her.

"Is he dead?" she asked, staring at the mountain of flesh on the ground before her. Mark didn't move.

"I don't know," he answered, the iron rod he had used to strike the man clutched in his hand. Lia looked at Mark vacantly and slowly reached for the weapon. He let her take it, and she gazed again at the man who had violated her.

Uncontrollable frustration overwhelmed her at the helplessness she felt, at her inability to change what had happened, and she felt as though she would burst. Her skin tensed and burned with rage as though her very soul itself was trying to claw its way out of her defiled body. Her eyes filled with blood, and with a quiet grunt she raised the rod and brought it down upon the man's head. She did it again, and again, a mixture of blinding fury and tears pouring from her with each blow.

A sticky, dark puddle of brain and blood pooled around the broken, mashed pieces of flesh melting into the cobblestone street, each strike causing the man's face to become more and more mangled. She was in a frenzy, hacking away at the disgusting creature before her. She could see nothing; her mind was numb, and Mark couldn't hide the satisfaction on his face as he watched her flail at the bloody carcass.

After what seemed an eternity, Mark finally stopped her.

"Lia, he's dead," he said, catching her arm. She pulled away, trying to continue her attack. "He's dead!" Mark repeated, prying the rod away from her. Lia's face was covered in tears, and her breath came in labored heaves. "Come, Lia, we need to go." Peering out of the alley to make sure no one was nearby, Mark took her hand and led her away.

They walked together in silence. Mark kept pace beside her, his hand resting gently on her back. Lia couldn't look at him, shame beginning to fill her heart. Her eyes, dry and unblinking, began to overflow with tears. A sob escaped from her lips, and Mark took her by the arm.

"We're almost there, Lia," he said, his voice low. "See? Your home is just there." He gestured, and Lia focused on the familiar chimney brightly lit by the moonlight.

Home.

She stopped.

"I can't," she said, pulling away. "I can't, not yet. Leave me be, I want to stay here for a while." Lia was frozen in the road, her feet planted stubbornly as Mark tried to move her forward. "Leave me!" she repeated. Pausing to look at her, he sighed.

"I'll not leave you here, Lia," Mark said firmly. "I'll wait here with you." She shook her head in protest and began to speak, but he raised his finger to her lips. "I'll not leave you!" he repeated, silencing her objections with a look. Still holding her hand, he turned to a stand of walnut trees near the road.

"There's a bench there," Mark told her, gesturing towards the trees. Lia nodded, allowing him to lead her from the road and onto the grass.

Beams of moonlight streamed through the full branches of the trees, coming to rest where they sat, and each breeze filled the air with the gentle rustling of fluttering leaves. Lia was silent, trying to erase the smell of the man's body from her memory, trying to mentally cleanse her skin from the feel of his touch. She glanced at Mark, wondering if he was repulsed by her after seeing what had happened.

Mark's eyes wandered, looking around absently at nothing in particular, worry creasing his face but obviously unsure of what to say. They sat in silence for a while before he ventured to speak.

"Are you sure you're not hurt?" he asked quietly. Lia shook her head, looking away.

"I'm not hurt," she answered. "I've but a few scratches that I can tell, nothing more." She peeked at Mark again, and this time he was watching her with a concerned look.

"But are you all right?"

Lia's shoulders, held upright and proud, sagged at his question. She felt her lip tremble, and she took a ragged breath.

"I'm fine," she answered, steeling herself. "I'll be fine." A thought occurred to her, and her face turned white. "Are you going to tell?" she asked him, her voice betraying her fear. She could only imagine what would happen if the townspeople found out.

"Of course not!" Mark told her quickly, giving her a reassuring look. Silence. He spoke again.

"I'm sorry I wasn't there sooner," he said. Lia felt a sudden burst of laughter leave her throat with a flat-sounding bray.

"Just so long as you weren't there any later," she said, her face cracking into a wry smile at the thought of what may have been in store for her. "It was lucky for once that you were following me." Her breath caught in her throat.

She had cursed and screamed at him for almost a year because he never left her alone, and now she was grateful he hadn't listened to her. If it hadn't been for him finding her she may very well be dead.

"Mark, I'm sorry," Lia began, her voice wavering. "If you hadn't been following me…"

"Hush, love," he whispered, silencing her as he quickly brushed her hair out of her eyes. Her mouth hung open as she tried to think of what to say, how to apologize to him for the way she had treated him, but her thoughts mixed together into a whirlwind of confusion before suddenly disappearing from her mind.

Lia closed her eyes and leaned forward, putting her hands up so she could rest her head, but Mark reached over and pulled her sideways into his arms. A flash of prideful resistance welled up within her, only to be quickly extinguished by the tears and exhaustion that overwhelmed her. She began to sob, her arms hanging limply at her sides while he held her tight.

They moved from the bench to the grass, and Lia laid her head against Mark's chest as he caressed her cheek. The night air gently cooled the streaks of warmth left behind by his fingertips as he traced the outline of her face, and the comfort of his touch along with the whisper of the night breeze eased her heart.

"Lia, it will be morning soon," Mark prodded her, his voice quiet. "Wake up, I need to get you home." Lia blinked her eyes against the night, a quick shiver running down her spine as she sighed.

"I don't want to go home," she told him, sitting up and crossing her arms. "I'm going to stay here." Mark stood to his feet.

"None of that, Lia," he scolded gently as he bent down to gather her into his arms. She buried her face in his neck as he carried her towards home. Her thoughts turned to her parents, and she whispered a prayer that her mother wasn't waiting up for her.

When they arrived at her house, Mark shifted her weight in his arms, then quietly lifted the latch and swung the door open. He moved slowly across the floor and towards the ladder leading up to her room, then he gently set her feet on the first rung. She let go of his neck and began to climb, his hand firmly resting on her back to steady her as he followed her up.

"Is that you, child?" her mother's sleepy voice called out. Lia cringed.

"It's me," she quietly replied.

"You are very late tonight, Lia," her mother chastised, then said nothing more.

When they reached the top of the ladder, Lia sagged onto the edge of her bed.

"I'll check on you tomorrow," Mark whispered, turning to leave. She reached out and took his hand, stopping him, overwhelmed by his gentle understanding and kindness.

"Mark..." she began, her voicing breaking. He smiled slightly and shook his head.

"Good night, Lia," he told her. He disappeared down the ladder, and she heard the faint sound of the front door shutting behind him as he let himself out. She sighed, and after a moment she got to her feet.

Lia lit a candle and looked down at herself. She was a mess. Her skirts were torn and shredded, and under Mark's shirt the scraps of her bodice were a hopeless tangle of frayed threads.

Removing her tattered dress, she could see large, deep, purple bruises on the insides of her thighs, and her breasts were scratched and bitten. Her face was, thankfully, almost untouched, with only a few small cuts and a single, fading handprint that stained her mouth from when she had been forcefully silenced. She was relieved, as it seemed that almost all evidence of her ordeal could be easily hidden under her clothing. She put on her nightdress and lay down on her bed, blowing out the candle.

She was exhausted, but peace did not come to her as easily as it had when she was with Mark. Each time she shut her eyes, she felt a panic take hold of her, and try as she might she could not will away the image of her attacker.

Her chest began to ache, and a lump formed in her throat. Each breath she took hurt her, as if her lungs were working against an invisible weight. Her eyes were dry, yet a deep, painful sob wracked her body. She caught her mouth, stifling the sound, but another came, and another. She pictured her parents below her, roused from their sleep by the shaking of her bed as she cried, and she did her best to lie motionless.

Her thoughts turned to Mark, and a wave of relief washed over her, momentarily chasing away the nightmare of the attack. She wished he had stayed there to watch over her. She closed her eyes, forcing herself to imagine that he was standing guard outside the house, and she fell asleep just as the sky was growing light with the oncoming morning.

• • •

CHAPTER FIVE

LIA SLEPT LATE the next morning. She awoke with a quiet groan, and as she stirred she felt as though her whole body had been torn to pieces. Her muscles were sore, and her legs and arms seemed to have been laid open to the bone. There was an odd ache between her legs, a pain she did not recognize, and she disgustedly realized it was the result of her body tearing as the man had entered her. Rolling out of her bed, she slowly stood to her feet and pulled back her nightdress to inspect her skin.

As if by magic, her arms and neck were spotted with new bruises, and her legs were the same. It was hard to turn her head, and she stiffly went about getting dressed. The events of the previous night almost seemed like a bad dream, a very vivid nightmare, save for her battered and sore body. She tried to push the memory from her mind.

She carefully looked at herself, checking to ensure that every scratch or bruise she could possibly cover was out of sight. She wore her hair down to hide her neck, and, after pulling the collar of her dress further up onto her shoulders, she decided she was ready.

Lia moved to check her windowsill for the gift Mark always left, and her cheeks flushed when she found a single, white rose waiting for her instead of the usual cast iron creation. She carefully broke each of the little thorns off of the rose's stem, then she tucked the blossom behind her ear. She smiled as she inspected her appearance once more, surprised at the sudden feeling of happiness that had overcome the sickness in her heart of a moment ago.

She descended the ladder into the kitchen where her mother was working, making preparations for the noon meal. Rachel glanced at Lia, nodding in her direction, and went back to her work.

"Good morning, Mum," Lia greeted her, reaching for a piece of bread. She bit into it, and a warmth washed over her. The taste of her mother's bread was something she had known since before she could remember, and now the comfort of the familiarity made her eyes sting. She gulped quickly, taking another bite of the honey-sweetened slice.

"Your father didn't go to the fields today," her mother began. "He went into town instead. There was a murder there last night."

News of a murder in the town usually didn't surprise Lia, but this time her heart skipped a beat. The bread she had been enjoying a moment ago lodged in her throat, and she gagged. Her mother looked at her in alarm; Lia's eyes watered, and she swallowed hard and coughed. She waved that she was fine, and her mother continued.

"A man, a patron at the tavern – perhaps you met him? – he was found in pieces next to the blacksmith's shop."

Lia tried to speak, dry crumbs of bread sticking in her mouth.

"In pieces?" she whispered, finding her voice. Rachel nodded.

"His head had been smashed in, and there was nothing left of his face," she explained. Lia felt cold.

"Do they know who did it?" she asked. Her mother shrugged.

"No, but the townspeople suspect a whore," Rachel answered.

Relief swept over Lia, and she relaxed.

"A whore?" she echoed. "Why do they believe it was a whore?" It would not take more than a moment for a whore to be convicted and executed for a murder, even if she was innocent. Her mother glanced at her.

"His pants were down," Rachel said matter-of-factly. "And he was exposed." Lia's skin crawled at the thought of the man's body against hers.

"But they aren't sure who it was," Rachel said, her hands working quickly to shell the beans she was working on. "The man was not robbed, he had well over thirty tokens. Surely a whore would have at least taken his money! Most are of the mind that it was a passing traveler who did it."

Lia shrugged, happy that the presence of the despicable creature's money ruled out the street women. She would have been bothered by the thought of someone else hanging for her deed, even if it was just a whore.

Brunbury had no magistrate or governor to punish those suspected of a crime. No, the townspeople handled criminals on their own, and in their own manner. Lia had witnessed many a miscreant's hanging or drowning, and she knew the townspeople were loath to accept an accused person's claims of innocence. Whores and beggars didn't stand a chance in this system of justice, and, ironically, the result was that whores and beggars almost never committed crimes for fear of the unfair treatment they would receive if they were to be accused.

Lia's mother changed the subject.

"Why didn't you go to work this morning?" Rachel asked. "Did Jem give you the day?" Lia looked away. "I asked you a question, child, and I expect an answer!" Her mother's voice began to rise.

"I didn't feel like going in today," Lia answered truthfully. She immediately regretted her honesty. Her mother stood to her feet, instantly angry.

"You must work!" Rachel said forcefully. Lia bristled, also standing.

"I hate that place!" Lia replied hotly. "You can't make me work there if I don't want to!"

Her mother reached out and slapped her across the face.

"Watch your tone with me, child!" Rachel cautioned, drawing back her hand again. "You've always loved the tavern! How did that change in a single day?" Lia backed away, seething.

"I don't want to work there anymore!" she exclaimed defiantly.

"You know we need the money!" Rachel shouted, her face growing red with anger. "Do you want us to starve just to pay for your dowry?" Lia sneered at her mother's words.

"I really don't give a damn," she snapped. "I'm not going back there!" Rachel opened her mouth to answer, but Lia turned and ran from the house, slamming the door behind her.

Lia spent the day alone in the hills. Her emotions ran wild; one moment she would be overcome with livid rage, while the next she was sobbing with uncontrollable sorrow and pain.

She was enraged at the terror she felt when she thought of the tavern; she had never felt fear like this before, and the weakness that overcame her when she thought of the man in the alley was paralyzing. Cursing and screaming at the sunny, cloud-filled sky didn't relieve the fury in her heart, and it felt as though the black hole of frustration and humiliation inside of her was growing larger and deeper by the moment. She could never tell her parents what had happened, and if she refused to go to work her father would beat her until she gave in. In a fit of childish stubbornness, Lia resolved in herself that she would just live in the fields, never to return home.

She felt vulnerable by herself, though, a feeling that was unfamiliar to her. Lia had always loved being alone, and the peace of the fields had always made her happy. Now, she found herself fighting off bouts of panic, constantly searching the treeline for unknown assailants. She thought of Mark and wondered where he was. She knew he would find her, like he always did, and the thought of him relaxed her. It was just a matter of time before he would come walking across the fields to sit with her.

The hours passed, but as the day grew later and later Mark didn't come. Lia watched the last dwindling streaks of fiery sunlight leave the horizon; the clouds, lit in shades of orange and pink, faded to hues of purple and blue with the oncoming night.

Then it was dark. Any security she had felt drained from within her, replaced with a cold wave of fear. The air had a cool edge to it, the warmth the sun had given it quickly ebbing away. The sweet-smelling grass, baked in the heat of the day, gathered moisture from the air, and a mist shrouded the ground.

Shadows came to life around her, and rustling in the brush made her jump. Every part of her body was attuned to the slightest movement or sound, and her ears strained to hear approaching footsteps. The mangled face of her attacker was on every tree and hidden in the windswept clouds of vapor rising from the grass, a ghoulish apparition creeping up to take her again. She couldn't move; her muscles were locked into place even as she willed herself to run. Where was Mark?

Lia's eyes caught movement in the trees, and this time she was sure that the man from the alley was coming to get her, that somehow her blows hadn't killed him and he had found her to satiate his vengeful lust. The shadow moved closer, and her heart pounded in her ears. A twig snapped, and her tensed muscles finally released. With a quiet cry, she found her legs and dashed towards her home, terrified to look back.

She ran through the trees, her dress catching on brush and twigs as she flew past. In her mind, each dark branch or bush were claws reaching for her, and when she tripped she was sure the shadow had gotten her. She ran until she couldn't breathe, panicking as her mind started to believe that she was trapped in the woods, when she finally saw the path leading out of the trees before her.

Sobbing in desperation, she fought her way to the road, willing herself forward, when suddenly a figure appeared in front of her.

"No!" Lia screamed, skidding to a stop and throwing her hands up in fear. "Get away from me!" She stumbled back and froze, just as terrified to flee back into the dark woods as she was of the man blocking her path.

"Lia, it's me!" Mark's voice called out, and with a cry of relief Lia launched herself into his arms. She gripped him tightly, unwilling to let go until her terror dissipated.

"What's wrong?" he asked her when she had calmed. "Was something chasing you?"

"I thought there was," Lia answered, catching her breath as her heartbeat slowed. "I waited for you in the fields and it got dark." Mark used his sleeve to wipe the tears from her face.

"I'm sorry," he apologized, putting his arm around her shoulders and leading her away from the edge of the woods. "I was being questioned in town."

"What do you mean?" Lia asked, confused. "About what?"

"About that dead bastard," Mark spat, his voice tinged with anger. "He was found right next to my shop, so they wanted to know if I'd killed him." He shrugged. "I guess someone saw him messing with you in the tavern, and they saw me storm out right afterwards, so they thought that maybe I had done it." Lia's face was white.

"What happened?" she asked quickly, fear entering her voice. "Are you safe?" Mark nodded, then cursed.

"Of course," he reassured her. "But it wasn't easy pretending to be upset that the filthy bastard was dead."

Lia's mouth went dry as she pictured the man's broken head.

"They think it was someone passing through town," Mark finished. "So you don't need to worry."

"Good," Lia answered absently. She stole a glance at him, wondering if he would laugh at the question burning on her tongue.

"Mark?" she asked timidly. "Are you sure he was dead?" His eyes sparkled.

"There is absolutely no doubt to be had," Mark told her. "I watched his body being scraped off the road, and some of him is still there. That man could not be any deader, believe me."

She let out a sigh of relief, and she and Mark walked in silence to the grove of trees where they had spent the previous night. They sat on the ground, and she leaned against him as they stared up at the stars in the clear, night sky.

"Thank you for the rose," Lia said, reaching up to touch where she had put it in her hair. It was gone now, lost in her frantic run through the woods. "I was surprised, you've never left me a real flower before."

"I didn't have time to make you something," he sheepishly explained. She snorted.

"I've always hated those little things!" she laughed. Mark was quiet for a moment, then he changed the subject.

"Did you get in trouble for being late last night?"

"No," Lia answered, rolling her eyes. "But this morning Mum wasn't happy with me for missing work. I don't care what she does to me, I won't set foot in that place again!"

"But you can't be afraid forever," Mark reasoned. "It's a good job with decent pay, and you shouldn't quit just because you're scared. But it's your choice, and no one else should make it for you." He paused for a moment. "You should have had a choice about the wedding, too," he added quietly. "I'm sorry." Lia was surprised.

"Why didn't you ever say that before?" she asked. Knowing that he was sorry she hadn't had a choice might have made him a bit more tolerable to her.

"I've wanted to!" Mark said, his body stiffening. "You wouldn't let me, remember?"

"How long would it have taken for you to say that?" she asked sarcastically, twisting around so she could look up at him. "All of a minute?"

"Well, you haven't exactly made it very easy to say much of anything," he countered. "I could barely get a word in between your screaming and cursing every time I tried talking to you!" She shifted uncomfortably at his tone. She didn't like hearing him upset, and she wished she hadn't said anything.

"I'm sorry," she told him quickly, hoping to calm him down. "Please, don't be angry." Mark's mouth dropped open.

"What?" he asked, staring at her in bewilderment. "Since when do you care if you make me mad?" Lia frowned, speechless. He was right, but she didn't have an answer.

"I don't know," she answered after a long pause. "Is that bad?"

"No, of course not," he told her. "I guess I just didn't expect it." He squeezed her tightly in his arms, and she closed her eyes.

They stayed there for a long while, sitting quietly while listening to the croaking of frogs mingle with the other sounds of the night. Finally, Mark sighed.

"It's getting late," he said, standing. "You need to get some rest." He helped her to her feet and took her hand, then the two of them began to walk towards her home.

When they got to the door, he bid her good night.

"Good night, Mark," Lia answered. "Will you come see me tomorrow?"

"You know I will," he told her. Smiling, she opened the door and went inside.

The kitchen was empty when Lia walked in, and she sat down hard on a chair. She leaned forward onto the tabletop, burying her face in her folded arms. Her skin began to crawl as the image of her attacker's face tried to force its way into her mind, and she struggled to keep the memory from showing itself. It was easy to keep her thoughts away when Mark was nearby, and she wished she was still with him. She heard her parents' bedroom door open, but she didn't move.

A hot flash of pain shot through her body, and Lia fell from the chair, screaming in shock and confusion. She glanced up to see her mother standing over her, brandishing a thick, green, willow switch. Her welted skin throbbing, Lia scooted away across the floor until her back was pressed against the far wall.

"Stop, Mum!" Lia cried, her eyes wide as she watched her mother advance towards her.

"You stupid child!" Rachel screeched, ignoring her daughter's words as she drew back the switch. "Where have you been?"

She struck again, drawing a bloody streak across Lia's forehead. Lia shielded her face from her mother's blows, feeling the sharp sting of the switch against her arms and legs. Rachel's breath came in short, wheezing gasps as she put her full strength into the beating. Lia wanted to get up and tear the switch from her mother's hand, but she couldn't move, her body suddenly feeling too weak to protest or fight back.

"Your father is beside himself!" Rachel shouted, lashing at Lia mercilessly. "You've barely been home for two days! He's at the tavern now, drinking himself into a stupor because of you! He knows you were with Mark; do you know what will happen to you if the townspeople find out you've been alone with your betrothed all night? Your father blamed me for your stupidity, he said that I've been too lenient with you!" Lia began to dull to the pain, the shock of each strike seeming distant.

"He's taken a room at the tavern!" Rachel shrieked, fear evident in her voice. "Your father may be sleeping under the same roof as a murderer because of your foolishness!" She threw the switch away in exasperation, stepping forward to kick Lia. Her foot caught the edge of Lia's skirts, exposing her legs, and Rachel caught sight of the bruises. She paused, shock filling her face as her rage turned to fear.

"What happened to you?" Rachel screeched.

The bruises on Lia's inner thighs looked black in the lamplight, and, suddenly emboldened, she stood to her feet and stripped off her dress. She stood naked before her mother, and as she watched Rachel's horrified expression turn to understanding the shame was too much for Lia to bear. She collapsed onto the floor after only a moment, her tears pouring unrestrained from her eyes. Her mother reached out and touched her bare shoulder, and Lia did not have the energy to recoil.

"Get up, child," Rachel said gently, her fury of only a moment ago forgotten as she picked up Lia's dress from where it had been tossed aside. Lia rose to sit but did not stand, and she limply obeyed her mother's prodding hands as they guided her dress back onto her body. She pulled her knees up to her chin, and the tears, which had slowed, rained down again.

"Mum," Lia breathed between sobs. "He took me! He took me in the alley! It wasn't a whore the dead man was with, it was me!" Her face contorted at the sound of the words, and with frantic hands she ripped at her hair. She felt as though her sobs were not enough to expend the emotions coursing through her, and she beat at her face, unable to bear the pain in her heart.

Rachel reached out to cradle her daughter's face. She knelt on the floor next to Lia for a long while in silence, and eventually Lia's sobs began to dissipate.

"You listen to me, Lia," Rachel said, her voice soft. "You will speak of this to no one. You will tell no one, not even Mark!" Lia took a deep, ragged breath.

"Mark found me," she whispered, averting her eyes in humiliation. "He saw me." Her mother grimaced, thinking for a moment before speaking again.

"He won't tell, Lia," she said reassuringly. "He cares for you too much." Lia nodded, trying to control herself.

"I know," she said, her shoulders heaving with each breath. "He already told me." A moment of smugness glowed in Lia's heart, and with a sudden calm she looked at her mother.

"I killed him," she said, her eyes bright. "I killed the bastard, there in the streets!" She was almost gleeful, and the surge of satisfaction she felt warmed her. Her mother's mouth twitched with a smile.

"I'd expect nothing else," Rachel said, pride welling in her voice. She stroked Lia's face, then moved to sit on the floor. Patting her lap as she had when Lia was a child, Rachel opened her arms, and Lia crawled into the comforting embrace she hadn't known since she was a little girl.

The strong, thin, familiar arms of her mother held her tight, and Lia closed her eyes. Rachel's voice sounded muddy as she spoke, the vibrations of her words carrying through her chest and into Lia's ear.

"You are brave, child," Rachel whispered, gently brushing at Lia's tear-soaked hair with her fingers. "Don't cry anymore, love. You're too brave and strong for these tears." Lia was confused.

"What about my shame, Mum?" she asked, yawning with the sudden desire to sleep. Her mother shushed her.

"Don't worry about that," Rachel told her firmly. "If Mark doesn't care it doesn't matter, and no one else will ever know." Lia began to drift off, the rise and fall of her mother's breathing lulling her to sleep.

• • •

CHAPTER SIX

LIA STOOD IN THE KITCHEN with her mother, both of them silent. The peace she had felt the night before, cradled on her mother's lap, had gone, and the more familiar stab of disgrace had filled her heart. With the morning had come a sense of awkwardness, and yet Lia felt a bond between her and her mother that she hadn't felt in years.

As a child, Lia and her mother had been close, and Lia's father, John, would often curse about being the only man in a house full of women. Then, when Lia was twelve years old, her mother became pregnant, and John swelled with the hope that he would finally have another man around. But when Rachel miscarried what did turn out to be a son, and she learned soon thereafter that she could no longer get pregnant, his hopes had been shattered.

Lia's father had always been gruff, but the knowledge that he would never have a son made him intolerable. Rachel, mourning the loss of both her child and her fertility, became withdrawn, causing Lia to bear part of the burden of her mother's sorrow. Now, as she and her mother worked side by side in the kitchen, the feeling of closeness between them that Lia had missed so much had returned, and she hoped her mother felt it, too.

They had woken up early, and Rachel had announced that they would bake pies that day. Lia was excited; pies were only for important occasions, and for Rachel to take pastry lard and fruit from their meager stores was, to Lia, a sign that her mother wouldn't cast her away.

A knock sounded at the door, and the women looked up from their work.

"Hello?" a voice called from outside. Lia recognized it instantly, and she went to the door.

"We're baking pies, Mark!" Lia told him excitedly. "Will you stay?" Mark shook his head.

"I can't," he answered, smiling at her happiness. "I have too much work to do. I just wanted to see if you were all right."

"I'm fine," Lia reassured him. "And I've told Mum what happened." Mark's eyes widened, and he glanced quickly at Rachel. Rachel pretended not to see, concentrating on her baking. He lowered his voice.

"Is she upset with you?" Mark asked quietly, stealing another glance at Lia's mother. Lia shrugged.

"I don't think so," she answered. "She's been very nice to me." His face brightened, and he touched Lia's cheek.

"Good," he said, then quickly dropped his arm to his side when he noticed Rachel watching him. "I'll come by to see you tomorrow." He turned to leave, then paused to dig in his pocket.

"Try not to hate this one, will you?" he said playfully, handing her a cast iron rose. Lia smiled and took the gift, smudging it with flour from her hands. "Goodbye, Mrs. Grey!" Mark called over his shoulder, and Rachel waved at him as he left.

"I'll see you tomorrow!" Lia called, watching him walk towards the road. She shut the door, and her mother looked at her quizzically.

"Well," Rachel mused, surprised. "How about that!"

"What?" Lia asked, slipping the rose into her apron pocket.

"I thought you would rather die than spend time with Mark!" Rachel exclaimed, amusement and confusion creasing her face. "Now you can't wait to see him?" Lia blushed.

"Well," she began, returning to her mother's side to finish rolling out pie crust. "I think I've changed my mind about him." She proceeded to tell Rachel about how Mark had found her and the time they had spent together.

"I don't know why," Lia finished, smiling to herself. "But after the other night I just feel closer to him."

"Are you sure it's not just because he helped you?" Rachel asked, frowning as she gave Lia a cautious look. "Are you sure it's not just because you've been hurt?" Lia shook her head vehemently.

"No, Mum, I'm sure," she answered. "I'm sure."

Even as she spoke the words, Lia felt doubt rise up within her, and she grew quiet, thinking. Her ability to tolerate Mark *had* changed rather suddenly, but why was that a bad thing? She had been plagued by the thought of marrying someone she hated, and at least now she could stand being around him. More importantly, the fact that he was still willing to marry her proved that he didn't see her as filthy, and it was reassuring to think that someone could want her despite her shame.

Rachel saw the pensive look on her daughter's face.

"Don't worry about it right now, child," she said, smiling at Lia. "Now, let's get these pies finished before your father comes home, shall we?"

The two women finished the baking, and by the time Lia's father returned from the fields three pretty berry pies dotted the windowsill of the kitchen, cooling next to the loaves of bread. The smell of hot, vegetable stew filled the house, but even the prospect of a good meal could not warm John Grey's cold countenance, and he glared at Lia as he washed up for dinner. It wasn't long after they sat down to eat that he began to speak.

"Lia," John said stoutly, his voice firm and loud. "I will not have any daughter of mine behaving in this manner." Lia stared at her half-eaten meal, her appetite instantly disappearing as she listened. Her father continued.

"You are the talk of the town yet again," he said, annoyance puckering his face. "I am putting my foot down! You'll not spend your nights alone with your betrothed, nor will you sell your kisses to the men in the tavern!" He scowled across the table at her.

Lia did not meet his gaze, poking at the food left in her bowl while her ears turned hot with embarrassment. He must have found out about her kisses during his night at the tavern. He turned to Lia's mother, expecting shock at what he had just said.

"Yes, Rachel, she's been selling herself to the men!" he growled, his eyes wide. "All evening I heard them lamenting the absence of the 'Ale-Wench' and her kisses, only to discover that they were speaking of my own daughter!" Rachel didn't answer, and John continued, wagging his finger in Lia's face.

"You're not married yet," he told her, finality in his words. "You *will* behave until then. And you *will* go to work. You're lucky Jem is kind, and he has agreed not to fire you. But you will work!"

Lia finally lifted her face, and her expression was full of insolence. Returning to the tavern would be her choice, not his.

"And if I won't?" she asked him defiantly.

"You will do as I say!" he shouted, shaking at his daughter's nerve. "I will have my way!" He lowered his voice. "And if you won't," he answered her, gripping the edge of the table until his fingertips turned white. "You'll not live under this roof any longer!"

Lia's mother quickly spoke.

"If you send her away I'll be going with her," Rachel told her husband, her eyes unwavering as she stared at him. "I won't have you send my daughter into the streets."

Her words were blunt, and it was obvious to John that an argument wouldn't change her mind. He leaned forward, and with an earth-shattering howl he swept his arm across the table, sending the dishes of food clattering. He fumed, his eyes moving from his wife's calm defiance to his daughter's determined stare. Without speaking, he moved back from the table, stomping loudly as he made his way to his room. The door slammed, and Lia turned to her mother.

Rachel's face was triumphant, and Lia smiled. She and her mother exchanged a look, and Rachel gave a quiet laugh.

"Perhaps you and I aren't that much different," she said, pinching Lia's cheek. "You just haven't the care or self-control to hide your opinions as I do." Lia smiled and helped her mother clean up the mess from the thrown dishes.

She couldn't breathe. Her lungs burned for air, and her eyes flew open to see the mangled face of her attacker.

No! *she screamed in her mind, frantically struggling against the weight of his body. She could see him clearly. The top half of his head was gone, and liquid from the empty hollows that were his eyes* oozed onto the raw meat of his cheeks. His mouth split into a cruel, mutilated grin, and Lia could see his swollen, bleeding tongue between his broken teeth and torn lips. Hunks of congealed blood dripped slowly from his ripped beard, smearing her skin with dark streaks.

"I'll have my coin's worth, whore!" he gurgled, and black blood seeped from his mouth. Lia couldn't move; it felt as though she were trapped in a pit of thick mud. She fought at him, her arms and hands weak and useless against him. He was like a massive rock holding her body down, and her nose filled with the fetid smell of rotting flesh.

You're dead! *she screamed in her mind, trying to convince herself that he wasn't real.* I know *you're dead! She shuddered in disgust as he touched her.*

"You'll never rid yourself of me!" he laughed as if he had heard her thoughts. His neck was split open from decay, the pieces of skin separating as he threw his head back with a roar. White maggots wriggled free, falling onto her bare skin, their tiny heads boring holes into her breasts as they began consuming her from the inside. She screamed again, her voice silent against the gnarled, decomposing hand he held against her mouth. She vomited, the contents of her stomach pouring from her nose.

"Don't you like your handiwork, whore?" he questioned. She began to choke, unable to draw a breath through the bile clogging her airways, and the foul liquid entered her lungs.

The man and his filth evaporated into the darkness as if he had never been there, and she turned onto her side, heaving and retching with a force she had never known. She lay there, naked, gasping for air, her mind unable to fathom what had happened. The *roar of her blood pulsing through her veins faded, and there was utter silence. The fear that had gripped her only a moment before began to ebb away as her breathing finally relaxed into a slow, steady, rhythm.*

A cry rang out in the silence, a sharp, helpless sound almost like that of a mewing kitten. Lia felt a tug at her heart, and she stood quickly, forgetting her fear and nakedness. In the distance, she could see the flame of a candle piercing the darkness with its light, and she cautiously moved forward. The cry came again, and Lia felt a desperation in her feet. She began to run, and as she came close she could see a small, dirty bundle bathed in the candle's soft glow.

Without hesitation, she leaned down, feeling in her heart that whatever it was belonged to her. She pulled back the linen, and the small, angelic face of an infant stared up at her. She cooed gently, holding the tiny form against the warmth of her body, bouncing and rocking slowly to comfort its cries. She brushed her fingers against its soft cheeks, and its beautiful, gray eyes closed in sleep. She stared down at the tiny face, awestruck, when, almost like melting wax, it began to change, the features twisting and contorting. Horrified, she watched as the peaceful, sleeping face of the baby she had gazed at but a moment ago transformed into the unblemished face of her attacker, its body elongating and stretching until it resembled a toddler.

"You'll never rid yourself of me!" the baby cried in a rough, gritty voice, and she flung it away from her. It began to crawl towards her, laughing at her fear.

"NEVER!" it howled, screeching with glee. Lia screamed.

"Lia!"

She could feel hands gripping her shoulders, and she fought against whatever was holding her.

"Lia, wake up!" Her mother was shaking her violently, trying to rouse her from her dream. Lia bolted upright, her nightdress drenched, fearfully searching for the evil creature of her dreams.

"Get away!" she shrieked, kicking wildly, her nightmare still clinging to the outer edges of her mind. She wailed in terror, and Rachel slapped her.

"Lia, it's me!"

Lia focused blankly on her mother's face. Her mind did not recognize her, and she recoiled from her mother's touch.

"You must wake up!" Rachel commanded her, and finally reality dawned on Lia's face. She looked at her mother's concerned eyes and the worried tears beginning to form there.

"Mum?" Lia gasped, bewildered. Rachel took her hand, squeezing it tight.

"Yes, child, you're safe, I'm right here," she promised, and Lia's face crumpled in agony. She trembled at the still-vivid memory of the nightmare, and Rachel held her as she cried. Lia couldn't even begin to explain what she had seen.

Her mother shushed her, rocking back and forth to comfort her just as Lia had comforted the child in her dream.

"Just forget it," Rachel whispered. "You're here, you're safe."

"What's the trouble up there?" Lia heard her father yell. "Is it not enough that we must spend every waking moment of our day worrying about Lia, but now also our sleep?" He stood at the bottom of the ladder, and when he didn't get an answer he stomped away in a huff.

"You just ignore him, Lia," her mother instructed. "You calm down, you're fine." Lia took a deep breath, her tears slowing.

She looked at her straw mattress. She had wet herself, and the pungent odor of hot urine rose from her stained bed. Her mother dismissed Lia's embarrassment with a shake of her head, and she quickly descended the ladder. Lia perched on the edge of her bed, her hands covering her face.

A moment later, Rachel reappeared, a stack of winter quilts balanced on her shoulder.

"Here, child," she said, setting them on the floor. "We won't worry about this tonight." She helped Lia move the thick mattress off its wooden frame, and with nimble hands Rachel crafted a soft cushion of quilts for Lia to sleep on.

"I don't have another nightdress," Lia told her, her eyes vacant. Again Rachel disappeared, and this time when she returned she had on her work dress, the nightdress she had just been wearing clutched in her hand. She gave it to Lia, the fabric still warm, and with a grateful sigh Lia quickly changed.

"Go to sleep, love," Rachel told her, dusting off the small stool Lia kept in her room. "I will sit here till you sleep." Her mother's presence calmed her, and Lia fell into a deep, dreamless sleep.

• • •

CHAPTER SEVEN

THE NEXT FEW DAYS were miserable. The nightmares came each night to torment Lia's sleep, but at least they didn't wake her the way the first one had. She was grateful to have no memory of the horror of her dreams, but she still dreaded sleep.

She didn't try to go wandering in the hills, preferring to stay close to her mother's comfort. Rachel was gentle and understanding, and Lia had seen her mother's sad eyes watching her on several occasions.

Lia was reassured by her mother's support and obvious concern, and despite the indignity and humiliation of what had happened she was glad she had told her mother the truth about the attack. Her father ignored both of them, eating his meals in silence before retiring early to bed, but neither of them cared. Lia wondered, once, if her father would behave differently if he knew what had happened to her, but she quickly put the thought out of her head. He was much too hotheaded to ever understand, and she knew he could never find out.

Mark visited often, and Lia ignored her father's warnings about spending time with him. They spent their evenings alone on the bench in the clearing near her home, staying there until the early morning hours, and she was content with the comfort she felt in his presence.

Too soon, Rachel informed Lia that it was time for her to return to work.

"I don't want to go!" Lia pleaded, feeling like an unhappy child. "Please, Mum, don't make me go back!" Rachel was firm.

"You must work, Lia," she said, her decision final. "You can't be afraid forever, and you know we need your earnings. I can't help your father in the fields."

After the miscarriage, Rachel hadn't been able to work tending crops, as the heat and strain would cause her to faint. She had been the town's midwife for years, and she made a little money from that, but there weren't many pregnant women in the town so her opportunities to earn money had been limited.

Lia's eyes flashed, and she set her jaw stubbornly. She opened her mouth to speak, intending to argue, but her words disappeared from her tongue when she caught sight of her mother's pained expression. She could clearly see that Rachel didn't want to send her back, and she realized that her mother wouldn't force her to go unless they truly did need the money. With a grunt of displeasure, Lia crossed her arms and nodded.

Lia awoke early the next morning and readied herself for work. She was uneasy at the thought of going to the tavern, but she would obey her mother's instructions.

When Lia arrived at the tavern, Jem greeted her in his usual manner, but instead of joking with him, she just stood there as he yelled.

"Useless, that's what you are!" he told her. "I'll fire you for sure! Days of moldy bread and watery brine, you're lucky I at least have ale to sell to the men!"

When she didn't respond, Jem tilted his head, puzzled.

"What's gotten into you, girl?" he asked, scratching his jowls. "Where's your fight gone to?" Lia was silent, and Jem waved her off. "You've gone soft, wench!" he called as she walked to the kitchen, making one last attempt at rile her. She didn't answer, and he gave a grunt of displeasure. He did not bother her again.

Dusk came too soon. The evening meal began as usual, and Jem called her from the kitchen.

"Lia, get yourself out here!" he yelled. She pretended not to hear as she peered through the kitchen door at the room full of men. She didn't want to walk among them, she didn't want to be near them.

"Lia!" Jem screamed. "I'll not call you again!"

Feeling her heart begin to race, she finally obeyed, gingerly stepping into the room and filling the empty bowls as fast as she could. She was turning to disappear back into the kitchen when one of the men grabbed her arm.

"Will you sell me a kiss, lovely?" he rasped. Lia pulled away, fear gripping her as her pounding heart leaped into her throat, and she had her dagger in hand before she could think.

"I'm not a whore!" Lia screamed at the man's shocked face, and the tavern fell silent. The sharp tip of her knife rested on the man's throat. "Don't touch me!"

Jem dragged himself to her side.

"Lia!" he said, ushering her away. "What's gotten into you? I can't have you threatening the men!" She wrested away from him, fury filling her.

"But they can touch me and ask for me, that you can have?" she asked, glaring at him. Jem shrugged.

"But Lia, you've always sold your kisses," he reminded her. "Do you think it's just your cooking and my ale that they come for?" Lia's face was blank, then realization dawned on her.

"What do you mean?" she asked, breathless at the thought of what he was saying.

"You're a fresh-faced innocent, a pretty plaything for them to look at, and they can steal a touch to dream about for less than the cost of a street whore," Jem answered.

"But that doesn't mean they can take me," Lia whispered. "They can't just take me." She had grown accustomed to feeling shame, but this time it came in a different color. If she had taught the men she was for sale, then perhaps the fault of her attack was hers. She was stunned at the thought, and grief filled her. Jem patted her back.

"Here, girl, take your leave," he said. "I don't know what's gotten into you! Go." He pointed to the back door, shaking his head with disappointment. "Just be here all the earlier in the morning."

Outside the tavern, Lia felt exposed. She stayed to the middle of the road, carefully looking about her for any sign of movement.

Stop being ridiculous, Lia, she told herself. *Mark will be watching you.* A panic took hold of her as she remembered that she had left the tavern early, realizing that Mark wouldn't know she was already on her way home. She stopped to fearfully search the dark street behind her, then, seeing no one, she swallowed hard and began to walk again. As she approached the blacksmith's shop and memory of the shadowed alley, her pace quickened, dread catching in her throat.

The sound of footsteps drew her attention, and she poised to run.

"Who's there?" Lia inquired of the darkness, her palms growing sweaty as terror stabbed at her heart.

"It's me, Lia," Mark said, stepping out of the shadows and into the dim light of the evening. "Who'd you think it was?" He cringed at his words, quickly apologizing. "I didn't mean to scare you, I'm sorry." Relieved, Lia began to calm.

Then, only a moment later, she suddenly felt her face began to burn, and she looked away, unable to meet Mark's gaze. It was one thing to spend the evenings with him close to her home, but being in this place with him again made her feel ashamed and naked.

Lia tried to speak, but her humiliation took her voice, and she choked. Mark watched her fidget with discomfort.

"What's wrong?" he asked. She was acutely aware of his stare, and she could bear it no longer.

"Stop looking at me!" Lia exclaimed. He was confused.

"Why?"

"You know why!" she answered hotly. She could only imagine how she must have looked to him that night, her dress in ribbons and her pale flesh starkly shining in the dark of the alley. The thought made her cringe, and she knew her face couldn't possibly convey any more embarrassment. He thought a moment, quickly realizing what she was referring to, and he shrugged her off.

"Stop being ridiculous, Lia," Mark told her, a disarming smile on his face. "I haven't thought about *that*, and besides, you weren't bothered about it the last time we talked!" She was surprised that he had caught her meaning, but her ears still burned with shame. He sighed.

"You're off work early," he said, trying to change the subject. Lia instantly bristled at his words.

"What of it?" she snapped. Mark was perplexed by her anger, and he tried to calm her.

"It was just a question, Lia," he soothed, reaching for her. "I was only asking."

"Well, don't!" She pulled away. "I don't need you to ask about me, thank you very much!" She glared at him, enraged at the mixed flurry of emotions she felt welling up inside of her. She wanted him to hold her, but at the same time she wanted to hit him. "Just leave me alone!"

"Okay, I'll leave you alone if you want me to," Mark told her evenly, trying to hide his confusion. "Can I at least walk you home?" Now Lia's anger turned to fear.

"So that's it?" she asked, narrowing her eyes as she fought against the lump growing in her throat. "All those months I tried to keep you away from me, and now I just have to ask you once and you'll leave me alone? Am I not good enough for you now?" Mark's eyes widened.

"What are you talking about?" he demanded. "I just want you to be happy! If you want me to leave you alone I will, but that doesn't mean I want to!"

"Don't lie to me!" Lia screamed, pushing him. "You think I'm filthy, don't you? You've just been pretending to love me, to care about me! You can't stand me *now*, can you?" Mark stepped close to her, shushing her.

"Please, Lia, don't be so loud," he cautioned, eyeing the darkened buildings. "The townspeople will hear!"

"I don't give a damn about the townspeople!" Her voice grew louder. "Why does it matter if everyone hears? Are you ashamed of being seen with me?"

"You're being ridiculous!" Mark exclaimed, turning away from her. "Absolutely ridiculous!" He walked to the blacksmith's shop and disappeared through the doorway, leaving her alone on the street. She stood there a moment, torn, before following him.

The forge's fire burned bright, and a long piece of iron was heating in the blaze. Lia could see that the white-hot end of the metal was twisted into a delicate pattern, and she knew Mark had been working on yet another trinket to leave on her windowsill.

"I see you've been hard at work, making another useless charm," she said, her voice rife with spite as she tried to rile him. She couldn't help wondering what he was making, but she wouldn't let her anger fade.

"Why did you ever start making them to begin with?" Lia snapped, glaring at him.

"It gives me something to do," Mark answered, twirling the workpiece in the fire and purposefully avoiding her eyes. "While I wait to see you."

"You're pitiful!" Lia blurted. "You mean to tell me you can't find anything else to occupy your mind?" Mark took offense at her belittling tone.

"Didn't you believe me?" he asked, his eyes boring holes into hers. "I told you how I loved you! Did you think I was lying?"

He clenched his jaw. "Do you believe me to be a fool, Lia?" he continued, his voice taut with frustration. She took a step back as he came towards her. "Do you believe it's easy for me to feel this way for you? You have made it so difficult for me to love you, and yet here I stand, hopelessly yours!" His face was pained.

"I don't understand you, Lia!" he exclaimed, his voice breaking. "I thought you were starting to care about me. Why did you spend all of these days with me, wanting my company, only to turn around and act like this? You let me hold you, be near you, and now this? I don't understand!"

"So you think I'm a whore now, don't you?" Lia asked, seething. "Because I let you near me?" Mark threw up his hands in frustration.

"Where are you getting this? When have I ever said anything of the sort?"

"You didn't have to say it, Mark!" she simpered. "It's obvious!"

He whirled around, moving close and grasping her shoulders in his strong hands.

"What's wrong, Lia?" Mark demanded. "Why are you acting like this? What happened?" His eyes were bright with worry, his voice tinged with fear. "I love you, Lia, I don't think anything bad about you! Can't we forget about this? Just let me walk you home!"

"I can walk myself home!" Lia spat, trying to pull away from him. "I don't need you!"

Mark fell silent, his mouth hanging open with speechlessness. She glared at him, then, with a single, quick motion, he pulled her into his arms. He held her tightly against him.

"It's okay, Lia," he whispered gently. "Whatever it is, it's okay. I'll always be here for you, I promise." Her arms were stiff at her sides, but her heart swelled with emotion. She began to cry.

"It's my fault, isn't it?" Lia breathed between sobs. "I sold my kisses to the men, it's my fault this happened!" Mark hushed her.

"No, love," he told her firmly, taking her face in his hands. His eyes bored deeply into hers as he spoke. "It's not your fault. You didn't do this, believe me. Please believe me, Lia." She wanted to believe him, more than anything, but Jem's words rang in her ears.

• • •

CHAPTER EIGHT

LIA GOT UP FOR WORK the next day, but she didn't go to the tavern. Instead, she spent her day in the hills, quiet and alone. This time her fear was controllable, but she found no comfort in the laughing of the creek or the warmth of the sun.

She tried desperately to convince herself that it wasn't her fault that she had been attacked, and while her mind knew it was true she still felt that she held some blame. Her heart ached, but she realized she had no more tears to cry. She stood in the tall grasses, steeping in her guilt.

The face of the man from the alley screamed in hers every time she closed her eyes, and no matter how hard she tried she couldn't escape his taunts. It was as if her nightmares were torturing her even when she was awake. There was no escape, and she knew it.

A rumble of thunder jolted her from her misery. She looked up to see that gray storm clouds had moved in, unnoticed, to crowd the sun. Lightning flashed across the sky, and a light drizzle of rain began to fall. Lia took refuge under a weeping willow tree when the rain started to pour, and another deep peal of thunder filled her ears. She closed her eyes at the sound of the splashing raindrops, happy that the dull roar of the chilly thunderstorm drowned out her thoughts.

Lia was soaked through by the time she made it home, and her father was waiting for her when she arrived.

"You ungrateful child!" John cried, taking hold of Lia's wet hair and dragging her over to a chair. "Sit!"

Lia obeyed, strands of her hair still clutched in her father's hand. She touched her head, and when she looked she could see blood staining her fingers. A small river of rainwater streamed from the hem of her drenched skirts, turning the floor dark as it pooled under her chair. She jumped as her father slammed his fists on the table.

"Do you realize what you've done?" John shouted, the veins in his forehead bulging. "All day I've heard nothing but talk about you!" Lia wasn't sure what he meant.

"What kind of talk, Papa?" she asked.

"Don't speak!" he roared. "Don't say a word!" She stood in anger, but her mother pushed her back down, her eyes warning Lia to keep calm.

"Mark called off your engagement, Lia!" John howled. He wouldn't even look at her, seeming to scream at the space above her head rather than at her.

"He what?" she blurted in surprise. "Why?" Her father's eyes bulged at her question.

"What do you mean, why?" He looked as though he would explode. "The people are saying that you've been whoring yourself in the streets! You were heard arguing with some man last night, and don't you deny it! Of course Mark withdrew his oath! How can you expect any man to want a whore?"

Lia slowly shook her head in protest, trying to stutter an answer, but she was silenced by another look from her mother.

"Don't you see, Lia?" her father moaned, holding his head in his hands dejectedly. "You're ruined! You will never marry now!" She was stunned, her ears deaf to her father's words.

Despite the time she and Mark had spent together over the past days, Lia was relieved to hear that the wedding was called off. Even so, the knowledge that he didn't want her anymore made her feel betrayed and worthless, and her heart began to ache.

She shook her head in confusion. But it made no sense; Mark hadn't given her any indication that he was intending to call off their engagement, and just last night he had promised to always be there for her. Then her eyes grew wide. The only thing that made sense was that he had been lying to her, and she had stupidly believed his lies.

"The bastard!" Lia fumed under her breath.

Her father's fist connected with the side of her face.

"Curse me, will you!" he bellowed. She gave him a blank stare, and he drew back his hand again.

"Don't touch her, John!" her mother yelled. "Don't you do it again!" John looked at his wife with sullen contempt.

"I'll not have her disrespect me, Rachel!" he shouted. "I'll beat her senseless, I will!"

"Lay another hand on her!" Rachel dared, threatening him. "You'll deal with a coldness you've never known before, husband!" John looked at his wife's determined face, and he lowered his arm.

He rested his hands on the table, shaking his head in anger. Rachel spoke.

"Jem was here, Lia, a short time ago," her mother told her gently. "He said you threatened a man at the tavern last night, and you didn't go in to work today. He gave the last of your wages to your father, and he said that you are not to go to the tavern again." Lia looked at her mother, unsurprised at the news.

"He wanted you to know that he will always care for you," her mother continued. "But he can't have you menace his customers and miss work." Rachel cut her words off quickly, pursing her lips to silence herself. Lia looked at her mother, knowing there was more to be said. She didn't have to ask.

"You forget, my dear Rachel, Jem's *other* reason," John added sarcastically. "He was very clear; he can't employ a woman believed to be a whore!" Lia was incredulous, and indignant rage filled her.

"I'm not a whore!" she screamed, slamming her fist against the table. "I don't believe this! I've done nothing wrong! I wasn't with another man, I was with Mark! He was walking me home!"

"You've brought this upon yourself!" her father told her without pity. "If you had just behaved properly! If you had controlled yourself this would not be!" His voice grew lower as he spoke, and Lia could tell that this anger was spent. "I will take you to work with me in the fields tomorrow, Lia," he said, waving her off. "Go to bed."

Lia woodenly got to her feet and silently climbed the ladder to her room. Standing next to her bed, she felt the uncontrollable desire to throw a fit, to have a tantrum like a child.

Breathing hard, she changed into her nightdress. She wouldn't sleep, she knew. She thought of Mark, and the cloud that had settled onto her mind darkened as she cursed him.

Lia's father woke her before the sunrise, hurriedly telling her to get up for the day's work. She stumbled from her bed, bleary eyed, and began to get dressed. She and her father ate their breakfast in silence, then set out for the fields.

She hadn't worked there in almost a year, and her heart was heavy with dread. No longer would she get her meals for free; no, now she would work her fingers to the bone for a measly bowl of watery soup. She turned up her nose in scorn as she walked. She hated the fields.

She remembered the day she had gotten her job with Jem at the tavern. Mark, in one of his efforts to please her, had given her a token so she could buy herself a ribbon from a passing street vendor. She had thrown it back in his face, telling him that her use for a token had nothing to do with dress goods.

Mark asked her what she would use it for, and Lia had angrily told him that her father would use it to prepare for the wedding that had been thrust upon her family, as there was no money for such things. Then she had run away from him, wandering about the town before heading back towards home.

Jem had called out to her as she passed the tavern, sarcastically asking if her mother would be willing to work in a den of thieves, because the slop he prepared was not fit for dogs and even the scourge who stayed at the inn wouldn't eat it. Surprised, Lia had answered, telling him that she herself was a better cook than her mother, and she did not mind the company of thieves. Jem laughed and offered her a job in his kitchen, and so had begun her employment. Lia smiled to herself, remembering how new and exciting it had been to start her job there. Nothing at all like the anxious feeling of dread she had now.

Arriving at the field, her father handed her one of the tools he had been carrying and led her to their family's portion of land. The sun was coming up over the horizon, and the ground stretched before her dismally. The air smelled and tasted of earth, and she spat in disgust. Across the way, she could see other people arriving to tend their own plots, and she reluctantly began to dig potatoes.

The week that followed was a blur. For six days, Lia woke before the sun, returning home when the light had gone from the sky with only enough time and energy to eat a hurried meal before collapsing in bed from exhaustion. Her father was silent while they worked, refusing to speak to her, and Lia was left alone with her aching back and racing thoughts.

Lia brooded on Mark, anger and misery coursing through her at the knowledge that he didn't want her. She had been foolish to believe that he didn't see her as disgusting, and her heart sank as she realized just how much his desire for her had helped to prevent her from seeing herself as worthless. Her anger and shame grew, and she forgot the pain in her hands and fingers as she tore into the dirt, swearing that she would cut out Mark's heart if she ever saw him again.

The days grew warm early, and Lia's dress was quickly soaked with sweat each morning. Today, there was not a cloud in the sky, and the heat of early September beat down on her as she worked. She straightened for a moment, looking at the bright sun ascending into the sky. It had seemed an eternity, but only a few hours had passed since she had arrived at the fields.

Bending again, Lia caught a glimpse of her father. He was standing a short distance away, a group of the other workers surrounding him. She could see his hands gesturing wildly, and she could tell he was not happy.

She continued working until noon, then her father called her to the trees to rest and eat their meal. He was quiet as he ate, obviously lost in thought. Lia did not try to converse with him, eating in silence and grateful that she didn't have to speak.

When they were finished eating, her father sighed.

"Lia," he began, and she could hear that he was angry. She cringed, waiting for him to begin another tirade about her behavior and reputation. "You must return home," he said. She smiled, instantly surprised and relieved.

"Thank you, Papa!" Lia exclaimed, giving him a quick hug. "I hate the fields!" He was quiet, then spoke again, snapping off each of his words curtly.

"You needn't worry about that any longer," he said. "You won't be coming back." Before she could ask, he continued. "Lia, the others here don't want to work with you." He would not look at her, and she felt that in his heart he agreed with them. "They told me they would not stand for someone like you being on this land, working side by side with honorable folk."

"I've been working alongside those *honorable* folk for a week!" Lia protested, trying to understand. "And they just now say something?" She had been grateful for permission to leave the fields, but not for this reason.

"The talk is getting worse," her father told her. "Someone said you were seen walking the streets with the whores." Lia's eyes flashed with anger, and she turned towards the people still working in the field. Her father stopped her.

"Don't, Lia," he said. "Your wages from the tavern are lost, and I haven't time to think about anything other than making sure we don't starve. Will you seek to destroy me even more? Is it not enough that I have been cursed with the burden of two useless women?" His eyes were tired and dull as he looked at her, his face emotionless.

"But Papa," Lia protested. "I'm not what they say I am!" Her father did not speak, and with a heavy hand he prodded her in the direction of home.

"Tell your mother I'll be home at the usual time," he said as she began to walk. Full of loathing, Lia obediently started towards home, casting a final, hateful glare at the field and its occupants.

Lia wandered the woods, not wanting to return home just yet. Alone with her thoughts, she realized just how much she truly hated the townspeople.

Honorable folk, she thought, scoffing. They were unforgiving fools. And now, she couldn't even help provide for her family because of their ridiculous gossip. Her father was right, she *was* useless.

Lia made her way to the creek. She laughed mockingly, her voice carrying over the trickling water, then she cursed as she kicked at the grass.

"Pigs, they are," she said to the frogs. "Every one of them, filthy pigs!"

"Who are you speaking of, love?" an unfamiliar voice rang out. Lia jumped, her heart instantly racing, and she whipped her head around, searching for the source of the voice. Fear crept up her spine, and she took hold of the handle of her dagger.

"Over here, love," the voice spoke again, and she turned to see a handsome young man standing on the other side of the creek.

"Who are you?" Lia demanded, her mouth going dry as she moved to get a better view through the tall reeds.

She had never seen him before, and she knew he was a stranger to Brunbury. His eyes, peering out at her from underneath a shock of tawny hair, were a deep, emerald green, and from his stance she could tell that he was thickly muscled underneath the loose, linen shirt and rough, brown trousers he wore. He smiled at her with a boyish charm, but Lia wasn't comforted by the kindness of his face. She was completely alone with this stranger, vulnerable and exposed, and she knew she didn't stand a chance against him even with her dagger.

"I'm Thomas," he replied, extending his hand. Realizing that he was too far away for a handshake, he lifted it into a wave instead, laughing. Lia squinted her eyes against the sun. "Why are you out here alone?" he asked.

"Why are *you* out here alone?" she echoed warily. He looked at the sky thoughtfully, scratching his clean-shaven chin.

"I don't believe I know," he answered. "But right now I'm speaking with a pretty girl, so I suppose nothing else matters." Lia forgot her fear for a moment, unable to refrain from smiling at his words.

"Are you afraid, love?" Thomas asked, nodding in her direction as his eyes gave a quick glance at her hand. "I'd bet you have a knife hidden in those skirts with the way you're gripping at them." Lia's heart stopped, and the back of her neck began to tingle with goosebumps.

"I don't know what you're talking about," she lied, her voice cracking as she glanced behind her. Her legs tensed, and she prepared to run. He raised a brow, giving her a knowing look.

"You don't?" he asked with mock surprise. "And I suppose you're not thinking about running, either, now are you?" It was as if he was reading her mind, and Lia was thrown off by his words.

"What if I am?" she countered, and Thomas chuckled.

"Go ahead," he challenged, his eyes sparkling with a playful gleam. "But before you do, will you at least tell me what I've done to scare you away?" He was calm and confident, and Lia found that she didn't know how to respond. She was speechless, and Thomas, seeing her confusion, forced a sorrowful expression.

"Just go," he said, feigning sadness as he dismissed her with a wave. "I suppose I'll just have to spend the rest of my days tormented by the memory of the beautiful girl who wouldn't even give me her name."

Lia needed no further prompting, and she turned to run. A thought flashed through her mind, and she stopped after only a few steps, looking back to eye him suspiciously.

"Are you going to chase after me?" Lia asked him bluntly, and his face lit up with a mischievous grin.

"No, love, of course not," he replied. He winked at her. "Not unless you want me to, that is." Frustration washed over her, and she stomped her foot in the grass.

"Can't you stop joking for even a moment?" she demanded, scowling at him. "I'm being serious!"

"So was I, love," he answered, winking again. Lia wasn't sure what to do, and they stood there in silence, staring at each other.

"Well," Thomas said finally, sighing. "This is fun, isn't it?" He pursed his lips thoughtfully. "So are we going to spend the entire day like this? We'll both have to leave sometime, you know." Lia scoffed, glaring at him, but she didn't answer. She felt trapped, and her mind raced as she tried to think. Thomas grew serious.

"If I wanted to hurt you," he informed her, trying to reason with her. "I would have done so already. I'm very fast, you know, and I could easily catch you." Lia bristled.

"I'd like to see you try!" she retorted indignantly, then she clapped her hand over her mouth. She couldn't believe what she had just said, and her eyes grew wide with horror. Thomas broke into pealing laughter at the look on her face.

"I won't try, love, I promise!" he exclaimed, wiping his eyes as he tried to regain control of his mirth. "Just tell me, why are you afraid?" She thought for a moment, trying to come up with a reply.

"I...I don't know you," Lia finally stammered, and Thomas gave a firm nod of his head.

"You're absolutely right," he agreed. "I'm Thomas Greene, and it's a pleasure to meet you." He bowed with an exaggerated flourish, then he straightened and looked at her expectantly. "And you are?" he prompted. She set her jaw, considering. He didn't seem to be a threat, and though she didn't want to admit it he was probably right about being able to hurt her if he wanted to.

"Lia," she answered quietly. "Lia Grey."

"There!" Thomas crowed happily, grinning broadly. "That wasn't so bad! And now that we're friends you have no reason to be afraid!" His enthusiasm was catching, and Lia felt her guard begin to drop.

"There's more to being friends that just exchanging names!" she pointed out, and Thomas nodded eagerly.

"You're right again," he told her. "But how are we to accomplish that with *me* all the way over here and *you* all the way over there?"

"I'm not even sure if I *want* to be your friend," Lia countered, and his face fell with disappointment.

Even as she spoke the words, she knew they weren't true. Despite her fear, Thomas had intrigued her during their short exchange, and she realized that his charming demeanor had won her over. She relaxed, smiling at him, and he immediately perked up.

"I believe you might be warming up to me," he said, eyeing her, and Lia felt her face grow hot. "Now, with the lady's kind permission, may I join you on that side of the creek?" He bowed again, and this time Lia responded with a slight curtsy and a nod of her head.

Thomas backed up, preparing to make a running leap over the narrow creek. As he jumped, his boot caught on the bank, and he fell face-first into the shallow, murky water. Lia gave a shriek of delighted amusement as she watched him struggle to his feet. His face was lit with excitement, and she couldn't help mirroring his enthusiasm. It felt good to laugh.

"Where are you from?" Lia asked him when he had climbed out of the creek.

"Darrowharty," Thomas told her, giving his head a vigorous shake and sending droplets of water in every direction. "About ten days' travel from here." She had never heard of the place.

"What brings you this way?" she asked, giggling as she dodged the spray from his wet hair.

"I came to find you," he answered, looking her right in the eye. Lia's stomach turned over in her belly, and her face flushed with embarrassment at his words.

"Where are you staying?" she asked, quickly changing the subject.

"I plan to take a room in town," Thomas said. "I heard of an inn, the Laughing Vixen. I had intended to board there." Lia scrunched her nose in disgust.

"If you value your life, you'll steer clear of that place for board," she told him. "I used to work there, and I'll tell you that many a soul was robbed and bled in those rooms." She paused, thinking. Jem's filthy rooms were terrible, and even her family's barn was better. The thought gave her an idea, and she glanced at Thomas.

"My family is poor," Lia began unapologetically. "But if you've nowhere to stay I'm sure we can find a place for you." He looked shocked.

"I've only just met you!" Thomas exclaimed. "And already you try to get me under the same roof as you?" He grinned at her.

"No, sir," she responded curtly, crushing his smile. "I was actually thinking about the barn." He threw his head back in laughter.

"And make my bed with a bunch of animals?" he cried, amused at her suggestion. Lia shrugged, feigning dismissiveness.

"If you'd rather try your luck at the tavern, you go right ahead," she told him, turning and beginning to walk away.

Lia hoped he would take the bait. She had made seven tokens a week when she worked at the tavern, and Jem charged two tokens a night for his disgusting rooms. Giving Thomas a place to sleep would more than replace the wages she had lost when Jem fired her, and she held her breath, listening for a response.

"No, love, I was joking," Thomas called after her, and she smiled triumphantly as she heard his footsteps moving quickly to catch up. "I'll take your word for it."

"Then let's go," Lia said, slowing down to wait for him. He jogged to her side. "I'll introduce you to my mother and father." Thomas nodded, then began digging in his pocket.

"To pay you for your family's kindness," he said, offering Lia several gold tokens. She stopped in her tracks. Gold tokens were not commonplace, and to have him offer her that many shocked her.

"Put them away!" Lia said in a hushed whisper, quickly folding his fingers over the coins. "Don't let anyone see!"

"Lia," Thomas laughed. "There's no one to see!" He was right, they were still alone.

"You'll be robbed, Thomas!" she told him, her voice tinged with concern. He was confused.

"But why?" he asked. "It's nothing but a few tokens!"

"*Gold* tokens, Thomas!" Lia stressed. "We don't see many of them here!"

It was true. Gold tokens held twenty times the value of a silver token, and it was rare to see anyone with that much coin. Carrying silver meant the coins could be divided up and hidden away from prying eyes more easily, and the carrier did not need to be concerned with making much change. Her mind raced.

"You're not a thief, are you?" she asked bluntly. Thomas was indignant.

"Of course not!" he answered. "This isn't much money, I don't understand!" Lia dismissed him.

"Just don't let anyone else see," she told him. He held out the coins to her again.

"I won't, but only if you take these," he promised. Lia was tempted by the pretty shine of the coins as he held them out to her. Giving in, she accepted the tokens.

"Come on!" she said, pulling him along. "Mum won't be happy if we're late!"

• • •

CHAPTER NINE

RACHEL WASN'T HAPPY despite them arriving on time. She was outside the house, dumping a pot of washwater, when Lia and Thomas walked up. Eyeing the stranger, she turned in a huff to go inside.

Lia's father was a bit more welcoming, curious about the visitor.

"What brings you here, Thomas?" he asked after Lia introduced them.

"I've come here for Lia," Thomas answered, winking at her. Lia's father laughed at the joke, then he pulled Thomas out into the yard to speak with him. Lia went into the house, where Rachel scolded her.

"Have you learned nothing, Lia?" she demanded. "Who is this man?" Her face was lined with worry, and the type of fear racing through her mind was evident. Lia was indignant.

"I didn't *try* to meet him, Mum!" she protested, rolling her eyes. "I was at the creek, and he just appeared!"

"And why didn't you leave?" Rachel huffed.

"It wouldn't have mattered!" Lia exclaimed hotly, echoing what Thomas had told her at the creek. "I was completely alone. If he had wanted to hurt me he could have easily done so!"

"And so you bring him home?" her mother cried, shaking her head in disbelief. "What if he's a thief?" Lia grinned, reaching into her apron pocket.

"I don't think he's a thief, Mum," she said, holding out the gold tokens Thomas had given her. "He said he was looking for a place to stay, and when I told him he might be able to sleep in the barn he insisted on paying me with *these*!" The gold coins seemed to glow in Lia's hand, and Rachel inhaled sharply at the sight of the money.

"Put those away, child!" she hissed, looking around anxiously. "What kind of man offers that much coin for a barn to sleep in? What else does he expect from you?"

"I don't think he's like that at all!" Lia told her, her face bright with excitement. "He seems very nice, and he's a gentleman, too!" She began to tell her mother how they had met.

Rachel listened silently, looking out the window to where Thomas and Lia's father were talking. After a moment, she shook her head, and she quickly looked away.

"I don't like him," she told Lia. "There's something about him that's not quite right." Lia rolled her eyes.

"Well," she said, hands on her hips. "You don't have to like him to keep his money!" She could see Thomas laughing as he spoke with her father, and when he glanced at the house she waved wildly. Thomas gave a slight wave, a half-smile on his face, before turning back to his conversation.

"We *do* need the money," Rachel slowly agreed, pursing her lips in thought. "And I suppose it won't hurt to let him stay a few nights." Lia smiled happily, glad that she had managed to find a way to earn a bit of money for her family. Her father's words from earlier that day rang in her ears, and she hoped that now he would change his mind about her uselessness.

Lia went up to her room to change out of her dirt-smeared work clothes. As she pulled a clean dress over her head, she heard a knock at the front door. Her mother's hushed, concerned tone drifted up the ladder, and Lia grew quiet as she strained to listen. She recognized the visitor's voice, and her face turned red as her blood instantly began to boil. With her dress hanging off her shoulders, she raced down the ladder.

"How dare you show your face here!" Lia screamed, picking up a wooden bowl off the table to hurl at Mark. "How dare you!"

"Lace your dress!" Rachel hissed, stepping in front of her. Lia pushed her mother out of the way.

"Lia, let me explain!" Mark said, putting his hands up to calm her. "It's not what you think!"

"You've turned the whole town against me!" she screeched, throwing the bowl. It narrowly missed Mark's head, shattering on the edge of the door instead. Rachel retreated quickly to the corner of the room as Lia continued.

"That's not my fault!" Mark countered, his voice rising. "No one's even talking about the wedding! Everyone's talking about you selling yourself in the tavern!" Lia took hold of her mother's kitchen knife this time, her eyes bulging.

"So it's my fault!" she shrieked, stepping towards him. "You're blaming me for this? You're calling me a whore?" Mark stood his ground.

"No, Lia!" he yelled in frustration. "If you'd just let me explain–"

"You don't need to explain anything, you bastard!" Lia raised the knife. "You're no different than anyone else in this Godforsaken town, you think just as little of me as the rest!"

"That's not true!" Mark answered, trying to reason with her. "I did it because –"

"What's the trouble?" Thomas interrupted, standing behind Mark in the open doorway. "What's going on?"

"Get him out of here, Thomas, before I stab his eyes out!" Lia screamed, her body shaking. "I'll kill him!" Thomas put his hand on Mark's shoulder.

"Come, friend, I think she means it," Thomas said, amusement dancing in his eyes. Mark shrugged Thomas off, ignoring him.

"It's not what you think," Mark told Lia, his voice calm. "I just wanted to prove to you that I love you."

"Hear the boy out, Lia!" her father called from outside, standing a safe distance away.

"Didn't you hear the lady?" Thomas said, taking hold of Mark's shoulder again and ignoring Lia's father. "I believe she wants you to leave."

"Take your hand off me," Mark told Thomas coldly, his eyes still locked on Lia. "My business is with her, not with you."

"I'm afraid I can't do that, friend," Thomas answered, his jaw set. Lia was somewhat surprised at Thomas' willingness to stand up to Mark, and she felt even more justified in her anger. She scowled at Mark, her knuckles turning white as she gripped the knife tightly.

"Put the knife down!" Rachel called from the corner of the room. Lia ignored her.

"Let me talk with you," Mark pleaded. "Just give me a few minutes, then I'll go."

"*Now*, friend," Thomas prompted. "I'll not ask again." Mark didn't move, waiting for a response from Lia. Her eyes narrowed, and her lips pulled back into a snarl.

"Leave!" she commanded, taking another step forward. "I'll kill you, I swear I will!"

"I love you, Lia," Mark said, his voice soft. "I'll always love you, and I'm sorry if I...."

"None of that," Thomas interrupted again. "Let's go!" He pulled Mark out of the doorway and gave him a shove.

"This doesn't concern you," Mark informed Thomas, glaring at him. "Leave me be." Thomas put up his fists.

"Then I'll have to make you leave," he said. Mark grimaced, glancing at Lia. She stood in the doorway, watching with a smirk on her face. Then, without warning, Thomas' fist caught the side of Mark's head with a staggering blow punctuated by a loud crack.

Mark didn't even budge. His eyes instantly sparkled, and his lips turned up in a slight smile that sent an unexpected chill of excitement up Lia's spine. He turned to face Thomas, who was readying for another strike, and with a single, quick motion Mark jabbed. His blow landed squarely in the center of Thomas' face. Thomas' mouth dropped open as Mark spun on his heel and turned towards the road.

"I just wanted to explain, Lia," he said.

As Mark walked away, Thomas crumpled to the ground. Lia watched Mark leave, frozen in place, before tearing her eyes away to look with disgust at Thomas' limp figure. He was flat on his back in the dirt, out cold as blood streamed from his already swollen nose.

When Thomas came to, Lia and Rachel did their best to clean him up. The front of his shirt was soaked with blood and his eyes were both turning black, but aside from his hurt pride, swollen nose, and momentary grogginess he claimed to be otherwise unhurt. Lia felt an odd sense of pride at the thought that Mark had beaten him with only one blow, but she focused on Thomas' injuries instead, trying to force any thoughts of Mark out of her mind.

After they fussed and fretted about him for a good while, Thomas finally convinced Lia and her mother that he was fine, and everyone sat down to eat. Their meal passed with laughter and lightheartedness despite the earlier events, a stark contrast to the dismal evenings of the past few days.

When they were finished eating, Lia's father walked Thomas out to the barn.

"Good night, Lia," Thomas said before leaving the house, grinning like an enamored youth through his bruised face. Lia flushed with color, aware of her mother and father's watchful eyes, and after bidding him goodnight she darted up the ladder to her room.

A few moments after lying down in her bed, Lia heard the front door open, and she held her breath, straining to listen. She could hear her mother's murmuring voice, and Lia was grateful for once that her father lacked the ability to keep his voice quiet.

"Rachel, he's captivated by our Lia!" John exclaimed, to which Rachel loudly shushed him. "He's a strong boy, a bright young man, and to hear him speak he and his family are very well off!" John could not contain himself. "To think that just today I was lamenting my accursed fate, yet now I stand here telling you that I believe this young Thomas might soon want to *marry* our daughter, shame and all! And he's a surprisingly good sport, he wasn't put off in the least by Mark's fist!" Lia could hear her father's feet stomp in the unmistakable rhythm of a jig. Rachel began to speak, her voice rising with dismay.

"I don't like him, John," she told her husband. "What do you know of him?"

"What does it matter?" John asked. "Any man that will have Lia now is good enough for me!"

"I don't like him," Rachel repeated. "I don't think he's right for her. I don't think he's a good man."

"I don't care, Rachel," John dismissed her. "If he asks for her hand I will give it! If she marries her shame will be gone, and we can put this whole ordeal behind us!"

A sad smile crossed Lia's face as she listened to her father's excitement. The voices of her parents drifted out of range and turned into distorted vibrations, and Lia rolled over onto her side. Thinking of marriage after everything that had happened felt like a burden, but her father sounded so sure of himself, and his words echoed in her mind. If she married, her shame would be gone.

The image of Thomas lying on the ground unconscious from Mark's blow flashed through her mind unexpectedly, and a giggle burst from her throat. She clapped her hand over her mouth to silence it, and she fell asleep with a smile on her face.

She was drowning, her hands clawing desperately at the water as she tried to swim. For a moment, her head broke the turbulent surface of the dark, murky blackness, and she gasped a breath before being sucked back under the waves. Her mind panicked, and she opened her eyes against the sting of the water.

Where am I? *she screamed in her head, confusion mingling with despair. Shadows danced gleefully, floating in ethereal wisps of smoke, and she could hear their cackling as she fought. They put out their sharp, needle-like fingers and dug into her flesh, dragging her down as she thrashed.*

Let go! *she begged into the darkness.* Let go of me! I want to live! *The creatures reached into her mind, laughing as they listened to her thoughts. Her lungs burned, and when she could take it no longer she pulled in a deep, agonizing breath of the cold. The water rushed in, filling her body, and she could feel herself losing consciousness. As she sank, her body turning to ice, she thought she saw the moon's reflection shining down at her. She closed her eyes, disappearing into the nothingness below her.*

Horrible pain shot through her body, and her eyes flew open in shock. She screamed, convulsing in anguish. She was no longer in the water, but was lying on the ground in a void of blackness. Next to her was a brightly lit candle, its flame glowing softly against the total darkness. She gazed up in confusion, and found herself wondering where the moon had gone. Another wave of pain wracked her being, and she curled into a ball, her voice hoarse from her cries and screams of agony.

Black hands reached out of the pitch dark around her, their fingers shredding her skin as they pulled at her. With a cruel, unforgiving grasp, they untwisted her curled body until she was stretched flat over the ground. She was naked, and streams of sweat poured from her skin. Her insides burned with an intense flame; she looked down, and a cold, vaporous finger traced a line across her stomach.

In the wake of its touch, something seemed to come alive within her. She watched in horror as her skin rippled and moved as if a demon was trying to break free from inside of her. She screamed aloud, and slimy fingers stifled her cry.

Sharp claws of white bone tore at her abdomen, scraping deep, bleeding furrows into her belly. The thin fingers took hold of her skin, ripping and pulling until her flesh tore, and from the wound thick, yellow pus and pale white mucous spilled. The pain was unbearable, and she could feel a violent writhing tearing her from within. Black worms wriggled out of her, squirming across her skin in slippery streaks. Streams of blood poured from her body, and something began to emerge from the gaping hole in her gut.

The hands released her, reaching instead to pull at the creature struggling to free itself from her body. Her eyes widened in terror as a face rose from the mutilated opening in her skin, and she could not bear the horror of what was happening to her. She squeezed her eyes shut against the gruesome sight, when suddenly it was over and the pain was gone.

A cry rang out against the silence as she caught her breath, afraid to look at her destroyed body. Her hands fearfully reached down to touch her belly, but to her surprise there was no wound. She opened her eyes. The small flame of the candle burned steadily, and she felt herself become calm. The cry came again, and her heart warmed at the sound. She looked, and a dirty, white bundle had appeared on the ground before her.

A baby's gurgle rose from the bundle of rags, and without a thought she reached for it, lifting it into her arms. She rocked the tiny infant, her heart swelling with adoration. The baby's mouth opened in a tiny yawn, and its gray eyes stared up at her in quiet tranquility. She smiled. The baby clutched her finger in its little hand as it began to drift into sleep, and she felt a serene happiness well up inside of her from a place in her heart she did not know existed.

A voice drifted towards her out of the darkness, and she cocked her head to listen. She clutched the baby tight to her chest, fear gripping her as the sound came closer. A shadow moved, brushing her skin as it passed, and she dropped to her knees. She cradled the baby protectively as her eyes searched the darkness for the apparition she knew was there, and in the stillness she could see glowing, emerald orbs staring at her, unmoving. Fear squeezed her heart, and she pulled the sleeping baby close, trying to hide it from whatever was crouching just out of reach of the candle's light.

"Who's out there?" she called, her blood pulsing loudly in her ears. She strained to see, and in a flash the eyes were gone. Immediately forgetting her fear, she relaxed again, peaceful, a smile playing on her lips as she gazed upon the beautiful face of the baby.

A shriek from the darkness pierced her soul, and cold hands reached out to pluck the child from her arms, pulling its sleeping form into the shadows. Terror flooded her and she froze, afraid to leave the safety of the candle's meager light. She stretched out her arms, groping and reaching in futile desperation for the sleeping child. Peals of laughter echoed around her, and she whimpered quietly as the sound of slow footsteps resonated in the distance. The cry of the baby called to her, and her heart faltered. She did not want to go. The cry came again, and she could not bear it; abandoning the candle's light, she ventured into the darkness.

"Baby?" she whispered, her voice pained with desperation. "Come back to me, sweetheart!" She stood in silence, unable to see through the inky blackness surrounding her.

"What are you searching for, love?" a voice rang out, and she jumped. A lantern appeared, dimly illuminating a man's figure as he stood motionless only a few yards away. She couldn't see his face; his features were hidden in the shadows save for his glittering eyes.

He cradled the baby in his arms, and her heart leaped.

"Please," she begged, extending her arms. "Please, give him back to me!" The man gave a cruel laugh, and as the light began to fade she could see his green eyes narrow.

"This bastard child?" he asked innocently. She nodded fiercely. "Why would you want a bastard child?"

Before she could answer, in the last moments of the dying light, she saw the man raise the baby above his head and hurl it towards the ground, the tiny body striking with a sickening thud. Her insides exploded into pieces, and a wail of excruciating sorrow burst from her throat. A dark stream of sticky black liquid ran from the tiny broken form, and she felt as though she could not breathe from the grief. The light was gone, and as she screamed in uncontrollable, gut-wrenching sobs she could hear the man laughing in the darkness.

Lia's pillow was soaked in tears when she jolted awake. She quickly realized that the horror was just a dream, but the sorrow didn't fade. With a bloodcurdling cry of anguish, her tears began afresh, and her very spirit was filled with an unbearable pain. Her body trembled and shook; her arms yearned to hold the child of her nightmare, and although her eyes were open she could still see the baby's broken body lying on the ground. She heard her mother's door fly open, and a moment later Rachel's head appeared at the top of the ladder.

"Lia!" Rachel's concerned voice cried, stepping quickly to the side of the bed. "What's wrong?" She searched Lia's swollen face, worry creasing her forehead.

"Shut that child up!" John's bleary voice yelled. "Someone's got to get some sleep around here!" Rachel ignored him, but he wouldn't give up. "Silence her or I'll come up there and do it myself!" John demanded, and Lia could hear the creak of his step on the ladder.

"Don't you take another step, John Grey!" Rachel shouted down at him, her hands covering Lia's ears to shield her from the loudness of her voice. "Go back to bed, you leave us be!"

"How can I sleep with this going on?" John whined, but Rachel didn't answer him. She caressed Lia's face, a feeling of complete helplessness overwhelming her.

"Tell me how to help you, Lia," she begged, her voice breaking at the sound of her child's cries. "Tell me what to do!"

Lia couldn't speak; she lay on her bed curled into a ball, clutching her stomach as each sob seemed to tear her muscles apart. The wails that emanated from within her expelled a tiny portion of her heartache, but when her lungs expanded to take in another breath it seemed that whatever misery had gone out of her was sucked right back inside of her.

"The baby..." she cried haltingly through clenched teeth. She could say no more, and Rachel rocked her, trying to soothe her.

Lia's chest contracted with each cry as the breath left her. There was a pause, her lungs completely emptying with the force of her scream, before her chest would swell again as she gasped for air. Her cries didn't subside despite her mother's touch, and when she finally fell asleep from exhaustion her sobs continued to wrack her body even as she slept.

• • •

CHAPTER TEN

LIA STARED AT THE PUFFY FACE that appeared in her mirror when she awoke. Two dark shadows had affixed themselves below her tired eyes, and her cheeks were red and burned, the result of sleeping in her own salty tears. Her nose was sore, and she knew the pain in her chest was from her sobs. Lia touched her chafed skin, frowning at her reflection.

Her mother had stayed next to her for the rest of the night in an attempt to offer some comfort, and what little was left of the night had passed in peace. Now, as Lia descended into the kitchen, her mother stood quickly to greet her.

"Are you all right?" Rachel asked, disheveled as though she hadn't slept at all. Her hair was mussed and her skin had dark cast to it.

"I'm fine," Lia sighed. "Just tired, that's all."

"You woke as though the devil himself were coming for you!" her mother exclaimed, searching Lia's face. "What on earth did you dream about?" Lia shrugged.

"I don't remember," she said, squinting as she tried to recall even the smallest bit of the nightmare. She shook her head, giving up after only a moment. "It's just like all of my dreams, I don't remember any of it." Unhappy with her inability to offer a better explanation, but too tired to think about it any longer, Lia began to help her mother in the kitchen.

Later that day, Lia found herself overcome with boredom as she lay on her bed, staring at the ceiling. Thomas had gone into the fields with her father that morning, and she had nothing to do as she awaited his return. Even the thought of wandering the hills wasn't appealing. She sighed, sitting up and scuffling her feet across the floor.

Her foot bumped up against the edge of her money box, which was hidden under her bed, and the coins inside jingled cheerfully. She pulled the box out, opening it and staring down at the tokens.

Each time Jem had paid her for her work at the tavern, she had faithfully deposited all of her weekly wages into the box, and now the box was half full. She had already taken enough out of her savings to buy two nice bolts of fabric to make her wedding dress, and half of the remainder would have gone to buy meat and drink for the marriage celebration. The rest would have been used as a dowry, money meant to accompany Lia as she left her parents' home and built her own home with Mark. She wouldn't need her silver any more, not with the gold coins Thomas had given her and now that the wedding had been called off.

Lia tipped the box, spilling the tokens onto her quilt, and she slowly began counting them into neat piles. Sighing, she reached out and scattered the coins, then fell back onto her bed.

"Lia!" her mother called from downstairs. "Get down here and help me with dinner!" Lia sighed again, and slowly sat up to put the coins back in their box.

"What are we having?" she asked her mother, already knowing the answer.

"Vegetable soup!" came the response. Lia cringed, her mouth dry at the thought of how bland her mother's soup would taste. If only they had some meat, but she knew it was too expensive for her parents to buy. She stared at the box of coins.

"Get down here!" Rachel shouted. "I'll not call you again!" Without another thought, Lia snatched a few silver tokens from her money box and hastily shoved them into her apron pocket.

"Coming!" she answered as she pushed the box back into its place.

Rachel was kneading bread dough.

"Help me," her mother told her, tearing off a hunk of dough for Lia to knead. "Help me with this." Lia shook her head.

"I'm going to town, Mum!" she said, turning to leave.

"You're going to help me, Lia!" Rachel insisted, giving her a firm look. There were dark circles under her eyes, the result of staying awake all night at Lia's bedside. Lia opened the door.

"No, I'm not!" she informed her mother. "I'm going to buy us some meat!" Lia looked back, seeing Rachel's tired, frustrated glare. Ignoring her, Lia shut the door and began to walk towards the town.

She hadn't gone to town since Mark had called off the wedding, and with each step Lia dreaded encountering the townspeople, wondering how they would respond if they saw her. She walked slowly, taking her time, but it wasn't long before she reached the first buildings. Her step quickened as she passed the blacksmith's shop, hoping that Mark wouldn't see her walk by and draw attention to her presence.

The butcher's shop was on the other side of town. She made her way to the squat little shack, and the smell of rotting entrails wafted towards her as she approached. Stepping onto the rickety porch, Lia pushed the door open.

Pieces of meat hung from the sharp tines of a rack on the wall, congealed blood dripping onto the floor to form stinking, blackening pools. Jennings, a short, squinty-eyed man with hair the color and consistency of chopped straw, was standing at the counter, counting money with his red, calloused fingers.

The blood from his victims burned his skin, turning his hands and forearms a perpetual crimson. His stained apron stretched tightly over his massive, round belly, the small piece of fabric offering little protection for his large girth. His clothes were evidence of this fact; the sides of his pants and shirt were streaked with stains from where he had missed the apron while wiping his hands.

Jennings' supply of meat was limited, and each day's stock was different. Some days he had beef, others he had pork or goat, and still others he may only have a few scrawny chickens, but he rarely, if ever, had more than one type of meat available at once. Lia had always suspected that he kept any choice cuts for himself while offering only tough, stringy, overpriced scraps to his customers, which would explain his portliness.

Lia greeted him as she had each day when purchasing meat for the tavern.

"Jennings, you fat bastard!" she smiled, giving him a small wave as she walked up to the counter. "What poor creature have you chopped up today?"

Jennings looked up in surprise at her words, but instead of breaking into a smile and answering with a similar greeting, he scowled at her.

"You shouldn't be here!" he said, pointing one of his thick, red fingers at her. "I won't have my business tainted by the likes of you!" Lia's smile froze on her face. She had expected this, but part of her had hoped she would be wrong and Jennings wouldn't treat her differently.

"I've always bought meat here!" she exclaimed, trying to reason with him. Jennings shook his head.

"Not anymore, you don't!" he told her, waving her to leave. "If I'm seen selling to you I'll lose my business!"

"What's so bad about me?" Lia asked fiercely, taking her tokens out of her pocket and holding them out. "I've got money, just like everyone else!" Jennings softened for a moment at Lia's reaction, and a hint of their old rapport shone in his eyes.

"Ahh, you stupid wench," he sighed. "Why'd you have to go get yourself into this mess?"

"I didn't do anything, Jennings, I swear it!" Lia exclaimed. "I don't deserve this!"

"It doesn't matter, girl," he told her, pity on his face. "Once the town believes it, there's no fixing it. You know that." He hardened again. "You leave now and don't come back, you hear?"

"I'll leave," Lia responded, setting her jaw. "And I won't come back. But I'm going to buy meat first." Jennings looked pained, but he had known her long enough to see that she was determined. He turned to the rack of meat and removed a small animal haunch, then he deftly wrapped it in a scrap of paper. He held it out to her, and she snatched it from him.

"How much?" she asked, seething. Jennings pursed his lips, then let out a breath and winked.

"You go ahead and never mind," he told her, turning away. "Every business in this town gives a little charity to the whores when no one's looking, so why can't I?" Lia grimaced, ready to snap back, before realizing that Jennings was trying to be kind. She rolled her eyes as she turned to leave.

"You're still an ugly bastard," she called over her shoulder, slamming the door behind her.

The evening was getting late, and the streets were mostly empty. When Lia was almost to the edge of town, she saw a small group of people standing near the tavern. They watched her as she passed. She stared straight ahead, trying to ignore them, when out of the corner of her eye she saw one of them pick up a rock.

"You're not welcome here!" the man yelled, throwing the stone at Lia. "You go wait in the whore's alley till nightfall with the rest of your kind!" Lia dodged quickly, then she straightened, rage instantly filling her.

"Miserable dog!" she screamed, standing on her toes. "I've walked these streets every day of my life, and now you treat me like this!"

"We don't want you here!" another person chimed in, and the small crowd moved in to surround her. Lia glared at them, bending down to pick up her own rock to throw, when she saw the simpering faces of Margaret and her sister, Helen. The two girls hated Lia, bitter at the knowledge that she had caught Mark's eye instead of one of them, and now they smiled at her mockingly.

"You need to leave, whore!" Margaret sang, turning up her nose. "The day is for respectable folk, not women like you!"

"The whores in the alley will have a place for you!" Helen chimed in. "Go home!"

The stone in Lia's hand began to burn, and with a cry of rage she pulled back her arm to let it fly. Just as she was about to send it sailing into Helen's smug face, she caught sight of Mark.

Lia paused when she saw him; he was standing in the door of the blacksmith's shop, watching her, the worry creasing his forehead evident even from a distance. His expression stunned her, and she momentarily forgot her anger towards him.

Their eyes locked, and he cautioned her with a firm shake of his head. Mark was afraid for her, she could see, and the reason for his fear flashed through her mind. She was considered a whore now, and a whore assaulting a townsperson was punishable by death.

She gritted her teeth, hearing her jaw grind as she tried to control her rage. She dropped the stone and held her head high as she began to walk again, the crowd of people laughing and jeering. Fuming as she left, she murdered Helen and Margaret a thousand times in her head, tearing them to pieces and leaving them in bits for the dogs and birds to eat.

• • •

CHAPTER ELEVEN

OVER THE NEXT SEVERAL WEEKS, Lia stayed close to home, never wandering too far for fear of being seen and harassed by the townspeople. She was bitter and angry at the way they had treated her, but Thomas' cheerful presence offered her comfort. He was a ready companion, acting as though nothing was more important to him than spending time with her, and it was soon very obvious that he liked her. She felt as if she had known him forever, and his company made her all but forget about Mark and the way the town had shunned her.

Her father was delighted at the turn of events, and as the days passed he grew more and more convinced that Thomas would soon ask for her hand. Lia, for her part, couldn't help being encouraged by her father's enthusiasm, and she soon realized that she was beginning to share in his excitement.

Thomas was sweet and romantic, constantly telling her how beautiful she was, and it wasn't long before she felt comfortable enough to allow him to accompany her on walks in the hills and meadows. He would pick wildflowers for her as they walked, and she found herself drinking in every compliment he gave her, unlike the annoying ramblings Mark had offered.

In all the time they had spent together, Thomas had not told her anything about himself, seeming to prefer silence or nonsense to serious conversation, but Lia's curiosity about him was beginning to get the better of her. As they lay in a sunbaked field one October afternoon, she tried to think of how to broach the subject.

Thomas chewed absently on a long stalk of dry grass, his head propped on one hand as he gazed at Lia's face. She was lying on her back, her eyes closed, enjoying the warmth of the sun on her skin in contrast to the cool, autumn air.

"You're beautiful, love," Thomas said, startling her as he broke the silence.

"You always say that," she answered, rolling onto her side to look to him. "Sometimes I wonder if it's because you have nothing else to say." He looked hurt.

"I have plenty to say," he replied, taking the grass from his mouth. "But that's all I ever manage to get out." He took her hand in his, his fingers gently rubbing her skin. "I do think of other things to speak of," he continued. "But I get too overwhelmed by your beauty." Lia smiled, closing her eyes again, then she sat up quickly. Thomas looked at her with a puzzled expression, surprised at the suddenness of her movement. She frowned.

"Thomas," she began. "Why haven't you told me about yourself?" He chuckled, sitting up as well.

"You've never asked me, love," he answered. Lia looked at him expectantly, and Thomas went on.

"Well," he said thoughtfully. "You already know I'm from Darrowharty." She nodded impatiently. "Where to begin?" He pondered a moment before speaking again.

"I'm the son of a lord," he told her. "My family governs an entire township." Lia was surprised. She had known he was wealthy, but it had never occurred to her that he might hold power as well.

Thomas laughed uncomfortably at the look of amazement on her face.

"It's not that bad," he reassured her. "It's not like I'm royalty or anything. My father governs but the one town, while my uncles oversee three or more provinces each." He grew quiet, thinking, then shrugged.

"I don't know what you want me to tell you, love!" he said. "I'm afraid I'll bore you!" Lia shook her head.

"I want to hear it all," she told him. "I won't be bored, I promise!" He smiled at her eager face.

"Tell me what you'd like to know," he said, giving in. "Then at least I'll have a place to begin!" She paused thoughtfully.

"What's your home like?" Lia finally asked.

"The estate?" Thomas shrugged. "It's big, much bigger than your home." Lia's eyes grew wide as she listened.

"The servants are always busy, cooking and cleaning and making ready for parties and events," he continued, yawning. "The peasants work as groundskeepers, cutting the grass and caring for the gardens before going to work on their own crops and chores. As for me, I spend my days in the stables and lazing about in the orchards."

"I think it's nice that your family employs the peasants," Lia noted. "If only we had someone here to do the same for us." Thomas burst into laughter at her comment, and she felt embarrassed.

"What's so funny?" she asked him, her mouth twisting into a pout. "Why are you laughing at me?" He calmed himself.

"Employ the peasants?" he said, stifling another chuckle. "Why would *we* employ the peasants!" He dissolved into laughter again, and Lia's frustration built. She scowled at him.

"Well, why not?" she yelled. "What's so bad about employing peasants?" Thomas stopped laughing at the sight of her face, coughing awkwardly before speaking.

"Lia," he said. "We don't employ the peasants! They pay *us*!" She was shocked at the thought.

"Why on earth would they pay you?" she asked him. "What do you do for them?" His face grew serious.

"We provide them with protection," he informed her, his voice patronizing and proud. "We lease them land to grow their crops, and for a fair price! They pay us for the right to live there, and for the right to have a good life. Lia," he said, looking at her. "If we didn't own them they would be poor like Brunbury!" She was indignant.

"*Own* them?" she screeched. "What do you mean, you *own* them?" Thomas sighed in exasperation.

"Yes, Lia, we own the peasants, and the servants, and the land," he answered her, rolling his eyes at her ignorance. "The land belongs to us, and does it not stand to reason that those who reside on our land would also belong to us?" Lia thought a moment. She supposed it did make sense, albeit in a very unappealing way.

"I wouldn't have it," she said, shaking her head. "But I suppose if those in your town choose to live there that would be their own decision. How did you and your family come to own the land?" Thomas gave her a disbelieving stare.

"Don't you know?" he asked. "The same way all lords and governors come to own their land!" He laughed at her blank look. "We came upon the town with our droves of servants and laid claim to it. It's not that hard," he finished. "The only ones living there were the peasants, and they couldn't fight us if they wanted to."

"Just like that?" Lia asked, bewildered at the thought. "You came and took the land as easy as that?" Thomas nodded, unhappy with her dismay.

"Why are you so worried about the peasants?" he asked. Her eyes flashed.

"Don't you realize, Thomas?" she asked him. "*I'm* a peasant!" Understanding dawned on his face, and he gently touched her cheek.

"Lia," he told her, his voice reassuring. "You're not the same as them!" She shook her head fiercely.

"What makes me so different?" she wanted to know, an unexpected hopelessness filling her. "What would stop you from viewing me as nothing but a worthless piece of property?"

"Ah," Thomas said, a smile dancing on his lips. "So that's why you're concerned." Lia looked down at her hands, and he moved closer to her. He leaned towards her, his lips brushing against her cheek. She tensed instinctively from his closeness, her heart pounding as her hands began to sweat. She was uncomfortable, but she didn't move away.

"Lia," Thomas whispered into her ear. "You don't have to worry about that."

"And why not?" she asked him, refusing to look at him. His breath was warm against her skin as he spoke.

"Because, Lia," he said, placing his hand on her cheek. "I don't see you as a peasant." He reached up and moved a stray wisp of hair back behind her ear. "All I see is a woman I love."

Lia's heart stopped at his words, and she froze, slowly lifting her face to meet his gaze. He was close, so close, and she felt herself drowning in the depth of his eyes.

"I love you, Lia," Thomas said, his voice steady and firm. Then his lips were pressed against hers, and his strong arms held her tightly against him as he kissed her. Her body glowed with heat at his touch, and she felt that she loved him, too. She kissed him back, feeling like she was floating on a cloud.

Thomas decided to visit the tavern the next evening, much to Lia's dismay. She tried to talk him out of it, but he was determined.

"I have to have a moment to myself, Lia," he said. She pouted.

"But I thought you loved spending time with me!" she protested, hurt. Thomas laughed.

"I always want to spend time with you!" he reassured her. "But you can't expect me to stay by your side every single second of the day!" She reluctantly gave in, and Thomas walked towards the town, whistling his usual cheery tune.

With Thomas gone, Lia felt a broody frustration rise up within her, and it grew with each passing hour. She sat in silence at the dinner table later that night, her mood foul and her face sour. Her father chastised her.

"You can't expect the man to spend all his time in the company of a woman, Lia!" John said, exasperated at her attitude. "What's gotten into you?" She shrugged, glaring at her food.

"I don't see what's taking him so long!" she snapped finally. Her mother looked at her.

"Don't you remember working at the tavern?" Rachel asked gently. "It was often very late before you came home."

"I don't care!" Lia huffed. "He should be back already!" Her father slammed a fist on the table.

"I won't have the peace of the past weeks tainted by your mood, child!" he shouted. "Calm yourself!" She glowered, unable to keep quiet.

"So as long as Thomas is around you're happy, but when you're stuck with the company of your useless women you act like a brute?" she asked her father, her tone challenging. Rachel gave Lia a hard look.

"Silence, Lia!" she commanded. "You know your father has never thought of us that way!" Lia scraped her chair against the floor as she jumped to her feet.

"Yes, he does!" she screamed. "He told me in the fields! He said he was burdened with two useless women, and I know he wishes he was at the tavern with Thomas instead of stuck here with us!" Lia stormed up the ladder to her room.

She lay awake until the early morning hours. The moon was high in the night sky before she heard Thomas' whistle coming down the road, and Lia looked out the window. He was stumbling, his steps wobbly with his drunkenness, and when he tripped and fell he struggled to his feet, cursing loudly. She draped her shawl over her nightdress and quietly stole down the ladder, letting herself out the front door and going to meet him.

"Ah, my lovely Lia!" Thomas sang, his words slurred. He staggered towards her, putting his arms around her and leaning on her for support. Lia felt her knees buckle under his weight, and she pushed him off of her.

"Give us a kiss, love!" He leaned forward heavily and Lia stepped back, disgusted at the smell of his breath.

"You're completely drunk!" she exclaimed. Thomas laughed.

"Of course I'm drunk, wench!" he crooned. "Why else would I go into town?" She felt rage well up inside of her.

"Don't call me a wench, Thomas!" Lia hissed. "Where were you? The tavern closed hours ago!" He threw up his hands.

"I don't know where I was, love!" he told her with glee. "But if you happen to find out be sure to tell me!" He doubled over with laughter, losing his balance and falling to the ground. He sat there, his hair and clothes disheveled, unable to control his giggling. Lia stomped her foot in frustration.

"Can't you keep quiet for a moment?" she demanded. Thomas put his hands up to calm her.

"Okay, yes, I'll be quiet," he chuckled. "Just tell me what you want, love, and I'll do it." He grabbed her hand and yanked her to the ground beside him, then he put his arms around her waist, hugging her tightly. "Give us a kiss, love, and I'll be at your beck and call!" Lia could barely understand his words, and she wrenched away from his grasp. He crawled towards her, reaching for her.

"Go to bed, Thomas," she told him, her voice low. "I'll talk to you tomorrow." He groaned in dismay.

"Come to bed with me," he pleaded. "I'll be nice, I promise!" Lia was overcome with the urge to slap him. Restraining herself, she turned away.

"Go to bed," she repeated through clenched teeth. "I'll talk with you in the morning." She began to walk away.

"You and I are the talk of the town, you know!" he called to her retreating back. Lia stopped, turning to him.

"What do you mean?" she asked. Thomas lay back on the ground.

"I believe I will sleep right here," he decided. She walked towards him, standing over his prone figure.

"What do you mean?" Lia repeated. "Why are we the talk of the town?" Thomas closed his eyes, starting to fall asleep, and she kicked him.

"Ow!" he howled. "Why'd you do that?" She put her hands on her hips, and he looked up at her blankly.

"I'll not ask again," Lia told him. He blinked a few times, remembering her question.

"You're a whore," Thomas said simply. "And you and I have been spending an awful lot of time together. Alone." He cackled loudly. "And what do you think they believe we've been doing the whole time?" He closed his eyes again, and she left him there.

Lia walked in the light of the moon, finding herself at the creek. Making herself comfortable, she lay back in the grass, listening to the sound of the water. She frowned, too overwhelmed by the anger still burning hot in her chest to be afraid of the dark. Mark would never have done this. But perhaps Thomas' behavior was normal; after all, she reasoned, the men she had encountered at the tavern were the same way. Still, she was angry.

As the moon rose higher and higher in the sky, she finally let herself be lulled to sleep by the sound of the trickling creek.

● ● ●

CHAPTER TWELVE

LIA AWOKE TO THE SOUND of splashing. She groggily opened her eyes to see Mark standing next to the creek, throwing rocks into the water. She sat up, finding herself oddly relieved to see him.

"What are you doing here?" Lia asked sleepily, rubbing her eyes. Mark turned to look at her.

"Good morning," he said, tossing a stone. It plopped into the water and he picked up another. "Where's Thomas?" Lia lay back down and covered her face with her arm.

"Probably passed out in the barn," she told him, sighing. "He spent the night at the tavern." Mark sneered.

"The fool," he hissed, throwing the rock angrily. It sailed over the narrow creek and into the reeds on the opposite bank.

"I know," Lia agreed, a satisfied smirk on her face. It was nice to hear that someone shared her opinion. "He couldn't even walk last night!"

"That's not what I meant," Mark corrected her, reaching for another rock. "He should be grateful that he has you, not wallowing in ale at the tavern." She uncovered her face and glared at him, irritated by his words.

"Like you were?" she asked tersely, her eyes filled with resentment. "When you called off the wedding?" He dropped his stone mid-throw and sighed.

"You never let me explain, Lia," he began.

"It doesn't matter," she said quickly, interrupting him as she stood to her feet. "Don't start, I really don't want to talk about it." Mark was obviously frustrated, but he gathered himself and cleared his throat.

"I need to talk to you about Thomas," he began. Lia cocked her head warily.

"What business is he of yours?" she asked, eyeing him.

"You'll not want to hear it," Mark warned her. She waved off his concern, motioning for him to speak. He averted his eyes. "Thomas doesn't care for you the way you may believe he does," he said quietly. Lia rolled her eyes and scoffed.

"I don't really care about your opinion," she said, turning away. "Or what you think I believe." Mark grabbed her arm, stopping her.

"You don't understand!" he explained, trying to make her listen as she pulled away. "I saw him last night!" Lia's heart skipped a beat. She slowly raised her eyes to look at Mark's worried face, and with clenched teeth she spoke.

"What did you see?" she asked, her voice low. He shook his head and sighed.

"I saw him leave the tavern, Lia," Mark began quietly. "He went into the whore's alley." Her face flushed with heat, but her skin was numb and cold.

It was generally acceptable for single men to visit whores, but it was despicable for a married or betrothed man to spend time with such filth. While Thomas was neither married nor officially betrothed, he had told Lia that he loved her, and the thought of him giving his attentions to some worthless street woman was unbearable.

"I….I don't believe you," Lia stammered, her eyes wide with shock as she stared at Mark. "I don't believe you!"

"It's true, Lia," Mark whispered. He stepped towards her, taking her hand. "He doesn't care for you."

Lia fell silent, trying to think. Her mind raced, and her chest began to ache. Mark watched her with concerned eyes, and she suddenly grew defensive, not wanting him to see how upset she was. She met his gaze, her eyes steely.

"Don't worry about me, Mark," Lia said finally, forcing a smile. "I have to go." She turned to leave, but a sudden pang of curiosity stopped her. She paused.

"Mark," Lia asked, her back towards him. "Why did you call off the wedding?" He was silent for a moment before answering.

"I wanted you to have a choice," he said. She turned to look at him, puzzlement on her face.

"What do you mean?"

"You would have married me because you had to," Mark continued. "I wanted you to finally have a choice."

"Why would you do that?" Lia asked, incredulous. "You knew what the townspeople would think!" Mark shrugged.

"I don't care about the damn townspeople," he told her. He stared at her, unblinking, searching her eyes. "I didn't think you did, either." He gave her a slight smile, then turned and reached towards the ground for a pebble. As Lia walked away, she could hear the plunk it made as he tossed it into the creek.

She made her way home, mulling over Mark's reasons for calling off the wedding. Lia was still angry at him, incredulous that he hadn't even talked to her about his plans before withdrawing his oath, but his explanation for why he had done so struck her deeply.

He had wanted so badly to marry her, yet he was willing to risk her rejection by giving her a choice. As she approached her house, though, her thoughts shifted to what he had said about Thomas, and she felt anger begin to pulse through her veins.

Lia threw the barn doors open to see Thomas sprawled out in the hay, snoring loudly. His clothes were awry and wrinkled, and even from her place near the door she could smell the lingering odor of ale rising off of him. Watching him sleep, she was overwhelmed with the desire to stomp his face in.

As much as she didn't want to believe it, she could almost picture Thomas staggering in the streets, his arms holding tightly to a whore as he whistled and sang in a drunken stupor. Her blood boiled with rage and betrayal, and she kicked him hard to rouse him from his sleep.

"Ow!" Thomas shouted, sitting up quickly to clutch his ribs. "Why'd you do that?"

Lia put her hands on her hips and scowled at him. He looked up at her, angry and bleary eyed. Seeing her enraged glare, though, he relaxed only a moment later, a smile playing on his lips.

"Lia!" he crooned. "Come give us a kiss!" She backed away, stomping her foot.

"And where were you all night?" Lia demanded. Thomas smiled wider, then seemed to think better of it and forced a dumbfounded expression.

"I don't know," he claimed. "I don't remember anything after the swill Jem served for dinner!" His eyes sparkled as he stared up at her, trying to keep a straight face. Lia was not amused.

"How could you be gone all night?" she yelled, kicking at him again. Thomas lay back in the straw, closing his eyes.

"I don't know, love!" he exclaimed. Lia seethed, and before she could stop herself she began to speak.

"You were with a whore, you bastard!" she screamed at him. Thomas' eyes flew open at her words, and he jumped to his feet.

"Why would you say that?" he demanded, his voice filled with hurt and confusion at her accusation. "You weren't there, how could you possibly know?"

"Mark told me!" Lia said defiantly. "He saw you in the streets!" Thomas gave her an incredulous look, then his eyes grew wide with shock.

"When were you with Mark?" he asked slowly. "What were you doing with him?" There was suspicion in his voice, and Lia could not believe her ears.

"I would never do something behind your back!" she exclaimed, offended by his insinuation. Thomas pursed his lips, his eyes full of betrayal.

"Then why were you with him?" he countered, shaking his head sadly. "Why would you spend time with him after I..." His voice broke. "...after I told you that I love you?"

Lia opened her mouth to speak, but paused. Thomas' eyes were damp as he blinked back the tears forming in them, and she didn't know what to think. He seemed honest and sincere, and she felt her anger begin to fade. Perhaps Mark had been mistaken; after all, he never said he actually *saw* Thomas with a whore.

"You still haven't accounted for your late night," Lia said finally, her voice growing calm. "The tavern was long closed before you came home." Thomas caught her hand, looking at her earnestly.

"I don't remember last night," he began, his voice soft. "But I swear to you, I would never visit a whore. I love you too much for that, drunk or not. Will you believe me?" Lia sighed, and she felt herself give in to him.

"Yes," she said, relaxing. "I believe you."

"I'm glad to hear that, love," he said happily, squeezing her hand. "Now," he rubbed his stomach. "Is there food in the house? I'm starved!" Lia nodded, and Thomas held her hand as they walked to the house.

• • •

CHAPTER THIRTEEN

THE AIR GREW COLDER as October turned into a snowy November. Thomas didn't go back to the tavern, spending each evening at home, and Lia was convinced that Mark had been wrong about him. A subtle fear gnawed away at her heart, though; he claimed to love her, but he still hadn't said a single word about asking for her hand. Somehow she felt that a proposal from him would further prove that Mark had been mistaken, and she spent her days trying to think of a way to prompt Thomas to ask for her.

Thomas frequently made trips into town during the day, and when he came back he always brought her a gift of some sort. Today, he had brought her a bag of molasses taffy, her favorite, and they lay in the warm barn slowly savoring the smooth sweetness of the treat.

"Thomas," Lia said, looking at him as he lay in the straw. "Do you remember that day in the fields?" Thomas didn't move, his eyes closed as he prepared to take a nap.

"What day was that, love?" he asked absently, his voice heavy with sleep and sticky from candy. "Let me rest a moment, Lia, I'm tired." She would not be put off.

"Don't you remember, Thomas?" He sighed and rolled over to face her.

"Remind me, love, and I'll remember," he told her. Lia squirmed.

"We were in the fields," she prodded. He laughed.

"We spent a lot of time in the fields, Lia!" Thomas chuckled. "How am I to remember one single day out of dozens?" She huffed.

"Well, it was a special day to me," she told him. "It was the first day you told me how you felt about me." Thomas looked bewildered.

"And what did I tell you, love?" he asked, suddenly irritated. "Out with it, and spare us from this nonsense game of yours!" Lia was frustrated with his tone. She had hoped that he would know what she was talking about, and she didn't want to have to tell him.

"It doesn't matter," she said quickly. "Just take your nap." She leaned back in the straw, fuming as she stared up at the dark rafters of the barn, and Thomas closed his eyes. After a few moments, Lia tried again.

"It was the first time you kissed me," she said. Thomas smiled, moving onto his side and propping his head up on his hand.

"Ah, now I remember!" he said, his eyes sparkling. "That was a special day for me, too!" Lia was relieved, but Thomas didn't go on.

"Do you remember what you told me?" she asked him. He shrugged, and his face became thoughtful.

"Hmm," he said pensively. "What was it? And you say it was something important, something special to you?" She nodded. Thomas was quiet as Lia's irritation grew, then he snapped his fingers.

"How could I forget!" he exclaimed. "I told you how beautiful you are!" She frowned, and he furrowed his brow as he went back to thinking. His face lit up again.

"I told you how beautiful you are," he repeated. "*And* it was the first time I told you how much I love you!" Lia's scowl disappeared as she laughed.

"Yes!" she crowed gleefully. Thomas leaned in for a kiss, but she pushed him away. He was disappointed.

"Give us a kiss, love, won't you?" he begged her, his voice sweet. Lia shook her head, giving him a coy look, and he twisted his mouth into a pout. His eyes began to gleam as he studied her face, and he grinned slyly. "What do I have to do?" he asked. Lia had wanted him to ask just that. She pretended to think, but she already knew.

"Well," she said, looking away. "You might continue your train of thought from that day." Thomas looked at her blankly, then understanding dawned on him.

"I see," he said, chuckling. Lia smiled, and he took her hand.

"Did you know that I realized I loved you the first time I saw you?" Thomas asked, his voice dripping with honey. She shook her head, enjoying the moment. "I did, though, love, I knew!"

"How could you possibly know?" Lia asked him playfully. Thomas' face became serious, and he gazed at her softly.

"You were the most beautiful creature I'd ever seen," he said. She waited for him to continue, but he just stared into her eyes.

"So it was just my beauty that did it?" she asked, pretending to be hurt. He quickly spoke again.

"And everything else about you!" he added. "You're such a sweet girl, Lia, and I can't help but love you!" She smiled, but she wasn't warmed. Sweet was a word no one had ever used to describe her. Thomas put his hand to her cheek.

"I've been thinking about this for quite some time," he said quietly. She knew what was coming, but she didn't feel the excitement she had expected.

"Lia," Thomas began, kissing her hand. "I would like to ask your father if I may marry you." A slight smile touched her lips, yet she was filled with dismay. She had thought this moment would be happier. Thomas stared at her, waiting for a response, and, swallowing hard, Lia feigned joyfulness.

"Yes!" she cried hollowly, tightly wrapping her arms around his neck. "Will you ask Papa tonight?" Thomas nodded quickly, unwrapping himself from her grip.

"Yes, love!" he promised. "Tonight. Now," he said, taking her face in his hands. "I believe you owe me something!" Lia didn't feel like kissing him, but she didn't pull away.

They stared at each other in silence. Thomas didn't seem any different than he had before his proposal, almost as though it didn't matter to him either way, and Lia couldn't help remembering how Mark hadn't been able to contain his excitement for weeks after her father had given him her hand. She tried to ignore the feeling of discomfort that gnawed at her, forcing a smile as Thomas pulled her close and kissed her again. This is what she had wanted, but Lia wondered why she was having to convince herself to be happy. She closed her eyes as Thomas held her in his arms, forcing herself to stop thinking about the confusion in her heart as she slowly drifted off to sleep.

It was dark when Lia awoke. Thomas was no longer by her side, and for a moment she was afraid.

"Thomas?" she called into the darkness. There was no answer, and she was hurt and angry that he had left her alone. She rushed to the house to find it empty save for her mother.

"Where's Thomas?" Lia demanded. Her mother was surprised.

"He's not here," Rachel answered. "He's gone into town with your father." Lia's heart jumped into her throat as her mother pulled a chair out from the table and gestured for Lia to sit down to eat.

"I wonder if Thomas has already asked him!" Lia exclaimed breathlessly. Her voice betrayed her enthusiasm, and her mother raised a quizzical brow.

"What do you mean?" Rachel asked cautiously, turning to fill a bowl with bread and soup. The excitement Lia hadn't felt earlier began to rush through her, and she beamed with happiness.

"Thomas told me he would ask for my hand today, Mum!" Lia exclaimed. Rachel did not look happy.

"I hope you know what you're asking for, child," she said softly. "I don't believe you know him well enough to marry him." Lia was disappointed with her mother's caution.

"And you truly believe I knew Mark any better?" Lia asked, pursing her lips as she rolled her eyes at her mother's tone. "He followed me around, yes, and he was an incessant bother, but that doesn't mean I knew him! I didn't love Mark, but I truly do love Thomas! Why can't you just be excited for me? Why must you try to ruin my happiness?" Rachel sighed.

"Despite what you might believe, Lia," she said. "Your father considered carefully before giving Mark your hand."

"He just didn't consider *me* before giving my hand," Lia interjected. Her mother ignored her.

"He would not give your hand to a man he did not trust," Rachel said. "He knew Mark to be honest and true, and he knew Mark would care for you." She looked at Lia thoughtfully. "This Thomas of yours, how are we to know he's trustworthy? We've barely known him a few short months." Lia opened her mouth to respond, but her mother stopped her.

"It doesn't matter now, Lia," Rachel said dismissively. "Your father's only concern is that you marry; he will not care to whom. He will give you to Thomas if Thomas asks him." Lia smiled. "I just hope you're certain, Lia," her mother finished. "Now eat your dinner."

Lia poked at her food, but she didn't eat. She was much too nervous, and she found herself glancing out the window every so often, waiting for Thomas and her father to come home. She grew impatient as time passed, and Rachel became tired of her pacing and whining.

"Go to bed, Lia!" Rachel commanded.

"I'm not tired, Mum!" Lia protested. "I slept late in the barn!"

"I did not ask, child," Rachel told her firmly. "I'm sure your father will wake you when he returns." Rachel rolled her eyes, thinking of her husband's noisy footsteps and loud voice. "Go to bed," she repeated. Lia grudgingly obeyed, stomping up the ladder to her room and readying herself for bed. She lay there, wide awake, listening intently for any sound of the returning men.

She dozed, unintentionally, for several hours before jolting awake. There was no light shining up into her room from the kitchen, and Lia knew her mother had already gone to bed. She looked out her window, sighing. The men had not yet returned. Falling back onto her bed in a huff, Lia crossed her arms, cursing them.

She closed her eyes, beginning to drift back to sleep, when she thought she heard Thomas' whistle in the distance. She sat up quickly. There it was again, she was sure of it! Lia looked out her window a second time, straining her eyes in the darkness. She could just make out two figures slowly coming up the road, and now she could hear a gruff, incoherent voice singing along to Thomas' tune. They were drunk, the two of them leaning against each other as they walked through the crisp snow, swaying and tottering as they laughed.

"Mum!" Lia called downstairs. "They're back!" Rachel threw her bedroom door open in an instant, and Lia couldn't help wondering if her mother had been as anxious for the men's return as she was.

The whistling and singing turned into slurred speech and laughter, and Lia could hear Thomas and her father approach the house. She peeked down into the kitchen, feeling her excitement grow.

The door burst open a moment later.

"Wife!" Lia's father bellowed. "Where's my dinner, wife?" Rachel stood in the kitchen, glaring at her husband in disapproval.

"Fetch it yourself!" she snapped, her voice stern. "You come home at this hour and expect me to wait on you?" John laughed at his wife's anger, turning to Thomas.

"This is what's in store for you!" John chortled, slapping Thomas on the back. "As stubborn as a mule, this one is, and Lia is just the same! Are you sure you still want her?" He and Thomas dissolved into laughter at the joke.

"Who else will take her?" Thomas asked, wiping his eyes. Lia burned at his comment.

"Daughter!" John called. He stumbled as he turned, catching himself on a chair. "Lia, get down here!" Lia flew down the ladder, tripping on the last step and falling in a heap on the floor. She stood up quickly, only mildly embarrassed.

"Yes, Papa?" she asked him, straightening her nightdress. John began to laugh again.

"Well!" he mused to Thomas. "You should have seen her when Mark came to call! She lit out through that door, her nightdress flapping in the wind and barefoot, before even hearing what he had to say!" John slapped his knee in amusement at the memory. "Let's hope her reaction this time is a sign of good luck, shall we, my boy?" He and Thomas howled, both doubled over as they shook with laughter. Lia's face turned red, her blood beginning to boil.

"Get on with it, will you?" she shouted at the two cackling men. "I'll not stand here all night!" Trying to control themselves, they looked at her, their faces crimson from their hysterics.

"Lia," John began, pulling her towards him and putting his arm around her shoulders. He gave her a squeeze, almost suffocating her with his grasp. "This Thomas fellow has asked me for your hand!" Lia smiled, her heartbeat speeding up. "And I've told him he can have it!" She looked at Thomas. A stupid, dazed grin played on his lips as he swayed, trying to keep his balance.

"Give your betrothed a kiss now, love!" Thomas sang. He reached for her, swinging wildly as he tried to find her hand. Lia recoiled, unable to swallow the repulsion that welled up in her throat. "Aren't you happy, Lia?" Thomas asked her incoherently, trying to look into her eyes. "You're going to be my wife!"

Lia's excitement was instantly and effectively stifled by Thomas' foolishness, and the sound of his words overwhelmed her with a sudden, uncontrollable disgust. Reaching for her again, Thomas pulled her towards him and lost his balance, the two of them landing on the floor in a heap. Lia kicked at him, cursing loudly.

"Get off me!" she shouted angrily. Thomas laughed, rolling over on top of her and kissing her hard on the mouth. Her mother gasped in disapproval, but John waved dismissively.

"Ah, Rachel," Lia's father laughed. "They'll be married in a month, don't you worry your pretty head about these two!" Rachel gave her husband a withering glare.

"You go to the barn!" she commanded, pointing to the door. "I'll talk to you in the morning when you've sobered up!" John's spirits fell, and he glowered at his wife.

"In the barn?" he roared. "In the cold?" He was flabbergasted at the thought.

"In the barn!" Lia's mother yelled, pointing stiffly at the door. "Go!"

"Stubborn woman!" John shouted. "You'll be the death of me, you will!" He bent down and took hold of Thomas. "Let's go, boy!" he said, dragging Thomas towards the door. "Save something for your wedding night!" Thomas waved playfully as he was pulled outside, winking at Lia as the door shut behind them.

"Are you sure this is what you want, Lia?" Rachel asked again, shaking her head in irritation at the condition of the men.

"I'm sure, Mum," Lia answered quietly, trying to convince herself more than her mother. She knew her mother didn't believe her, and Lia's heart suddenly felt heavy. Rachel shook her head, turning to go to bed.

"I hope so, child," she said quietly. "I hope so."

• • •

Chapter Fourteen

They announced the wedding on Lia's seventeenth birthday, and three days later Mark left town.

"He's gone, Lia," her mother told her, frowning.

"What do you mean, he's gone?" Lia asked, surprised and taken aback. "Why would he leave? Why wouldn't he say goodbye?"

"Think about it, Lia," Rachel said, rolling her eyes at Lia's naiveté. "That boy loved you, and you're marrying someone else. You tell me, why do you think he left?"

"But he should have said goodbye!" Lia cried. "He should have at least said goodbye!"

"He wanted to, Lia," her mother said gently. "But he didn't feel like he could."

"How do you know?" Lia demanded. "You saw him, didn't you? You talked to him!"

"Yes, I did," Rachel answered, looking away. "He told me to tell you that he loves you, and that he's sorry."

"Didn't he want to see me?" Lia was confused and disappointed, unsure of what to think. Mark had never been gone; while she hadn't seen him since that day at the creek, the news of his departure brought with it the realization that, despite the events of the past months, there had been comfort in knowing he was close by. She always knew that if she really needed him she could find him, and knowing that he had left made her feel inexplicably vulnerable and lost.

"He did, Lia," her mother told her. "But he chose not to. You must understand, child, that boy was heartbroken. You can't fault him for his weakness."

"What weakness?" Lia asked, incredulous. Her mother gave her a sad look.

"You, Lia," she answered simply.

Thomas had agreed to marry Lia in mid-December, a little less than a month away, and a flurry of preparations ensued. The dress she would have worn to marry Mark was partially unfinished, and now she stayed up late each night with her mother to finish sewing. Lia's father was in high spirits, spending his days in town bragging about the upcoming wedding and making sure that everyone knew that Lia's shame would soon be a thing of the past. Thomas stayed by his side, spending coin after coin on useless baubles for the marriage celebration.

After about a week of long days and nights, Lia began to feel tired and ill. She didn't think anything of it, attributing the sick feeling in her stomach to her lack of sleep, but when she awoke one morning feeling as though her insides had been stirred into a frenzy she knew something was wrong.

"Mum!" Lia called weakly, the watery contents of her stomach rising in her throat. "Mum!" Rachel climbed up the ladder to Lia's room, and she was immediately surprised by her daughter's green face.

"What's gotten into you, child?" Rachel exclaimed as Lia lay motionless in bed. Descending the stairs, she quickly grabbed a bowl from the kitchen, returning and handing it to Lia just in time. Lia vomited, her body arching as her stomach emptied itself.

"What have you eaten?" her mother asked, feeling Lia's forehead for signs of a fever. "What have you gotten into?" Lia threw up again, gasping as she caught her breath.

"I don't know!" she cried, her empty stomach hurting. "I haven't eaten anything different than anyone else!" She groaned as she lay there, her arm across her face. "I don't know what's wrong!" Rachel thought a moment, then her face darkened.

"Lia," she asked quietly. "When was the last time you saw your monthly blood?" Lia shrugged, her stomach rising into her throat again.

"I don't know!" she whimpered. "I was working at the tavern still, I think!" Her shoulders heaved as she swallowed hard. "Why does that matter?" Rachel's face was white, and Lia looked at her in surprise, instantly afraid. "What's wrong, Mum?"

"Lift up your skirts," her mother commanded. Lia hesitated, and Rachel took hold of the nightdress herself, quickly raising it to expose Lia's legs and stomach.

"Mum!" Lia exclaimed, embarrassed and indignant. "What are you doing?" Her mother's strong fingers kneaded and prodded her abdomen as Lia turned on her side to vomit. Fear shadowed Rachel's face.

"No," she whispered to herself, taking a step back. She thought a moment, then, with a swift motion and flash of her hand, she inserted her fingers, pressing on Lia's abdomen from both the inside and outside as Lia was stunned speechless.

It was over in a quick moment, and Rachel yanked the nightdress back down, a grave look on her face, while Lia gave a cry of shock and horror at what her mother had done. Rachel ignored her, wiping her hands on her apron.

"What have you and Thomas been up to all those days alone in the fields?" Rachel demanded, crossing her arms.

"What do you mean?" Lia asked, still stunned by her mother's actions and incredulous at the insinuation. "Do you think that because I was taken I would suddenly be willing to give myself freely to a man?"

"You're telling me the truth?" Rachel asked severely. Lia nodded, and Rachel sat down next to her. "Lia," she said, shaking her head sadly. She fell silent.

"What, Mum?" Lia asked, fearful at her mother's tone. "What's wrong?"

"You're with child," Rachel told her quietly, avoiding her gaze. "You're pregnant."

Lia felt her throat close tight, and she couldn't breathe. She reached down to the place her mother had felt, and as Lia pressed her normally soft belly she could feel a slight firmness there that she had never felt before. Her stomach churned and she threw up again.

"No," she whispered, coughing, unwilling to believe it. "No! I'm getting married, I'm going to be happy! You're wrong!" Hot tears welled up in her eyes, and a sinking feeling mixed with the nausea in the pit of her stomach. Her eyes pleaded with her mother, begging her to be wrong, begging her to take back her words. Rachel shook her head.

"I'm not wrong, Lia," she said. "I wish I was, but I'm not. I've midwifed for enough women to know what a pregnancy feels like." Lia looked at her mother, her eyes wild.

"What can I do?" she asked desperately. "What can I do?"

"What are you talking about, child?" Rachel breathed, aghast as she caught Lia's meaning.

"Mum, how can I get rid of it?" Lia reached for her mother's hand, her fingers squeezing tight. "I don't want this horrible creature! I don't want it inside of me!" She lit upon an idea, and a glimmer of hope appeared in her eyes. "The healer, Mum!" Lia exclaimed. "Can she help me?"

The town did not have a doctor, only a wise woman who knew the remedies of the forest, and for a small price she would prepare a healing mixture of herbs to treat whatever ailments the townspeople suffered from. Surely she would have something to cure this affliction!

"No, Lia!" her mother exclaimed. "She can give you herbs, but there's no promise they will work!"

"I can try, though, can't I?" Lia cried.

"You can try," Rachel cautioned. "But if the dead child doesn't come out it could rot inside of you, killing you! Or you could give birth to a deformed monster, and you will be forced to care for the beast all your days!" Rachel shuddered. "There was a boy in my town, when I was a child," she said. "He had no eyes, Lia! His mother had tried the concoction of the wise woman, and instead of emptying her womb it cursed her with a sightless child!"

"There must be something I can do!" Lia desperately searched her mother's face. "Please, Mum, tell me how to fix this!"

"I'm sorry, child," Rachel said sadly. "Only God can take this from you, either through an untimely loss or when you give birth." Lia could not contain her sorrow, and she began to sob.

"How can I marry?" she cried. "Now Thomas is sure to know! I can't hide *this* from him!" Lia had intended to cut herself on her wedding night to mimic her purity blood, but too much time had passed since her attack for her to claim the child was Thomas', even if they married that very day. She didn't know what to do, and as her cries of sorrow and frustration grew louder she wished she could just disappear.

After she had managed to stop crying, Lia went to the fields to think. Thomas had gone to town, as usual, and for once she was glad that he wasn't there. She wanted to be alone; she had to pull herself together before he returned, but doing so soon seemed impossible.

She couldn't contain the disgust she felt at the thought of having her attacker's child inside of her. Lia looked down at her belly, bile rising in her throat, and she was overcome with the urge to take hold of a knife and hack the creature out of her. Heaving again, her rage and frustration built into an inferno, and she bit her lip until it bled in an effort to stifle her screams.

The metallic taste of her blood filled her mouth, and she threw up thick mucus from her empty stomach. She tried to calm herself against the fresh wave of tears and nausea that washed over her, but her mind was too frantic with the knowledge of her affliction. She began to wail, every muscle in her body tensing with the pain she felt in her heart. It was not enough that she had been taken, it was not enough that she was called a whore by the town. Now she would be forever burdened with the memory of what had happened to her, a daily reminder contained in the face of the filthy creature inside of her. And Thomas would want nothing to do with her once he found out, she just knew it.

Lia lay back in the cold snow and rolled onto her stomach. Burying her face in the frozen drift, her cries were muffled in the brilliant, sunlit crystals of ice and brittle, frosted grasses under her. The fear she felt at having to tell Thomas about her condition paled in comparison to the thought of having to bring the child into the world, and her heart wrenched at the knowledge that she couldn't rid herself of the parasite within her.

She sat up and began to beat at her stomach, feeling in her heart that the child would bear the face of her assailant, but when a sharp pain stabbed through her abdomen she stopped, fearful of her mother's words. While she would give anything to destroy the being in her womb, she could not stand the thought of the slow death that would result if it were to die and fester inside of her. She would not give the bastard who had done this to her the satisfaction of her death, wherever he may be.

"I will hate you, you little beast!" Lia promised, addressing the baby inside of her as her overwhelmed mind grew focused. "I'll count the days till you're gone from me, then I'll leave you to die in the woods!" She smiled at the thought, picturing her attacker as a small, rotting corpse decaying in the forest. She put a hand on her abdomen, disgust crawling over her skin like flies.

Lia found herself waiting for Mark to appear as he always did when she was alone or upset, but she knew he wouldn't come this time. Emotionally drained and her tears used up, she realized that part of her almost wished she was still engaged to him. At least she could tell him about her condition without fear of losing him. The irony of her predicament was not lost on her, and she chuckled bitterly. She shielded her eyes, looking up at the sun. It was getting late, and she sighed with hopelessness and dread as she began to walk back home.

Thomas was still gone when she got back, and Lia spent the evening awaiting his return. As the night came and the moon rose high, her frustration at Thomas' absence grew. She still couldn't imagine how she would tell him about her affliction, but she wanted him near her, she wanted the comfort of his company.

Her mother's pitying glances followed her throughout dinner, and Lia went to bed early. She lay huddled under her winter quilt, listening to the muted, hushed voices of her parents. She hoped her mother wouldn't tell her father.

Lia heard her parents go to bed, yet as the house grew silent and the hours crept by Thomas still hadn't come home. Alone with her thoughts, her mind raced, and she bitterly remembered what Mark had told her about the last time Thomas stayed out all night. She had believed the explanation she was given, choosing to take Thomas' word over Mark's, but now she couldn't shake the nagging voice of suspicion that had managed to take root inside of her head. She argued with herself until she felt as though she were going insane, trying to unsuccessfully convince her heart that she had no reason to be concerned with Thomas' whereabouts.

Finally, she couldn't stand another moment. She threw the covers back and leaped to her feet with a sudden determination. Shivering against the cold, Lia pulled her dress on and wrapped her shawl tightly over her head and shoulders. She tiptoed down the ladder and into the kitchen, then took her shoes from their place by the front door and quietly let herself outside. The winter air bit at her face, but as Lia marched towards town her blood warmed and she forgot the cold. She was nervous; there was only one way to confirm her suspicions, but she had never been to the whore's alley before.

Lia approached the town, her palms beginning to sweat, and her pace slowed. She trudged through the frozen, moonlit streets and past the tavern's darkened windows, then hesitated at the street corner. She strained her ears, the familiar fear from the night of her attack clutching her heart. Mark wasn't there; he couldn't save her this time if another monster tried to take her in the dark. Swallowing hard, Lia did her best to stifle the memories welling up in her mind, and, setting her jaw, she turned the corner.

As she walked, Lia could see dim lights in the distance. Her heart raced faster and faster with dread and excitement as every step carried her deeper into the place she had been warned to stay away from since before she could remember. As she neared the lights and stepped off the cobblestone street, it was as though she was entering an entirely different world.

The place was more of a shanty town than an alley. On either side of a rotting, boardwalk street were tiny, ramshackle huts, pieced together from scraps of splintered wood and salvaged remnants of Brunbury's abandoned buildings. Snow layered the sunken, makeshift roofs of each shack, giving the place a ghostly and dead appearance.

Steaming liquid boiled over small fires, the contents of the large, black cauldrons billowing thick clouds of foul-smelling vapor into the cold air. Lia stepped close to one, curious, and held her breath as she peeked quickly into the pot. It was some sort of food, and as the broth boiled the skinned bodies of what looked like small rodents rose to the surface of the vile concoction before sinking again. For a moment, she wondered why someone would cook outside in such weather, but the homes were so tiny they wouldn't have room for a fire large enough to cook over, and imagining of the smell of the soup trapped in the enclosed space of the shacks made her gag.

There was a lantern perched atop a short post outside of each of the homes, and it didn't take her long to realize that the small flames were a signal: a lit lantern meant the whore was available, and an unlit one indicated she was indisposed. Lia could see the dark shapes of men coming and going out of the shacks, and when she recognized some of the faces she turned away with embarrassment. Many of them were men she had served while working at the tavern, and of the men she recognized almost all had wives and children.

A thin woman stood in front of one of the huts, her filthy, yellow dress stained and torn, her face drawn and pale in the light of her burning lantern. Her hollow eyes fixed on Lia, and with a sideways smile the woman nodded a greeting.

"Never seen the likes of you, honey!" she said. "You taking up a post?" Lia averted her eyes, shaking her head as she moved on.

"Then you're looking for your man?" the woman called, and Lia stopped.

"Yes," she answered quietly, stepping towards the woman. "His name is Thomas."

"There are no names here, girl," the woman told her, coughing. She hacked, a guttural sound from deep in her throat, then spat. "What's he look like?"

"He has green eyes," Lia said, pausing. She clenched her teeth, unsure if what she was thinking was actually true but deciding to say it anyway. "And he pays with gold."

"Aaahh," the woman's face lit up with recognition. "The rich boy! He's the only one that visits us during the day!" Lia's heart sank, and the cold she felt wasn't from the winter air. She realized that Thomas' daily visits to the town weren't just to buy gifts and candy for her, and the thought sickened her.

"Check with Elly, down at the end," the woman continued. "He likes her. But then," she laughed, throwing her head back as her voice cracked into a shrill cackle, her open mouth exposing blackened, broken teeth. "He likes all of us." The woman jerked her head towards the end of the street, and Lia numbly moved in the direction she had indicated.

"What's your price, lovely?" a man asked as she passed by. Lia tried to ignore him, but he put out a hand to stop her. She glanced at him, trying to sidestep his touch, and her mouth dropped open in shock. It was Margaret and Helen's father. He smiled widely when he recognized her, and his eyes grew bright.

"Lia!" he sang as he moved closer to her. "I never thought I would ever have the chance!" Confused, she backed away.

"What do you mean?" Lia stammered. "A chance for what?"

"I'll triple your price!" he told her, grabbing her and holding her against him. "When the others find out you're here…." His voice trailed off as he licked his lips. "Well, let's just say you've danced through the dreams of many a man in this town!" He gestured towards the passing shadows of the other men with his free hand, still clutching her with the other. "You'll make a far better living that any of these other whores!" he crowed. She wrenched away from him, catching his meaning.

"Leave me alone!" Lia exclaimed, unable to contain her disgust. Turning quickly, she began to run, leaving him standing there in open-mouthed disappointment.

She neared the end of the row of houses, and she immediately knew which one Thomas was in. The lantern on its post was unlit, and the walls of the shack did little to stifle the cries of a woman punctuated by Thomas' grunts. Lia felt sick. She slowly walked up to the shack, and through a torn, makeshift curtain she could just barely see inside.

There was a bassinet in the corner of the tiny room, and the hands of a baby could be seen waving about just above the edge. A little girl, maybe four years old, with a sweet face and wispy, dark hair, sat on the floor, playing with scraps of tin. Lia moved to the side to get a better view, and she could now clearly see Thomas and the whore.

The woman's breasts were engorged and swollen, the sensitive skin cracked and bleeding. Her pregnant belly was huge, its wide girth striped with red lines from where her skin had stretched thin. Lia instinctively touched her own stomach, feeling its flatness, and a wave of nausea caused her throat to burn. The woman's eyes were shut tight; although her cries seemed to portray ecstasy, she winced in pain with every movement, and her expression was one of sorrow and humiliation. Somehow, Lia knew that she herself had worn that same look the night she had been attacked, and her body began to shake as her mind conjured up the image in vivid clarity.

Revulsion filled Lia's soul, and she turned suddenly to vomit. Bent at the waist, she could feel her blood rush to her head to settle, pounding, in her ears, and her vision went hazy. She wanted to scream. After what seemed an eternity, she struggled upright and turned away, unable to force herself to look at the abominable sight again.

As she straightened, a burly man appeared next to her, craning his neck for a look through the window. His fat belly shook as he shifted his massive weight from one foot to another with anticipation. His red, frostbitten nose dripped mucus, and Lia shielded her own nose from the stench of feces that wafted from his clothing.

"Is he almost done?" the man wondered aloud, his voice gruff and impatient, his eyes hungry and unblinking as he stared at Thomas and the whore. He stamped his feet, obviously in a hurry, when he noticed Lia standing there.

"Go away," he told her, blowing on his cold fingers. "I don't want you, I'm waiting for the little one." She glanced back through the window. This time, she was blind to the sight of Thomas, and all she could see was the little girl that played inside, the 'little one' as the man had said. Lia bared her teeth, her lips curling in utter abhorrence at the bastard's vile intentions. Unable to bear the thought of staying there another moment, she turned and fled.

Lia staggered home, choking as she tried to breathe, blinded by tears of horror and shock. When her house was in sight, she stopped, her shallow breaths clouding in the cold air as she tried to calm down. She rested her hands on her knees, and she felt her legs buckle. She dragged herself to the snow-covered clearing, the same place Mark had comforted her the nights after she had met the man in the alley, and, her strength gone, she began to sob.

The pain in her heart was more than she could bear, and her tears did little to relieve the sorrow she felt. She cried for herself, for the despair that overwhelmed her, and her stupid foolishness for believing that Thomas loved her. She cried because of her attack, and the fact that she could not change what had taken place or the presence of the abominable creature inside of her. And, in the same breath, she cried for the pregnant whore and the sweet-faced child, trying her best not to think of the disgusting, fat man and what he might be doing to the little girl.

That disgusting man. She clenched her fists until her fingernails cut into her palms, hearing her jaw squeak loudly as her teeth ground together. Her tears renewed, but this time rage, not sorrow, filled her being. Thomas was just as disgusting as her attacker, using the street women just as she herself had been used. Pressing her now-bleeding hands over her mouth, Lia screamed; the sound, although muffled, rang out across the snow and through the leafless, ice-glazed skeletons of the walnut trees.

She rolled over in the snow and gazed up at the clear, winter sky. The light of the half-moon illuminated the night, its bright luminescence soaking into her blue-tinged skin. She shivered, finally noticing the cold that had seeped into her body.

Sitting up as she prepared to go home, Lia glanced towards the little bench on which Mark had held her all those months ago. She wished he was there to comfort her again, and she couldn't help the feeling of longing creeping over her. Sighing, she stood to her feet and began to trudge home, her heart heavy and her mind overwhelmed with the emotions and pain the evening had brought.

● ● ●

CHAPTER FIFTEEN

LIA OPENED HER EYES, slowly remembering the events of the night before. The fitful sleep she had managed did nothing to alleviate the disgust in her heart at the thought of Thomas, and she swallowed hard against the nausea that washed over her. She wasn't sure if the sick feeling in her stomach was because of the creature inside of her or because of the memory of the whore's alley, but it made no difference either way.

A twinge of dread mingled with the taste of bile accumulating in her mouth, and she got dressed while trying to contain the anger that threatened to erupt from within her at the thought of having to speak with her betrothed.

"You slept late today, Lia," her mother said, looking up from her work as Lia descended the ladder. Rachel was darning socks, her needle flying quickly through the thick, woolen fabric. Lia nodded, pursing her lips. Her eyes instantly flashed with a smoldering rage as she formed the words on her tongue.

"I'm not marrying Thomas," she announced through gritted teeth. Rachel's hands dropped and her mouth opened with surprise.

"What?"

"I'm not marrying him, Mum," Lia repeated, cursing as her blood began to boil. "He's a filthy, disgusting bastard!"

"Thank God!" her mother cried with relief, clapping her hands together, too overwhelmed with joy to notice Lia's reddening face. "I was so afraid you wouldn't come to your senses!"

"Is he in the barn?" Lia asked as she moved towards the door, her fists clenched. "I'm going to tell him to leave!"

"I think so," her mother answered breathlessly, her brow raised quizzically. "But what happened, what changed your mind?"

"I went into town last night, into the whore's alley," Lia spat, cursing again, and her mother's eyes grew wide. "I won't tell you any more, I can't stand the thought!" Rachel nodded gravely, then she smiled with happiness.

"I knew he wasn't right for you, child," she said as Lia opened the door. "I'm can't begin to tell you how happy you've made me!"

Thomas wasn't asleep. He was reclining in the straw piled high in the corner of the barn, lazily smoking a pipe. He looked up as Lia entered.

"Hello, love!" he sang, his face bright despite the shadows of sleeplessness that darkened his eyes. "Will you give us a kiss?"

"You need to leave, Thomas," Lia told him firmly, crossing her arms and ignoring his question. "You won't be staying here any longer." Thomas' eyes narrowed, flashing with a sudden anger at her words. He studied her face for a long moment, thinking, then he forced himself to feign calm.

"What's the matter, love?" He stood to his feet, holding out his hand. "What's wrong?"

"You already know!" Lia shouted, unable to contain herself. He shook his head, maintaining his ignorance, and opened his mouth to protest. She stopped him, unwilling to let him speak. "I went to find you last night!" she told him, hatred poisoning her words. "I saw you with the pregnant whore, I saw you!" His face darkened dangerously.

"You followed me?" Thomas asked, incredulous. "You *followed* me?" He moved towards her, his body tensed with anger.

"I went to *find* you," Lia corrected, clenching her hands. "And I found you, all right!" She rose up onto her tiptoes, jabbing her pointed finger towards him to emphasize her words. "You need to leave, Thomas! Get out!"

"But I love you, Lia!" Thomas' voice was desperate and sweet, but his face was threatening. "Please, let's talk about this! Let's not do anything you might regret!" Lia gave a short, flat-sounding laugh.

"Anything that *I* might regret?" she howled. "The only thing I regret is not realizing how worthless you are sooner!"

"Worthless!" he hissed. "I am the son of a *lord*!"

"You're the son of a dog, Thomas!" Lia retorted, her lip curling. "I will never know how I could have been too blind to see you for what you really are!"

"How dare you!" He leaped towards her to grab her, his fingers digging into her shoulders. "No peasant speaks to me that way!" He shook her, his nose inches away from hers. She scoffed defiantly.

"Now I'm a peasant, Thomas?" Lia asked, her voice dripping with sarcasm. "There's no end to the lies you've told, is there? Get out! NOW!" He shook his head in refusal, lowering his voice.

"I've spent too much time trying to win you," Thomas whispered fiercely through gritted teeth. "I won't have my efforts wasted!" He gripped her tightly against him, and his hands moved to her waist.

Lia's anger evaporated in a single instant, replaced immediately with cold fear. Her heart began to beat faster as her muscles tensed.

"What are you talking about?" she asked, her voice hollow. "What efforts?"

"I've wanted you from the moment I laid eyes on you!" Thomas answered, his voice husky as his demeanor suddenly took on a cold, calculating darkness. It was as if the person she had known him to be had vanished; it had been nothing but a shadow, a façade, and now she could see him for who he really was.

"You think I went through all this trouble because I *love* you?" Thomas laughed mockingly, his eyes wild and piercing. "Every girl I've laid eyes on has thrown herself at my feet, begging for me, but not you! You've made me work for my bread, and I willingly played your game, but I won't walk away empty handed!"

"And the wedding?" Lia asked him, her thoughts racing. She knew, now, that he had lied to her, but she hadn't even thought to consider that every single moment of their time together had just been some sort of ploy. Thomas rolled his eyes.

"Why should I care about a wedding?" he snarled. "If a marriage is all it takes to get what I want, then by all means I'll do it! Winning your bed was a trophy, a challenge, a prize that would have been so much sweeter if I'd won." He laughed at her stunned face, his chest swelling with pride at the cleverness of his plan. "But now…." His voice trailed off, and the gleam in his eyes betrayed his intentions.

Lia screamed, wrenching herself free and trying to run, but he was too quick. Throwing her to the ground, Thomas pinned her down, his fingers deftly unlacing her dress.

"Get off me!" she screeched, fighting against him. He ignored her, lifting her skirts, and she screamed again, terrified as she felt his hands on her skin. She pushed at him, flailing, but she couldn't stop him. "Stop, Thomas!" She was frantic, twisting and writhing as she tried to get away. He was silent as he pawed at her, and she couldn't get out from under him.

Thomas' mouth was hard as he forcefully kissed her, and she could feel him swell with excitement and desire. He bit her, his teeth sharp, and she began clawing him, grabbing at his face. He was unfazed despite the deep, red furrows her fingernails scratched into his skin.

He had found his place, and Lia went numb. Fear suddenly paralyzed her, her mind flashing back to the night in the alley. As her thoughts clouded, her dazed mind remembered Mark. Mark would be watching. She relaxed, her body limp, silently waiting in her dream-like trance for him to arrive and pull Thomas off of her.

As Thomas steadied himself, he rested his forearm on her throat, and the sudden loss of breath jolted her back to reality.

"No!" Lia roared, her lifeless form suddenly surging with energy. "NO!" Arching her body, she managed to get her arm under him, and with every ounce of her strength she rolled him off of her. She leaped to her feet, backing towards the door.

Thomas crouched in the hay, his clothes undone and his eyes fiery. Without a word, he launched himself at her. Lia sidestepped his attack, looking desperately at the door. She knew she wouldn't make it, even if she ran. Searching through her skirts, she tried to find her dagger.

"Looking for this?" Thomas taunted, holding up the small knife. Lia's face drained; she must have dropped it while she was fighting him off.

"Leave me alone, Thomas!" she cautioned him, gauging the distance to the door. He sneered.

"I'm very fast," he grinned wickedly, advancing towards her. "You know you can't outrun me. Why must you be so difficult?"

"Mark was right about you!" Lia shouted, trying to keep her eyes on him while she looked for a weapon. "You're a worthless bastard!" Thomas' face filled with rage, and he lunged at her again. She saw the handle of a pitchfork protruding from under the hay, and she snatched in quickly, brandishing it in his face. He stopped just short of being impaled, and he chuckled.

"Now, Lia," Thomas scolded, smiling cruelly. "Why must you play games?" He put his hands up, backing away slowly, then he charged. She moved the pitchfork again, but this time he was too fast. Tackling her to the ground, he was under her skirts again in an instant, ignoring her flailing hands as he moved into place.

Lia felt him tense with anticipation, and, knowing it was only a matter of seconds before he conquered her, she screamed with one last effort.

"NO!" she screeched, tearing at his face, and an instant later she felt the gratifying squish of his eyeball bursting under her clawing fingers.

Thomas howled in pain, leaping to his feet and staggering back, his hand clutching at the raw hole that had once been his left eye.

"My eye!" he shrieked, horrified at what she'd done. He removed his hand for a moment, only to clamp it right back in place. "I can't see!"

Lia was on her feet in an instant and she grabbed the pitchfork again, backing away as she watched him thrash about in pain. Her dress hung loosely from her shoulders, and she was covered in Thomas' blood. He froze suddenly, his hand dropping from his face, and she could see that his left eye was destroyed, the clear slime from his useless eyeball dripping down his cheek. With a final cry, he collapsed onto the ground in shock, and Lia turned to run.

Her mother looked up in surprise as Lia slammed the door shut and bolted it, breathing hard with the pitchfork still clutched tightly in her hands.

"What happened to you?" Rachel gasped, fear on her face as she jumped to her feet. She looked at the pitchfork. "What did he do?" As Lia's fear slowly faded, she let out a victorious shout.

"*Nothing*, Mum!" she answered proudly, breathing heavily. "He did *nothing*!" Rachel watched her with concerned eyes. "He tried to take me!" Lia exclaimed, her face alight with fiery triumph. "But I took his eye!" She doubled over with laughter, giggling in senseless mirth. When she finally calmed enough to think clearly, she told her mother what had happened.

"He'll be out for blood," Rachel said cautiously after Lia finished. "He'll not let this go."

"I don't care," Lia said, smiling proudly. She knew her mother was right, but all she could think of was the look of horror on Thomas' face when he realized what she'd done to him.

The loud slam of the barn door rang out, and when Lia and her mother looked out the window they could see Thomas heading down the road towards town. His steps were unsteady and he was bare-chested in the cold, his shirt wrapped tightly around his head. Lia closed her eyes for a moment, feeling that somehow a small piece of her that had been taken by the man in the alley had been given back to her through her victory over Thomas.

• • •

Chapter Sixteen

THE MORNING EXCITEMENT soon became a pensive silence, and Lia didn't speak as she helped her mother in the house. The rush of jubilance that had filled her after her encounter with Thomas had ebbed away, leaving in its place a deep feeling of guilt. She should have listened to Mark, and she wished he hadn't left town so she could apologize to him for doubting him. He had always looked after her, and she should have trusted him.

The sound of a pounding fist on the front door jolted Lia from her thoughts, and she moved quickly across the floor to see who was there. She was greeted by Jem's massive bulk huffing and puffing as he leaned against the door frame, barely able to hold himself up as he tried to catch his breath.

"Lia!" he panted, his face crimson and dripping sweat. She couldn't believe her eyes. Jem hardly ever set foot outside the town, and here he was looking as though he had actually *ran* the entire way to her doorstep! She couldn't contain her amusement at the sight of him, his curly brown locks of dirty hair plastered to his forehead, and he sucked at the air as he drew in long, rasping breaths.

"Why are you here, you ugly bastard?" Lia asked him with the same playful tone she had used during her time working at the tavern. He waved her off.

"They're coming!" Jem wheezed, gasping. "The townspeople are coming for you!" She chuckled, exchanging a look with her mother.

"Who's coming for me?" Lia asked him, smiling. He was a sight to behold, a massive behemoth of red flesh. "How much have you had to drink today?" Jem glared at her, his face serious.

"That Thomas fellow," he told her, his labored breaths calming. "He's told everyone what you did!" Lia's skin crawled, and she scoffed in disgust.

"Why should I worry about what he's told them?" she sneered. "That bastard can go hang for all I care!" Fear filled Jem's eyes.

"You're the one that'll hang!" he exclaimed, straightening. "They're coming for you, Lia!" Rachel stepped in.

"What are you going on about?" she demanded, concern etching her face. Jem took a deep breath, trying to get his words out.

"She attacked him, Rachel!" he shouted, trying to make them understand. "You know the penalty! They'll kill her for that!" Rachel's face turned white with alarm. Jem continued, his hands gesturing wildly as he spoke.

"Don't you see?" he bellowed, turning to Lia. "You're a whore! You've maimed a man, and now they're coming for you!"

The reality of what he was saying began to sink in, and now terror flooded her body. In the eyes of the townspeople, Thomas' filthy corpse, no matter what he had done, was of far more worth than the life of a whore. She began to tremble, panic taking hold of her. Rachel thought quickly.

"You must leave!" she hissed, pushing Lia into the house. "Hurry! Go gather your things!"

"Where will I go?" Lia asked, her voice frantic. "I've never left Brunbury!" Rachel dismissed her.

"I don't know, but you can't stay here!" she insisted, her eyes fierce. "I won't have my child killed by a bloodthirsty mob! Quick, get your things!" Lia rushed up the ladder to her room, spreading her quilt open on the bed and putting her few belongings in the center of it. She could hear her mother still talking to Jem.

"How did you find out?" Rachel asked.

"One of the townspeople came into the tavern," Jem answered. "He wanted to know if I would join them!" Rachel inhaled sharply.

"How much time do we have?"

"Not much," Jem told her. "They were almost ready to come this way when I left. They were all gathered in the street near the center of town, and they weren't in the mood to wait!"

"Go back to the tavern," Rachel told Jem. "I'm in your debt for the warning."

"I'll always care for your Lia," Jem said wistfully. "She's the best cook I've ever laid eyes on!" Rachel leaned in through the door, her voice impatient.

"Come, Lia!" she called. "You must go, right now!" Lia started down the ladder, then turned and grabbed her money box. She opened the lid and pulled out a handful of coins, tossing them onto her bed and hoping her mother would find them, then she put the box into her quilt. With one last look at her room, she hurried down into the kitchen.

"I have no food!" Lia cried as she ran towards the door. Rachel gestured to the loaves of bread.

"Take those!" she commanded, falling silent. She cocked her head, listening, then stood on her toes and peered down the road. "Oh, hurry child!" she screeched as Lia threw the bread in with her other things. "They're coming, I can hear them!" Lia's heart stopped at her mother's words, and, holding her rolled up quilt, she ran out the door. Her mother gave her a quick hug, staring into her eyes in anguish. Lia felt her heart tear in half.

"Find Mark," her mother commanded, her eyes boring holes into Lia's. "You must find him! You won't survive, not in your condition, not without Mark! You'll end up a whore in the streets!" Lia tried to listen to what her mother was telling her, but her mind couldn't focus.

"I don't want to leave!" she managed to choke out, her throat dry as she struggled to think. "I'll just hide in the fields…"

"No, Lia!" Rachel snapped, interrupting. "You don't know what you're saying! They'll find you!" Lia gave a feeble nod. "You can't come back here!" Rachel took hold of Lia's face. "Swear to me! Promise me you won't come back!" Lia swallowed hard.

"I swear," she whispered numbly. Her mother stared into her eyes for a moment longer, then she smiled.

"I love you, child," she whispered, hugging Lia again. "Now go! Find Mark, and send word back to me!" Lia darted away as fast as her legs could carry her.

She could hear the voices of the approaching townspeople, and she knew they would easily follow her footprints in the snow if she tried to make it to the road. Lia went the opposite direction instead, following the well-trodden path the cattle took to the watering pond. She stopped just as she entered the woods a short distance from her home, and she buried herself in a dense thicket of thorns. The brambles tore at her skin and clothes, and she clenched her teeth against the pain. She could hear the crowd from where she was, and she held her breath, listening.

"Where is she?" someone demanded. "Where's your whore, Rachel Grey?" Lia strained her ears for her mother's reply.

"She's not here!" Rachel answered loudly, her voice filled with loathing. "And I'll thank you to leave my property!"

"She's lying!" the cry went up, and Lia could hear the townspeople's feet stomping with excitement. "Search the house!" She could imagine them tearing through her home, and rage overwhelmed her. Another voice rang out, and her blood turned to fire in her veins.

"We'll find her, Rachel!" Thomas swore, his voice cracking feebly as he spoke. "She won't get away from the justice that's coming to her!" Lia felt like screaming, livid at the sound of his voice. She could imagine herself leaping on top him, her teeth latching onto his throat as she ripped and tore at his flesh. She wanted to watch the light leave his remaining eye, and it took every ounce of her being to keep silent. Her anger turned to pride when she heard Thomas' next words.

"You put that down, Rachel!" he hollered, fear in his voice. Somehow, Lia knew her mother was threatening him with the very same pitchfork she herself had brandished, and her heart swelled.

"Are you afraid, you worthless pig?" Rachel screamed. "You should be! You tried to take my daughter, you sat in my home pretending to be a friend, and now you have the gall to set foot here again?" She laughed maniacally, and Lia could almost see her mother's wild eyes. "These other folk can search my house and I won't stop them," Rachel continued. "But if you don't get your filthy corpse off my property they'll be hanging *me* for murder!" Rachel addressed the crowd. "I won't interfere with your search," she promised. "As long as this son of a bastard cow leaves now!" Lia could hear a quiet murmur, then a cry of pain.

"Put your hands on me again, Thomas Greene!" her mother challenged, and Lia could hear Thomas scream. Satisfaction filled her, and she wished she could see his face.

"You stabbed me!" Thomas wailed.

"Get out of here!" someone commanded. "We'll handle this without you, Thomas!"

"You'll regret this, Rachel," Thomas promised, and Lia tried to contain her glee at hearing the rage in his voice.

Someone must have alerted Lia's father to what was happening, because it wasn't long before she heard his gruff voice join the din of the searching crowd.

"What's the meaning of this?" he yelled. Lia felt a twinge of pain. She hadn't said goodbye to him, and she hoped her mother would bid farewell in her stead.

"Tell us where Lia is!" a voice answered him.

"Why?" John demanded, infuriated. "What's she done now?"

"She attacked Thomas Greene, John!" someone called out. "She put out his eye!"

"What? Why?" John asked, his voice confused and indignant. Lia's mother must have answered, as his next words were an unintelligible string of curses all ending with Thomas' name. Lia felt almost sorry for her father. He had been so happy and excited to have another man around, and although he wouldn't ever admit it she knew he would be hurt by what Thomas had turned out to be.

The search continued for almost an hour, until finally one of the townspeople spoke.

"She's not here," the man said, disappointment in his voice. "But I know she wanders the hills during the day!"

"Let's go!" someone prodded. "We'll find her!" Lia could hear the crowd moving away, and she breathed a sigh of relief.

Lia waited in silence until nightfall, shivering in the frosty air, then she carefully untangled herself from the thicket of thorns. The full moon was hidden behind a thick blanket of fast-moving clouds, offering just enough light for her to see the silhouette of her home in the distance. It was cold. She was tempted to go back, to see her mother and father one more time, but she knew it would be unwise to do so. The townspeople were no doubt watching, hoping she would do just that so they could catch her. She tiptoed through the woods, giving the town a wide berth as she made her way to the road.

Lia knew the closest town was Hollendale, but she didn't know how long it would take her to get there. She wished she had listened more closely when Jem gave directions to travelers passing through town, but try as she might she couldn't remember anything other than that she needed to follow the main road.

The path was well-travelled, and the deep ruts formed by wagon wheels and horses' hooves had frozen into hard ridges and holes. She could feel the uneven ground under the soles of her shoes as she walked, and after only a short time blisters began to form on the bottoms of her feet. She was used to roaming the fields, not the rough terrain she was now walking on.

Lia's foot caught the edge of a large pothole and she tripped, her arms outstretched before her as she tried to catch herself. She landed hard, feeling the sting of the ice-encrusted dirt as it scraped the skin from her face. She was stunned for a moment, lying motionless on the ground, and she realized that she didn't want to move. She didn't want to think about the journey ahead, and the thought of leaving the only home she had ever known was unbearable.

Finally forcing herself to her knees, Lia slowly picked herself up, her arms feeling as though they would give way. She searched the dark road for her belongings, now scattered across the cold ground, and gathered her quilt into her arms. Straightening her shoulders, she took a deep breath, trying to muster her courage.

"You're too strong for tears, Lia," she told herself, her voice trembling. She turned to look behind her, but the town had long since disappeared into the darkness. Her vision began to blur, but she shook her head in defiance. The clouds in the night sky had parted, and the moonlight revealed a stoic gleam in her eyes. She held her head high. The blisters on her feet had broken, and she could feel the moisture from her burning skin clinging to the insides of her shoes. She ignored the pain and began to walk again, her chest swelling.

She thought of Thomas, and rage filled her heart. He had brought the town to her home, and he had almost succeeded in having her killed because of her scorn for him. She laughed aloud, her confidence returning. He was sadly mistaken if he had believed he could take her that easily.

"You're such a sweet girl, Lia," she mocked him in a high voice, remembering Thomas' words from the day he had proposed to her. She frowned regretfully, wishing she had killed him. In her mind, she could almost see the blood seeping from the perfectly spaced wounds, the tines of the pitchfork stained red as she stood over him, watching him bleed. She began to walk faster, her hurting feet forgotten.

Although Lia didn't know much about the towns outside of Brunbury, she knew enough to realize that she needed to find Mark, as her mother had instructed. If the other towns were anything like her own, an unmarried, pregnant woman would be shunned and fated to make a living in the streets.

She cursed herself again for not listening to Mark that day at the creek, sighing regretfully, then she smiled to herself a moment later at the thought of seeing him again. She knew that despite the pain she had caused him he would welcome her with open arms. Although she was setting out for the unknown and unfamiliar, she was comforted to think that she would at least know Mark. She began to jog, her spirits slightly lifted.

Lia walked all night. When the dark sky began to lighten into a navy blue she stopped, exhausted, and she moved into the thick trees lining the road to find a place to sleep. As she made her way into the woods, she heard a rustling and loud crashing, and for a moment her heart jumped into her throat. She squinted her eyes in the gradually-lightening night, then she sighed in relief. A deer jumped out of the thick brush and bounded away, disturbed from its sleep by the sound of her trampling feet approaching.

She took a few more steps, and as she ducked under a low hanging branch she stepped into a hollowed out space in the snow-laden grass. She smiled; the deer's bed would become hers, and it was perfectly hidden from sight under the tree branches and overgrowth. Tired and sore, she wrapped herself in her quilt and fell asleep.

• • •

CHAPTER SEVENTEEN

THE SUN WAS HIGH in the sky when Lia awoke. She lay there for a moment, blinking slowly as the blanket of sleep lifted from her mind. She thought she heard voices drifting towards her from the road, but she couldn't quite make out what was being said. Listening absently to the sound, she closed her eyes again, not quite ready to wake up and continue on her way. The voices grew louder, and now she could hear the two men clearly. Lia cringed and tried to bury herself deeper in the hollowed grass, holding her breath. She recognized the voices.

"She's not gotten very far, I promise you," said Lewis, the town's cobbler, standing only a few yards away. Lia shivered, cowering in the beam of sunlight that shone through the trees and onto the blue fabric of her dress. Trying to quietly move out of the light, she put her weight on a twig and heard it snap under her. She froze, afraid to make a sound. The men continued speaking, still oblivious to her presence.

"She didn't just disappear!" Toby exclaimed. He was their neighbor, a man Lia had known since she was a child. "She wasn't in the fields, and we've searched high and low in the town. Where else could she be if not on one of the roads?"

"The wench is smart, if not anything," a third voice said, and Lia's face flushed with anger. "And you say they've already checked the southern road from Brunbury?"

"We've checked all the roads, Thomas!" Lewis answered, exasperated. "I'm tired and hungry, and no whore's worth a whole night's searching! As long as she's not in the town I'm happy, and she won't dare set foot back there again in this lifetime!"

"I agree!" Toby added. "Let's go back and get some sleep!"

"And you two have no problem letting a worthless whore get the better of you?" Thomas demanded, the anger rising in his voice. "I've no intention of letting her get away with this!"

"Then you go ahead on your own," Toby told him. "I'm not searching any longer! For all we know she's hiding out in the woods near her home, waiting for us to forget about her!" There was a moment of silence, then Thomas spoke again.

"You may be right," he agreed thoughtfully. "We'll post more people on the road next to the house to keep an eye out for her. She's a resourceful one, and I've no doubt she could stay out there for days."

"Then we're going back?" Lewis asked hopefully. Thomas gave a muttered answer, and Lia could hear their footsteps as they walked away. She exhaled quietly, thankful they were gone, then chuckled to herself, glad the fools had lost a night's sleep over her. Stretching out on her quilt, she closed her eyes, deciding to give them a few hours to return to town before continuing on her way.

Late afternoon came quickly, and she had trouble finding the motivation to drag herself to her feet to start walking again. Lia was well-rested, but she wasn't looking forward to another night's walk. After eating a bit of the now-stale bread her mother had given her, she stood to her feet and carefully made her way back to the road. Cautiously looking back and forth before leaving the woods, she stepped onto the road and began to walk.

The winter day was warm, and the snow was steadily melting. Lia made good time in the light, able to avoid the misshapen areas of the road that would have slowed her. She was so absorbed in placing her feet that she almost didn't notice a man ride up next to her.

She looked up, fear and surprise on her face, then she quickly smiled sweetly at him. She didn't recognize him, which she was glad for, and he had a pleasant face under the brim of his stained hat. Anxiety filled her nonetheless, and she wanted to run into the woods and hide, feeling naked without her dagger.

She silently begged him not to stop, but as she averted her eyes from his stare he slowed.

"Hello there!" the man called down from atop his black and white mare. Lia's mind raced, trying to think of what to say.

"Hello," she greeted him quietly, trying to hide her nervousness. He kept pace next to her, and she began to blush.

"What's a little lady like yourself doing out here all alone?" he asked, amused. Lia smiled at him again, feigning confidence.

"I'm on my way to town," she told him, looking away.

"Where's your escort?" he asked cheerfully, his eyes unblinking as he looked her up and down. She shot him a glance.

"I didn't know I needed one," she answered innocently. She swallowed hard and tried to change the subject. "Where are you headed to?"

"I'm coming from Shelton," he said. "Going on to Overfield." This time her smile was genuine. Shelton was east of Brunbury, and she knew he wouldn't have passed through her town.

"Is that far?" she asked, wishing he would continue on his way. He nodded.

"Overfield's about a week's travel from this very spot," he told her, finally looking away from her. "Are you going the same way?" Lia shook her head.

"No," she said, not wanting to tell him where she was headed. He looked at her expectantly, but she didn't continue.

"You're not a very talkative thing, now are you?" he grinned, glancing back at the road. The steady clop of the horse's steps was loud, but the racing of her heart was all she could hear.

"You expect me to tell a strange man where I'm going?" she told him, forcing a laugh. "I don't know you!" She had thought he might take her hint, but instead he became serious.

"You'd better watch yourself out here all alone," he cautioned, eyeing her. "You might get snapped up by some big strong man like me with that pretty smile of yours." He winked at her, and she felt like throwing up.

"Thank you, sir," Lia said, giving a little curtsy. "Looking out for someone like me." He nodded, looking her up and down once more.

"Good luck on your journey," he said, nudging his horse. Reassured by his obvious intention to continue on his way, Lia stopped him.

"Can you tell me how far to Hollendale?" she asked quickly. He grinned widely.

"So Hollendale, for you, is it?" Laughing, he moved his horse to a trot. "About three more days, love!" he called over his shoulder. "Good luck to you, and be careful now!"

"Thank you!" she shouted at his back, and he gave a quick wave.

Lia breathed a sigh of relief as she watched him leave. She would have to be more careful; it was just pure luck that he hadn't been someone who had passed through her town. She continued walking, this time being less mindful of her feet and paying more attention to her surroundings. Three more days.

Night came quickly, and as the last bit of light disappeared from the sky Lia heard a peal of thunder. Looking up, she noticed clouds rolling in, hiding the moon and stars from sight. A breeze picked up, blowing her skirts gently. She began to walk faster, praying that the weather would keep, but within an hour she was leaning forward into strong gusts of wind, trying to stay upright as she shivered in the cold.

As she walked, freezing rain began to fall, and the path soon became an icy, muddy swamp. Puddles of slush formed in the craters and troughs in the road, and she breathed hard, straining to lift her feet with each step. Finally, her legs burning from the effort, she stopped, frustrated, tired, and freezing. She wasn't making much progress against the wind and ice, and continuing was almost impossible.

Lia moved from the road, knowing she had to find shelter from the cold. She wiped her eyes and squinted into the darkness, trying to see where she was going. She thought she saw the treeline in the distance, and she slowly made her way in that direction. After a short while, her outstretched hands felt the rough bark of a tree, and as she entered the thick woods the cover of dense branches slowed the rain.

She crouched under a bush, quickly opening her wet quilt and removing her oilpaper-wrapped candle and matches. Her hands were numb and shaky, but thankfully the matches weren't wet and she managed to light the wick of the candle. Shielding the flame with her hand, Lia shone the light around her, looking for a place to wait out the storm. The weak flame revealed little against the rain and darkness, and, after clumsily wrapping her belongings back up, she began to walk again.

Her candle sputtered as drops of water leaked through her cupped, frozen fingers and threatened to extinguish her small light. The sound of the sleeting rain filled her ears, and she knew she was wandering further from the road than she wanted to. She searched the darkness for a place to stop, feeling lost, and despair filled her heart.

Fighting off tears, Lia struggled forward, wishing she was back at home. The mossy ground was slick with ice, and she stumbled on the slippery rocks protruding from the earth. She took a few more steps, only to fall face-first into a small, rushing stream of freezing water, the light of her candle instantly gone. She jumped to her feet, gasping as the frigid water took her breath away, then she staggered forward and tried to stand.

She cried out in pain, the top of her head hitting hard against something above her. Bewildered, she reached up to feel what she had struck. Her fingers brushed against a smooth surface, and she quickly realized that she had stepped into a rock crevice. She smiled, suddenly relieved, and tried not to dance with joy.

Abandoning caution, she moved deeper inside and out of the rain, again digging through her water-logged quilt for her matches. She was fortunate; the oilpaper packet was mostly dry despite her fall, and it didn't take her long to relight her candle. The bright flame illuminated the small space she was in, and she looked around.

The crevice wasn't very deep, but Lia immediately noticed that the wind didn't reach her there. She was shivering uncontrollably, and she quickly slipped out of her dress to wring it out before laying it flat. The ground was dry, and she spread out her quilt to lie down.

The wool quilt was scratchy against her bare skin, but she was too tired to care, and when her teeth stopped chattering she began to doze. Just as she was drifting off to sleep, an odd feeling filled her stomach, and she snapped awake in anticipation, thinking she might be getting ready to throw up.

Lia lay there, flat on her back and completely still, waiting for her insides to calm. She didn't quite feel like vomiting, but she also didn't recognize the sensation in her abdomen. It felt as if someone had released dozens of butterflies inside her, and their wings were gently fluttering as they tried to escape her belly. The feeling was almost like a combination of both nervousness and excitement, yet she couldn't identify which. She held her breath, concentrating, and gingerly pressed her fingers into her skin.

She felt the firm bump in her belly, and revulsion filled her as she jerked her hand away quickly. She grimaced with disgust, and the fluttering stopped. Shrugging dismissively, she closed her eyes, but after only a few moments the feeling returned, and a sudden realization dawned on her as she remembered something her mother had once said about swimming butterflies.

Lia's eyes grew wide. She was feeling the baby move, she knew, and she couldn't help imagining tiny feet and hands gently brushing her insides as it twisted and turned in her belly. In an instant, her disgust was forgotten and replaced with wonder. She touched her abdomen again, awestruck, and her heart began to race. She was captivated by the feeling.

A giggle escaped her, and she clapped her hand over her mouth to silence herself. Forcing a frown, she tried to remember her anger, unwilling to admit her excitement, but she couldn't contain herself. She laughed quietly, her voice bouncing off the rock walls. She had regarded the pregnancy as more of a condition or affliction that anything else, not fully considering until that moment that the result of her predicament would be a living, breathing child.

Lia closed her eyes and smiled, breathing deeply of the cold, rain-scented air. Her hand rested on her belly, and she thought of Mark. She couldn't help wondering what he would think when she told him about the pregnancy. She rolled onto her side, blowing out the candle. She wished he was there with her. The steady pattering of raindrops lulled her to sleep quickly, and she slept soundly through the night.

When Lia woke up, the sky was still drizzling, and a heavy fog shrouded the ground. The morning air was cold and dreary, and her body ached as she sat up. The weather had warmed slightly, and almost all of the ice from the night before had disappeared. Water dripped down in front of the entrance to the small cave, and as she gazed out through the opening and into the trees her stomach growled.

She glanced over at where she had piled her things the night before, and she saw the soggy mess her remaining bread had become from the rain. She sighed, extending her arm towards it, considering whether she wanted to eat it anyway. She still had a few days until she would be in Hollendale, and she knew she couldn't count on finding a place to stop for food on the way. Grimacing, she poked at the disintegrating mass. Just the thought of eating it turned her stomach.

Lia felt the fabric of her dress, and she wasn't surprised that it was still very wet. She shivered in anticipation, knowing how cold it would feel when she put it on. Crossing her arms in a frustrated pout, she didn't want to move.

Sighing, she finally shook the quilt off her shoulders, shrinking back from the cold bite of the air. She stood and pulled her dress on, then quickly wrapped herself back in her quilt to warm up. The skirt felt frozen against her legs, and goosebumps raced over her skin. After a moment, though, the wet cloth warmed slightly, and she stood to her feet and gathered her things.

Lia stepped over the small stream that she had fallen in the night before and out into the misting rain. She looked around, and her heart sank. She didn't remember where the road was.

She tried to force herself to stay calm against the panic that threatened to overwhelm her. She began to walk, ducking under low hanging branches she didn't remember from the night before. When she didn't reach the road after a few moments, she knew she was lost.

She began to run, frantic, and her stomach sank into the soles of her sore, wet feet. Despair filled her, and tears of frustration and anger welled in her eyes. It was hopeless; the road was nowhere to be seen. Tiring quickly, she collapsed on a rain-soaked log to rest and catch her breath.

She looked up, then let out a cry of relief. She could see the road just a short distance away, and she leaped to her feet, sniffling and chuckling to herself. She climbed up the slight embankment separating her from the road, and she started on her way, walking in the bowed-down grass next to the road to avoid the thick sludge the path had become.

The drizzling rain stopped mid-morning, and by early afternoon the dark, gray clouds had lightened slightly. Lia's stomach growled loudly in her ears, and she knew she would have to find something to eat soon. She eyed the muddy grasses next to the road, wondering, for a moment, how they would taste, when the scent of burning wood wafted by her nose. She glanced up.

In the distance, she could see smoke rising out of the chimney of a small, broken-down cottage, and she felt a twinge of hope as she started running.

"Hello!" Lia cried, pounding on the door. Through the window, she could see vegetables on the table inside. "Hello! Is anyone here?"

There was no answer, and she sank onto the doorstep. She rested her chin on her hands, sighing deeply, and her stomach announced itself again. An idea came to her, and she dug into her money box to pull out a few silver tokens before standing to her feet and trying the door.

It swung open easily. Moving quickly, she helped herself to two heads of cabbage and a few beets, leaving the silver coins in their place. She rolled the vegetables up in her quilt and shut the door behind her.

Guilt tugged at her heart as she hurried away. She had paid for the food, but somehow she still felt that she'd done something wrong. Even so, she was proud of herself; despite her situation, she had been honest.

Once she was out of sight of the house, Lia couldn't stand it any longer. She sat down in the mud and water on the side of the road and began tearing the leaves off one of the cabbages, chewing only slightly before swallowing. She hated cabbage, but she was grateful for it this time. Before long, almost half of it was gone, and she took a breath, instantly feeling better. After finding a somewhat clean puddle to drink from, she contentedly began walking again.

The sky thundered as night fell, and Lia quickly moved off the road to find a place to sleep. She didn't want to have to search for shelter in the dark as she had the night before, and within a short time she found a tall, wide, hollow tree. She bedded down just as the freezing rain began to fall again, and aside from a slow trickle of water running down the inside of the trunk she was able to stay relatively dry. She fell asleep to the flutters in her belly, feeling strangely happy despite her surroundings.

When she woke up, the late-November sun was shining brightly, and she made good time throughout the whole day. The road was still waterlogged and wet, but with the rain gone the surface was slowly firming up. The only people she encountered were a small family, a man and his wife with their two children heading the opposite direction. Lia had asked where they were coming from, but all four of them had ignored her. She had been a bit disappointed and bewildered, wondering why they hadn't answered her cheerful greeting.

Later that night, as Lia was preparing to sleep on the rocky shore of a lake a short distance from the road, she looked at herself in the tiny mirror she had brought with her. In the light of her small fire, she almost didn't recognize herself. Her hair was caked with dirt and her face was filthy, covered with scratches and scabs from when she had crawled through the woods to find shelter. She looked down at her torn dress, and she started to laugh. No wonder the family on the road hadn't answered her; she was a fright to behold.

By her count, she would be arriving in Hollendale sometime the next day, and she knew she would draw stares with the way she looked. She glanced at the lake, the reflection of the orange flames of her fire dancing on the dark peaks of the rippling waves, and she shivered as she contemplated a bath. She could just imagine how cold the water would feel on her tired skin. Sighing, she willed herself to get up to at least wash her face, but she couldn't seem to move. Her feet were warm and throbbing, and the icy water would ease the swelling and pain, but she couldn't find the motivation to get up.

Her stomach growled at her, reminding her that her food was gone. She hoped Hollendale was close, otherwise she'd be going hungry the next day. She stared up at the night sky, listening to the gentle splash of the water as she closed her eyes.

The sun hadn't yet risen when Lia got up. She forced herself to wash her face, splashing the freezing water onto her skin. It took her breath away, and she ran back to her quilt to warm up after she was finished. Her hair was impossible; she tried running her comb through it and ripped out a good handful in the process. She gave up quickly, her scalp sore after only a few strokes, willing to be content with the somewhat smooth appearance she had managed to give her tangled mane. Her dress was another issue; she couldn't do anything about the rips and tears, and she refused to take it off to wash it clean.

She walked all day, her stomach grumbling and growling at her the whole time. It was late in the afternoon when she came across a worn-out sign, the words barely legible. She shielded her eyes with her hands, squinting to read what it said:

HOLLENDALE – 10 MILES

Excitement filled her, and she rocked back and forth on the balls of her aching feet with happiness. Only ten more miles and she would be there; a few hours and she'd find Mark. The sun was setting low in the sky when the town came into sight, and she began to run.

• • •

CHAPTER EIGHTEEN

THE TOWN OF HOLLENDALE was much bigger than Brunbury, and Lia stared, openmouthed, at the dozens of tall, dark, wooden buildings squeezed in tightly next to each other. The cobblestone streets were filled with people, and young boys roamed from corner to corner lighting the streetlamps. A thick layer of sludge sat in the gutters carved into each side of the road, and the foul odor of excrement and waste permeated the air.

Despite the stench, Lia was mesmerized. She had never seen so many people in one place before; Jem's tavern, even on its busiest night, couldn't hold a candle to the hustle and bustle of Hollendale. Everyone seemed to be in a hurry, unlike Brunbury's leisurely pace, and Lia's heart quickened with the fast steps of the people around her.

She was a stranger there, and although she didn't feel odd being around the unfamiliar faces surrounding her, it seemed that everyone noticed that she was out of place. As the people passed her in the streets, they turned up their noses, scoffing and rolling their eyes. Lia was confused; she couldn't understand why they were so unfriendly. She knew she didn't look very nice compared to most of the people she passed, but, at least in her opinion, she didn't look like a beggar, either.

"Excuse me," she asked, putting out her hand to stop someone. "Can you tell me where the blacksmith's shop is?"

"Leave me be!" the woman snapped, twisting out of the way.

"I just needed directions!" Lia angrily called, but the woman ignored her. She stood there for a moment, fuming, then she turned to find someone else to ask.

As she spun around, she found herself face-to-face with a tall man wearing a gray, flannel suit and a round, black hat. He tapped his wooden club impatiently against his worn, leather boots as he glared at her with narrowed, suspicious eyes.

"Can I help you?" he asked curtly, his voice gruff under his thick mustache. Lia smiled, cocking her head.

"Yes sir," she began, her voice sweet. "I'm looking for the blacksmith's shop. Can you point the way?" He eyed her cautiously, looking her up and down.

"You've just come in, haven't you?" he demanded, his eyes flashing when she nodded. "Where's your man?" Exasperation filled her. She just wanted to know where the damn blacksmith's shop was, and she couldn't understand why it was any of this fellow's business if she had a man with her.

"I don't believe I'd like to tell you that," Lia told him, crossing her arms. "As you've said, I'm new here and I don't know you or what your intentions might be!" The man straightened up, squaring his shoulders indignantly.

"I'm a watchman for this town!" he bellowed hotly, looming over her. "You answer me, girl!" She cringed, thinking quickly.

"I'm looking for my.....betrothed," Lia lied, forcing an innocent grin. "I think he might be at the blacksmith's shop." The man was not convinced.

"Listen, girl," he began impatiently. "We don't tolerate single women in this town! You won't find work here, and you'll end up begging or whoring in the streets!" Lia's eyes met his with a defiant glare.

"I'm not looking for work!" she told him firmly. She concentrated, trying to force tears. It wasn't a hard thing to do. "I'm looking for my betrothed!" The watchman scoffed, then paused at the sight of her now-watering eyes. "You must believe me!" She wiped her eyes with an exaggerated flourish.

"What's your betrothed's name, girl?" he demanded, not quite persuaded.

"Mark Samuels," Lia answered, and the watchman nodded immediately.

"Yes," he said thoughtfully. "That name does sound familiar…" His voice trailed off, and Lia stared at him expectantly.

"Is he here?" she asked eagerly. The man didn't speak, then he met her gaze.

"You don't have the look of a whore," he said, musing more to himself than speaking to her. He turned to leave.

The town had grown dark save for the light of the streetlamps, and the rush of the streets was calming. Lia put out her hand to stop him.

"Please," she pleaded. "Can't you just tell me the way to the blacksmith's?" The watchman stopped.

"It's that way," he finally told her, pointing.

She almost ran right past the blacksmith's shop. The smell of hot metal and burning embers stopped her, and she threw open the door to the squat building.

"Mark?" Lia called out anxiously. The dim light of the shop revealed a large, heavyset man standing by the blacksmith's fire. He was startled by her voice.

"Who's there?" he demanded. "What do you want?" He squinted, trying to see who had barged in, then his greasy, broad face broke into a gap-toothed smile. "Well, come in, come in!" he crooned, setting down his work. "I've always time for a little play!" Lia made a face, taking a step back as he moved towards her.

"I....I'm looking for Mark," she told him, grimacing with disgust. "Is Mark Samuels here?" The man threw his head back, laughing.

"A picky whore?" he chuckled, thundering across the room. "I'll pay double for a woman as pretty as you!" He came closer, and Lia backed out of the door.

"I'm not for sale!" she shouted angrily. "I'm looking for my betrothed!" The man stopped, his red-rimmed eyes glowering at her.

"That Mark wasn't engaged," he hissed. "You're a liar, that's for sure." Uninterested in her now that he knew she couldn't be bought, he turned to waddle back to his workstation.

"My name is Lia," she ventured, stepping back into the shop and moving towards the man. "Is Mark here?" His eyes lit up, and he stared at her.

"*You're* Lia?" he asked, drinking her in. She was uncomfortable under his gaze, but she didn't care. "You're the woman Mark was so flustered about?" She was surprised that this man knew of her.

"Yes!" she answered quickly, wishing the fool would just answer her question. "I'm Lia Grey! You know of Mark; can you tell me where I can find him?"

"He's not here," the man said simply. "He's gone on to another town."

Lia sank down onto a small stool, her head in her hands. She had been sure she would find Mark here, and disappointment settled thickly in her heart at the thought of having to continue her journey. She looked up at the man, tears stinging her eyes.

"Do you know where he's gone to?" she asked despairingly. "Do you know where I can find him?" The man ignored her, and after waiting a moment without receiving a reply, Lia stood to leave. Just as she walked outside, the man answered her.

"He was awful upset about you, girl," he called to her, and she stopped. "He was brokenhearted, that's what he was." She frowned, staring down at her feet. Mark had done so much for her, and he didn't deserve the hurt she had repaid his kindness with.

"What do you mean?" Lia asked quietly. "How do you know?"

"It wasn't hard to see," he told her. "He was always moping about, and always muttering on and on about his beautiful Lia. I reckon the poor fool didn't know you were coming after him?" He smirked, amused at how upset she was.

"I just need to find him," she whispered. "When was he here?"

"A bit more than a week ago, at least," he answered. "Maybe a little longer than that." She was surprised.

"He wasn't here for long then, was he?" Lia asked, quickly adding up the days. The man shook his head.

"I'm Paul," he introduced himself, extending his hand. Lia eyed him warily, and he rolled his eyes at her caution. "Where are you staying, girl?" She shrugged.

"I don't know," she answered, suddenly remembering her hunger. "I'd be thankful if you had some food, though."

"Of course you would," Paul sneered. "Now I'm a charity, is that it?" She was offended.

"I'll gladly pay you for it!" Lia told him proudly, holding her chin high. "I don't expect a handout from you!" His eyes gleamed at her tone.

"I can see why that fool Mark liked you," he said, laughing quietly. "You're a spirited one, I can tell that for sure!" She glared at him.

"Will you sell me food or not?" she demanded, her hands on her hips. He chuckled, waving her to a table in the corner of the shop.

"Any friend of Mark's is a friend of mine," he told her, pointing at a bowl of cheese and bread. "Even if you *did* do him terrible. That boy was one talented smith, and I was sad to see him go." He gestured towards a wall hung with various items. "He managed to make most of those in just the short time he was here," Paul told her regretfully. "I wish the boy had stayed, I made a pretty coin selling his work. Especially the little pieces, the animals and flowers and the like. Don't have many of those left."

Lia stared at the wall as she took a bite of cheese, her eyes unfocused. She wished she still had the rose Mark had made for her. When she blinked, she caught sight of a small trinket on the wall, and she moved closer to look at it.

"How much for this?" she asked. She gingerly touched the small cast iron maiden, the little figure's hair blowing back as she spun in a dance in the waving grass. Sitting under her leaping feet was a small laughing fox, and Lia could see the loving detail Mark had worked into his art. She knew he had made it with her in mind.

"It's one of the last pretty ones I have left," Paul informed her, glancing at her. "But I'll let you have it for..." he paused, gauging her level of interest before giving the price. "...for seven silvers."

"I'll take it," Lia told him, her eyes searching the other items on the wall. Her gaze rested on a dagger, almost identical to the one Thomas had taken from her, and she ran her fingertips over the hilt. *M.S.* was stamped on the blade with Mark's intricate crest, and she knew she wanted it as well. "I'll have the dagger, too," she said, taking it from the wall. "I'll give you four more silvers for it." Paul grunted in acknowledgement.

"And where will you stay tonight?" he asked her again. Lia sighed.

"The streets, I suppose," she answered quietly. "I've no other place, and I don't know where I'd find lodging at this time of night." Paul coughed deeply, hacking hard before spitting on the ground.

"For another three silvers you can sleep in the hay," he told her, seizing his chance to make a little more money. She gave him a fierce look, and he put his hands up defensively. "I won't bother you, love," he snickered. "You have my word."

Lia thought for a moment. The idea of sleeping under the same roof as Paul was not appealing, but she couldn't help feeling that the blacksmith's shop was at least a little safer than spending the night exposed in the streets. Besides, she reasoned, if Mark had been willing to work here, Paul had to be at least a little trustworthy. Mark would not have shared a workplace with him otherwise. She pursed her lips, making up her mind.

"And I now have a dagger," Lia told Paul pointedly. "I thank you for your kindness."

• • •

CHAPTER NINETEEN

LIA DIDN'T WANT TO LINGER in Hollendale, and when she awoke the next morning she immediately prepared to leave.

"Do you have any idea where Mark may have headed to?" she asked Paul. He shrugged.

"Perhaps on to Woodston," he replied. "It's further north, about three days."

"Where can I buy food?"

"The market, on your way out of town," he answered. Lia thanked him, then bid him farewell and went on her way.

After buying food at the market, Lia headed north. The food was expensive; she could have gotten twice as much in Brunbury for the same cost. The journey was uneventful, though, and aside from exhaustion and her cold feet and hands she arrived in Woodston none the worse for wear.

There was a large wall surrounding the town, and a gatekeeper whom everyone entering had to pass by. It looked like people were paying a toll before being permitted to enter, so she moved back from the road to take a handful of silver tokens out of her money box before taking her place in line.

When it was her turn, the gatekeeper eyed her impatiently.

"Ten silver tokens to stay!" he growled, his slender, drawn face scowling at her as he looked her up and down. He thrust his hand out, waiting for her to pay. "And it's twenty–"

"But I'm not staying!" she interrupted, not wanting to part with that much money. "I'm only passing through! I'm looking for someone, I won't be here long!"

"If you'd shut up and let me speak," the man snapped, his crooked, yellowed teeth caked with old, decaying food. "It's twenty to pass through."

"How does it cost even more just to pass through?" Lia demanded.

"Hurry it up!" someone from behind her called. "I've got business to attend to!"

"I'll just refuse you entry, then," the gatekeeper threatened, ignoring the grumbling person, and she quickly shook her head, paying the man almost all of the silver she had taken from her money box.

"And you'll need this," the man continued, scribbling on a small piece of paper. "You must present this to the gatekeeper on the other side of town, otherwise you won't be permitted to leave." Lia cocked her head, wondering why she would need a piece of paper just to leave town, but she was too angry to question the man. She snatched the paper from him, glaring, and walked into the town. She was immediately shocked by what she saw.

Everyone was filthy and thin, obviously poor, their clothing hanging in tatters as they made their way about their business. Lia stood out in the crowd, not because she was dirty, as she had in Hollendale, but rather because she wasn't dirty enough.

As she walked down the main street, she heard a noise coming from next to one of the buildings. She looked, then quickly averted her eyes. A man stood behind a woman, moving quickly, and Lia realized that in this place there was no such thing as the whore's alley as there had been in Brunbury. Here, the men and women obviously had no misgivings about doing their unmentionables in plain sight, and for a moment she was almost grateful she had grown up in Brunbury rather than in this place. For all its faults, at least her own town would not permit the endeavors she was now seeing to take place in view of the public. The temporary feeling of appreciation dissipated only a few seconds later, however, and she scowled, her face burning with anger, as she remembered how eager the very same people she had been raised with had been to kill her.

Lia bumped into a man, then looked up quickly to apologize.

"Excuse me," she said, flashing a smile.

"I've no interest, whore," the man answered gruffly, waving her off. "Go peddle to the other men."

"No, you misunderstand," she explained, putting out her hand to stop him. He slapped her away, pointing his finger in her face.

"Don't touch me!" he warned, glaring at her with steely, gray eyes. "I'll have you thrown in jail, accosting a gentleman!"

"I'm not doing anything!" Lia protested, stepping back. The man was perturbed, but seemed to relax when she moved away. "Can you tell me where the blacksmith's shop is?" she asked quickly.

"Down that street," the man huffed, pointing. He straightened his dark green jacket. "Then turn left at the corner. You'll see it." He went on his way, ignoring her muttered thanks.

The blacksmith's shop was easy to find. She swung the door open, seeing a large, tall man working the bellows.

"Hello!" Lia called, and the man turned.

"Well, hello there!" he answered, licking his lips unashamedly. "And what can I do for you?"

"I'm looking for a blacksmith named Mark Samuels," she told him, trying to ignore his hungry stare. "Is he here?"

"He was," the man said, turning back towards his work. "He left the same day he arrived." Lia cursed.

"Why?" she asked, frustration filling her voice. "Did he say where he was going?"

"He said he wouldn't rest his head in a town owned by the Greene family," the blacksmith told her, chuckling to himself. "Can't say I much blame him. They're a bunch of greedy bastards, that's what they are." Lia's mouth went dry. A chill of fear raced up her spine, and her body went numb for a split second.

The Greene family. *Thomas'* family.

"Did he say where he was going?" she repeated, barely managing to get the words out.

"On to Maplegreen," the man told her.

"Is that town owned by the Greene family, too?" Lia croaked. The man laughed.

"This Mark you're looking for asked the same question," he answered. "No, it's not. And to answer what I suppose your next question will be, it's five days' travel from here, due east."

"Thank you for your help," she told him. "I'll be going now." She walked out, her heart racing.

Lia couldn't believe that she hadn't thought of asking about the governance of the town, especially after what Thomas had told her about his family's lands. Knowing that Thomas' family owned the place made the filth understandable, and someone as despicable as Thomas would have no problem with such a public display of the livelihood of the whores.

She quickly made her way to the center of town, hurriedly searching for a food vendor while fighting against the panic that was telling her to run and leave this place far behind her. She didn't want to stay there another moment, and she actually welcomed the thought of spending a long, freezing night on the road.

The last rays of sunlight sank below the tops of the buildings as she moved through the crowd, and Lia heard a crier take up a call.

"CUR-few!" the young boy yelled, his voice ringing out with a haunting cadence. The streets began to empty. An uneasiness came over her, and she felt lost and exposed.

"You!" a tall man shouted at her. "Come here!" Lia turned to run, instantly afraid, but there was nowhere to go. She froze, eyes wide, as he approached.

"Didn't you hear the crier?" he snapped. He wore a blue uniform jacket with a small, round medallion that said 'CONSTABLE'. She shrugged and stammered, unsure of what to say.

"Yes....yes, but I…"

"Speak up, girl!" the constable commanded. Lia cleared her throat.

"I don't know where to spend the night," she said, forcing an easy tone. "I've just arrived, could you tell me where I might find lodging?" He gave her a hard look.

"There's the Dancing Maiden, right over there." He gestured. "But be quick about it," he told her, jabbing his finger into her chest. "Or I'll take you before Lord Greene! You're not to be on the streets after curfew unless you're whoring!"

"Why?" Lia asked, bewildered at the unreasonable rule. "Why are the whores allowed on the streets, but no one else is?" Irritated at her question, the man rolled his eyes.

"Half of a whore's earnings are paid as a tax," he snapped patronizingly. "Of course Lord Greene wouldn't interfere with the livelihood of those making him money! Now," he thrust his finger in her face. "Take up a corner or take up a room, it makes no difference to me, but make up your mind and quickly!" He spun on the heel of his black, oiled boots and walked away.

Lia seethed, wondering if she should ignore the man's instructions and head towards the gate to leave, but she quickly decided it wasn't worth the risk. If Thomas had managed to send word of her to his family here, and if she were arrested and her identity discovered, she knew she would be trapped. Frustrated, Lia made her way to the inn.

The Dancing Maiden was an inn, to put it kindly. The rotting timbers of the roof looked as though they may collapse at any given moment, and the floorboards creaked and sagged as she walked across them. The place was busy, and as she watched the men laugh and fall over themselves Lia could almost hear someone cry for the Ale-Wench. An ache unexpectedly appeared in her throat. This place, despite her situation, reminded her of Jem's tavern, and she realized how much she missed home.

"You!" a man bellowed. "Don't be peddling yourself in here!" Lia turned towards the voice.

Her heart leaped into her throat at the sight of the man, his red beard and pock-marked face instantly jolting her memory. Her stomach turned, and she could almost hear the huffing breath as her attacker pinned her down in the alley; her body cringed as she again felt herself tear against the force of his entry. She imagined his foul stench and his grating, hissing voice.

You'll not take my coin without earning it, whore!

"Are you deaf, girl?" the man growled, reaching for her. Lia stumbled back, throwing her hands up to shield her face.

"Get away!" she croaked, her voice barely a whisper. "Leave me alone!" He cocked his head.

"Crazy, are you?" he grunted, rolling his eyes. "Every night, some crazy whore...." Giving his jowls a shake, he pointed at the door. "Go on, get out of here!" She began to back away, swallowing hard.

He's dead, Lia, she reminded herself. *This isn't* him, *he's dead.* She snapped back to reality, firmly fixing her gaze on the man's face as she forced herself to believe that his resemblance to her attacker was mere coincidence.

"Are you the owner?" Lia asked.

"Depends on who's asking," the man answered, frowning at her.

"I...I need a room."

"A room, is it?" he laughed. "And where is your benefactor?" She shook her head.

"It's just me," she answered quietly, keeping her distance from the man.

"Twelve silvers," he told her, wiping his nose on his sleeve. The cloth was streaked with yellow mucous, and Lia fought the urge to gag. The room was six times as expensive as Jem's rooms, but she was too flustered to even think of haggling over the price.

"Not until I see the room," she managed to say, her voice stronger as she found her nerve.

"Not until I see your coin," he countered, eyeing her. "And I'd better not find you sneaking customers in, either!"

"I'll give you eight silvers now," Lia bargained, realizing she would have to get into her money box for more. There was nowhere private enough for her to do so without someone seeing. "Then four more in the morning." She held the coins in her palm, and the man scratched his chin. He nodded, grinning to expose his rotting teeth.

"Upstairs, lass," he told her, beckoning her to follow. He started up a small staircase, and Lia's heart pounded. Through her skirts, she could feel the handle of the dagger she had bought in Hollendale, and she held it tightly as she climbed the rickety steps.

There was a small landing at the top, and a narrow hall with rooms on either side.

"Are you opposed to bunking with another?" the man asked her.

"I want my own room," Lia told him firmly. "Do the doors lock?"

"Have you anything worth stealing?" The man eyed her again.

"My life," she replied, to which the man laughed heartily. He stopped in front of a tiny, crooked door.

"Right here will do you," he told her, holding out his hand. "Give me my coins, and it's all yours. But," he cautioned, narrowing his eyes. "If you even think of leaving without paying me the rest, I'll have the constable arrest you before you can get halfway to the gate!"

"I'll not cheat you," she promised, handing him the coins. She opened the door to the room and quickly shut it behind her.

The dingy, small room stank of death, and Lia immediately felt swindled that she had paid so much money for such a disgusting place. The only furnishings were a chair and a broken bed frame; there was no mattress, not even a blanket, which, given the condition of the room, was probably a blessing. A feces-caked chamberpot sat in the corner, its contents festering and brewing into a fetid ooze. She covered her face, trying not to breathe.

After a few moments, her nose adjusted slightly to the stench, and she tiptoed across the stained floor to the tiny window, throwing it open despite the cold air that blew in. She took in several breaths, then stepped back to the door to bolt it.

The bolt wouldn't move, and Lia threw her full weight against it, trying to slide it into place. She grunted, pulling and pushing at the latch; then, with a snap, the nails holding it in place gave way, sending her to her knees. She lost her balance and fell over, coming to rest seated firmly on the damp, stinking floor. She opened her hand, and she could see the broken pieces of the bolt in the dim light of the street lanterns that made its way through the grimy window.

Tears of frustration welled up in her eyes as she searched the room, trying to think of something else to use to lock the door, when her eyes settled on the chair and the bed frame. She swallowed hard. Perhaps she could make them work.

Standing to her feet, she grabbed hold of the wooden bed, stifling a cry when a large rat ran out from underneath the frame. She dragged the heavy bed towards the door, pushing it firmly into place, then she took the chair and balanced it atop the frame. She stood back, feeling slightly better. Now, if anyone should try to enter, the bed would deter them and the chair would fall, hopefully waking her.

Lia spread her quilt out, then, striking a match, she lit her candle and affixed it to the floor with a few drops of melted wax. She curled into a ball and closed her eyes, trying not to cry. The flutters in her stomach were back, but the excitement they had elicited before was no longer aroused.

In the meager light of the candle, she took out the little figurine she had bought in Hollendale, running her fingers over the happy face of the dancing girl. She knew it was supposed to be her, and she smiled slightly at the thought. This was how Mark saw her; this is what he imagined. How beautifully he had captured her dance, and she wished she was still carefree enough to laugh and frolic as she used to.

With a sigh, Lia removed her dagger from her skirts and clutched it to her chest. It was almost identical to the one Thomas had taken from her, and she cursed herself again for letting him get away. She smiled regretfully to herself, imagining how she would have cleaned up the blood after dragging his body to the woods for the wild dogs to eat. Closing her eyes, she drifted off into a light sleep.

The loud clatter of the chair falling from its perch startled her awake, and she blinked in the darkness. Her candle had gone out, and the room was black. The bed frame scraped against the floor as someone pushed at the door, and Lia leaped to her feet, the sleep instantly gone from her eyes.

"Go away!" she yelled, slamming her body against the door to force it shut.

"Don't be like that, lovely!" a drunken voice crooned from behind the door, pushing at it again. "I just want a word with you!" The man dissolved into hysterics, his fingers poking through the crack. "Just a word!"

"Leave me alone!" Lia screamed, throwing her weight against the door again. The man's fingers were caught between the wood and the door frame, and with a howl of pain he yanked his hand back, cursing. "Go away!" she repeated. She could hear mumbled obscenities coming from the hallway, and she held her breath as she listened intently. Heavy footsteps stomped away, getting quieter and quieter until fading completely. Lia leaned against the bed frame, sagging onto the floor. It was a long time before she finally dozed off again.

• • •

Chapter Twenty

LIA HAD FALLEN ASLEEP sitting up, leaning against the door, and when she awoke her body was stiff and sore. Her bladder was uncomfortably full, and with a grimace of disgust she looked at the putrid chamberpot. Unable to muster the courage to use the disgusting thing but quickly losing control, Lia finally crouched on the floor, lifting her skirts to relieve herself. The liquid seeped through the floorboards, and she tried not to feel guilty. The place was already filthy, she reasoned to herself, so what difference did it make?

Lia gathered her things, hoping the smell of the place would eventually dissipate from her quilt and clothing. She opened her money box to count her coins, and she realized that she didn't have much silver left. Sighing, she took the last of her silver tokens and a single gold coin from her money box, deciding that she should ask the gatekeeper to change her gold before she left town, then she opened the door.

Making her way downstairs, Lia was stopped by the owner of the inn.

"My money, lass?" he asked her, holding out his hand. Lia obligingly dropped four silver tokens in his outstretched palm, then, without a word, turned to leave.

"Aren't you forgetting something?" the man prompted her, putting his hand on her shoulder to stop her.

"What do you mean?" Lia asked, confused. "We agreed on twelve tokens, and I've paid you. Now I'll be on my way."

"But I warned you not to have any company last night, now didn't I?" he scolded, gleaming at her. "And I know I heard someone at your door last night."

"Someone tried to break into my room!" she told him hotly. "Whoever it was wasn't there because of my invitation!"

"A likely excuse," the man dismissed her. "How much did you make? Five tokens? Ten?"

"I made nothing!" Lia hissed, agitation rising up within her. "Let me go, I've paid you what I promised!"

"I want another five silvers, lass," the owner of the inn told her, glaring at her. "Or I'll report you to the constable and he'll take you before Lord Greene!"

"Why would he do that?" she demanded. "I've done nothing wrong!"

"You have to pay your tax," the man said, grinning. "Every whore has to, and if I tell him you're trying to keep from paying you'll be taken before the lord! Now," he lowered his voice, holding out his hand. "Take your pick! Either go before the governance, or give me what I want!" Lia gritted her teeth, hearing them grind loudly in her ears. Her face turned red with anger as she handed the man five more silver tokens.

"I thank you, lass!" he crowed, touching his head and giving a slight bow. "Wise choice, that was!" She stormed out of the inn, happy, at least, that she had used the bastard's floor as a chamberpot.

Lia made her way to the center of town to buy food for the five day walk to Maplegreen. There wasn't much available, and most of the food was rotting and wilted or half frozen and mushy. After perusing several market stands, she settled on buying a few loaves of bread, some cheese, and two bunches of rubbery, sick-looking carrots. She knew it wasn't enough, and that she would most likely go hungry for the last day or so of her journey, but she would rather deal with hunger pangs than eat rotting food.

"Eleven silvers, girl," the proprietor, a short woman will stringy, straw-colored hair and abscessed skin told her. Lia's eyes bulged at the price.

"But I've bought so little!" she exclaimed. "Will you take nine?" She only had nine silver tokens left, and she felt uncomfortable about using her gold token.

"Eleven," the woman answered coldly. "Take it or leave it, girl. My prices are lower than the others, and if you'd rather pay more you're welcome to take your business to them!" Lia thought a moment. The only alternative would be to go get change from the gatekeeper first, but she didn't want to linger in the town any longer than she had to. Besides, everything was so expensive in this town, so perhaps using gold was less risky than it was in Brunbury. With a grunt of displeasure, she handed the woman her gold token.

The woman's eyes lit up at the sight of the coin, and Lia instantly felt that she had made a terrible mistake. She forced herself to ignore the worry rising up within her, reminding herself that within just a short time she would be leaving the accursed town, and she took her change from the woman's outstretched hand.

"Do you have a sack, at least?" Lia asked, and the woman reached under the table on which she displayed her wares. She produced a very large, surprisingly clean-looking flour sack.

'That'll cost you one more," she told Lia, and Lia didn't argue. Placing her food into the sack, she began to walk to the gate on the far side of town.

She didn't make it far.

"Don't move, my pretty," a voice hissed in her ear, and Lia felt a sharp stab of pain in her back as a wave of fear washed over her skin. A man took hold of her arm, and before she could react he roughly pulled her into an alleyway. Her body flushed with terror at the thought of what the man wanted, and she choked on the scream rising in her throat.

He spun her around, and now he pressed the blade of his knife to her throat. The woman from the market stand was with him.

"I'll slit your gullet if you move," the man warned her, his yellowed eyes flashing. His thin, grizzled face was sickly and gray, and he looked as though he hadn't eaten in weeks. He coughed loudly in her face. "You know what we want."

The woman moved forward and snatched Lia's bundled quilt, the money box and its contents clattering to the ground with her belongings. The man's face brightened at the sight of the coins, and, without thinking, Lia tried to take advantage of his momentary distraction.

Reaching for her dagger, she shoved the man away. She opened her mouth to scream, but her eyes suddenly went dark as stars filled her vision.

"Try that again, wench!" the woman cackled, dropping the rock she had used to strike Lia's head. "No one will take notice of your rotting corpse until the stench becomes unbearable! The whores will just step over you to do their business, and the dogs will lick the flesh from your bones!"

"That's everything I have!" Lia begged groggily, trying to appeal to the couple. "Please, just leave me a few silvers!"

"It's your own damn fault for paying with gold," the woman told her, chuckling to herself as she quickly counted Lia's money. "Haven't you any sense? You'll know better next time, now, won't you?"

"What's this?" The man was holding the piece of paper Lia had gotten from the gatekeeper. He stared at it, his face bright with excitement. "It's an exit pass!"

"Give it here!" the woman snapped, reaching for it. "I'm the one who told you about her. You keep the money, and I'll have that for myself!"

"But I won't be able to leave without it!" Lia wailed, trying to focus through her blurred vision. "You don't understand, I'm just passing through!"

"Then you'll just have to change your plans!" the man chuckled, tucking the slip of paper into his jacket. "Everyone's trying to leave this place, and this pass is worth more than your coin!"

"They only cost twenty silvers," Lia explained desperately, regaining her clarity. "Can't you just buy one from the gatekeeper?"

"If only!" the woman laughed sarcastically, rolling her eyes and putting her arm around the man. "We're residents here. There's an exit tax of a thousand silvers for a citizen to leave, but now that I have *this*," she stepped back quickly, and in her fingers she held

Lia's pass. "I'll be leaving today!" The man patted his pocket, realizing the woman's deft hands had taken the paper from him.

"I'll kill you for that!" he growled, stepping towards the woman. "I'll bleed you dry!"

"How are you going to follow me?" the woman laughed as she darted away. "*You* don't have a pass, now do you!" The man followed her, cursing, leaving Lia lying in the street.

She dragged herself to her feet, leaning against a building for support. Her head pounded, and as she reached up to touch her skull she could feel warm droplets of blood leaking from the gash the rock had torn into her scalp. She looked down at the ground, her few belongings scattered across the dirty, cobblestone street. She shivered, and with a heavy heart she began to gather her things. At least she still had the food.

She made her way back to the entry gate. The gatekeeper was the same man she had seen the day before; surely he would remember her, and she could only hope that he would help her. There was no one awaiting entry through the gate, and Lia stepped towards him.

"Excuse me," she said, forcing a smile. The man glowered at her, unhappy that she was bothering him.

"What do you want?" he asked snidely, turning away.

"My pass has been stolen," she told him. "And I was hoping you could write me another."

"Ha!" the gatekeeper barked, obviously amused at Lia's request. "Like hell I will!" She clenched her fists in anger but tried to remain calm.

"Don't you remember me from yesterday?" she asked sweetly, and the gatekeeper looked at her again.

"Can't say that I do," he answered, his voice dull and disinterested. Hot fear raced through her, and her throat closed with panic.

"Please!" she exclaimed, stomping her foot with urgency. "You have to remember!"

"Nope," he told her, uncaring. Lia seethed. It took every ounce of her strength to keep from throwing herself at the man and stabbing him through the heart, but she managed to force herself to turn away.

"You know," the man called, and Lia paused. There was a familiar gleam in his eye, and she knew what he was going to say. "I might be prompted to remember."

"And how might I do that?" she asked flatly.

"Well," he said, drawing the word out, pretending to think. "I get awful lonely over here, all by myself." She sneered, scowling at him.

"If it were really that simple, wouldn't everyone do that to get out?" she snapped.

"You're an awful pretty little thing, though, aren't you?" he mused, his voice dripping honey. "Haven't seen anyone who turns me quite the same way, especially not the whores in this place. I could lose my life over this, you understand, I'd be doing you a service." His chest swelled with self-importance at the thought, then his voice lowered as he smirked. "In more ways than one."

Lia was disgusted, not just at the gatekeeper's offer, but also at the consideration she was actually giving him. She realized what she was contemplating and she fiercely shook her head, glaring at him.

"I'd have to be at death's door before bedding with you!" she exclaimed, her lip raising into a snarl. "I'll find another way!"

"Suit yourself," the gatekeeper shrugged. He chuckled sarcastically. "You could always try the constable."

Lia searched the crowds, looking for a constable. She desperately wanted to avoid drawing attention to herself, and she had a feeling that she wouldn't receive any help, but it seemed to be her only choice. She recognized the same man who had directed her to the Dancing Maiden the previous day, and she approached him.

"Can you help me?" she asked. He scowled at her, listening as she explained what had happened.

"You'll have to take your issue to Lord Greene's nephew," the constable told her, waving her off. Lia's heart sank with dread.

"Nephew?" she asked weakly. The constable nodded.

"Lord Greene left this morning," he answered quickly. "To attend to important business. His nephew, Thomas, is in charge." Her predicament was hopeless, and she wanted to curl into a ball and scream.

Lia wandered the streets, trying to make herself as inconspicuous as possible as she searched for a way out of the town. It was impossible; the only way in or out was through the gates, and the wall surrounding the town was too high to even think of climbing.

Night fell, and the cry announcing curfew rang through the streets. Lia remembered what she had been told, that after curfew she would either need to take up a corner or find a place to stay. She didn't know what to do, and as the minutes slowly passed she felt an increasing urgency to get off the streets. She began to walk towards the far gate, hoping she wouldn't be bothered.

"Get off the street!" a constable called towards her as he approached her. "Or take up your post!" She smiled disarmingly, nodding, and hurried away. He didn't follow, and when Lia was sure he couldn't see her she ducked into an empty alley.

She huddled in the darkness, feeling exposed. The space was narrow, the two buildings on either side less than an arm's length apart. The alley was closed, the outside wall that surrounded the town forming a dead end. She wondered if she could just stay there all night, avoiding detection, when she heard the click-clacking of boots approaching.

As quietly as she could, Lia peeked out of her hiding place and looked. A constable was walking slowly towards her, carrying a lantern and shining it briefly into each alley he passed. She backed up quickly, crouching in the far corner, her mind racing. There was no way out. Her fingers brushed her dagger, but she decided against it. Thinking quickly, she settled on a story.

She would claim that, when she had finished with a customer, he had left her there without paying after hitting her on the head. Lia touched the now-scabbing wound from where the thief had struck her, praying that her lie would work. There was no other choice but to try.

The footsteps came closer, and Lia stood to her feet, knowing she would soon be found. She leaned heavily against one of the buildings, nervously lifting her foot and tapping it against the opposite wall. Her knee locked, and now she was braced between the two surfaces. An idea flashed through her mind, and she knew how she would get away from the approaching street patrol and out of the town.

Hurriedly, Lia stuffed her quilt into her food sack and tied the end of the sack into a loop. Draping it over her neck, she braced herself again between the two walls, and, whispering a prayer, she began to move her feet. She slowly began to ascend, the force of her back and her feet against the hard surfaces giving her the leverage to walk up the walls.

The constable's footsteps echoed in the empty streets, and Lia moved even faster. She looked down, and she could see the lanternlight begin to illuminate the darkness of the alley below her. She pushed herself further up the wall, her heart pounding, then she looked again.

Something broke free under Lia's foot, and she held her breath as the sound of the falling object rang out in the silence. Cursing in her mind, and sure the constable had heard the noise, she heaved herself upward with one final effort. Reaching the top of the wall, she quickly disappeared onto the roof of the adjacent building and flattened her body against the clay tiles.

She froze, waiting. The footsteps paused, and Lia could see the light from the lantern shining up between the two buildings. After what seemed an eternity, the light moved, and she could hear the steady steps continue as the man resumed his patrol. She let her breath out slowly, momentarily relieved.

Lia crawled across the roof until she reached the edge where it met the exterior wall that surrounded the town. She hadn't thought of how she would get down, and when she looked she realized how far away the ground was from her perch, the surface of the earth almost invisible in the darkness. She would have to jump. As she gathered her courage and prepared to make the leap, she remembered the day she had raced Mark to the roof of the cobbler's shop.

She smiled, her eyes shining with determination. She had beaten him that day, and she was going to beat this damn town, wall or no wall. As she stared down at the far-away ground, she remembered how it had felt falling from the cobbler's roof. She braced herself, preparing for the inevitable pain, and, after tossing her sack, she leaped into the nothingness.

Her ankle felt like it had exploded when she landed on the rocky ground, and she couldn't help letting out a quiet shriek of agony.

"Over there!" a voice called, and Lia quickly realized that there was a patrol outside the wall as well as within.

Picking herself up, she tried to run, her foot buckling under her weight. Grimacing, she bit down hard on her lip, and she took another step. Her ankle screamed at her, white hot pain shooting up her leg. She could hear the sound of people approaching, and as she looked behind her the glow of lanterns was steadily coming closer.

She thought of Thomas, and the satisfied grin that would break across his face when he saw her. He would drag her to his bed, and what she had managed to stop him from doing in the barn would inevitably happen. Steeling herself, she fought off the pain and began to run.

Lia flew across the ground as fast as she could, her ankle throbbing with blinding fury with each stride. She ignored the excruciating agony, and as the pursuit of the men faded into the distance she felt like shouting with triumph. She kept running, finally stopping when her now-swollen ankle wouldn't let her go any further.

Limping as she made her way into the trees, she lit her candle. She found a rock overhang hidden behind a thick, tangled veil of leafless vines, and she collapsed with exhaustion to the ground, barely managing to stave off sleep long enough to wrap herself in her quilt.

• • •

Chapter Twenty-One

Her twisted ankle hindered her progress towards Maplegreen, and the going was slow for the first few days. On the fourth day, Lia was able to increase her pace, but she had lost valuable time, and when her food ran out she was much further away from her destination than she had planned. Tired, hungry, and cold, she trudged along the road, hoping that as she crested each hill she would see the town in the distance.

After six days of walking, the weather turned. The early-December snow and ice pelted her as she stumbled on the road, wrapped in her blanket with her shoulder bent against the wind. She was grateful for the numbing effect the cold had on her still-aching ankle, but her appreciation ended there. Her freezing skin burned as she walked, and she fell asleep that night tormented by despair. She knew she wouldn't survive much longer unless she found the town.

She awoke to a pristine, white landscape, the sun shining brightly despite the blanket of gray clouds filling the sky. The icy wind whipped at her face, and she could barely muster the energy to shake herself from sleep. She was grateful, at least, that her stomach had stopped hurting; she had finally grown accustomed to the pangs caused by its emptiness.

Lia trudged on for hours, and the sun was high in the sky when she reached the top of yet another steep hill. She paused to catch her breath, gazing with tired eyes at the snow-covered road that stretched before her. She blinked, and she realized that she could just barely see a town tucked into the valley below her. Her shoulders sagged, and she felt like sobbing with relief.

Lia's joy at finally reaching the town overshadowed the knowledge that she had no money, and she wasted no time stopping someone for directions.

"Where's the blacksmith's shop?" she asked quickly, ignoring the dirty glare the woman gave her.

"Use your eyes!" the woman commanded, pointing. The blacksmith's shop was several yards from where Lia stood, and she ran the short distance, bursting through the door.

The blacksmith looked up at her in surprise, pausing mid-strike in his work.

"Is Mark here?" Lia blurted. "Mark Samuels?"

"Never heard of him," the blacksmith answered, raising his brow with concern. "Are you all right, girl?"

Lia's face had drained of color, her skin instantly breaking out into a cold sweat in the warmth of the shop. She turned to leave, reaching out to push the door open, but her hand missed the door handle and she collapsed.

When she came to, she was still in the blacksmith's shop, lying on the floor. She blinked, the heat of the forge causing her hands and feet to tingle and burn as they warmed thoroughly for the first time in days. She could hear the metallic clanking of the blacksmith's hammer, and as her vision cleared she got a good look at the man.

His thick arms flexed as he swung his hammer, striking his workpiece. His short, blond hair appeared gray with its coat of soot from the fire, and his face was smudged from where he had wiped the sweat from his brow with dirty hands. He was tall, and when he glanced towards her Lia could see that his dark, brown eyes seemed kind and bright. He smiled.

"You're awake," the man said, setting down his workpiece and moving towards her. "I was just wondering to myself if you were going to die here!" Lia sat up slowly, instinctively checking to make sure her clothing was still in place. It didn't seem that she had been disturbed from where she had fallen, for which she was both relieved and grateful.

"No," she answered. "I'm still alive." He laughed, giving her a strange look. She stared at him blankly.

"I thought for sure he would be here," she said, her voice distant.

"Who is 'he'?" the man asked. Lia frowned sadly.

"My betrothed."

"He can't be worth much," the blacksmith mused. "Leaving a young lady like yourself out in the cold without telling you where he's gone."

"I don't think he ever dreamed I'd try to find him," she muttered under her breath.

"I'm Garrett," the man said, extending his hand. "Garrett Daniels." Lia cautiously returned the gesture, shaking his hand. He seemed nice, and she was too tired to be afraid of him. He hadn't done anything to her when she fainted despite having the perfect opportunity to do so, and he didn't terrify her. That's all she had the energy to care about.

"Lia Grey," she told him. Her stomach growled, and she ventured a question.

"I haven't any money," she began, a twinge of anger stabbing her heart as she remembered the thieves. "I was robbed in the last town I passed through. But I wonder if you might have a bit of food you could spare."

"Not only half-frozen, but starved as well," Garrett mused, narrowing his eyes. "Robbed, huh? You're not just spinning a story to get a free meal, are you?"

"I'm too tired to spin a story," Lia sighed, slumping against the wall. Her eyes glimmered slightly as she met his gaze, pride welling in her chest. "But I *can* tell a tale if I've got a mind to!"

"I might be interested to find out what kind of tales," he smiled before disappearing into a back room.

When Garrett returned, he had a large hunk of bread.

"I think I can spare a little food, just this once," he said. He held the bread out, but pulled back as she reached for it. "Just this once," he repeated, giving her a stern look. Lia nodded gratefully as he handed it to her. He went back to his work, letting her eat.

Her stomach full, she stood to her feet.

"I suppose I'll have to move on," Lia told Garrett, thanking him for the food. "Where's the next town?"

"Depends on where you want to go," he answered, looking up and stepping towards her. "There's a town in every direction." Her heart sank as she paused to think.

"I don't know," she said finally, throwing up her hands in defeat. "I don't know where the damn fool would have gone! He passed through Hollendale, and the blacksmith in Woodston suggested I might find him here. But if you haven't seen him," Garrett shook his head again, confirming that he hadn't. "Then I don't know where to look."

"Might I give you a bit of advice?" Garrett asked. She nodded, and he continued. "See if you can't find some work before you set out again. You said you haven't any money." He paused, giving her a hard look. She met his gaze, and he grunted, reading her answer from her expression. "So unless you plan to steal, you're going to need to earn some coin." She shook her head vehemently.

"I don't intend to steal," she told him firmly. He went on, his next words causing her to brighten.

"Why don't you send word on to the other towns, rather than visiting them yourself? Is there any reason you can't stay here for a short while, or at least until the weather warms?"

"I think that's an excellent idea!" Lia exclaimed, her spirits lifting. She hadn't thought of doing that, but given her predicament it seemed to be the best option. "Where do you think I might find work?"

"Just ask around," Garrett instructed her. "We're a travelling town, there's always a job here or there."

"What about here?" she joked, forgetting herself in her excitement. Her eyes instantly grew wide; she couldn't believe she had asked him that question. He laughed, lightly slapping her on the back. Her face prickled with fear at the touch, her ears ringing with the blood that rushed to her head.

"What would you do here, love?" he chuckled, looking her up and down. "I don't even think you'd be strong enough to work the bellows!" She sighed with relief, glad this man hadn't assumed from her poorly-worded statement that she was a whore.

"I've got some experience as a cook," Lia told him. "Is there an inn or a tavern here?"

"Right down the street," Garrett answered. "And if you're any good, I'm sure they'll have a position for you!" He grimaced, pretending to gag. "What the current cook makes isn't fit for dogs!" Lia smiled, thinking of how she had gotten her job with Jem. She thanked Garrett, waving as she stepped outside.

The Golden Barrel Inn was much larger than Jem's tavern, and as Lia entered she was assaulted by a horrible stench. She immediately weighed her options, unsure if she even wanted to consider working in a place that reeked as badly as this one, but after a quick look around she realized where the smell was coming from. Smoke poured out of an open doorway, and she could hear the sound of a heated argument, disrupted by fits of violent coughing, drifting towards her with the smoke.

The patrons seemed oblivious to the goings on, the large crowd of men drinking and carrying on as though nothing were out of place. At first glance, it didn't appear that the inn's owner was in sight, so, holding her breath, Lia approached the billowing smoke and the raised voices.

"You'll burn the place down!" a man screamed, gasping as he spoke.

"I won't!" the raspy voice of a woman retorted.

"I can't feed the men this swill!" the first voice countered, coughing and hacking. "A body could die from the smell alone!"

"Then cook it yourself!" the woman howled. "You'll not find another to work in this pigsty!"

Lia's eyes smarted from the smoke, and she blinked, trying to make out the two figures standing toe-to-toe. A fire blazed under a large, cast iron pot, and the contents, obviously burnt beyond recognition, were the source of the stinking cloud. She waited as patiently as she could for one of them to notice her, but after only a few moments she could bear it no longer.

Seeing the back door, Lia took hold of an empty burlap sack and used it to grasp the handle of the pot. Lifting the heavy cauldron from its place on the fire, she staggered forward, kicked the back door open, and dropped it into the street. The loud crash it made as it hit the ground startled the arguing man and woman, and they turned their attention to her, their eyes livid.

"Who are you!" the man shouted, pointing his finger at her and daring her to respond.

"My name is Lia," she answered evenly, placing her hands on her hips.

"Get out of my kitchen!" the woman screamed, moving towards Lia threateningly. The smoke had already begun to clear, wafting out the still-open back door and revealing a fat, heavyset, bearded woman and an equally large, bearded man.

"I'm looking for the owner," Lia said, backing away slightly.

"That would be me," the man told her, his voice calming. "I'm Rene, and this," he spat, gesturing wildly at the fat woman. "This is my blasted cook, Gretchen!"

Gretchen was hefty and held the appearance of a man, her broad shoulders set proudly as she seethed at Rene's words. Her hands and face were caked with filth, and her eyes were aflame with loathing.

"I'll quit, you ungrateful bastard!" Gretchen shrieked, stomping her foot. Lia could almost feel the entire building shake with the weight of the woman.

"Then quit!" Rene answered. "The men would rather starve!" In a huff, Gretchen turned and waddled away as quickly as she could, muttering to herself as she went.

"And don't come back!" Rene called after her, to which she responded with a string of curses. "Now," he continued, directing his attention to Lia. "What can I do for you?"

"Well," Lia began, amusement on her face. "I'm looking for a job."

"I'm glad to be rid of you!" Rene shouted suddenly in response to the loud slam of the inn's door, his gray eyes burning once again. He hadn't heard Lia's words, cursing under his breath. "Stupid, fat whore!"

"Has she worked here long?" Lia asked, trying to stifle a smile.

"For too long," Rene answered, rubbing his temples. He pushed his shaggy, brown hair off of his forehead. "I fire her at least twice a week, and she quits just as often." He sighed. "But she's the only one who can put together something even remotely edible, and even that's just a matter of opinion and how drunk the fool eating her cooking is. Answer me this, if you can," he continued, frustration edging his voice. "Entrails are supposed to be rinsed and cleaned before they're cooked, aren't they?" Lia wrinkled her nose with disgust.

"I suppose, if you don't mind the taste of shit, you can leave them unwashed, but I prefer not to eat or prepare entrails one way or the other," she answered, swallowing hard and making a face.

"That's what *I* said!" Rene crowed triumphantly, grinning from ear to ear. "But that dammed fool of a woman insists on making them! Makes the food taste like something a cat threw up!"

"If you don't mind me saying so," Lia said mischievously. "I think the taste may have been from her hands, not what she was cooking." Rene dissolved into laughter, bending over and slapping his knee loudly at her joke. Then, after pulling himself together from his momentary elation, he again addressed her reason for being there. "What can I help you with?"

"I think I might be able to help *you*," Lia told him. "I'm passing through town, and I need to make a little money before I leave. I'm a damn good cook," she said hurriedly at his dismissive expression. He eyed her suspiciously.

"That's what they all say," he answered. "Then I have to call the undertaker, and Gretchen won't let me live in peace for weeks afterward!"

"I really am!" Lia insisted, her mouth twisting into a pout.

"Tell you what," Rene began, a thoughtful expression on his broad face. "Gretchen won't be back until tomorrow, and I've nothing to serve the men. You cook tonight, and if it's any good I'll give you a job."

"With what pay?" Lia asked, and he waved her off.

"We'll discuss that later," he promised. "After we find out if the customers survive your cooking." She quickly agreed.

• • •

Chapter Twenty-Two

LIA BUSIED HERSELF in the kitchen, falling into the old routine she had grown used to while working at Jem's tavern. The place was filthy and she didn't have time to clean, but she did her best to ensure that the thick layer of grime covering everything didn't make it into the food she was preparing.

When the smell of baking bread and boiling stew began to waft out of the kitchen, Rene became curious, and he poked his head inside to see what she was doing.

"Well," he told her, a dumbfounded expression on his face. "Well!" Lia took his short comment as a good sign, and the food was soon done cooking.

She peeked out of the kitchen at the horde of men filling the inn, and she swallowed hard against the anxiety rising in her throat. She remembered her last night at Jem's tavern and how terrifying it had been just to walk amongst the men, but she knew that her fear was nothing compared to her need for a job.

Sighing with dread, she thought of what Mark and her mother had said, and she tried to gather her courage. She couldn't be afraid forever. Giving her dagger a reassuring pat, she loaded her serving bowl and bread onto a large tray and stepped out.

"What's this?" one man called, obviously surprised to see Lia instead of Gretchen. "It smells good enough to eat, and the wench isn't bad, either!" Forcing herself to stay calm, she quietly and quickly began serving the meal. It wasn't long before the room was filled with the loud compliments of the men, and she blushed deeply as she refilled her tray to serve the men seconds.

After the patrons had been served, Rene met her in the kitchen, cautiously eyeing the food.

"Not a one of them has keeled over yet," he observed, gesturing towards the customers. "But I'll have to wait till morning to be sure." Rene eyed the food again, contemplating, then he shrugged. "I think I might be bold enough to give it a try, even so," he decided.

"It won't poison you, I promise," Lia reassured him, dishing him up a bowl of stew and tearing off a large hunk of bread. Rene leaned against the kitchen counter and tentatively tasted the food. He chewed for a moment, then began voraciously slurping the stew. She smiled. She knew she had gotten the job.

"Lia!" a familiar voice called, and she turned to see Garrett standing at the door. "I see you've been successful in your job search!" He smiled broadly, his eyes twinkling.

"I believe I have!" Lia responded excitedly. "And I'll gladly repay you for your earlier kindness. That is, if you're hungry." She laughed when he nodded, and she served him a bowl.

"Now, just you wait," Rene protested through his food, spewing small bits across the counter. "You can't just give one of my meals away!"

"If it hadn't been for him, I wouldn't be here!" Lia answered, meeting Rene's stare as she handed Garrett his food. "Quit griping and eat!" Rene seemed unsure of how to respond, then, with a quick shrug and a muttered curse, he began stuffing his mouth again.

When the meal was over and after Lia had collected the dishes, she took up the issue of lodging and pay with Rene.

"At the last tavern," she lied. "I made eighteen tokens a week. But if you'll give me lodging as well, I'll only expect sixteen."

"Highway robbery!" Rene spluttered, his eyeballs bulging out of his skull. "I'll pay you twelve, with a room!" She paused, thinking quickly.

"Fourteen, and you have a deal," she countered.

"Done!" Rene shouted before she had even finished speaking. Lia smiled to herself. Not only was she making twice as much as she had back home, but now she would have a room, too.

"And I'll take my meals from what I cook," she added. Rene opened his mouth to protest, but, catching her determined glare, he thought better of it and nodded in agreement. "What room shall I have?" she asked smugly, happy with the deal she had struck.

Rene led her upstairs, and Lia was relieved to see that the rooms there were in much better condition than the one she had rented in Woodston, complete with not only a bed frame but also a somewhat decent-looking mattress. She asked Rene for a lantern, which he readily provided, before bidding him goodnight.

There was a bolt on the door, albeit flimsy, but she was satisfied that she would be relatively safe throughout the night. She made mental note to speak with Garrett the next day to have him make her a better lock.

She spread her quilt out on the bed and lay down. For the first time since she had left home, Lia felt safe, and she drifted off to sleep to the tickle of butterfly wings in her stomach and the comfort of a well-fed belly.

The next morning, all hell broke loose.

"What do you mean, fired?" roared the fat cook, Gretchen, the timbers of the inn's roof shaking at the force of her voice. "You can't fire me!"

"This new girl is a better cook than you!" Rene told the woman, his eyes wild, easily matching Gretchen's volume and tone. "I made more money last night on just one meal than I have in a week from your cooking!"

Lia tiptoed down the stairs, trying to see what was happening. Gretchen stood near the front door of the inn, her broad face crimson, her carrot-orange hair seeming to burst into flames with her rage. She caught sight of Lia, and she forgot about Rene.

"You thieving whore!" she screamed, launching her massive bulk at Lia. "I'll kill you, wench, I swear I will!" Lia froze, unsure of how to escape the behemoth hurtling in her direction. She was trapped; the door of her room would do little to protect her from the angry woman, and she couldn't get off the stairs to run. She withdrew her dagger, brandishing it in hopes that the woman would stop, but it was to no avail.

In an instant, Lia was on the floor with Gretchen's thick fingers wrapped around her throat.

"Get off her, Gretchen!" Rene screeched, pounding up the stairs. "You'll kill her!"

In her mind, the stench of sour ale filled Lia's nose, and she could feel the weight of the man from the alley pinning her down. In a panicked daze, she searched wildly for something to use to defend herself, and her groping fingers found the staircase baluster.

She pulled with all her strength as she gasped for air, and the baluster broke free. Her vision was going dark, and Lia swung the makeshift weapon with all her might. It struck the woman squarely on the back of the head, and Lia felt the tight grip suddenly loosen.

Heaving, Lia managed to struggle out from under the now-limp body, and she stood to her feet, staring down at the woman's bleeding head. Gretchen didn't move, and Lia backed away, opening her hand and hearing the hollow clatter of the baluster dropping to the floor.

"Gretchen?" Rene called, his wide, dirty face creased with worry as he rolled the large woman over and slapped her. "Gretchen!" He turned and gave Lia a grave look. "She's dead, I think," he said, his voice a hushed whisper of awe.

In shock, Lia allowed herself to be pushed and jostled out of the way as several men moved into position to lift the dead woman. As she watched, they carried the body down the stairs and out the door.

Lia sank down onto one of the steps, staring blankly.

"Don't you worry," Rene told her quickly, reaching out and patting her shoulder. She shrank away, and he pulled his hand back. "Don't you worry," he said again. "We all saw it, she attacked you. I'll talk to the governance, don't worry." He began to rush down the stairs, then paused.

"Go ahead and start cooking," he prompted her. "I'll handle this." Lia numbly obeyed.

The hours passed, and Lia fought to contain the worry that filled her. She was afraid; she knew the woman would have killed her, but she didn't know what justice was in this unfamiliar town. In Brunbury, while she wouldn't have been executed, the blood on her hands would have sorely limited any hope of making an honest living. Lia choked back tears, hoping that her good fortune wouldn't be spoiled by the fat woman's rage.

Her thoughts were interrupted by Garrett.

"I heard what happened," he said, knocking once on the edge of the door before entering the kitchen. Lia jumped, surprised, then clapped her hands to her face.

"What's going to happen?" she gasped, her eyes dark. "Are they coming for me?" Garrett hushed her, moving to her side.

"No," he told her, smiling. "As a matter of fact, everyone's rather impressed that someone as small as you managed to keep from getting killed!" Lia let out a sigh of relief, relaxing.

"I didn't mean to hurt her," she told Garrett, going back to her work. She was making meat pies for the evening meal, and dozens of pans of unbaked crusts covered every flat surface in the kitchen. She ladled the meat filling into the pastries and sealed the pies with a second crust, then began sliding them into the oven to bake.

"If you hadn't done what you did, she would have killed you," Garrett told her, admiration in his voice. "Perhaps I was wrong to say you wouldn't be strong enough to work the bellows." He chuckled, referring to the day before when she had joked about working in his shop. "You've got quite an arm on you!" Lia cracked a grin, straightening after slipping the last of the first set of pies into the oven.

"Thank you," she told him playfully, giving a small bow. "Just keep that in mind if you ever consider upsetting me!" She was partially serious, and she found herself hoping that her new reputation would help prevent any future bothers.

Lia was comfortable at the inn, and over the next few weeks she quickly became used to her surroundings. She had sent word on to the other towns inquiring about Mark, but there had been no answer. Despite the nagging feeling that lingered in the back of her mind, prompting her to move on, she was not anxious to again experience the long, tired, cold nights she had spent on the road, and she was content to remain in the town.

Garrett was a kind companion to her, and Lia was set at ease by the fact that he didn't give her any indication of being interested in her. He hadn't once commented on her looks or flirted with her, and it surprised her in a way; she wasn't used to being around a man who didn't try to give her attention. He reminded her a little of Mark, and she enjoyed the company he offered.

In her spare time, Lia would sit in the warmth of the blacksmith's shop, talking and laughing with Garrett. She didn't tell him much about herself, restraining her portion of their conversations to superficial things, but he spoke openly and freely with her.

Garrett had come to Maplegreen several years before, apprenticing under the old blacksmith that had worked there. When the man had died, Garrett took over the business. Maplegreen was a busy town; there was always more than enough work for him to do, and it didn't seem that he had taken much time to think about anything other than his job. He had a beau once, a young woman who had stolen his heart, but she had shunned him, much like Lia had shunned Mark. The woman had left town with another man, leaving Garrett heartbroken and alone. Despite the years that had passed, he still seemed pained over it as he told Lia the story, and she couldn't help feeling sorry for him.

On a snowy day in early January, Lia went to see Garrett at the blacksmith's shop. Rene had given her the day off, happy at how much money he had been making from her cooking. She had protested at first, telling him that she couldn't afford to lose some of her pay just to have a break, but he had promised her that he wouldn't reduce her wages.

When she got there, Garrett had immediately disappeared into another room, and he returned wearing a jacket and boots.

"Why are you bundled up?" Lia asked him, bewildered by his attire. She wondered if he was trying to hint to her that he didn't want her there. "Are you going somewhere?" Garrett seemed uneasy, and he shifted his weight from side to side.

"Well," he began, his voice cracking. He cleared his throat. "I thought I might take a break for a little while." She gazed at him quizzically, then shrugged.

"Makes sense," she decided. "You work hard, and you deserve a break." Garrett grew quiet, and an awkward silence ensued.

"So do you want me to leave?" she finally asked, slightly disappointed by the thought. She would have to spend the day alone in her room at the inn if he didn't want her to stay. Garrett cleared his throat again, shaking his head quickly.

"There's a creek," he told her, glancing down at his feet. "It's very nice in the winter, especially with the snow. I thought we might go for a walk. Unless," he added quickly. "You don't feel like it." She thought of the creek at home, her safe haven from the worries of the world. It might be nice to see the place Garrett spoke of.

"How far is it?" she asked cautiously, unsure if she trusted him enough to venture off alone with him.

"Not far at all," he answered, pointing in a general direction. "It's still inside the town, just a minute or two away, if even that. It's really close." He was talking fast, and his nervousness made her smile.

"Sure," she said, shrugging off her concern. "I'll go." They stepped out into the cold and began to walk.

Garrett had been truthful; the creek was very close. Still, Lia couldn't help feeling a bit nervous at the thought of being alone with him, and she shifted her weight uneasily.

"Are you all right?" Garrett asked, and she looked up at him in surprise. He must have noticed her discomfort.

"I'm fine," she replied quickly, smiling.

"Hello, Garrett!" a man shouted out, startling her. Garrett turned and waved, and Lia relaxed. They were in full view of any passing townspeople, she realized. She didn't need to be afraid. She sighed and looked around, drinking in the winter scenery.

The reeds lining the bank were bent over with a heavy layer of ice, and the bright red winter berries that grew on low bushes near the water's edge were strikingly bold against the pure white snow. The creek was frozen solid, and the little pointed V's from the feet of birds crisscrossed its surface with tiny trails.

Lia breathed deeply of the crisp, clean air, grateful for a moment of peace. She glanced at Garrett, and was suddenly aware of his eyes gazing at her. Her cheeks flushed.

"Why are you staring at me?" she asked him bluntly. He looked away.

"I don't know," he said, shrugging before looking at her again. He swallowed hard. "You're beautiful, you know?" It was half a question, half a statement, and Lia was taken off guard.

"Thank you," she stammered. "Mark always tells me the same thing." She eyed him cautiously, unsure of what to think.

"I know you must miss him," Garrett continued, his voice low. He took a deep breath. "But Lia, you don't even know where he is. Don't you think you could be happy with me?"

Lia couldn't hide her shock. She hadn't suspected, not even in the slightest, that Garrett had feelings for her, and she didn't know how to respond.

"I don't really know you, Garrett," she told him finally. "Don't you think I should at least get to know you before answering a question like that?"

"I feel like I've known you all my life," he countered. "I had hoped you felt the same way." Lia shook her head, seeing the heartbreak on his face.

"I'm sorry, Garrett," she told him gently. "I just...I don't...." Her words trailed off, and she averted her eyes, wishing she had stayed at the inn. His face fell, and he stepped back.

"It's okay," Garrett told her, disappointment in his voice. "I just thought....well, it doesn't matter, just forget it."

"Are you still my friend, Garrett?" Lia asked him, and he nodded quickly. She smiled, relieved that the uncomfortable exchange seemed to be over, and she stepped forward to put a reassuring hand on his arm.

With a sudden, unexpected motion, Garrett took hold of her and pulled her tight to him. Her heart stopped, and her body flushed with heat, but he released her only a split second later. He pushed her away, his mouth agape and his eyes wide.

The embrace had lasted only a moment, over before Lia could blink. She was glad to be free of his grip, but she was puzzled by his reaction. Following his shocked gaze, she realized that he was staring at her midsection, and her eyes filled with fear. He must have felt her growing belly.

"Please!" Lia begged, reaching for his hand. "Please, don't say anything!"

"You're pregnant?" Garrett asked incredulously, pulling away. "You're *pregnant*?" She shushed him.

"It's not what you think!" she told him, her voice low as she glanced around. She hoped no one was watching, and she wondered if she could convince him to keep her secret. He began to back away, pain and betrayal in his eyes. "Just listen to me!" she begged.

"I thought you were different!" he exclaimed, scowling at her with disappointment and anger. "I thought you were an honest woman!"

"I didn't have a choice, Garrett," Lia tried to explain, hoping he would understand. "I was attacked!"

She watched his face as she spoke, waiting for him to soften, but his expression stayed cold, and helplessness filled her as she realized he didn't care about what she was telling him. She put up her hands in defeat.

"I suppose none of this matters to you, does it?" she said quietly, shaking her head. Garrett turned away from her.

"Does your Mark know?" he asked, disgust rising in his voice.

"Mark found me," she said, not caring if he knew the details. "But he doesn't know about the baby."

"He won't have you," Garrett told her coldly, beginning to walk away. She didn't answer; she knew he was wrong, but saying so wouldn't matter. Her stomach sank as she watched him disappear from sight.

She remained by the frozen creek for a long while, thinking. From what she had seen, Maplegreen was much like Brunbury in its opinions, and she knew what would happen if the townspeople found out that she was pregnant. Sighing deeply, she decided to return to the inn.

Her heart sank the instant she arrived, and Lia knew that Garrett hadn't kept her secret. All of her belongings were piled in a heap on the ground outside of the inn, and she quickly bent down to gather them up. Swinging the bundle over her shoulder, she pushed the door open.

Rene met her, barring her path.

"What's the meaning of this?" Lia demanded, feigning ignorance.

"You've ruined me, that's what!" he wailed. "Now I have no cook!" Rene gripped his head in his hands, looking pained. "You can't work here, girl," he told her. "If word gets around that I've employed a pregnant whore, I'll be run out of business!"

"I'm not a whore!" she protested. "Why does everyone accuse me of something they know nothing about?"

"Are you, in fact, pregnant?" Rene asked, and Lia pursed her lips. She finally gave a slight nod, and he began to wail again.

"I'm ruined!"

"Just shut up, you old fool!" Lia hissed, rolling her eyes with annoyance at his theatrics.

"You don't understand!" he began, trying to get ahold of himself. "Half my business is from the town's men! If their wives find out I've employed a pregnant whor--- *woman*," he quickly corrected himself before continuing. "They will forbid their husbands from setting foot in my inn! I'll end up on the streets, starving to death!"

"And what about me?" Lia demanded, scowling. "Doesn't it matter that I'll end up on the streets the same way?"

"You said you were only passing through," Rene reminded her. "So go on, move along. I live here, this is where I earn my bread. I can't just up and leave!"

"Thank you, Garrett, you bastard!" she muttered under her breath, quickly realizing that arguing with Rene would be pointless. "I'll go up to my room," she said, her voice louder. "I need to get my money."

"I have it here," Rene told her, stopping her from ascending the stairs. He handed her the coins. "And I've added your pay for this week, too."

"I haven't worked a full week," she reminded him rudely. "I wouldn't want it to get out that you've been doing favors for whores." He rolled his eyes.

"I don't like it any more than you do," he said, grimacing. "Your cooking is some of the best I've ever had." Waving her to leave, he turned. "Go on, get out of here." He placed his hand over his face dramatically, muttering to himself about Gretchen. Lia slammed the door behind her.

• • •

CHAPTER TWENTY-THREE

LIA SANK DOWN ONTO the street corner, contemplating what she would do. She had counted her money a dozen times already, and she knew had barely enough for a journey to another town. She didn't have much of a choice, though, and after buying some bread and cheese she began to walk.

The town of Blackmoor was the closest town, only two days east of Maplegreen, as compared to the others which were each more than a week's walk. Lia had already asked about the governance there, and she knew it was not controlled by Thomas or his relatives. It was still early, so she hoped she would arrive the next day if she made good time, which she was determined to do.

It wasn't long before she was freezing, and with every cold, puffing breath Lia cursed Garrett and his foolish jealousy, and her own stupidity for letting her guard down. She swore to herself that it would never happen again, vowing that Mark would be the only man she'd ever trust.

She spent a sleepless night on the side of the road, shivering. There wasn't much for shelter, so she huddled under an overhanging bush, its branches bowed and filled with snow and ice, but it did little more than block the wind. At first light, she began to walk again, trying to keep track of the hours and impatient to reach Blackmoor. She hoped she would find Mark in this new town, or a job like she had in Maplegreen.

When Lia arrived in Blackmoor that evening, and like she had at her previous destinations, she made her way to the blacksmith's shop. She found it easily without needing directions, but she was instantly disheartened to see that the door was barred and the windows were shuttered. It was obvious that no one worked there, and disappointment settled thickly in her heart.

Sighing, she looked across the street. A battered sign declared the name of the town's inn, a broken down shack called the Black Dragon. She rolled her eyes at the name, slightly amused that such a rickety place could be called something so foreboding.

Lia swung the inn's door open, and a frail-looking woman greeted her.

"What can I help you with, dearie?" the old woman wheezed, flashing a toothless smile. Lia forced a pleasant expression.

"I'm looking for work," she answered, approaching the woman.

"Not many stay here long enough to work," the woman replied warily. "Are you looking for a place to settle down or just passing through?"

"I'm looking for my betrothed," Lia told her. "His name is Mark Samuels. He's a blacksmith."

"No blacksmith here," the woman said, eyeing her. "Is this man of yours responsible for your condition?" Lia gave her a questioning look. "I have eyes, haven't I?" the woman laughed. "It's not hard to see!" She pointed at Lia's midsection, and Lia instinctively raised her hands to cover her belly. The woman laughed again.

"Can't do much to hide that, now can you?" she cackled. "Did he disappear after learning what he'd done to you?" Lia was speechless for a moment before finding her voice, unsure of how to respond.

"He didn't abandon me, if that's what you mean," Lia finally answered. "He left for other reasons, and now I'm trying to find him."

"That's what all men say, dearie," the woman chuckled, then frowned. "The only work you'll find here is whoring."

"There's nothing else?" Lia asked, annoyed at the woman's comment about Mark. "Anything?"

"Any jobs you might have found will be sorely limited by *that*," the woman answered, pointing at Lia's belly. She shrugged. "Even whoring in that condition won't make you much of a living." The woman's words stung her ears, and Lia's face crumpled with dismay at the meaning they held. She didn't know what she would do if she couldn't find work.

"What about lodging?" Lia asked finally. "And food?"

"I've got food to sell," the woman answered. "But no lodging, not for a woman in your condition." Lia nodded grimly, fully understanding.

Lia spent the night in front of the inn, shivering in the cold. She didn't sleep, instead lying huddled near a lamppost, waiting for dawn as she tried to stifle her fear of the noises that echoed out of the shadowed darkness of the alleyways. Stiff and sore from the uncomfortable night, she was grateful when the black sky finally began to gradually lighten into a pale, golden pink. She waited for the inn to open, and after paying for an overpriced, meager breakfast, Lia began making her way from door to door, asking for work.

As she walked the streets, she could tell that Blackmoor was strict. There was an empty set of stocks and a whipping post in the town square, and she shuddered as she passed a looming, wooden gallows. There was a jail as well, and a group of incarcerated men laughed and jeered at her from behind corroded, blackened bars as she went by. She wondered if justice in this town was the same as in Brunbury, or if people accused of crimes were actually given fair treatment.

The town was huge, and Lia was hopeful that there would be work somewhere among the seemingly endless rows of buildings and houses lining the streets. But despite the many businesses, she soon realized that the woman at the inn had spoken the truth; there were no jobs for a single woman in the town. Only one man seemed interested, offering her ten silver tokens a day to keep his books, but when his wife appeared and saw Lia's pregnant belly the job offer was quickly withdrawn.

Night fell, and Lia had nowhere to go. She sat at a table in the inn, trying to make her meal of sourdough bread and watery soup last as long as she could, savoring each moment she had within the safety of the walls of the building. But the inn slowly emptied as the night grew late, and when she caught the stare of the inn's owner Lia finally stood to her feet, taking the clear hint that it was time for her to leave. The heavy wooden door of the Black Dragon closed and bolted behind her, and she was alone.

Lia sighed heavily. She eyed the place near the lamppost where she had spent the previous night, contemplating whether she wanted to stay there again, but after realizing how tired she was and that she wouldn't be able to stay awake to keep watch in such an exposed place, she decided to look for somewhere else to make her bed. Despite the fear rising in her belly, she turned the corner and began to walk into the darkened streets.

Dread sat heavy on her shoulders as she ventured deeper into the alleyways, terrified of what she might find as she kept going down the narrow, cobblestone streets. To her surprise, though, Lia heard the sound of laughing and singing drift towards her as she walked. It sounded like a party, and she couldn't help the curiosity that was aroused within her. Why would there be festivities in the middle of the night, she wondered, and in the cold, winter streets for that matter?

She could see a pinpoint of light appear at the far end of the street ahead of her, the glow growing brighter and brighter, drawing her in. As Lia approached the sounds of merriment, she stepped out of the dark night and into a raucous liveliness.

The alley was a dead end, formed at the end of the street on the outskirts of the town. There was a muddy, frozen path stretching off to the left and right of where the paved portion of the street stopped, which Lia supposed went on to encircle the entire perimeter of the town. Small shacks lined the edge of the path, and lights shone through cracks in their battened windows.

Lanterns were strung up across the street, casting a warm but dim light upon the jubilant dancing of the men and women there. A fire burned brightly in the center of the street, and a few men were breaking up old pieces of furniture and wooden boxes to feed to the hungry flames.

It was obvious that the dancing women were whores, but they didn't appear as dismal and dreary as all the other whores Lia had seen before. Their skirts were bright and colorful, and they laughed with drunken mirth as they staggered and sang with the men who hung on their shoulders. There were tables set up in the snow, the barrels atop them spurting ale into waiting mugs. To Lia, it appeared to be an outdoor tavern, and the patrons didn't seem to mind the night and freezing weather one bit. She shivered as she watched, her eyes bright with surprise and wonder at the scene before her.

"Hello, lovely!" a man crooned, suddenly materializing in front of her. She jumped, startled from her momentary reverie, and he reached out to grab her arm.

"Let go of me!" Lia hissed, pulling away. The man smiled a toothless grin, his dirty face creased with greasy excitement.

"You're much prettier than all of *them*," he slurred, grabbing her again. A few other men took notice of her, and now she was surrounded by a small, hungry group.

"Leave me alone!" Lia screeched loudly, backing away. Her heart pounded out of her chest, and she was no longer mesmerized by the place. "Leave me alone!"

The singing and dancing had stopped, but Lia didn't notice, too focused on the men closing in on her. The whores turned their attention to the commotion as well, upset that they had lost the attention of the men. The women glared at Lia, slowly moving towards her.

Wide-eyed as she backed away from the people, Lia's wonderment of only a few moments ago was forgotten and replaced with anxiety now that she was suddenly the center of attention. She felt cornered, and when she realized that her escape was barred by one of the men she began to panic. Dropping her quilt, she withdrew her dagger, determination filling her as she set her jaw.

"I'll not warn you again!" she yelled, desperation in her voice as she spun around, brandishing her knife at the group encircling her. "Leave me alone!"

"I only want a bit of fun, lovely!" someone said behind her, and Lia felt a hand on her backside. "Tell me your price, I'll gladly pay!"

With a cry, she whirled around and slashed at the man who had touched her, and a satisfying yelp of pain rang out. Blood seeped from the man's palm, and she narrowed her eyes as she met his angry gaze.

"Let me leave!" she demanded. "I don't want trouble, but I *will* give it!" A roar of laughter rang out from the crowd, and even the eyes of the bleeding man began to crinkle from amusement.

"I'll have her first!" someone else said, and Lia braced herself for a fight. She would die before she let them lay another hand on her.

"All right, back off!" a woman commanded, and the men parted for a moment as a pretty young whore approached. Her sky-blue eyes flashed, and she waved the men away. "She doesn't want your attention! Go back to your wenches, and let her be!"

The men paused, then slowly moved away as they obeyed the whore's words. A moment later, the singing and laughter began again, and Lia let out a cautious breath of relief. She eyed the woman who had spoken up for her.

"Thank you," Lia said, picking up her bundle and stepping back, anxious to leave. "I'll be going now." The whore chuckled, putting her hands on her slender hips as she looked Lia up and down. Her skin glowed with vibrancy, and despite Lia's upset she was almost surprised at the woman's beauty.

"That was quite a show," the woman said, smiling. "Did you honestly think you stood a chance if they had really wanted to give you a fight?" Lia pursed her lips.

"I would have died trying," she answered resolutely, and the woman laughed.

"I'm Belle," she introduced herself, extending her hand. Warily, Lia took it.

"Lia," she replied. She turned to leave, but Belle stopped her.

"Never seen you before," Belle said. "What brings you to our part of town?" Lia shook her head, not wanting to answer.

"Nothing," she replied. "I'll be going."

"Well, something had to bring you here!" Belle exclaimed. "I won't bite, I promise. What do you need? Are you looking for work?" Lia shook her head firmly, and Belle smirked, rolling her eyes. "Too good for our line of business, is that it?"

Suddenly feeling as though she had offended Belle, Lia tried to think of a response.

"No...yes...I mean..." she stammered. She took a breath, thinking for a moment before continuing. "I'm not a whore," she said finally. "I just need a place to stay and some honest work."

"Ha!" Belle chortled. "Honest work! You say you're not a whore?" She gestured at Lia's belly. "You didn't have a problem getting yourself into *that*, now did you!" Lia's face flushed with embarrassment and frustration.

"I didn't ask for this!" she replied indignantly. She spat, glowering at Belle. "All I did was walk home!" Belle's face was blank for a moment, but became sympathetic as understanding sank in. She frowned, and reached out a hand.

"I'm sorry, dear," she said quietly. "I assumed it had happened in the normal course of things."

"Normal!" Lia scoffed. "I don't know the meaning." Belle's eyes grew soft, and longing filled her face.

"There's nothing quite like it," she whispered, her voice distant. "It's not at all like *this*." She gestured towards the whores in the street and shook her head. Glancing at Lia, she shrugged, brightening again.

"There's no *honest* work for a woman in your condition," she continued matter-of-factly, trying to force a smile. "And you'll not get help from anyone else. But if you'd like, I can offer you a place to stay until you get your bearings. I won't feed you, though, you're on your own with that." Lia cocked her head, confused and guarded.

"Why would you help me if no one else will?" she asked.

"I remember being in your place," Belle answered. Lia looked at her expectantly, and Belle went on. "I came here a few years ago with my husband, and when he died I had nowhere else to turn but here."

"Were you pregnant?" Lia wanted to know. Belle nodded, and Lia cringed, remembering the child of the whore in Brunbury. Sadness furrowed Belle's brow.

"He died," she said quietly. "My milk didn't come in right, and I didn't make enough money to pay a wet nurse."

Lia touched her own belly. She wasn't sure how she felt about the baby anymore. Part of her was still disgusted by the creature, but part of her was excited, too. Whatever the case, while she didn't know if she would love it, she had decided she didn't want it to die. Hearing Belle's words troubled her, and she couldn't help worrying that her child's fate would be the same if she didn't find Mark or work before she gave birth.

"I'm sorry," Lia breathed. Belle smiled dismissively.

"Nothing can be done about it," she said. Her face grew dark for a moment. "And it was probably for the best, this is no place for a child." She beckoned Lia to follow, leading the way towards her home.

Belle lived in one of the small shacks lining the muddy outer road, and Lia was pleasantly surprised to see that it was rather nice inside. While the building itself appeared rickety at first, it was warm and much larger than expected.

Noticing Lia's reaction, Belle explained.

"I'm the magistrate's mistress," she said, making a face. "The others don't like me much for it, but I'm not stuck up like they say. They're all just jealous because I make more money than them."

"How much more?" Lia asked. Belle paused, giving Lia a long look.

"Enough," she finally said. "My belly stays full and I want for little." Lia was confused.

"Then why don't you stay in town?" she asked. "You'd have enough for a better home, wouldn't you?" Belle scoffed, rolling her eyes.

"I would if I could," she said, loathing in her voice. "But this damn town and its damn rules won't allow it."

"It doesn't seem that bad," Lia told her, thinking of Brunbury's rigidity in respect to the whores. "Are you allowed out during the day?" Belle nodded, and Lia went on to describe the whore's alley and the restrictions in her own town.

"Perhaps I don't have it as bad as I thought," Belle mused when Lia was done explaining. "We aren't permitted to stay near where the respectable folk live, but we can go wherever we want and buy food from any of the businesses." She changed the subject. "How do you expect to eat?"

"I have a little money," she told Belle. "I don't know what I'll do after that." Belle smiled.

"Well, I don't expect you'll have any trouble finding customers after that show you gave the men," she said.

"I've no intention of whoring," Lia answered quickly. "I'll find another way." Belle shook her head.

"I don't see how," she said. "There aren't any other jobs, I promise you that." Lia grew quiet, feeling hopelessness well up inside of her again. "I wish you luck, though," Belle added, noticing Lia's disheartened expression.

"How long can I stay with you?" Lia asked. Belle shrugged.

"As long as you need to," she answered. "You seem nice, and I do get lonely sometimes."

"How much?" Lia wanted to know, and Belle shook her head.

"Just keep yourself tidy," she said. "That's all I ask."

Lia was overcome by Belle's words, and she couldn't express the gratitude she felt for the help. A whore, a woman who lived a life scorned and used by the people of the town, still had some kindness to give.

"Thank you," Lia whispered, her eyes suddenly brimming with tears. Belle dismissed her gratitude with a smile.

"Now," she said. "I've told you my story. It's time, I think, for you to tell me yours."

• • •

Chapter Twenty-Four

BELLE DIDN'T DO BUSINESS with the other men, explaining that her services were reserved only for the magistrate, and unless she was summoned she was free to do as she wished. A covered wagon would appear in front of her home, at which time Belle was to immediately accompany the driver to the magistrate's house.

The magistrate only sent for her a few times a month, when his wife was gone, and Belle never knew when to expect to be called upon. As a result, she had to stay close to home, and she spent her idle time dancing and drinking with the other whores and the men each night.

Lia spent her days in town, looking for work, and when night fell she locked herself in the house. She was uncomfortable and nervous about venturing out into the street with Belle, but as the week passed she couldn't help beginning to feel left out. She could see the dancing and hear the laughter of the drunken people, and she wanted to feel the same happiness they felt. She didn't say anything, refusing to admit her desire to go, but Belle noticed the envious look on Lia's face one night as she prepared to leave.

"You can come with me, you know," she told Lia. Lia made a face, shaking her head.

"I don't think so," she answered. Belle cocked her head.

"And *I* think you want to," she sang knowingly, reading Lia's expression. "You don't have to miss out on the fun just because you aren't for sale." Lia grew quiet, thinking.

"The men will think I'm a whore," she said fearfully. "I don't want to be taken." Belle laughed at Lia's concern.

"They won't take you, Lia!" she said reassuringly. "They'll ask for your price, but they won't take you!" Lia considered Belle's words, but she wasn't convinced.

"No," she said, shaking her head again. "No, Belle, I think I'll just stay here."

"Come on, go with me," Belle urged, rolling her eyes at Lia's hesitance. "It's not good for you to be cooped up all the time! You haven't been outside for days, Lia, you need to have some fun!"

"No, I don't think so," Lia repeated. "I'm going to get some rest." Belle put her hands on her hips, studying Lia's face, then she stamped her foot.

"You're coming," she decided, giving Lia a firm look. "You'll be fine, I promise. Just stay close to me." Her confidence was persuading. "Besides," Belle went on. "There *are* some benefits to being the magistrate's whore. None of the men want me to whisper to the governance about them, so as long as you're with me you can be sure that you'll be all right." Lia was uneasy, but she believed Belle, and she reluctantly allowed herself to be pulled outside.

The night was cold, but Lia's nervousness warmed her. There had been snow the day before, and it had been trampled into a dirty, icy mess under the feet of the whores and their men. Despite many of them slipping and falling to the ground in their drunkenness, the people carried on without a thought, laughing and giggling each time someone fell before helping the bruised person back to their feet.

Belle was right about the men asking Lia for her price, and a few of them flocked around her almost immediately. After the first several minutes, and with Belle's help, the men's interest in Lia was dispelled by a few curses and one well-placed slap, and she wasn't bothered again. She clung to Belle nonetheless, worried that if she moved even a few feet away she would be whisked away into the darkness.

"When I said stay by my side, I didn't mean to stand on top of me!" Belle exclaimed. "Here, take this!" She was holding a mug of rum, and now she thrust it in Lia's face.

"I've never had it before," Lia told her, turning up her nose.

"It'll take the edge off," Belle insisted. "Just a few sips." Lia thought for a moment, looking back and forth between Belle's expectant face and the rum. Finally, she took the mug and raised it to her lips.

The strong liquid burned her throat, instantly doubling her over into a fit of coughing. Belle laughed heartily, her eyes bright as she watched Lia try to breathe.

"Gets you deep down, doesn't it?" she chortled when Lia finally straightened. "Take another pull." Lia obeyed, feeling the warmth travel from her stomach and into the tips of her fingers and toes.

With each sip of rum, Lia grew more and more comfortable with her surroundings. She began to wobble slightly, and a wave of elation washed over her. Grinning sheepishly at the landscape, she was surprised to see that everything was tilting back and forth. She giggled, watching the snow covered ground move and dance in front of her.

Casting off any remaining shred of apprehension, Lia took hold of Belle's hands and began to dance, feeling almost as giddy and free as she had when she had danced in the tavern at home. She threw her head back in laughter as she spun in an endless circle, and she didn't even notice when Belle passed her off to one of the young men there.

Then the dance ended, and so did Lia's drunken happiness.

Despite the fact that she was no longer moving, Lia was overcome with the sensation that she was still spinning. Staggering backwards, she felt that something was terribly wrong.

"Belle," she gasped, trying to balance. The lanterns were flying in circles, and her eyes desperately followed their movement in an effort to orient herself. It didn't work, and she teetered to one side.

Wobbling uncontrollably, she lost her balance and fell flat on her face. She swallowed hard, then, only a moment later, her mouth filled with the contents of her stomach. Struggling to her knees, she threw up.

She tried to catch her breath before vomiting again, and through her daze of drunkenness she could hear Belle's laughter ringing out above the cries of disgust and amusement that came from the other people who witnessed what had happened.

"I think she's had enough!" Belle cackled as Lia began to fall over again. "No, love, don't lie down! You'll get it all over your dress!" Lia's body was numb, but somewhere in the distance she could feel Belle's hands take hold of her arms.

"Let's get you home!" Belle laughed.

The next morning, Lia awoke completely miserable. Belle's eyes sparkled with amusement.

"You had a time last night, didn't you!" she exclaimed, pointing and giggling at Lia's drawn, pale face. Lia groaned, holding her head after collapsing into a chair next to the small kitchen table. Belle chuckled, pulling a flask from her skirts.

"Here," she said, offering Lia a sip. Lia refused, but Belle wouldn't be put off. "It'll make the spinning stop," she promised, and with a grimace of disgust Lia took the flask.

"I feel like a horse is sitting on my head!" Lia wailed, closing her eyes.

"You had a bit too much," Belle told her. "Next time you'll have to take it easier."

"There won't be a next time!" Lia swore, to which Belle scoffed.

"That's what they all say," she sang knowingly. "You should try to eat something." That sobered Lia up rather quickly, and she straightened.

"I don't have any money left," she told Belle. Belle stiffened.

"What are you going to do?" she asked, turning away from Lia.

"I had hoped that maybe I could borrow some from you until I find work," Lia answered. She waited for a response, watching Belle closely. Belle rested her hands against the wall, growing quiet, then she turned to face Lia.

"That will never happen, Lia," she said softly. "I would be feeding you forever." Lia's face reddened with anger.

"Yes, it will!" she insisted. "I'll find something!" Belle shook her head.

"No, Lia," she said, giving her a firm look. "You won't. You know it just as well as I do, and I told you from the beginning that I would give you a place to stay but no food."

"I can't do it!" Lia cried despairingly. "I can't become a whore!"

"But *I* can be?" Belle demanded, narrowing her eyes with sudden anger. "You have no problem letting me whore myself to pay for your meals, you have no problem benefitting from *my* humiliation, but you can't step up and do what needs to be done yourself? Have you no pride? Do you want to live on the shame and charity of someone else?"

Looking down at her hands, Lia felt tears sting her eyes. She knew Belle was right; it wasn't fair for her to expect the woman who had shown her such kindness to do even more.

"I'm sorry, Belle," Lia whispered. "I won't ask you again." Belle pursed her lips, calming herself, then she gave a quiet laugh.

"Here, Lia," she said, reaching into her apron pocket. "Just this once, I'll give you a few silvers. But after this," she cautioned, holding the coins in her outstretched palm. "You'll be on your own." Lia eyed the coins.

"And if you're right?" she asked before taking the tokens. "What if I can't pay you back?"

"It's a gift," Belle told her. "My thanks for your companionship."

Lia didn't ask Belle for money or food, even after going hungry for two days. The townspeople were growing annoyed by her daily job inquiries, and she began to despair. She walked by the blacksmith's shop every day, still hoping that she would find Mark, but it remained empty and abandoned.

Finally, Lia found herself seated on the corner in the town square, her hands outstretched and her eyes downcast, begging for coins. She shivered in the cold and pulled her quilt, which she had wrapped around herself for warmth, tighter against her body. Her stomach growled angrily as the smell food wafted towards her from the warm homes of the townspeople, and she sighed.

Just when she was ready to give up, she felt the cold, smooth surfaces of two coins drop into her cupped hands, and she looked up. A tall, grizzled man wearing a plaid overcoat stood before her, his dark eyes staring at her.

"Thank you," Lia told him, immediately thinking of food. She could buy a bit of bread, which would fill her belly for a least a short time. The man looked at her expectantly, glancing over at a shadowed side street before meeting her now-worried gaze.

"Well?" he asked, his voice impatient. Lia forced a smile.

"Thank you," she repeated firmly, hoping he would understand. He did.

"Give them back," he demanded, thrusting his hand in Lia's face. "I don't give charity."

"But I haven't eaten in days," she protested, hoping he would have sympathy for her. The man glared at her, then, without another word, he strode away.

Elated at her good fortune, Lia stood to her feet and quickly bought bread with the tokens, swallowing down the small, warm roll in only a few bites. It was gone too quickly, but at least her stomach didn't hurt as much, and she resumed her place on the corner feeling encouraged. She wouldn't starve if she had the same luck at least a few times a day, and she almost felt like whistling.

Two dark shadows suddenly appeared before her, and she was surprised to see that her benefactor had returned.

"Here she is!" the man exclaimed unhappily, pointing at Lia. A constable stood next to him, frowning down at her.

"You robbed this man?" he demanded, glaring. Lia was shocked, and she shook her head fiercely.

"Of course not!" she answered, indignant. "He *gave* me money!"

"I did nothing of the sort!" the man replied hotly. "I paid for a service I was never given!"

"Did you perform?" the constable asked. Lia's mouth dropped open.

"I'm not a whore!" she cried. "I was just sitting here, the same as I was when you walked up! I never once said I would do anything in exchange for a coin!"

"You're begging, then?" the constable asked, narrowing his eyes. She nodded, and the constable grabbed her by the hair. "Begging isn't allowed here!" he growled, pulling her to her feet.

"Every town has beggars!" Lia snapped, reaching up to pry at the hands ripping at her skull.

"Not this one!" the constable answered. "People work for their bread here! Give this man his money!"

"I don't have it!" she screeched, wincing in pain. "I bought food!" The expectant man's face turned red with anger, and the constable let go of Lia's hair to grab her arm.

"Then you'll do as expected," he told her, gesturing to the angry man. "Or you'll spend a night in the jail!"

The man's eyes brightened at the constable's words, and he looked at her with anticipation. Revulsion turned Lia's stomach as rage darkened her face. She stomped her foot.

"Take me to jail!" she shouted. "I'd rather spend a night in hell than a minute doing that bastard's bidding!"

The constable punched her in the face, splitting her lip, and her mouth filled with warm blood.

"You won't talk to a gentleman that way!" he hissed, drawing his hand back to strike again. Lia was stunned. "Apologize!" Unsure of what would happen if she refused, Lia obeyed, glaring as she muttered a quiet apology.

"Now," the constable continued, waving at the disgruntled man to be on his way. "You've made your choice! Let's go." Still holding tight to her arm, the constable dragged Lia down the street.

The heavy wooden door to the town's jail was heaved open, and Lia was thrown inside. Her feet sank into the thick slime covering the stone floor, a deep layer of human waste and dead, decaying insects and rodents. The smell was overpowering, and Lia's lungs burned with the first breath she took in, her throat closing as she choked on the filthy air. She heard the door lock behind her, and the constable spoke with the jailer.

"One night," he said before going on his way. Lia looked around.

Her eyes adjusted to the dim, and she could see the black shapes of people huddled in the darkness. The sound of coughing echoed off the wet, stone walls, and groaning from sick, feverish prisoners gave the place a deathly eeriness. She was almost afraid to move, but after a moment she took a step, hoping to get closer to one of the open, barred windows and the fresh air that wafted through.

Her feet made a sucking noise as she fought her way over the uneven surface, but, thankfully, the spot she had in mind was slightly higher than where most of the prisoners were gathered, and the muck wasn't as deep. A pile of filthy straw sat in the corner, and she could hear the loud squeaks of mice and rats coming from within the stack.

She looked through the bars, feeling the cold air on her face as she took in several deep breaths.

"You have a blanket," a hoarse voice said, and Lia whirled around to see a skinny woman standing behind her. "I want that blanket." The woman's face was thin, and she grinned slyly, baring her broken, jagged teeth.

Lia's heart thumped in her chest as she grasped the woman's intentions.

"It's mine," she said, pressing her back against the dank wall. "You can't have it."

"You don't understand," the woman chuckled, stepping towards her. "I mean to have it."

The woman's hand shot out in the blink of an eye, grabbing hold of Lia's face and digging dirty fingernails into the soft flesh of her cheeks. Lia was stunned for a moment, then, with a scream, she twisted around and shoved the woman away. The other prisoners watched in the meager light that streamed through the barred window, their eyes blank, as the woman launched herself again at Lia, biting and clawing with a determined fury.

Lia fought back, punching the woman repeatedly in the face. She caught hold of the filthy, flailing arms and forced them upward and back, hearing the woman's ear-piercing shriek and the crunch of bone. Gaining more leverage, Lia shoved the woman, sending her flying, then stepped back and crossed her arms defiantly.

"It's mine!" Lia repeated, breathing hard. The woman scowled, her face twisted with pain, and Lia knew she had broken the woman's arms. She smiled triumphantly as she watched the woman shrink into the shadows.

Settling back into her place near the window, Lia pretended to ignore the other prisoners. Her eyes shone brightly as the sun settled beneath the horizon and the moon rose; she unblinkingly kept watch throughout the night, counting the hours until she would be released. She thought of home, and how much she missed her parents, and how miserable she felt. Cursing under her breath, she wished she had never met Thomas, or that she had been wise enough to listen to her mother about how untrustworthy he was.

Lia wondered if Belle was worried about her, and she sighed again. Fighting sleep, her heavy eyes were just beginning to close when the first hint of the cold light of winter sun peeked over the town's rooftops, brightening the foul darkness of the place and prompting her to stand to her feet. It wouldn't be long now before she was freed.

• • •

Chapter Twenty-Five

"WHERE HAVE YOU BEEN!" Belle demanded when Lia stumbled through the door. Lia didn't look at her, shuffling to her bed and collapsing. She lay there, face down, relief flooding her.

"Jail," Lia responded, her voice muffled by her pillow.

"What did you do?" Belle asked, surprised. "I thought something had happened to you!"

"I was begging," Lia answered, rolling over slightly to glance at Belle's concerned face. She closed her eyes, then her mind registered what she had seen. Bolting upright, Lia leaped from the bed and rushed to Belle's side.

"My God, Belle! What happened to you?"

Belle shrank away, turning her back. Her face was swollen and covered with red welts. Her dress was torn, and the fabric was mussed and dirty. Bits of dried blood clung to her golden, blond hair, the wound from which it had come stretching across her cheek before disappearing under her disheveled tresses. Lia was speechless, and after a long moment Belle faced her, wincing in pain.

"I was called to the magistrate," she told Lia simply, as though no other explanation was needed.

"Did you do something wrong?" Lia cried, trying to understand. Belle chuckled.

"Sometimes satisfying a man's wants involves a little more than the usual expectations," she answered.

"What do you mean?" Lia exclaimed, dumbfounded.

"The magistrate enjoys a bit of roughhousing," Belle explained, moving gingerly towards a chair. Lia quickly jumped ahead of her, pulling the chair out. Belle sat down heavily, her body stiff. "That's why he has a mistress. He can't do *this* to his wife." Lia's mind reeled.

"And you let him?" she asked, incredulous. "You let him do this to you?"

"Yes and no," Belle chuckled bitterly, shaking her head. She immediately stopped, obviously pained by the slight movement. "I'm supposed to fight back. The more I fight the worse it is, but I don't get paid unless I do." Lia sank onto the chair across from Belle, still trying to grasp what she had been told.

"Don't go to him!" Lia said, finally finding her words. "Just quit!"

"And starve?" Belle snapped, anger in her voice. "Do you know how many men it takes to make enough money to live?" Lia gave her a dumbfounded expression, and Belle softened. "At least eight a night, Lia," Belle told her gently. "Twelve if I want to make enough to keep living here instead of in one of the smaller places. Food is expensive here, you know that. But working for the magistrate once or twice every few weeks gives me enough to last over a month, and then some!"

"But he hurt you!" Lia protested weakly.

"Not much," Belle told her, forcing a disarming smile. "He doesn't do anything that won't heal before the next time he calls for me." She changed the subject, wrinkling her nose. "Jail, huh? I suppose we've both had a night to remember. What happened?"

Lia told her the story, and Belle tried to chuckle before grimacing against the pain.

"A night in jail for two tokens?" she asked, rolling her eyes. "*That* was worth it." She sighed. "It's been a tough day, so don't worry about food right now, Lia. I'll buy dinner tonight."

The evening passed in somber silence, and Belle went to bed after only a few hours. Lia stayed awake, sitting at the kitchen table as she sipped from a flask of rum. She was worried about her friend, but she didn't feel like she could do anything to help. As the rum began to cloud her mind, Lia decided to do her best to stop thinking about it.

Lia passed a bakery stand, eyeing the golden, fresh-baked rolls that were being sold there. She hadn't eaten in three days, and the ache in her stomach was made worse by the sight and smell of food. Although tempted, she didn't dare ask Belle for a handout, especially not after seeing the agony she suffered through to earn money.

Instead, Lia had spent her days searching the waste bins of the townspeople for scraps of food. There wasn't much to be found, barely more than a morsel of moldy cheese if she was lucky, and the bits she had managed to dig out of the rubbish did little to stave off her hunger.

Now, her mouth watered as she stared at the warm bread. She sighed, turning to continue home, when she noticed that the bread vendor had his back turned. Pangs of hunger stabbed at her belly, prodding her, and she couldn't resist.

Her hand flashed out and snatched a roll. Turning quickly, she moved away, trembling as she raised the bread to her lips.

"There!" the vendor yelled, his face full of wrath as he pointed at Lia. The constable at his side glared at her, but she didn't care. She began to run, shoving the bread into her mouth and hurriedly chewing as she tried to get away, but she was too weak to move fast enough. She had just managed to swallow the last bite before the constable grabbed hold of her arm.

"Thief!" the vendor howled. Lia stood quietly, her head hanging, as the man told the constable what she had done. She didn't deny the accusation, knowing full well that she had been caught red-handed.

The constable asked the vendor what he thought her punishment should be, and she straightened up, instantly afraid of what she heard next.

"Brand her a thief!" the vendor demanded. "That'll teach her to steal from honest folk!"

"No!" Lia cried in protest. "I won't do it again!" Her eyes pleaded with the man, hoping he would let her go. "I'm starving, I haven't eaten in days!"

"Why should I care?" the vendor snarled. "Starving or not, you've no right to steal from me!" He gestured to the constable. "Take her!"

"Don't brand me!" she begged. "Please, anything but that!" The vendor thought a moment, then he smirked.

"A day and a half in the stocks," he said, and the constable's eyes widened.

"You'd do better to take the brand, girl," the constable told her. "You'll freeze to death spending even a single night there."

"Where will I be burned?" Lia asked, taken aback by the constable's reaction.

"Your forehead," he replied. "But you'd rather be alive and disfigured than frozen—"

"The stocks," Lia answered, choosing quickly. "I'll take the stocks." The vendor grunted in satisfaction, and the constable led her away.

The stocks were in the center of the town. As they approached the wooden device, the constable took a set of keys from his pocket. He opened the two locks at either end and removed the top board, then he gestured to Lia. She was afraid, but anything was better than being branded.

"You've made your choice," he told her as Lia nervously leaned forward, placing her hands and neck into the hollowed spaces. He set the second board in place, and a moment later she was trapped, held securely between the wooden slats.

Instantly realizing her vulnerable position, she began to panic.

"I'll be taken in the night!" Lia cried, her blood aflame with terror. "There's no one to stop someone from taking me!" The constable gave her a stern look, annoyed at her hysterics.

"Silence!" he commanded. "It's a crime punishable by death to attack a criminal in the stocks!" She calmed momentarily at his words, before fear again clouded her mind.

"Who cares about a thief?" she wailed.

"The law apparently does," he told her, turning to leave. "Don't say I didn't warn you, girl. I'll be collecting your frozen body before your time is through." He crossed to one side of the darkened street and began to walk slowly, taking up his patrol.

"Why does it matter to you?" Lia called after him bitterly, frustrated at his words. He acted as though he was worried about her, yet willingly locked her up anyway. He ignored her, disappearing into the haze that had settled onto the snowy streets.

She shivered as the cold cut at her bare skin, but despite the freezing temperatures she was warm with the heat of fear and dread. She wanted to scream. Worried, though, that she would draw the attention of someone else who didn't care about the law that was supposed to protect her, she managed to keep mostly silent save for the quiet whimpers that escaped her tightly clenched jaw.

As she tried to get comfortable, Lia quickly realized why the stocks were considered a punishment. Within just a short time, her back began to ache, and her wrists and neck started chafing against the rough wood as she fidgeted. As the night wore on, the weather grew colder, and her teeth were soon chattering, the sharp sound echoing through the darkness. She sighed, already wishing she had taken the brand. She tried to focus on the coming dawn, but as pins and needles shot up her legs and into her buttocks she quickly lost her determination.

Tears began to pour down her cheeks, but even crying brought her no comfort. Instead, her runny nose stung in the cold air, and she couldn't reach her face to wipe it. Her bladder was full, and she didn't even try to hold it in, wetting herself there in the streets. The wind quickly chilled her soaked skirts, adding to the utter misery she already felt.

Lia began to feel lightheaded as time dragged by. Her eyes grew heavy as she tried to stay awake, doing her best to count the minutes and hours until the sun's rays would warm her and mark the passing of the night, but despite her efforts her lids closed.

"Is she dead?" a muddy voice asked, and Lia stirred slightly. Opening her eyes against the morning sun, she could see a short, squat woman standing in front of her, the concerned, round face inches away from hers.

"Ahh," the woman said. "There you are." Lia's mouth was dry, and her lips cracked as she tried to speak.

"I'm cold," she rasped, coughing as the words cut the inside of her parched throat.

"No doubt, dear," the woman answered. "It's a crying shame, a young, pretty thing like you dying in the stocks."

"I'm not dead," Lia whispered, her vision blurring from the pain in her back as she tried to move. "Not yet."

"Well, it's my job to feed you till you are," the woman said happily, a steaming bowl of thick, brown gruel in her hands. "You'll not die of starvation at least, not on my watch."

The events of the night had caused Lia to forget her hunger, but now the smell of the food the woman had brought reawakened the pangs in her stomach, and her eyes brightened for a moment. The woman raised a heaping spoonful of the slop to Lia's lips, and she opened her mouth.

She immediately choked, spewing it out forcefully, surprising both the woman and herself.

"It's hot," Lia croaked. "Too hot!"

"Take it or leave it!" the woman said firmly, her bubbly demeanor visibly dampened by the sticky gruel Lia had spit all over her. "Would you rather have nothing?"

"No," Lia said quickly, opening her mouth for another bite. She swallowed, ignoring the pain caused by the scalding porridge as it slid down her throat. It settled heavily in her belly, and Lia instantly felt warmer.

"Now," the woman said as Lia finished the last of the food. "I'll be back tonight, at suppertime." Without another word, the woman turned and left.

It was the first of February, and the winter forgot its cold that day. The warm sun beat down on Lia, thawing her hands and feet and even drawing a bead of sweat on her brow. She was thankful for the warmth, thinking how nice it would be if the coming night stayed this mild.

The townspeople ignored her, save for a few children who stopped to point and laugh. The snow melted around her, running in quick rivulets down through the gutters and onto the streets, and the sound of its splashing reminded her of the creek at home. She was comforted slightly despite the pain she was in, and she began to daydream of the fields. Closing her eyes, she remembered the soft grasses and the clouds she had lazily counted every chance she had back home.

Night fell, and despite Lia's hopes the cold returned with the darkness. It wasn't long before she was shivering uncontrollably, and the hot gruel the woman had brought turned sour in her stomach.

Her bowels began to grow heavy as her body quickly processed the food she had eaten, and now she realized that she wouldn't be able to control herself until she was set free. She squeezed her muscles, fighting against the pressure, but it was no use. Her mouth twisted in disgust as she felt the thick muck slide down her legs, and even though there was no one nearby her face still flushed with embarrassment. It had been years since she had messed herself, and she was mortified.

The hours passed, and Lia suddenly grew warm, feeling the uncontrollable shivering that had wracked her body cease. She dozed off, smiling to herself as her whole being began to glow with heat.

"You still alive, lass?" a voice rang out, and Lia opened her aching eyes. It was the same constable who had locked her in the stocks.

"Yes," Lia answered, her jaw tight from the cold. He took out a gold pocketwatch, squinting at the face and the time it told.

"You're in a bad way, girl," the constable told her grimly. "When your skin takes on the color of midnight snow, that's when you know you're not long for this world." Lia smiled at him, her thoughts just as frozen as her hands, and she was almost happy to hear his words.

"It's about time," she mumbled.

"I think so," the constable agreed. "It's been right about a day and a half, don't you think?" Lia nodded sleepily, barely noticing as he took his keys out and opened the stocks.

She fell over, her dead limbs reviving in a vengeful fury of agony. Her body screamed at her, and she cried out. The constable hushed her.

"I'll lose my job, girl!" he exclaimed, warily looking about. "You're not due for release until dawn, but that's still four hours away!" Lia managed to nod, using all of her willpower to keep from shrieking in pain, too grateful to question his kindness.

"Take a moment," the constable told her. "Then get yourself out of here, you understand?"

Lia nodded again. She rolled over onto her back, allowing gravity to straighten her bent body. It was a long time before she could get up.

Belle was waiting for her.

"I heard about you, Lia," she said, shaking her head in disapproval. "You shouldn't have stolen, not in this town." Lia didn't want to hear it, and she collapsed onto her bed.

Early the next afternoon, Lia finally forced herself to wake up. She was sore, and it took her several tries before her body would respond to her attempts at movement. Belle heard her stirring.

"Finally," she said, exasperated. "I thought you'd never wake up!" Lia struggled to her feet.

"I wish I hadn't," Lia groaned. "I hurt all over!"

"The stocks will do that to you," Belle grimaced, shuddering. "I spent two days there once. At least it was summertime, though." Lia tried to stretch, but quickly gave up when lightning bolts of pain shot up her spine.

"I need to clean my dress," Lia said. "And bathe." Belle nodded.

"Yes, you do!" she agreed, sniffing and turning up her nose. "I'll take you to the river, that's where we all do our washing."

Lia followed her through town, and soon they arrived at the river. A rushing torrent of black water roared past them, a dark, violent snake moving quickly between two muddy banks. Lia was flabbergasted with disbelief.

"How can I bathe here?" she asked incredulously. "I'll be swept away!" She stared at the turbulent water, and Belle laughed.

"Over here," she beckoned, walking down the shoreline and under a wooden bridge. Lia followed, and on the other side of the low structure was a small pool into which the water flowed, swirling about and calming before trickling back out to rejoin the fast moving river.

"I'll stand watch," Belle promised as Lia stripped off her clothes. "You don't want to be caught naked by the wrong man." She chuckled at Lia's questioning face. "Some of the men wait for us here," Belle explained. "Most just watch, but a few will always try to get something for nothing."

Lia stepped into the freezing water, shuddering as the cold took her breath away. She washed quickly, then did her best to scrub her dress clean. Shivering and wet, she wrung the water from her clothing before slipping it back on. Her teeth chattered, the wet cloth clinging to her skin as she and Belle made their way back to town.

• • •

Chapter Twenty-Six

LIA WAITED AS LONG as she could, but after another three days had passed she couldn't take it anymore. She paced back and forth while Belle watched, trying to reassure her.

"It's not that bad," Belle said, pursing her lips at Lia's tearful agitation.

"You don't understand!" Lia cried, throwing up her hands. "I can't do this, I just can't!"

"You don't have a choice, Lia," Belle told her, shaking her head. "I know what you're feeling, I've been there too." Lia turned and quickly moved to Belle's side, kneeling beside her chair.

"Can't you help me?" Lia begged, desperation in her voice. "Please, Belle, won't you do that?"

"No, Lia!" Belle exclaimed, shaking her head. "I can't afford to feed us both!" Lia jumped up, ripping at her hair with her hands.

"I can't do this!" she cried, whimpering as she spoke. "Please, Belle, I can't!"

"Listen, Lia," Belle told her after a moment's pause. "You're going to have to. But this is what I'll do." Lia held her breath, listening.

"You make at least four silvers a night," Belle began. Lia's face crumpled in dismay, knowing the price of a whore was only two silvers. That meant she would have to take at least two customers a night, and her mouth began to salivate with nausea as her stomach turned.

"And," Belle continued. "I'll combine it with my money and pay for everything else." Lia stopped for a moment, thinking about what she was being told. It was better than nothing.

Suddenly overcome with the desire to burst out laughing, Lia stifled a giggle. The outrageousness of Belle's offer sank into her mind; it didn't seem real that she was actually comforted by the nature of the consideration she was being given.

Her amusement didn't last long, though, and she fought back tears.

"I don't think I can do this, Belle," Lia said, choking back a sob. She couldn't believe what she was actually thinking of doing, and the thought made her blood run cold in her veins. She tried to sit, but missed the chair, landing heavily on the floor.

"Do you want to starve?" Belle asked, standing and reaching for Lia's hand. Lia ignored her, content to remain where she sat.

She remembered the horror of the man in the alley, and the way it had felt to be taken. Giving it, to her, would be worse than being taken against her will, even if it was done only to survive. Lia looked up at Belle, her eyes dazed and vacant as she slowly blinked. She didn't want to move.

"It's worth it," Belle told her finally. "Comforting a few men each night for the sake of your life, Lia, think about it!" Lia closed her eyes.

She wished that Mark would appear, that he would walk through the door and save her, but she knew better. No one could save her, and there was no escaping the choice she had to make. All that mattered was that she was hungry, and no one else was going to feed her.

Belle's hand was still outstretched, but Lia didn't take it. She stood to her feet on her own, straightening her shoulders with sudden determination.

"I can do this," Lia said, her voice firm. "I won't die in this damn town."

"That's it, Lia," Belle answered, her face sad but proud. "You can do it." Lia took a quick, deep breath and cracked her neck nervously.

"What am I supposed to do?" she asked hollowly. Belle shrugged.

"Just go out there and wait," she answered. "They'll come."

"But what am I supposed to do?" Lia repeated. Belle was puzzled for a moment until she caught Lia's meaning, and understanding filled her face.

"You come back here," Belle said. "Don't let him in or you'll be here forever. Go behind the house, and just turn around and close your eyes. He'll do the rest. It doesn't last long, most are in a hurry to get home to their wives." Lia swallowed against the bile rising in her throat.

"Will it hurt again?" she asked.

"Maybe," Belle answered, her words honest and unashamed. "It always will, at least sometimes. But you should be all right. Being pregnant helps with that." Steeling herself, Lia nodded.

"You'll be all right," Belle told her again. "Only take the nice looking ones until you get used to it. They've been waiting for you, and you'll have first pick tonight."

The men that thronged around Lia disgusted her. She wanted to tear them all to pieces, enraged that she was in the position to make the choice she faced. Sitting at a table with Belle, Lia gulped down a mug of rum, waiting impatiently for the incoherence it would bring.

"That one," Belle whispered, pointing. Lia looked, and she saw a young man staring at her. "The young ones are usually quick, and they're easier to tolerate."

Lia glanced away when she felt her nerves waver, worried that if she looked too closely at the man she wouldn't be able to go through with it. Belle gave her a questioning stare, and, setting her jaw, Lia nodded. Belle got up and whispered into the man's ear while Lia pretended not to notice, and after a few moments she felt a hand touch her shoulder.

Lia stood to her feet stiffly, turning her nose up with pride and loathing at the man. In another world she would have found him attractive, but now she had to force herself to keep from wondering if he had a wife at home.

"What's your price?" the man whispered in her ear, and Lia recoiled. Holding her breath, she managed a reply, quickly thinking of how popular she knew she was with the men.

"Eight," she told him. He opened his eyes in shock.

"Are you crazy?" he asked her, incredulous. "No whore's worth that much!"

"Then go back to your place and I'll find someone else," Lia snarled, trying to keep from vomiting.

"Five," he countered. Lia stopped walking, refusing to take another step. She glared at the man, insolent abhorrence on her face. He got her meaning. "Eight," he agreed quickly, and she started walking again.

As they neared Belle's house, Lia's heart pounded in her throat as her determination began to dissolve. She wanted to run, but her legs wouldn't work. Her skin crawled as she turned around, her back towards him, her face hot with shame as her breath came in short, tense, nervous puffs. As she felt the cold wind bite against her exposed legs, she squeezed her eyes shut.

Humiliation surged through her under the touch of his hands, and she fought back the sobs that threatened to escape her. The sensation she had felt for the first time that night in the alley came back to her, and it was just as gut-wrenching as she remembered it being. Tears trickled down her cheeks as she held her breath, waiting for it to end.

He was done quickly, and he tossed the eight silver tokens onto the ground before leaving her alone in the darkness. She knew he was going back to brag to the others about being the first to have bought the spirited girl with the dagger, and she shook with rage as she picked up the coins.

The anger turned to tears after only a moment, and the sobs she had managed to hold back broke free.

"No, Lia," she told herself, sniffling hard and taking deep breaths. "You're all right, you did it, you're fine." She calmed for a moment and cleared her throat, then her stomach convulsed with another wrenching cry.

"Are you all right?" Belle asked, suddenly appearing with a worried look on her face. Lia's empty, red-rimmed eyes met Belle's concerned gaze. "I didn't see you come out, I thought maybe...."

Belle's voice trailed off as she studied Lia in the darkness. The moonlight reflected off Lia's tears, her face glistening.

"Are you all right?" Belle repeated.

"I'm fine," Lia answered, wiping her face. "Here." She held her hand out, and when Belle took the coins and counted them amazement filled her face.

"Eight?" she asked in disbelief. "I suppose the men *do* think awfully highly of you! If you weren't pregnant I'd think that the magistrate would give you my job!" Lia looked up at her in fear, worried that the magistrate might take an interest in her.

"You're prettier than I am," Belle told her matter-of-factly. "But he'll not want a pregnant whore." Lia let the word sink in.

Whore.

While the magistrate might not want a pregnant whore, as Belle had said, the men in the streets didn't seem to mind, and Lia managed to get away with charging four to eight tokens each time she sold herself. The worst time of the day was right before she fell asleep, when her mind would conjure up the images of the men who had used her, and she did her best to drown her misery in the rum she choked down each night.

The days wore on, marked only by the tears Lia swallowed back as the men bought her. In the midst of her constant misery, she noticed that Belle had started to worry. At first, Lia thought it was because there wasn't enough money, but soon she realized it was because Belle knew the magistrate would be calling for her again.

Sure enough, the magistrate summoned Belle a few days later. As Lia watched the wagon disappear into the darkness, dread rose in her heart, and the hours dragged by as she waited for Belle to return.

Lia had made enough money the previous night to allow her the evening off, and she sat at the kitchen table, sipping from the flask of rum Belle had left behind. When the sky began to grow light, Lia finally nodded off, her head resting on the tabletop.

The door burst open, and Lia jumped, startled from the doze she had fallen into. The morning sun shone brightly through the door, and Lia shielded her eyes against it, squinting.

Belle's silhouette was framed in the sunlight, and after swinging the door shut she fell to the floor with a thud.

"Belle!"

Lia moved to her side, blinking as she tried to make sense of what she was seeing.

"I'm all right," Belle mumbled, her lips swollen and bleeding. Her face was a mess, beaten almost beyond recognition, and her ripped dress exposed her bruised ribs. "I'm all right."

"You can't keep doing this!" Lia shrieked. "You have to quit, Belle, he'll kill you!" Belle croaked out a hoarse chuckle, spitting blood from her mouth. She smiled, and Lia could see that at least two of her teeth were missing.

"The bastard ruined my face, Lia," Belle moaned, her smile turning into a cry of anguish. "I'll not make any money if I quit now!"

"But he'll kill you!" Lia cried. "Please, Belle, you can't go back!" She moved from Belle's side long enough to wet a cloth in the wash basin, then she gently dabbed at Belle's face, trying to clean the blood from her once-perfect skin.

"He's never done this before," Belle managed to whisper. She closed her eyes. "I'm going to sleep, I'll talk to you when I wake up."

"Let me help you to bed," Lia offered, grasping Belle's hand. Belle cried out in pain.

"No, Lia," she said, squeezing her eyes shut. "Just leave me here."

The next two weeks passed quickly. Belle refused to leave the house for the first few days, spending her time in a drunken stupor as her bruises ripened into blue and black masses.

When she finally sobered up, and much to Lia's relief, Belle announced that she wasn't going back to the magistrate. Instead, she joined Lia in the streets to make money with the other men. Belle had to lower her price to only a single silver token for the first week, while her face was at its worst, and she took more than a dozen customers a night. She was different; her demeanor was empty and detached, and Lia could tell that the magistrate had broken more than Belle's face.

One morning, when the two of them returned home a night's work, Belle told Lia to sit down.

"We're going to be on the streets soon," she said, pursing her lips. Lia felt her face grow hot with sudden fear.

"Why?" she asked. Belle sighed.

"I didn't get my pay from the last time I was with the magistrate, and now I won't be able to afford the rent here."

"But why didn't you get paid?" Lia asked, confused.

"I only got paid once a month," Belle explained. "The magistrate always had a sack of silver waiting for me when I first got there so he could be sure I would have to visit him again."

"Why didn't you tell me sooner?" Lia cried. "We could have gotten the money if we'd had more time!"

"I've been too drunk to think about it!" Belle answered, cursing. "I only remembered after hearing some of the other girls talking about making rent!"

"Isn't there anything left from last month?"

"I spent it all, Lia," Belle said quietly. "I've been helping you with food."

Lia felt her lip tremble, realizing, for the first time, just how much her friend had been doing to help her.

"This is my fault," she whispered, staring down at her feet. "I'm sorry, Belle, I—"

"No, Lia." Belle's expression was firm. "It's not your fault, it's mine. I remember what it was like when I first started, and I suppose I thought I could spare you from some of the misery I went through. You wouldn't give in, you tried everything before you finally turned to the men, and I admired you for that. I didn't last nearly as long, I went hungry for just one day before I gave in. I wanted to help you, and we'd be fine if the bastard magistrate hadn't gotten carried away."

A tear trickled down Lia's cheek, and her throat began to ache. She should have seen what Belle had been doing for her, she should have done more to help. She wiped her eyes and looked up.

"How much do we need?" she asked. Belle sighed.

"Too much," she answered. "Almost four hundred silvers."

"By when?"

"Day after tomorrow," Belle told her. Lia felt despair sink its cold fingers into her heart. There was no way they could make that much.

"Let's just move to a smaller place, then," she suggested.

"We can't," Belle told her. "Not without paying what we owe first."

Lia fell silent. It was barely March, and the weather was too unpredictable for them to risk living on the streets. Some nights might be mild if they were lucky, but it would be deadly if the weather turned. She eyed Belle, an idea forming in her mind.

"Could you go to the magistrate, take the money, and run?" Lia asked. Belle pursed her lips, thinking.

"Maybe," she finally said. "I'd have to be quick." She thought of something else, and her eyes widened with fear. "But he knows where I live! He'll come after me even if I get the money!"

Lia frowned, then her face brightened with sudden excitement.

"Then we'll leave this damn place!" she crowed, her eyes dancing. "The next town is only a few days away, and I know we can survive two or three nights on the road! We might be able to find real work, and maybe even lodging!"

"But if we don't, we'll still be on the streets," Belle pointed out.

"No, we won't," Lia countered. "We should have enough money to rent a place with the whores if we can't find anything else. And if I find Mark there, I know he'll give both of us a place to stay."

Belle looked away, considering, then she slowly nodded.

"It's worth a try," she quietly agreed. "It just might work."

"I'll take everyone who comes for me just in case you don't get the money," Lia promised, swallowing hard. "It's about time for the magistrate to call you again, isn't it?" Belle shuddered and nodded again.

"Then it's settled!" Lia said.

The two of them talked as they readied themselves for bed, hopeful that their plan would work. The thought of trying their luck in a new town had lifted their spirits, and they fell asleep with excitement in their hearts.

• • •

CHAPTER TWENTY-SEVEN

THE MAGISTRATE SENT HIS wagon for Belle the next night. As she watched the wagon drive away, Lia fought the urge to run after it. Instead, though, she turned her attention to the drunken men.

The night showed promise, and after a few hours Lia had made fifty silvers. She grew impatient and worried as she waited for Belle to return, but she ignored the feeling, focusing on work.

Lia shuddered as she pulled her skirts down, and the man turned to leave.

"Aren't you forgetting something?" she called, stopping him. He glared at her.

"I won't pay for a pregnant whore," he snarled, beginning to walk again. Lia grabbed his arm.

"You knew I was pregnant from the beginning!" she protested. "I need that money!"

"Why would I pay good silver for something so obviously used?" the man scoffed, spitting on her dress. Lia watched him stride away, her insides still throbbing from where he had spent his time, and her vision turned red.

With a furious scream, she attacked him.

"I earned my money!" she shrieked, trying to get to the man's eyes. "Give me my money!" The man howled in pain, fighting against her.

"Fine!" he shouted, and she paused in her assault. "Here!" He pulled a few coins from his money bag, throwing them on the ground. She let him go, and he ran away.

"Cheating bastard!" she hissed, counting the tokens. He had overpaid by three coins, and she smiled triumphantly. Belle would be back soon, and it was only a matter of time before they would be leaving the town behind them.

Lia rejoined the group of whores and immediately saw a squat, gray-haired man with a dirty face set his eyes on her. She cringed and forced a smile. She had promised Belle that she would take every man who asked for her, and she intended to keep her word.

Stifling her disgust, Lia stepped forward to approach the man, but she was stopped by a rough hand on her arm.

"Is this her?" a voice growled. She pulled away, glancing up to scowl at the person who had grabbed her, only to feel a hot shiver of fear race up her spine. It was a constable, and the man who had refused to pay her was standing next to him.

"That's her! She's the whore who attacked me!" the man wailed, holding his scratched and bleeding face. "Punish her! I want her hanged!"

Lia's heart stopped and her face turned white. Back home, the punishment for a whore assaulting a townsperson was death, and she should have known that this town would be the same.

"Please!" she begged, panic seizing her. "Please don't kill me! He wouldn't pay!" The constable began dragging her away, ignoring her hysterics.

"He wouldn't pay me!" she screamed, sobbing as she kicked and fought against him. "I'm sorry! Don't kill me!"

"Enough of that!" the constable commanded, slapping her. "You'll go quietly or I'll beat you senseless!" He turned to her accuser.

"There will be a public trial," the constable said. "You'll have to testify." The man's eyes grew wide; apparently he hadn't considered that.

"Forget it!" he answered. "My wife will find out!"

"Then do I let her go?" the constable demanded, stopping in his tracks and giving the man an annoyed look.

"All of her money," the man said, thinking quickly. "And brand her!"

The constable was searching her before she could blink, easily finding her bag of money. She was too relieved to protest, but her heart still sank as she watched the man hurry away in the darkness, her bag of coins clutched in his hand.

"Come, wench," the constable said, dragging her along. "You'll spend the night in jail, and you'll be branded tomorrow morning."

Lia had calmed considerably now that she knew she wasn't going to be killed, and her thoughts turned to replacing the money she had lost. She realized that her punishment was unavoidable, but there was no way she could wait until the morning to receive it.

"Listen to me!" she begged, hoping the constable would have mercy on her. "My friend and I will be left to freeze in the

282

streets if I don't get back to work. Please, do it tonight!" The constable glared at her, but something in her expression must have moved him.

"Fine," he said after a long pause. "Let's see if Sam's awake."

The constable led her to the jail, and for a moment Lia thought he had lied when he had agreed to have her branded that night. But instead of going to the front entrance, he escorted her around to the back where a small lean-to rested against the worn, brick wall of the building.

"Sam!" the constable called. "Are you there?" There was a light burning inside the lean-to, and the door was thrown open.

"Who's there?" a large shadow called, looming in the doorway.

"It's Jacob," the constable answered. "Do you have enough time to do a branding?" Sam scoffed.

"Are you daft?" he asked, incredulous. "It's the middle of the night!" Lia's heart sank, but the constable spoke again.

"I need it done tonight," he insisted. "Are the coals hot?"

"Well, now," Sam answered. "Just give me a minute and I'll take a look."

The door closed behind him, and a moment later he reappeared, a cloak pulled over his shoulders and a cap on his head. His dark eyes lit up when he saw Lia.

"A pretty one, isn't she?" he mused, taking hold of a long poker. "It's been a while since I've branded a woman, I thought all of them knew better than to end up here."

There was a large pit dug into the ground, and in the center of it Lia could see red coals come to life as Sam stirred them. Bright sparks rose into the cold air, and she gulped, dread leaving a bad taste in her mouth.

"X?" Sam rasped, apparently content with the heat of the coals. The constable nodded, and Sam reached towards a row of long-handled branding irons.

He selected an 'X', and Lia broke out in a cold sweat when she saw the size of the letter. It was much bigger than she had expected, appearing to be a little over an inch tall, and she wanted to run. She watched with ever-widening eyes as Sam buried the end of the brand in the center of the coals, waiting for it to grow hot enough to melt her skin, and something else occurred to her.

In just a few moments, her face would be ruined forever. No matter where she went, people would see the mark of a whore on her forehead, and any chance of finding honest work would be gone. Even working as a whore would be near impossible, as the men in the streets only paid so much for her because of her pretty looks. The realization made her breath catch in her throat.

She turned to the constable, desperation in her eyes.

"Not my forehead!" Lia gasped, again begging for mercy. "Please, I won't be able to make any money!" The constable glared at her.

"You don't understand," she pleaded. "We'll die on the streets! I need to work!" Grunting with annoyance, the constable sneered.

"Where, then?" he asked, much to both Lia and Sam's surprise. "And keep in mind that it must be visible!"

"You're losing your edge, Jacob!" Sam scolded, shaking his head. "Doing favors for a whore!" The constable silenced him with a stern glare, then turned back to Lia, waiting for a response. She didn't know what to say, and her mind raced as she tried to think.

"Here!" she said quickly, pulling her dress down. She pointed at the place right above her now-exposed breast. "Isn't this visible enough?" The constable pursed his lips, thinking, before finally nodding.

"Given your line of work," he reasoned. "I suppose that would be acceptable." Sam chuckled.

"I take it back," he said, smirking as he eyed Lia's chest. "Maybe you should give them all a choice!"

Ignoring the comment, the constable offered her a dirty rag, and she gave him a puzzled look.

"For your mouth," he explained. "So you don't scream."

Lia's heart pounded as she refused. Shrugging, the constable took his place behind her, holding her arms immobile as Sam removed the brand from the fire. Her chest heaved rapidly as her breathing increased, and she cringed with anticipation and fear as the hot brand moved closer to her skin. She squeezed her eyes shut and turned her face away.

White-hot, searing pain flooded her body, and she could feel her skin bubble under the burning heat. Her flesh turned to smoke, and she choked at the stench of her own cooked skin. A loud hiss filled the air as her skin melted, and she threw back her head, emitting an earth-shattering screech of agony that rang out into the dark night and empty streets. Her legs kicked as her body shuddered, and she heard the constable curse behind her as he tried to hold her still.

The brand lingered too long before pulling away from her skin, taking with it pieces of her flesh. Then it was over and she fell to the ground, her chest throbbing as she cried.

"Pull your dress up, girl," the constable told her. "Get out of here." Tearfully, she did as she was told.

Lia rushed back to the alley. She hoped Belle had returned while she was gone, but there was no sign of her at the house, and so Lia went back to work. For the rest of the night, she did her best to make more money, but the men had heard that she had attacked one of her customers. They avoided her, and her spirits sank. It would be impossible to make enough now, and all she could do was pray that Belle had found better luck.

When the night ended, Lia only had seventeen silvers, and she fought back tears as she made her way home. As she waited for Belle, she tried to remain hopeful that her friend would bring the rest of the money they needed.

Knowing they would have to make a quick getaway, Lia passed the time packing up the few belongings she and Belle would be taking with them, grimacing with disgust at the memory of all the men who had visited her that night. Her burned chest ached with loathing, but she tried to focus her thoughts on Belle's return and the journey ahead of them.

A loud thump sounded at the door, startling her. She smiled a moment later; she knew it was Belle, and all the worry and anxiety left her. Jumping to her feet, she ran to the door and threw it open.

Lia opened her mouth to scream, but no sound came out. Horror instantly drained all the breath from her body, and the passing seconds of her wide-eyed shock were marked only by the slow beats of her heart resonating in her ears.

Then she found her voice, and a cry leaked out of her in a low moan as she sank to her knees. She began to sob, her heart shattering as she fought to make sense of the sight before her.

Belle's cold eyes were blank and unseeing, and her pale, beautiful face was spattered with blood. Her throat was slashed so deeply that her head was turned in an impossible way, and stark, white tendons and torn flesh lay exposed through the gaping wound that had emptied her life and soul from her body.

"No," Lia whispered, gathering her friend into her arms. "No...please, Belle, no!" She closed her eyes, praying that she was trapped in a nightmare, but as she gazed down at Belle's dead face again she knew that what she was seeing was real.

She screamed, cradling Belle's lifeless form in her arms as she rocked back and forth. Her sobs tore into her stomach and back as blood stained her dress and hands a dark crimson. She cried until she couldn't breathe, her salty tears pouring down her cheeks and splashing onto Belle's skin.

Someone must have noticed what was going on, because it wasn't long before a small crowd gathered.

"You need to leave!" one of the whores whispered hurriedly. "If you stay here they'll suspect you did it!" Lia didn't move, unable to comprehend what she was being told, and the woman scoffed.

"Stupid whore," she cursed, turning away. Another woman repeated the warning.

"Get her inside and get out of here!" she hissed. "They'll hang you!" Lia looked up through her tears, her eyes blank. The woman kicked her, stunning her from her daze.

"Go!" the woman said again. "You'll be executed!"

Lia wiped her eyes and struggled to her feet. Somehow, she managed to follow the woman's instructions, pulling Belle's limp form inside the house and shutting the door. She stood in the middle of the floor, her mind sluggish and empty, then she moved into the kitchen and got a cloth and the washbasin.

Over the next several hours, Lia carefully cleaned the blood from Belle's skin. She was in a trance, almost unaware of her actions, and when she was done she took one of Belle's dresses out and laid it carefully on the bed. It was Belle's favorite, and tears again welled up in Lia's eyes as she remembered how beautiful her friend had looked in it. She stared down at the pretty, violet flowers that dotted the fabric, and she could almost hear Belle's laughter from the nights they had spent dancing in the streets.

Weeping quietly, Lia gently removed the bloodstained clothing Belle was wearing and replaced it with the clean dress. She sat at her friend's side for a long time, then, drawing a shuddering breath, she spoke.

"I'm sorry," she whispered, kissing Belle's cold cheek. "I never should have sent you back there."

Lia stood to her feet and walked towards the door, her money and few belongings forgotten in the midst of the numbness that blanketed her. The sun was beginning to set as she stepped out of the house, taking only her shawl with her.

Lia wandered the streets for the next three nights, and she huddled in the shadowed corners of the alleyways during the day. She was hollow inside, and even tears didn't come to her. Her stomach had remained empty, but she didn't notice the hunger pangs.

On the fourth night, the weather turned bitterly cold. Her body shivered uncontrollably in the falling snow, but she ignored the pain in her freezing hands and feet as she aimlessly walked in the darkness.

She made her way to the river and stood on the bridge, remembering when Belle had brought her there to wash her clothes. Barely a month had passed since that day, but it seemed like a lifetime ago. She gasped a sob.

Belle.

Lia's chest ached with sorrow. She had killed her friend, her beautiful Belle. The knowledge was too much, and she grasped the railing of the bridge for support as her body arched with the cries that tried to escape her throat.

She stared down at the dark water of the churning river, its surface frothing into tiny whitecaps. Without thinking, she climbed over the railing, balancing on the slippery ice under her tattered and worn shoes. It would be so easy to simply fall. Gazing up at the sky, she extended her arms to reach towards the falling snowflakes and closed her eyes.

She took a step.

She fell for what seemed like forever, then the river opened its gaping maw to swallow her whole. She plunged below the freezing water, instantly feeling the strength of the river take hold of her. For a moment, her head broke the turbulent surface of the dark, murky blackness, and she gasped a breath before being sucked back under the waves. Forcing herself to relax, she opened her mouth, preparing to breathe deep of the cold.

Then, just as suddenly as it had gripped her, the river let her go, and Lia felt her body drift to a stop as the water slowed. Looking around her in bewilderment, she began to laugh maniacally, disbelief filling her when she realized what had happened. She had been washed into the calm waters of the pool she had bathed in. Shaking her head and shuddering in her wet dress, she stood to her feet. Even her attempt to end her misery had failed.

She was lightheaded as she made her way back to the center of town. The stocks were empty and silent, and she thought of hot gruel. She sank to her knees.

There was something hard beneath her, and she absently felt for the object. From her skirt pocket, she withdrew the little figurine Mark had made, and she almost smiled as she ran her fingers over it. The little fox laughed as the girl danced, twirling and floating in the grassy fields.

Falling onto her back in the soft snow, she stared at the sky.

"I wish I was home," she said, closing her eyes. "I want to go home."

Lia walked through the streets, shivering in the softly falling snow. The yellow light of the streetlamps illuminated the sparkling flakes, following each crystalline flight before the cold flurries settled gently onto the ground, slowly accumulating into a smooth, white blanket shrouding the earth.

She crossed her blue-tinged arms in a feeble attempt at preserving what little was left of her body's warmth. Her bare feet left black impressions in the snow as she walked, each step seeming to steal a little more of her strength from her body. She was alone.

There was a quiet cry of pain, and she looked up. She could just barely make out the figure of a girl, almost completely covered in snow, huddled in the street.

Summoning the last of her strength, Lia moved towards the girl. She knelt, reaching out to touch the waxen, bare shoulder.

"Get up," she whispered urgently, shaking the girl. "You must get up!"

There was no answer; the girl lay motionless, ice clinging to her long, dark eyelashes.

"Please," Lia begged, shaking the girl again. "You'll die!"

The girl snapped awake and whipped her head around with a sharp, quick movement. Her eyes were empty and hollow, their blank stare boring holes into Lia's heart.

"Get up," the girl echoed in a doleful whisper. "You'll die!" Lia staggered back, aghast at the sight of the girl.

Her face was emaciated, her skin sunken in deep shadows where it clung to her cheekbones. Her hair hung in a tangled mass, the dark, frozen strands draped across her thin shoulders and neck. On her breast, a red 'X' glowed with an angry fire, the flames licking at her skin as they fed on her flesh.

She rose slowly, struggling to her feet.

"Get up," the haunting whisper said again. "You'll die!"

The girl's milky-white skin was transparent, and Lia could see her ribcage protruding through her flesh. As the girl moved closer, Lia inhaled sharply. She was pregnant, and Lia could see a baby writhing in agony through the translucent abdomen.

"Your baby!" Lia cried, pointing. As she watched, the unborn child began to die, its pink face and limbs slowly blackening in the cold womb of its mother.

The girl stared at her with an unwavering gaze, stepping closer. Lia had nowhere to go; the shadows had solidified behind her, and her back was pressed tightly against them. Her mouth hung open in horror as the girl moved close enough to touch her.

Holding out a frozen, brittle hand, the girl brushed her fingers against Lia's face.

"You'll die!" the girl wailed, her face crumpling in sorrow. "You'll die!"

Her eyes flew open as she jolted awake, and her breath caught in her throat as she looked around in bewildered shock. She was in a bed in someone's house. The room was dim and warm, and a thick, woolen blanket was pulled tight to her chin. A fire burned in the fireplace, and from what she could tell she was alone.

Confused and afraid, Lia pulled the blanket back to get up, only to be shocked once again. She was fully unclothed, and her eyes immediately searched the small room for her dress. Then, from her place on the bed, Lia could hear a door open in another part of the house, and she shrank down under the covers.

The bedroom door creaked open a moment later, and her blood rushed through her veins when she saw the tall figure of a man enter. She cowered, trying to make herself as small as possible, then she peeked out from under the blanket.

The man shook himself, small snowdrifts falling from his heavy coat and onto the floor, sticks of firewood cradled in his arms. He set the wood down and slipped out of his coat, then fed the fire until it blazed and roared. She didn't know what to think, and despite her efforts to stay quiet a small whimper escaped her. Pulling the blanket over her face again, Lia held her breath.

The man knew she was awake, and from her place under the covers she could hear his footsteps rapidly cross the short distance from the fireplace to her bedside. The bed flexed with his weight as he sat down next to her, and now Lia was sure of what was about to happen.

Her body shivered with dread, but she relaxed only a moment later. She didn't care what happened anymore. She could fight, but it would do no good, and it made no difference now if she was taken.

The man's weight shifted as he leaned towards her, and she set her jaw in anticipation. A light touch brushed her forehead as his fingers took hold of the edge of the blanket, and she closed her eyes as her face was exposed.

"Lia?" he whispered, gently placing his cool hand on her flushed cheek. "Are you awake?" She cringed instinctively at the sound of his voice, her mind unable to understand the words he had spoken.

"Lia?" he repeated.

After a moment of fearful silence, recognition sank in as she realized she knew his voice, and her eyes flew open to instantly fill with tears.

With a cry, Lia sat up and grabbed him, holding tight to him. She began to scream, wailing and sobbing with both misery and relief. He held her against him, his arms supporting her as she shook with anguish.

"I've got you, love," Mark whispered, kissing the top of her head as he cradled her and gently rocked back and forth. "I've got you."

• • •

Chapter Twenty-Eight

MARK HAD ARRIVED in Blackmoor only a few days before finding Lia, and he had immediately opened the empty blacksmith's shop. As the blacksmith, Mark was entitled to live in the home that adjoined the shop, and he wasted no time in making sure Lia was comfortable there.

The house was small, with one bedroom and a nice sized kitchen. There was a tiny living room, and the house's furnishings, while dusty, were in good condition. Lia was just thrilled to have somewhere to stay, and she thought the house was perfect despite Mark's modesty.

There was a door leading from the kitchen to the shop, which Lia thought was an excellent idea. The shop in Brunbury had been a fifteen minute walk from the home Mark had shared with his father, and, in Lia's opinion, this setup was much better. Mark hated it, though, saying that she wouldn't find it very convenient if a spark from the forge burned the place down.

Lia had been feverish for almost six days after Mark had found her, but her strength was slowly returning. Now, the two of them sat across from each other at the kitchen table, talking after she ate.

"I didn't look," Mark promised when Lia asked him about where her old dress had gone. He had bought her a new dress while she was still unconscious, a replacement for the tattered, worn thing she had been wearing. The dark red calico was bright and crisp; although, even with her pregnant belly, it was a bit too big.

Lia couldn't help imagining Mark trying to blindly remove her filthy, wet clothing, and she dissolved into a fit of laughter at the thought.

"I don't believe you," she told him when she calmed. He turned red and looked away.

"I have something for that," he said, gesturing towards her chest as he avoided her gaze. Lia didn't understand what he was talking about at first, giving him a quizzical look, before realizing he was referring to the red, scabbed 'X' above her breast. Now it was she who was embarrassed, knowing full well that he knew what the letter meant, and her face burned with shame. She managed to force a smile.

"I thought you said you didn't look!" she said, feigning amusement. Mark shrugged.

"It's not like your dress covers it," he answered simply. He stood and moved towards a cabinet, opening it and removing a small jar. Lia took it from him and eyed the dark, golden contents.

"It's honey," he told her, answering her unspoken question. "It'll heal in no time."

"Honey?" she asked. Her mother had always used chamomile for burns. She dipped her finger in the viscous substance. Cautiously, she dabbed a bit on her tongue, surprised to find that it was, indeed, honey. She gave him a suspicious look and chuckled. "Are you teasing me?"

Mark shook his head.

"I'm serious," he told her. "I'm around fire all day, Lia. Trust me, I know what I'm talking about." She shrugged, taking his word for it, and she quickly dabbed some on her burned chest. They fell silent again, then Mark spoke.

"Do you want to talk about it?" he asked timidly, purposefully avoiding her eyes. "You don't have to," he added quickly, glancing at her for a moment. "But if you want to..." His voice trailed off.

"Why?" Lia asked, her ears red with embarrassment as she searched his face, trying to read his expression. She wasn't sure how to respond to his question, and she couldn't help wondering if he was asking because he was ashamed of her. "Are you mad at me because of it? Because I was a whore?"

Mark gave her a confused look, cocking his head questioningly.

"Why would I be mad at you?" he asked. Lia shrugged.

"Disgusted, then," she replied, and Mark shook his head fiercely. His eyes bored holes into hers as he stared at her.

"No, Lia," he told her. "I could never feel that way about you. I just wanted you to know that you can talk about it. If you want to, anyway."

Her throat swelled with tears. He was already comforting her, and she felt a tiny bit of the darkness of the past months disappear from her heart.

"Does it still hurt?" Mark asked quietly, glancing at the burn. Lia instinctively reached up and tried to move her dress to cover it, looking away.

"A little," she answered, feeling him staring at her. He grimaced, then changed the subject.

"When will the baby come?" he asked. She gave him a sideways glance, shifting uncomfortably in her seat.

"Sometime in May, I think," she answered. A thought occurred to her. "It's not Thomas'," she added quickly. Mark shrugged off her concerned comment and smiled warmly.

"Congratulations, Lia," he said, and as she studied his face she was surprised to see sincerity there.

"What?" she asked, baffled by his response. "What do you mean, 'congratulations'?" Mark shrugged.

"Just what I said," he told her simply. "Aren't you excited?" Lia sighed heavily, twisting her mouth into a pensive frown.

"I don't know yet," she whispered. "I can't help feeling that I'll hate the little beast." Mark was taken aback.

"But you won't," he answered reassuringly. "You'll be a wonderful mother."

"What if I can't stand it?" Lia asked. "I wanted to kill it when I found out." Mark eyed her.

"Have you changed your mind?"

"I don't know," Lia answered. "Maybe. Yes, I think so, at least partly. I don't want it to die, but...." Her voice trailed off as she looked helplessly at Mark. He stared into her eyes, his face genuine as he managed to see right through her.

"Lia," he began, giving her a soft smile. "The baby will be beautiful." She didn't expect him to say that, and she was caught off guard.

"How do you know?" she demanded. "How can you tell me something like that, knowing where it came from?"

"It's a part of you," he answered, as if his explanation was enough to satisfy her question, and Lia's heart began to ache.

"But it's not just a part of me!" she cried, wrestling with her own mixed feelings.

"You're the only part that matters," Mark replied firmly. "And I, for one, will see nothing else."

As always, Lia couldn't comprehend his logic, and the gentle confidence with which he spoke amazed her. She was certain that anyone else in the world would hold nothing but disgust for her and for the bastard child growing within her, but not Mark. Despite the way she had treated him, she could still see the love he held for her within his gaze, and a stab of guilt brought tears to her eyes. She stood to her feet, moving to sit in the empty chair beside him.

"I owe you an apology, Mark," Lia said quietly, leaning towards him and resting her hand on his back. He stiffened at her touch, glancing up at her.

"For what?" he asked.

"I know I hurt you," she continued, her voice threatening to break. "You've always been there for me, and it wasn't fair for me to treat you the way I did. And I should have trusted you about Thomas, you were right about him."

Mark couldn't hide the surprise on his face.

"I...I...." he stammered, trying to think of how to respond. He fell silent for a moment, then smiled disarmingly. "It's okay, Lia," he told her. "I've had a lot of time to think since I've been gone, and I should have known I couldn't force you to have feelings for me. You've never been one to let anyone tell you what to do. Stubborn as a mule, as always." He winked at her playfully.

"I think I've come to realize that it was never meant to be between us," he continued, his voice hollow. "I just wish I had understood that a little sooner, then maybe we could have at least been friends." Lia shook her head, pained by the sorrow she heard in his words.

"You're a good man, Mark," she told him, taking his hand in hers. "I've done some thinking, too, and aside from annoying me to the point of death," she made a face, feigning dismay before giggling. "You've been more of a friend to me than I ever could have hoped." Mark was silent, processing her words, then he squeezed her hand tightly.

"I'm happy to hear you say that," he said, his eyes sparkling as he smiled at her. "So you don't hate me anymore?" Lia rolled her eyes.

"I never did hate you," she responded, and as she spoke she realized it was true. "I just thought I did. I was too stupid to see how much you really mean to me."

She wasn't expecting the suffocating embrace that came a moment later, but she relaxed in Mark's arms, closing her eyes against the warmth of his grasp. He let her go a few moments later and stood to his feet.

"I suppose I should to get to work," he said, sighing. "I'll be right outside. You should get some rest." He disappeared through the door, leaving her alone with her thoughts.

Lia went back to the bedroom, lying down and closing her eyes. A slight tingle of excitement ran up her spine as she considered what Mark had said about the baby. As she turned his words over in her mind, she began to wonder if she really would be a good mother.

A few days later, Lia found herself staring at the dwindling flour sack in the kitchen. Anxiety filled her at the sight of it, and she began to mentally make note of each and every food item in the house. She frowned as she calculated how many days the food would last, thinking of how to stretch the meals as far as possible, when a sudden realization dawned on her. She didn't have to ration her food anymore. Smiling, she grabbed her shawl and went out into the shop.

Mark looked up as she approached.

"I need to go get some things," Lia sang, trying to contain her happiness. "Can I have a few silvers?" He wiped his brow, his face breaking into an amused grin at her excitement.

"How much do you think you'll need?" Mark asked, stepping away from his workbench. He gestured for her to follow him as he walked into the house.

"Well," she mused, thinking. "We need flour, and cheese, and I'd like to buy some meat…"

He moved towards an end table and opened a drawer, taking out his moneybag.

"Do you think fifty will be enough?"

Lia's heart leaped into her throat for a moment, and she almost felt greedy at the thought of spending so much.

"I don't have to get it all now," she told him. "We only really need flour."

"It's fine, Lia," he told her, smiling reassuringly. "Get whatever you want. How much?"

"I think about fifty should do it," she answered. Mark began to count out the coins, then he stopped.

"Here," he said, handing her the bag. "Use as much as you need." Thanking him, she walked outside.

It was raining slightly, and Lia moved quickly to get her shopping done. It was liberating to buy as much food as she wanted to, and she realized too late that she had gotten a little carried away. She ended up having to pay a boy to help her carry the groceries home, and she felt a bit nervous when she returned with only twenty tokens left from what Mark had given her.

After putting the food away, she went out into the shop to give him his change.

"Did you get everything we need?" Mark asked, taking the moneybag from her. He weighed it in his hand, estimating how much she had spent. Lia nodded slowly as she watched his face, wondering how he would respond.

"I had to pay someone to help me carry it all home," she answered. "Maybe I spent too much?" He shook his head.

"It's fine," he told her. He gestured at his workbench. "I have a lot to do before I can take a break. Can you make something for lunch?"

"Sure," she told him, turning to go back inside. "I'll call you when it's done."

Lia felt a sob rise in her throat as she stared at the food she had bought. It had been so long since she had known the comfort of a well-stocked kitchen. She was overwhelmed with emotion, and she did her best to keep her tears from falling into the food as she cooked.

● ● ●

Chapter Twenty-Nine

THE DAYS PASSED AND TURNED into weeks, and April soon arrived. Mark's gentle understanding of what had happened during her time on the streets began to overshadow Lia's guilt and shame, making her feel almost whole again. She was content to be with him, and he was happy to provide for her.

It was almost as if all she had been through was just dream, a nightmare about things that had happened to someone else. While she knew, in her mind, that the horrors of the past months had really happened, the memories seemed distant, and she found herself thinking less and less about everything she had been through. Even the heartache of Belle's death had somehow faded, lost in the peace and comfort of feeling safe.

Lia quickly grew used to living with Mark, and she actually enjoyed spending time with him. Her one concern was her pregnancy, and she knew her time was fast approaching.

One morning after breakfast, she went out into the shop to talk to Mark about a midwife.

"Mark!" she called over the sound of his hammer striking against his workpiece. He paused, turning towards her.

"Are you okay?" he asked worriedly, glancing at her belly. She shrugged off his concern, reading his concerned face and gesturing at her swollen midsection.

"I'm fine," Lia reassured him. "That's what I wanted to ask you about." Mark raised a brow, a half smile on his lips.

"I don't know much about things like that," he replied jokingly, winking at her. "But ask away."

"Very funny," she chuckled, rolling her eyes. "You know what I mean. I need to see about a midwife, is that okay?"

"Of course," he answered. "Are you going now?"

"Yes," she answered, turning to leave. "I shouldn't be gone long."

"Let me know how it goes," Mark called over his shoulder as he resumed work. "And how much it will cost." Nodding, Lia disappeared into the house.

Readying herself quickly, Lia set out to visit the town's midwife. The woman's house wasn't far from the blacksmith's shop, and as Lia approached the large, squat building she could see a hand-carved plaque that read 'MIDWIFE – HEALER' affixed to the door. She knocked, and after a few moments a plump, middle-aged woman answered.

"Hello!" the woman greeted her, looking her up and down as she quickly realized why Lia was there. "I'm Mabel." She gave a sweep of her arm, inviting Lia to enter.

"Lia," she answered. "Nice to meet you."

Lia followed Mabel through a set of double doors and into a small sitting room.

"I'll take your shawl," Mabel offered, holding out her hand. Lia smiled and shook her head, kindly refusing as she sat down on one of the tattered, upholstered chairs in the room.

"From your size I'm assuming your time is close," Mabel said, studying Lia with her large, hazel eyes. "Do you know when you got pregnant?"

"The middle of August," Lia answered, looking around.

The home was fairly large, much bigger than where she and Mark lived, but it was very crowded with furniture and various knick-knacks. Mabel apparently loved cats, as there were dozens of wooden cat figurines gracing the many end tables and shelves in the room. There was a small, worn carpet-rug in the center of the floor, patterned with deep green and dark blue, and although it was pretty it seemed mismatched next to the burgundy color of the chairs. Mabel noticed Lia's wandering eyes and chuckled.

"My late husband was a carpenter and woodcarver," she explained, gesturing at the carvings. "I hate cats, but I don't have the heart to get rid of them now that he's gone. I lost all the others he made, so I suppose I'm stuck with these." Lia smiled politely, unsure of how to respond. "Now, let's continue," Mabel said, rapping her knuckles on the short, long table that sat between them to get Lia's attention. "Have you had any pain?"

After Lia had answered all of Mabel's questions, she was led down a short hallway into a small room with a large table.

"Climb up there," Mabel said, rolling up the sleeves of her brown and white dress. Lia obeyed, sitting on the edge of the table. "Lie down." As Lia leaned back, she knew what was coming, remembering her mother's examination. Her dress was pulled up to expose her swollen stomach, and she cringed as she felt the midwife's cold hands.

"My mother is a midwife," Lia said, making conversation as she tried to stifle her embarrassment. Mabel grunted in acknowledgment, withdrawing her fingers and wiping them on a cloth hanging from a hook on the wall. She then began to feel Lia's belly, murmuring with approval when the baby kicked her hands away.

"So did she tell you what to expect?" Mabel asked, gesturing for Lia to sit up. Lia nodded.

"A little," she answered. "I'm a bit afraid." Mabel threw her head back in laughter.

"Child," she said, shaking her head. "If you knew what was coming you'd be more than a bit afraid!" Lia's face drained, and anxiety filled her chest. Mabel gave her a pitying look. "This is your first one, I can tell." Lia nodded.

"Yes," she confirmed. "It's the first." Obviously amused, Mabel chuckled to herself, then she grew serious as she addressed business matters.

"My fee is two hundred silvers," Mabel told her. "This is the second week of April, so I'd say...." she paused, counting quickly on her fingers. "I'd say any time after the first week of May. I'll need to see you once a week until you go into labor, but any more often than that will cost you an extra twenty silvers a visit." She held out her hand to help Lia move off the table

As Lia slipped off the table, her shawl fell from her shoulders, and after straightening it she glanced up to see that Mabel's demeanor had suddenly changed. Lia gave her a questioning look.

"You're a whore!" Mabel hissed, narrowing her eyes as she pointed at Lia's chest. She had seen the brand, and Lia's heart sank, expecting to be told to leave. Mabel turned up her nose disdainfully, scowling. "I might have known. The price is double." Lia was surprised that the midwife wasn't kicking her out, but she was more shocked by the price.

"No whore could afford that!" Lia exclaimed, remembering how little the whores were paid. Mabel frowned.

"The ones who plan to keep their children manage to come up with the price," she said firmly, glaring at Lia. "I deal with a lot of hatred from the townspeople for birthing whores, only to have the women abandon their babies in the town. If there's no midwife the women and infants are more likely to die, which rids us of both a whore and a bastard child! No, I won't go to the trouble of attending unless you pay enough to show that you've no intention of burdening someone else with your bastard."

"First of all," Lia began, growing indignant. "I won't abandon my baby. And second of all, I'm not a whore." Mabel scoffed.

"I'm no fool!" she snapped. "I know what that letter means! And it's fresh, too, can't be much more than a month old!"

"I *was* a whore," Lia admitted, her mind racing. Despite Mark's steady work, she was sure he wouldn't be able to afford four hundred tokens for a midwife. "But I'm not anymore. I'm married." Mabel didn't believe her.

"And now you lie to me?" she said angrily, her face reddening. Her straw-colored hair was thinning, and Lia couldn't help noticing that Mabel's scalp had also turned crimson in her anger.

"It's the truth!" Lia quickly lied. "My husband left home without me some months ago, looking for work, and when I set out to follow him I couldn't find him! I had to turn to the streets, I would have starved!" Mabel grew quiet, considering Lia's explanation.

"You found him, then?" she asked. Her voice had softened slightly, but her face remained wary. Lia nodded vehemently. Thinking for a moment, Mabel shrugged. "I don't believe you," she said, and Lia's face fell. "But," she continued, holding up a finger. "You bring your husband with you next week, and we'll see." Lia quickly agreed, and Mabel gave her a packet of herbs to brew into tea each night.

"I'll bring him," Lia promised, stepping out the door and onto the street. Mabel snorted derisively and waved her off.

"How did it go at the midwife's?" Mark asked during dinner that night. Lia choked on her milk, spewing droplets of the pale liquid across the table. She didn't know how Mark would react to idea of pretending to be her husband, and she hadn't figured out how to tell him yet.

"Fine," Lia coughed, wiping her mouth and grinning widely at him. "She said the baby's doing fine, and I'm healthy." Forcing a smile, she took another sip of milk. "I'm due any time after the first week of May," she finished, echoing what the midwife had told her. She fell silent, taking a bite of food.

"And?" Mark prodded, gesturing for her to go on. "What about the price?" Lia took her time chewing, trying to ignore the nervous flutters in her stomach.

"Four hundred silvers," she told him, cringing as she gave him a sideways glance. His eyes widened, and he looked up at the ceiling, muttering to himself as his fingers rapidly moved. Lia could tell he was counting his money in his mind, and she waited patiently for him to finish. After a long moment, he gave her a grim look.

"That's a lot," he mused quietly, sighing. "I'll just have to put in extra hours."

"Well, you know," Lia began, drawing her words out. She paused, dropping her gaze for a moment before glancing back up at him. "It might only cost two hundred." Mark's eyes snapped forward to meet hers.

"How?" he asked, leaning forward in his seat. "I thought you just said it was four."

"That's the whore's price," Lia told him. "The midwife saw my letter. But I told her I wasn't a whore, I said that I was married. She'll only charge two hundred if I go to my next appointment with my husband."

"Well, that's a fine mess!" Mark exclaimed, shaking his head. "And when you don't bring this 'husband' of yours to your next appointment, what then? She'll know you lied to her and she might charge you even more!" Lia gave him a half smile.

"Not if my *husband* goes with me," she answered pointedly, eyeing him. "Are you busy next Wednesday?" She held her breath, waiting for a response.

Mark's face went blank and he froze, staring at her. When he didn't answer, she sighed.

"I understand, Mark," Lia told him quickly, giving him a knowing look. "It's no problem, I'll just tell her the truth the next time I see her."

"And spend two hundred extra tokens?" he rasped, finding his voice. He grinned, but she could see that his expression was pained. She wished she hadn't suggested it in the first place.

"You don't have to, Mark," she reassured him. "I'm sorry, I shouldn't have…"

"Lia," Mark interrupted, giving her a meaningful look. "I think I can tolerate being your husband for a single day." His eyes began to sparkle, and Lia's smile was genuine.

"Thank you, Mark," she said gratefully.

As promised, Mark accompanied Lia to the next appointment. She knocked on the door, and Mabel was surprised to see that Lia had actually brought a man with her.

"This is my husband, Mark Samuels," Lia introduced him, and she heard him swallow hard as he extended his hand in greeting. Mabel nodded suspiciously, looking Mark up and down, before taking his hand.

"He's a handsome one, isn't he?" Mabel mused, glancing at Lia with a twinkle in her eye. Lia blushed, staring up at Mark.

"That he is," Lia answered, taking his arm. Mark returned her gaze, smiling warmly, and he put his arm around her shoulders.

"All right, ladies," Mark scolded, embarrassment in his voice. "Enough of that, I've got to get back to work. Can I go?" Mabel put her hands on her hips and shook her head.

"How do I know she didn't just pay you to act like her husband?" she asked, frowning as she eyed him. "You'll stay until I give you leave." Mark opened his mouth to protest, but Mabel fixed him with a stern glare, and Lia followed her into the examination room.

The exam only took a few minutes, and Mark stood to his feet when the women returned.

"Are you all right?" he asked Lia, concern etching his face. She nodded.

"Everything's going as expected," Lia said cheerfully. Mark was on edge, but he was truly happy to hear that she was okay.

"How long have you been married, Mark?" Mabel asked, changing the subject. Lia had prepared him for this question, and he was ready with an answer.

"Since July of last year," he said. "It's kind of strange when you think that we're going to have our first baby before our first anniversary!" He sounded genuine, and Lia was impressed with his acting.

"Well, certain honeymoon activities do tend to result in babies," Mabel said, amused when Mark's face turned red. "And it just so happens that babies don't take as long to come around as anniversaries do. How long have you known your wife?" Mark looked up at the ceiling as he counted.

"Well," he answered. "Since I was seven, I think. So about fourteen years." Mabel was surprised.

"And how did you know you wanted to marry her?" she asked. Mark shifted his weight from one foot to the other, obviously uncomfortable with the question. Seeing the expectant look on the woman's face, he sighed with defeat.

"Do you see this?" he asked, turning his head. He pointed at the white, jagged scar that began above his right ear and continued down to the bottom of his earlobe. Mabel nodded hesitantly, confused, and Mark sighed.

"She won a race," he told her, his face beginning to glow with excitement. "I wasn't a very good sport about it, and she ended up with bloodied nose." Mabel inhaled sharply, giving him a disapproving look. "Oh, she got me back for it!" Mark reassured her, unable to hide his proud grin. His words began to flow easily as he quickly became absorbed in the reliving of his memory. "I'll never forget how stunned I was when I realized she was throwing rocks at me, much less when she caught me right in the ear with one the size of my fist! I looked back at her, scared to death, but when I saw her I didn't care if she hurled a dozen more rocks at me." Lia stared at him, entranced as she listened to his voice grow distant.

"The sun was setting behind her, and the light made her hair shine like it was on fire," Mark continued, clearing his throat. "Her eyes burned, and I felt like I couldn't move. My heart stopped beating, and somehow I just knew that I never wanted her to look at anyone else the way she looked at me that day." Lia was captivated by the feeling in his words.

"But I hated you that day, Mark," she interrupted softly. He shook his head, giving her a meaningful look.

"No," he said, his voice full of passion. "It wasn't hatred I saw. It was everything else. Your spirit and your fire. The boldness and confidence and impulsiveness that drove you to stand up to me, even though you knew people would speak badly of you. In that moment, you couldn't see anyone except for me, and it took my breath away. I didn't want you to ever see anyone else. That's when I knew."

Lia noticed that the room had fallen deathly silent. Mabel clutched her heart with her hand, obviously touched by the explanation, and Mark took a deep breath as he managed a relaxed grin. Lia's heart ached with an unfamiliar pain, and she felt for a moment that she was seeing a part of herself she had never seen before, the part of her that only Mark could see. She swallowed hard against the lump that had appeared in her throat, trying to clear her head, and she returned Mark's smile.

"I've never heard you say it quite like that," she breathed.

"You've never listened quite like that, either," Mark replied quietly, his voice tinged with bitterness as he dropped his gaze.

"It was beautiful," Lia told him, unable to refrain from taking his face in her hands and turning him to look at her. "I wish I'd listened before."

"Well," the midwife sighed, smiling as Lia and Mark turned to face her. "If the two of you are lying, that show you just put on was well worth the money I'd be losing out on." Mark turned red.

"Can we go?" he asked quickly, looking as though he might run out the door at any moment. "I've got a lot of work to do."

"Yes, by all means," Mabel said, ushering them towards the door. "Be back here next week, Lia Samuels."

•••

Chapter Thirty

HALF OF THE MIDWIFE'S PAYMENT was due a few days after Lia's third weekly visit, and when she dropped it off Lia was told that Mabel would make house calls for any future visits. But Mabel didn't arrive for the scheduled visit the following week, and after waiting for several hours Mark walked over to see what was keeping her. He returned shortly, a grave look on his face.

"There was a note on her door from early this morning," Mark told Lia, his voice grim. "It said that one of her family members in another town is ailing, and that she'll be back in three days." Worry creased his forehead, but Lia shrugged dismissively.

"Three days isn't very long," she said, trying to reassure him. "I'll be fine." Mark frowned, muttering a curse.

Lia was wrong, and the next night, while preparing dinner, she felt a wave of pain wash over her. Something inside of her felt like it had been ripped into pieces, and she couldn't help the cry of agony that echoed through the house as she tried not to fall to the floor. Mark was at her side in an instant, rushing in from the shop.

"What's wrong?" he asked fearfully, studying her face. Lia caught her breath and tried to calm, wincing as she straightened.

"I don't know," she gasped, the pain ebbing away. She wracked her brain, trying to remember everything Mabel had said.

Breathing deeply, she took a step, and Mark helped her to a chair. "The midwife said there might be some pain even before it's time, and that I shouldn't be worried unless I start bleeding or the pain keeps coming."

"Are you bleeding?" Mark blurted, his eyes wide. Lia gave him a look.

"I can't exactly tell right now," she told him. His face was flushed with concern, and he gestured quickly.

"Aren't you going to find out?" he asked impatiently, his voice hushed.

"If you don't mind watching me hike up my skirts," she answered, trying not to laugh at his flustered ignorance. "Where do you think I have to check?" Mark looked at her blankly before catching her meaning, then he turned red and averted his eyes.

"I knew that," he stammered, and she giggled at the embarrassment on his face. She patted his arm.

"I'll let you know if I need you," she told him, reaching for his hand. He pulled her to her feet and helped her to her room.

Four more days passed with agonizing lethargy, and Mark refused to let Lia leave her bed. He worried constantly about her, coming in from the shop and checking on her dozens of times each day. The midwife was already two days late, and Lia could feel an urgency rise up inside of her. She knew her baby would be coming soon.

On the fifth day, Mark woke her up at dawn. He had a number of deliveries to make, and he wanted to get an early start.

"I won't be back until the afternoon," Mark told her worriedly, reluctant to leave her alone. Lia was still half asleep, and she waved him off.

"I'll be fine," she murmured, closing her eyes. "Just go." She began to drift back off to sleep.

"Do you want me to bring you something to eat?" he asked. Her eyes opened slightly, and she shook her head.

"No," she muttered. "I'm not hungry."

"I could set it on the table," Mark said. "For when you wake up." She shook her head again and rolled over. He waited for a moment before walking out of her room, and she heard the door to the shop open and close.

Lia tried going back to sleep, but Mark had mentioned food and now she was starving. After lying in bed for over an hour, she finally sighed and sat up. Swinging her legs over the side of the bed, she stood to her feet, then she shuffled into the kitchen, wishing she had taken Mark up on his offer to cook before he left.

She reached for a packet of stale crackers, glancing at the basket of eggs on the counter. Her stomach growled. She didn't want crackers, she wanted eggs with a slice of fried ham and fresh, buttered bread. Her mouth began to water, and she thought for a moment. Mark would cook for her when he got back, but she wasn't sure if she could wait not only for him to return but also for the extra hour or so it would take for him to cook.

Lia glanced towards the door to the shop, thinking of the stack of firewood waiting just outside and the fire she would have to build before cooking. Sighing, she moved towards the door to get some wood.

The fire was soon blazing, and Lia worked quickly to finish kneading and shaping the bread dough. As she set the loaves aside to rise, she glanced up at the ceiling. Hanging from the rafters, just out of her reach, was a large ham.

She moved a chair and carefully stepped up, reaching above her head with the knife she was holding to cut off a thick slice of meat. The chair wobbled slightly, and Lia caught her breath. She put her arms out to her sides, trying to regain her balance, but her foot slipped off the edge of the chair. Inhaling sharply, she felt herself totter, and she lurched quickly in the opposite direction. The maneuver didn't work, and she let out a cry of wide-eyed fear as she fell, landing hard on her side.

She lay on the floor, stunned, her body momentarily numb. A stab of panic shot through her when she thought of the knife, then she breathed a sigh of relief when she saw that it had clattered to the floor a short distance away. Rolling onto her back, she closed her eyes and tried to calm her racing heart.

After a long moment, she tried to move to her knees. She didn't feel hurt, just a bit sore, and she braced her hand on the chair to lift herself to her feet. She slowly straightened.

A wave of ripping pain wracked her body, sending her right back to her knees with a scream of agony. Lia looked down in confusion; she didn't remember wetting herself, but a puddle of water pooled underneath her. Fearful dread filled her.

She glanced towards the window. The shutters were open, and the morning light streamed brightly through the glass. Mark had said that he would return in the afternoon, and Lia's heart sank as she realized that she still had at least a few more hours to wait.

Sweat began to bead on her forehead, and her insides felt as though they were being torn into pieces. Flexing her jaw, she thought of her bed and tried to stand again, but after another wave of pain wrenched through her she gave up, content to remain on the floor.

Time passed slowly, and Lia tried to keep herself calm. She found that if she focused hard enough, she could just barely keep from screaming as the waves of agony washed over her, letting out periodic moans instead. The ripping pain was coming more and more frequently, though, and she became increasingly frantic.

As her body told her to give in to the pressure building within her, Lia did her best to control herself, too terrified to consider giving in and bearing down. Then, in the midst of her desperate, choked sobs, she thought she heard a noise come from the shop. Holding her breath, she listened. The sound came again, and she was sure Mark had finally come home.

"Mark!" Lia tried to scream, her voice breaking as she set her jaw against the pain. She struggled to her feet for a moment, moving towards the door, only to double over again. "Mark!" Footsteps moved quickly on the other side of the door, and he appeared a moment later.

Mark turned white with fear when he saw Lia on the floor, her hair soaked with sweat and her face crumpled in agony. He rushed to her side, gathering her into his arms and carrying her to her room. Laying her gently on her bed, he stared down at her, terrified. He looked like he wanted to run and hide.

"I'll go see if the midwife's back!" Mark told her, moving towards the door.

"Don't you dare leave!" Lia screamed, her words turning into a wail. "There's no time!" He was scared.

"What do I do?" he cried, his face twisted with helpless panic.

"Cloths," Lia told him, her breath whistling through her teeth as she inhaled. She wailed again while Mark looked on, unable to move. "Clean cloths! Go!" Startled by her voice, he sprang into action.

His footsteps pounded against the floor as he ran, and she rolled her eyes when she heard the clattering of various items falling in the other room. Mark reappeared after only a few moments, clutching several clean, unstained sheets.

"Now what?" he asked, grimacing as she let out another cry.

Lia's mind raced as she tried to remember everything her mother had ever told her about childbirth, and she made a face as she glanced at Mark. There was no one else to check her, and she tried to think of the best way to tell him what he had to do.

Blinded by pain only a moment later, she abandoned any thoughts of tactfulness.

"You have to check inside me," Lia said, clenching her teeth. Mark stared at her blankly, then his expression changed.

"What do you mean?" he asked warily.

"What do you think I mean?" she screeched, her face red as perspiration stung her eyes. He was horrified.

"No!" he cried. Lia stiffened again, wincing, before glaring at him.

"I don't care how much it hurts!" she snarled. "I'll get up off this bed and strangle you if you don't!" She spread her legs, lifting her skirt, and Mark looked away. "I don't like it any more than you do!" she snapped. "Hurry up and get it over with!"

Mark moved towards her, and she breathlessly told him what he was trying to determine. He removed his fingers a moment later, swallowing hard. His face was pale and green, and Lia got the impression that he was either fighting the urge to vomit or trying to keep from passing out. She glared at him, and he steadied himself.

"Did you feel it?" she gasped. He nodded slightly, holding up his bloody fingers. She beckoned him to move closer, comparing his measurements to the size of her own hand.

"There's something hard," Mark told her, unable to refrain from shuddering. Lia was in too much pain to yell at him, concentrating instead on her breathing as she tried to prepare herself. It was time, and she quickly tried to explain his upcoming role, setting her jaw with determination as she braced herself.

Lia cried out in agony as she bore down hard. She could feel something stretch and tear inside of her as the head of her baby moved down slightly, and in its wake was a horrible, intense, burning pain. Pausing for a moment, she finally let her body's instincts take over, and when it signaled to her again she let out a blood-curdling scream as her muscles tensed.

Again and again Lia pushed; she was sure that her insides were ripping apart, shredding into bloody ribbons of flesh. It felt as though her bones were splitting, and she wished she was dead. As she caught her breath yet again, an indescribable impatience filled her, and somehow she knew she was almost done.

Mustering every last bit of strength in her body, she screamed again, the long, lingering wail trailing off as she felt the tiny creature slip out of her.

"I've got him!" Mark cried, and Lia's body was overcome with a sense of relief more profound than anything she had ever felt before. A pathetic, quiet cry rang out, and something inside of her soul ached. She had heard the sound before in her dreams.

Tears streamed down her sweat-soaked face as she watched Mark cradle the tiny infant, its small, wet body still attached to hers. Rapture filled his countenance as he stared at the baby, and he seemed unable to tear his eyes away from its crying form. She held her arms out, beckoning him to give the baby to her, but he was awestruck.

"Mark," Lia prompted, breathing hard. Shaken from his reverie, a dazed wonder still lingering in his eyes, he handed the child to her. She held her breath, afraid as she took her first peek at her baby's face.

She began to sob, and she realized that the burden that had weighed on her shoulders from the moment she had discovered her pregnancy was unfounded. The infant looked nothing like *him*; this baby was beautiful, and as Lia drank in each of his little features she could see that he favored her father.

When the afterbirth had passed from within her, Lia handed the baby to Mark. Ripping the sheets he had fetched into pieces, he gingerly wiped the baby's skin clean amid the desperate, tiny cries that rose from its little pink mouth, then he managed to tightly swaddle the frail, little body. Mark gave him back to her, and the baby suckled at her breasts, his cries quieting almost immediately.

The bed was soaked with blood and fluid, and Mark busied himself trying to clean up. He brought his cot into Lia's room, gently moving her, then he picked up the ruined straw mattress and hauled it out of the house. Darting back and forth like a startled deer, Mark rushed about, finding a new mattress cover and filling it with fresh straw.

Laying the sleeping baby down on the clean bed, Mark helped Lia out of her spoiled dress. Her blanket and pillow had been spared from the mess, tossed aside into a corner during the frenzy, and he covered her up as she settled onto the sweet-smelling bed.

Lia was exhausted, and she couldn't keep her eyes open. The baby was asleep in her arms, and now she, too, began to doze.

"He's beautiful, Lia," Mark whispered, lightly touching her forehead. She smiled at him.

"You did well," she breathed, her tired eyes grateful.

"Can I hold him?" Mark asked her, looking again at the infant. Lia nodded, and he carefully took the sleeping child from her. He smiled, captivated as the baby took hold of his finger.

"Get some sleep," Mark said, leaning over to pull the blanket further up under her chin. "I'll sit here with him." Lia wasted no time, falling asleep before he finished speaking.

• • •

Chapter Thirty-One

MARK TOOK THE NEXT FEW DAYS off work, spending his time waiting on Lia's every whim and doting on the baby. The midwife returned two days after the baby was born, and Mark left the house only long enough to demand his money back from her. Mabel refused, saying that each of the three visits cost twenty silvers and only offering a refund of forty coins, but Mark would not be put off, telling her that delivering the baby without her help was an ordeal worth much more than forty tokens. After he threatened to call a constable, Mabel finally gave in, and Mark returned home triumphant.

Any question Lia may have had about her feelings for her baby disappeared the moment she laid eyes on him, and she adored her child. Mark seemed to feel the same, and in between feedings he would appear at her side, asking to hold the infant.

After a few days, the issue of the baby's name came up, a detail forgotten in the excitement of adjusting to his arrival.

"I'd like to name him after my father," Lia said. Mark pursed his lips, nodding slightly.

"That's a good, strong name," he told her hesitantly. She could hear the strained twinge in his voice, and she glanced up at him.

"But...?" she asked, waiting for him to go on. Mark sighed.

"Don't take this the wrong way, Lia," he began. "I don't mean anything *else* by it, believe me. But remember, everyone thinks that we're married. I don't know how the townspeople will act if they find out we're not, and if you christen him with your father's name everyone will know."

"I thought you didn't care about the opinions of the damn townspeople," Lia countered, remembering what Mark had said about calling off their wedding. He shook his head, giving her an apologetic look.

"I used to think it didn't matter," he told her. "And I still wish I could believe that. But I was foolish, and I'm sorry for what you had to go through because of what I did. It's not fair." He gazed down at the sleeping baby. "I make good money here, and I can provide for all of us. How can we survive if we're shunned by the town?" Lia thought a moment. She knew he was right.

"John Samuels," she whispered, turning the name over on her tongue. Mark smiled, reaching out and brushing his fingertips against the baby's rosy cheeks.

"John Samuels," he echoed, and the pride in his voice was unmistakable.

The cool nights of May faded into a warm June, which, in turn, became a hot and humid July, and before Lia could blink John was seven weeks old. One night, while the baby was sleeping, she and Mark sat at the kitchen table eating a late dinner. John had been colicky for the past several evenings, and both of them were exhausted from his cries.

"I'm so glad he's finally asleep!" Lia exclaimed, rolling her eyes. "He's been driving me crazy!" Mark nodded fiercely.

"Me too," he agreed, cringing. "And just think, it'll start back up again in just a few hours."

"Don't remind me!" she moaned, hanging her head. "I can't wait till he starts sleeping through the night!"

"When will that be?" Mark asked eagerly.

"Another month, I think!" she quietly wailed. "At least you get to escape to the shop if you want to! I can't avoid the screaming no matter what, I have to feed him!" Mark gave her a pitying look. They fell silent, their meal finished but both of them too tired to get up and clear the table.

"Lia?" Mark began. She glanced up at him, her eyes heavy. "Hmm?"

He seemed reluctant to speak.

"What's going to happen with us?" he asked quietly. "Are we just going to live together like this forever?" She sighed. Part of her had wondered when this question would come up.

"I don't know," she replied. "I suppose it's up to you." Her shoulders sagged, and she leaned forward onto the tabletop, resting her face on her arms.

"I don't know what I would do without you, Mark," she continued, lifting her gaze and giving him a soft, grateful smile. "That seems to be the story of my life this past year. I don't know how much I can keep asking of you, but whatever you're willing to give I'll gladly accept." Mark raised a brow, studying her earnest expression.

"You've changed so much, Lia," he mused, a hint of awe in his voice. "If someone told me a year ago, or even a few months ago, that I'd ever hear you say what you just said, I would have thought them insane." Lia feigned hurt.

"Was I really that bad?" she pouted, frowning with dismay. Mark chuckled, nodding.

"You might have been," he told her, his eyes sparkling mischievously.

"You weren't exactly the easiest person to tolerate, though," she informed him, rolling her eyes as she smiled. "You followed me everywhere!"

"I know," he said. "I couldn't stand being away from you." He paused, eyeing her. "Can I ask you something?"

"Sure," she answered.

"Why didn't you love me?"

Lia drew in a deep breath, surprised by his question. She had never thought about it before, and she pursed her lips, unsure of how to answer.

"I don't know, Mark," she told him. "I suppose it's because all I could think about every time I saw you was how much I hated you."

"But you changed, remember?" Mark pointed out. "You actually wanted me around."

"I needed you, Mark," she tried to explain. "Being with you made me stop thinking about what happened to me."

"So is that why you're different this time, too?" he asked. "Because you need me?"

"No, it's not," she told him. "Well, I suppose that's part of it. Things are different now, though. You're my friend, and I care about you, I really do. And not just because I need you."

"But you loved Thomas, didn't you?" he asked. "What made you love him and not me?"

"I didn't really love him," Lia said. "I just thought I did." She frowned, trying to think. "I don't know why I was going to marry him. I was mad at you, and I was mad about how the townspeople were treating me. Thomas was sweet and made me feel special, and I fell for his lies. It was a mistake."

"Did I make you feel special?" Mark asked. She could tell what he was getting at, and she didn't like where the conversation was headed. The thought of trying to sort out her feelings was overwhelming, and she desperately wanted him to stop asking her questions.

"So much has happened," Lia told him, trying to hide her growing frustration. "I can't even think straight yet. You're my friend, and I appreciate everything you've done for me. Isn't that enough for now?"

"Of course, Lia," Mark answered quickly, taking her hint. "Just forget I mentioned it." He gave her a meaningful look. "And just so you know, you can stay with me as long as you need to."

Lia nodded and gave him a slight smile. She knew she would never be able to repay his kindness. A thought suddenly occurred to her, and her eyes grew wide.

"I forgot to send word to my parents!" she cried. "I was supposed to send them word after I found you, and I completely forgot!" Mark hushed her.

"We'll do it tomorrow," he quickly reassured her. "Don't worry." He yawned and rubbed his eyes. "We should get some sleep," he told her. "The baby's going to be waking up soon." Lia nodded in agreement, grimacing at the thought of John's screams.

"Good night, Lia," Mark said, heaving himself up from his chair. "Try to get some rest."

The following day, as promised, Mark sent word to Lia's parents. Brunbury was almost two weeks' journey from Blackmoor, so Lia knew it would be quite a while before she would receive a reply. Still, as the days passed and summer reached its peak, she could feel her impatience growing.

One afternoon, as July neared its end, she heard a commotion coming from Mark's shop. John had just fallen asleep after crying for hours from the heat of the day, and Lia was instantly irritated, worrying that the noise would wake him up. Marching towards the door, she flung it open, preparing to yell at Mark for being so loud.

She stopped in her tracks, surprised to see both him and another man hollering and jumping up and down with excitement, slapping each other on the back.

"What's going on?" Lia demanded, quickly stepping into the shop and closing the door. "The baby's sleeping!" The man turned to face her, and her heart caught in her throat. It was Ben Samuels, Mark's father.

"Lia!" he cried, his blue eyes dancing with happiness when he saw her. He threw his arms open and rushed towards her, sweeping her into a hug. "I'm so glad I found you two!" Lia's face lit up with hope, her eyes sparkling.

"Are my parents here?" she asked breathlessly, looking towards the street. "Did they come?" Ben's face instantly darkened, and he glanced at Mark. Just as suddenly, he went right back to smiling.

"No, child," Ben told her, shaking his head. "I left Brunbury shortly after you did. I haven't seen them since." Lia's heart sank, and tears welled up in her eyes. "But they told me to give you their love if I happened to find you," Ben added quickly, reaching out and cradling her face in his hands as his eyes grew soft. "You're more beautiful than I remember, the very image of your mother." He pinched her cheek playfully, but Lia could see that his eyes were mournful. Changing the subject, he turned to Mark.

"Is there any food lying about?" Ben asked, rubbing his stomach. "I haven't eaten in I don't know how long!" Mark nodded, glancing at Lia questioningly. She got his meaning, and turned to go back inside.

"I'll make you something," she said, opening the door. "Just try to be quiet, will you?"

Mark and Lia had already eaten lunch, but there weren't enough leftovers for a meal. Only a few slices of cold ham remained, so she reheated them while she fried some eggs and toasted a piece of bread. It didn't take long, and when the food was finished she opened the shop door, carrying Ben's plate and a mug of fresh milk.

She was taken aback as she approached the men, her forehead immediately creasing with worry. Mark's face was drawn with anger, and Ben spoke in a hushed whisper. Mark erased his enraged expression the moment he saw her, nodding in her direction with a quick smile, but Lia wasn't fooled.

"What's wrong?" she asked, handing the food to Ben.

"Thank you, child," he sighed, eyeing the plate hungrily and pretending not to hear her question. "I've been living on my own cooking for too long!" He took a bite, closing his eyes as he savored the taste. Lia turned to Mark.

"What's wrong?" she repeated, studying him. He smiled again, shrugging.

"Nothing," he said, his voice light. "We were just talking about work, that's all." Lia nodded slowly, pursing her lips. Mark wasn't a very good liar, and he began fidgeting under her suspicious stare.

"This is wonderful, Lia," Ben told her, his voice thick as he ate. She ignored him, knowing full well that he was trying to change the subject. She glanced back and forth between his face and Mark's as if she could somehow discover what they were hiding, but there was nothing to be found. Clenching her fists in irritation, she turned and went back into the house.

Lia tried to stay mad at the men for keeping their secret, but Mark's excitement at his father's arrival soon made her forget her frustration. Deciding to take the rest of the day off, Mark took Ben to the butcher's shop to buy some fresh meat, planning to make a special meal in celebration. John woke up from his nap while the men were gone, and when they came back Ben practically snatched him from her arms as Mark began dinner preparations.

"And who is this little man?" Ben sang, his wrinkled, tanned face lighting up with excitement. He cradled the baby, singing and talking quietly. "He's a handsome fellow, isn't he?" Ben glanced up at Lia and Mark, noticing that they had fallen silent. He gave Mark a look.

"Is he yours, son?" Ben asked bluntly. Lia stared at her feet, her face burning as she waited for Mark to tell his father about her attack.

"Yes," Mark answered, looking up from the vegetables he had been peeling. Her mouth dropped open in surprise. "His name is John Samuels." Mark met Lia's gaze, and she smiled gratefully.

"Shame on you," Ben scolded, sternly shaking his head at Mark. "I thought I'd raised you better than that." Mark eyes were proud as he looked at his father.

"You did," he replied, his face serious. "I just lost my head for a moment." Lia's heart burned, and she fought back the urge to tell Ben the truth. He couldn't have raised a better son.

"Ah, well," Ben sighed, looking down at the baby and grinning. "It happens to the best of us. At least I've got a handsome little grandson, now!" He babbled nonsensically, trying to make the baby smile. "He'll be working away at the bellows in no time!" Mark scoffed in amusement at his father's words.

"And you'll be there to teach him, won't you?" he asked, affectionately glancing at his father.

"Of course!" Ben exclaimed loudly, prompting a cry from the baby. Lia reached out to take him, but Ben pulled back, soothing the startled child without her help. "I know a thing or two about babies!" he said proudly, gesturing at Mark. "I raised that one from the very start, and look at how he turned out!" Lia couldn't help the sarcastic giggle that rose in her throat, and her eyes twinkled.

"That's not very reassuring!" she laughed, playfully reaching for her son again. Mark feigned a hurt look, and Lia moved to his side, putting her arm around him. "I'm only joking," she told him, her mouth twisting apologetically.

"Sure you are," Mark answered, pulling away.

"Do you want me to help?" she asked, gesturing at the food. Mark shook his head, motioning with a nod towards a chair.

"You relax, Lia," he told her. "I'll do the cooking tonight." She sat, happily watching the scene before her, and her heart swelled. Although she missed her parents, the ache in her chest had grown suddenly dull with the lighthearted atmosphere of the room.

• • •

Chapter Thirty-Two

For two days, Mark and his father spent hours in the shop, talking amongst themselves in urgent, quiet voices. Whenever Lia tried to join them or asked them what they were talking about, they would fall silent and change the subject. By the third day, every last shred of patience she possessed was used up.

After putting the baby down for a nap, she marched into the shop, opening her mouth to demand an explanation from the men about their secrecy. This time, though, they didn't try to hide their grave faces, and Ben beckoned her to approach as Mark stepped outside.

"We didn't want to worry you, Lia," Ben said, reaching out and putting his arm around her shoulders. She heard the gentle huffing and snorting of horses, and she glanced towards the shop's street entrance to see Mark guiding a wagon into the work space. Her face creased with confusion, and she looked up at Ben, waiting for him to explain.

"What's going on?" Lia asked cautiously, watching Mark close the shop doors. The horses stamped nervously in the sudden dim, and he turned towards her, setting his jaw grimly. He looked at his father, and it seemed that neither of them knew how to start. Ben finally took the initiative and began to speak.

"Thomas is looking for you and Mark," he told her, his eyes pained. "He was in Brunbury from the very beginning as a scout, trying to find out how easily his family could lay claim to the town, and less than a week after you left that's exactly what happened. Brunbury is under his control now."

Despite the severity of what she had just been told, Lia couldn't help the smug satisfaction that washed over her. The townspeople in Brunbury had chosen Thomas over her, trying to kill her for putting out his eye, and she smiled at the thought that the filthy pigs were finally getting what they deserved.

"Mark told me that you sent word to your parents telling them that you two are here," Ben continued. "Thomas will come looking for you. We have to leave, Lia." She felt her heart begin to race.

"Why does he want to find us?" she asked, a puzzled look on her face. "I don't understand." Ben looked at Mark helplessly.

"Because you rejected him," Mark answered quietly. "He's convinced that you shamed him by refusing to give yourself to him, and he's taken it as a personal insult to his *honor*." His voice dripped sarcasm, and he rolled his eyes mockingly. "And also because of what you did to his eye," he continued. "He can't abide the thought of a..." he paused and took a deep breath, his chest swelling with pride. "...of a *woman* getting away with disfiguring him." Lia scoffed incredulously.

"That part's his own damn fault, though!" she exclaimed, her eyes growing wide. "He tried to take me! I would think he'd be willing to admit at least that much!"

"But he won't," Ben told her, grimacing. "He's used to getting everything he wants, Lia, and he wanted you. No one stands up to him. You should have seen the men he brought with him when he took over the town! Almost a hundred of them, each twice his size, but all of them acted like scared children around the weak little bastard!" He spat, cursing. "I don't think the boy's father ever gave him a good lashing, that's for sure!"

"But what about Mark?" Lia asked. "He didn't do anything to Thomas, so why does he want Mark?" Ben scowled, eyeing his son.

"He believes you chose Mark over him," Ben said, shifting his gaze to her. Her face flushed, and she averted her eyes.

"I know," Mark chuckled sarcastically, and Lia was surprised to hear that there was no bitterness in his voice. "Ridiculous, isn't it?" Lia turned a deeper shade of crimson as she tried to think of the reply she somehow felt she needed to provide.

"I suppose," she stammered, staring at her feet. "Absolutely ridiculous."

"He's also rather upset about letting Mark off so easily after that fight," Ben added mockingly, referring to the day that Mark knocked Thomas out cold. He stifled a scornful laugh. "As if he'd stand a chance against my son! Look at these arms!" He reached over and lifted Mark's bare arm, gesturing at the size of his bicep, and she was helpless against the crimson embarrassment that burned over every inch of her skin. Rolling his eyes at his father's pride, Mark pulled away, his face red as he turned from Lia's gaze.

"How did you find out about all this?" she asked, changing the subject as she looked at Ben. His face darkened.

"Thomas gathered everyone into the tavern," he answered, scowling as he remembered. "He ranted and raved for hours about you and Mark, and how he was planning to set the record straight once and for all when he found the two of you."

"And how does he intend to do that?" Lia asked. "Did he forget his broken nose from the last time he tried to fight Mark? He doesn't stand a chance, that's already been proven!" Trying to fight off a fit of self-consciousness, Mark cleared his throat.

"He's going to bring all his men and kill me," he said matter-of-factly. "And he's going to carry you off to his estate and make you one of his wives." Lia's mouth dropped open.

"*One* of his wives?" she cried in disbelief. "How many does he have?" Ben gave her a pitying look.

"Come now, Lia," he gently scolded. "You couldn't have possibly believed you were the first and only girl Thomas had ever set his sights on! He's the son of a *lord*, after all! He gets whatever he wants, and that includes women! According to his drunken bragging, he has more than a dozen wives in his harem." Her ears burned, and she was embarrassed by her naïve ignorance.

"I didn't know that!" she shot back defensively, stomping her foot. "Do you think I would have ever considered him if I'd known?"

"It's all right, Lia," Mark told her quickly, gesturing for her to calm. "A lot of people were fooled by Thomas."

"But you weren't!" she angrily retorted.

"It doesn't matter now," he answered, changing the subject. "What matters is that we leave before he gets here." Lia fumed, but she knew Mark was right.

"Where are we going?" she asked, her shoulders sagging with defeat.

Ben had been on his way to Tannenbury before finding Lia and Mark, a town ten days' travel from Blackmoor. He had received word of a blacksmith's position in the town, and Mark agreed that they should try their luck there. Lia didn't mind the thought of leaving, but she was worried about how her parents would be able to contact her if they didn't know where she had gone. Ben reassured her that he would think of a way, and they busied themselves readying for the journey.

Their belongings were packed within a few hours, and Lia carried John outside, laying him gently in the cradle that had been secured in the back of the wagon. The baby was still asleep, resting comfortably, and she climbed in to sit beside him. Mark took his place on the driver's seat next to his father, hanging a lighted lantern on the hook above them before whistling to the horses.

The wagon lurched forward, and the sound of the wheels grating against the cobblestone streets filled the air. They reached the end of the paved street after only a short time, crossing onto the dusty, rutted dirt road and leaving the town of Blackmoor behind them. Despite the brooding anger that had settled over her heart with the knowledge that Thomas was searching for them, she couldn't help feeling a wave of happiness at finally escaping the town.

When the men had been packing up her room, Lia had found the little figurine of the laughing fox underneath the bed, lying, forgotten, in the dust, and now she clutched it tightly in her hand. She hadn't noticed losing it in the first place, but she was glad to have it. It was the only thing she had left from her journey, the only tangible memory she was taking with her. Her teeth chattered from the bumpy wagon ride, and Lia thought of Belle, tears stinging her eyes.

They made good time, stopping only to rest and tend to the horses. Lia stayed in the back of the wagon with John, while Mark and Ben sat in the driver's seat, taking turns at the reins. The heat of late July lingered heavily throughout the nights, and she stewed with jealousy as she lay in the suffocating warmth of the wagon with John by her side, hearing the men's soft voices as they travelled by the light of the stars.

The days passed slowly, and Lia felt herself growing increasingly agitated. By the eighth day, as John screamed inconsolably in the stifling heat of midafternoon, she found herself seriously considering throwing him out the back of the wagon.

"Mark!" Lia shouted. She could hear the two men laughing and talking, and now they fell silent.

"What's wrong?" Mark answered, turning around in his seat and peeking into the wagon. She gave him a poisonous glare.

"We need to stop!" she snarled, gesturing at the screaming baby. "I'm going to lose my mind if I don't get a breath of fresh air!"

"We can't, Lia, we need to keep moving, especially while it's still daylight," he told her sympathetically. "For all we know, Thomas may have found out where we're going, and he could be right behind us. Just a few more hours, then we'll take a break for dinner. I would open the wagon cover, but the dust would choke the baby."

"Good!" Lia roared, her flushed face streaked with sweat. Her dress was soaked, and her hair was a mess. "At least then he would shut up! We have to stop, or I swear, I'll jump out!" Mark was taken aback at her tone, and he disappeared from sight. A moment later, she heard Ben call the horses to a stop, and she leaped from the back of the wagon as the men climbed down from the driver's seat.

"Come here, little one," Ben sang, reaching for John. Without a moment's hesitation, Lia thrust the screaming child at him, and he immediately started rocking the baby and trying to soothe his cries.

There was a stream near the road, the shallow water shaded by a few large trees growing from the banks, and Lia stormed off to cool her feet. Cursing under her breath, she hiked her dress up and walked in until the water reached her knees, immediately enraged when she realized that the water was only slightly cooler than the humid, hot air.

Scowling, Lia glanced back at the wagon. Mark was unhitching the horses so they could drink from the stream, and when he saw her looking at him he rolled his eyes and turned away. She could feel smooth rocks under her feet, and she fought the urge to throw one at him. Kicking at the surface, she felt a pocket of ice-cold water right in front of her, and she moved forward a step.

The bottom of the stream bed seemed to drop off, and she considered jumping in and going for a swim. She paused, thinking. If her dress got wet, she knew the rest of the day would be even more unbearable, and she could just imagine steam rising from her clothes to cook her alive in the back of the scorchingly hot wagon.

"To hell with it," Lia hissed, setting her jaw. Splashing back to the bank, she started unlacing her dress.

As she began to slip out of the heavy fabric, Lia heard Ben call out to Mark, hurriedly speaking her name.

"What are you doing, Lia?" Mark shouted a moment later, disbelief in his voice. She turned towards him, seeing the shocked, wide-eyed stare he was giving her. Ben's back was turned, and he was gesturing to Mark to do the same.

"What does it look like?" she snapped, dropping her dress. Mark was stunned, thrown completely off-guard by her sudden nakedness, and he seemed unable to move as he stared at her. "Are you going to join me?" she demanded sarcastically, glaring at him with her hands on her hips. "Or are you just going to stare?"

Regaining his composure, Mark's face turned crimson, and he whirled around. Lia stepped into the water, laughing when she heard Ben poking fun at Mark for not turning his back faster, and when she reached the cold water she sighed with relief.

"Are you sure you don't want to take a swim?" she playfully called, her mood instantly improved. "The water's freezing right here!" Mark didn't answer, and she scoffed, holding her breath and diving below the surface.

Lia relaxed in the cool water, swimming back and forth for almost half an hour. Ben had managed to quiet John's cries, and all she could hear was the peaceful splashing of the stream. Mark paced anxiously near the wagon, glancing at the sun every few moments, but she ignored him. Finally, his patience worn thin, Mark told her it was time to get back on the road.

"We need to keep going, Lia!" he called. "We've already lost enough time!"

"It was worth it!" she said loudly, speaking to herself as she leaned back in the water. She didn't think Mark had heard her, but when she looked she saw that he was coming towards her, his countenance darkening. Astonished at his anger, she froze.

"It was worth it?" he echoed incredulously as he approached. "Thomas intends to kill me!" He picked up her dress and tossed it near the water's edge. "And do you think he'll have any interest in keeping John alive? It may mean nothing to you, but I don't want us caught just because you want to take a damn swim!"

Lia's mouth dropped open, completely stunned by the venom in Mark's voice. She frowned and stood, stepping towards the bank. She hadn't thought about that, and now she hung her head in shame at her lack of consideration. Mark turned away as she moved closer, and she sheepishly began to pull her dress on over her wet skin.

"I'm sorry," she mumbled, quickly tying the laces.

"Let's get going," Mark said brusquely, moving towards the wagon. "My father was able to put John to sleep, so at least there won't be any screaming."

Ben was resting in the back of the wagon, John cradled in his arms, and Lia smiled when she saw them.

"Ben," she whispered, and he opened his eyes slightly. "It's time to go." He sighed, closing his eyes again, and she had a thought. "Do you want to stay with the baby for a while?" she asked, and Ben quickly nodded. Her chest swelled with relief, glad to finally have a chance to ride in the front of the wagon and out of the suffocating heat.

Excited, she ran to the front of the wagon. Mark was already sitting in the driver's seat, and he made a strange face when he saw her.

"What are you doing?" he asked, watching her step up. Lia sat down next to him and grinned broadly.

"Your father's taking a nap with John," she answered happily, gesturing for Mark to start moving. "I get to ride with you." He didn't seem pleased by the news, and her spirits fell. "You don't want me to, do you?" she asked disappointedly.

"It's fine," he said quickly, stiffening and whistling at the horses. "Just so long as we can keep going."

The next few hours were painful. Mark pretended she didn't exist, ignoring her attempts at conversation, and by the time it began to get dark Lia's throat hurt from fighting off tears. She didn't understand why Mark was treating her this way, and why he wouldn't respond to hardly anything she said.

"Are you mad at me?" Lia finally asked, wondering why he was so quiet. Mark shook his head, giving her a reassuring smile, but she didn't believe him. "You and your father talk the whole time you're driving," she pointed out, crossing her arms. "But you haven't said a word to me."

"What's there to talk about?" Mark countered, shrugging. "I can't exactly go on and on about work with *you*, now can I?" Lia studied his face, then frowned

"What's wrong?" she asked, twisting her mouth into a pout. His jaw was set and his lips were pursed.

"Nothing," he mumbled in reply.

"Mark, you're a terrible liar," Lia told him firmly, crossing her arms. "Tell me what's wrong." There was silence, then he finally spoke.

"Sometimes you're really selfish, you know that?" Mark snapped suddenly, and her eyes grew wide.

"What?" she stammered, completely taken aback. He sighed heavily, and she could hear his teeth grinding as he tried to calm himself.

"I know you've had a tough time, Lia," Mark went on, his voice strained. "I understand that. But you throw a tantrum and risk our lives for a stupid swim?" The leather reins squeaked in his tightly-clenched fists.

"I already apologized about earlier!" Lia retorted, confused at his anger. Mark scoffed.

"Sorry wouldn't have made much of a difference if Thomas had shown up!" he hissed. "But all you could think of is yourself!" She didn't know how to respond, and they fell silent, both of them brooding.

"I already told you I'm sorry!" she repeated. "What else do you want from me?" Mark glanced away from the road long enough to glare at her.

"Maybe you could grow up a bit!" he replied hotly, and she couldn't hide the hurt on her face at his words. "Like I said, I understand what you went through, but..."

"How the hell could you even think you understand?" Lia snarled, her voice rising as the emotions she had locked away inside of her suddenly broke free. How dare he try to sympathize with her! "You couldn't possibly know!" Hot tears filled her eyes as indignant rage flooded her, and the words rushed out of her in a torrent.

"You don't know what it feels like to sell yourself for a bit of bread! You've never felt the shame, the utter humiliation, of so many different filthy hands touching you each night! Or what it's like to feel them tear you open to get their wants!" Mark opened his mouth to speak, but Lia wouldn't be interrupted.

"I close my eyes and I see *his* face, Mark!" She was practically screaming now, her voice ringing out and echoing in the evening air. Her chest hurt, and she could almost feel the weight of the dead bastard's bulk on top of her, suffocating her. She gasped a breath. "I still feel him inside me, and I know I'll never forget! Can you honestly tell me you know what that's like? Then, to stand in the cold and invite the bastards in, when all you want to do is curl up and die? I wish the river had taken me that night! I wish I had died! I wish you'd never found me! I wish..." Her voice trailed off into sobs, and she buried her face in her hands as her shoulders shook from her cries. It hurt so much to think about it, to relive the pain and terror she felt in the alley that night, and to admit that after being attacked she had willingly sold herself for a few coins.

"Lia," Mark whispered softly, reaching towards her. He put his arm around her shoulders and tried to pull her close to him, but she wrenched away.

"Stop the wagon," she managed to say, shuddering as she swallowed back a sob. "Just stop, now!" He immediately obeyed, and the wagon slowed to a halt.

Without another word, Lia jumped down from the seat and ran to the back of the wagon. She pulled back the dusty linen cover, ignoring Ben's wide-eyed, concerned stare.

"Get out!" she commanded, quickly wiping her face as she gestured for Ben to move.

"I'm sorry, Lia," Ben breathed. He stepped out of the wagon and reached for her, enveloping her in a tight embrace.

"Let me go!" Lia screamed, her voice muffled in his shoulder. Ben ignored her, and she flailed helplessly at him, fighting to break free. He was strong; he wouldn't let her go, and she finally allowed herself to collapse in his grasp, her tears flowing unrestrained.

"You go ahead and cry, love," Ben soothed, stroking her hair gently. "You ignore that foolheaded boy, you hear?"

"I'm so ashamed!" she wailed, beating at him with her fists. She couldn't think; her heart felt as though a red-hot blade had seared her very being. The humiliation she had felt on the streets was fresh again, and she wanted to sink through the ground and disappear. "I just want it to go away!" she cried. "I want to go home! I want my Mum, I don't want to be here anymore! I just want to go home!"

"I know, sweetheart, I know," Ben whispered, squeezing her tighter. "I'm sorry, love, I wish I could make this go away."

They stood there, motionless and silent save for Lia's sobs. John began to cry, and she managed to draw a deep, calming breath.

"I have to feed him," she choked out, pulling away from Ben. He held her a moment longer, giving her one final squeeze before releasing her.

"You ignore that boy of mine, you hear me?" he told her firmly, taking the end of his shirt and wiping her face. "You just forget him now, and worry about you and that little one in there." Lia's chin quivered as another wave of tears threatened to pour out of her, but she set her jaw and nodded. Ben leaned over and kissed her cheek, then he held his hand out to help her into the wagon.

They travelled through the night, stopping only to cook a quick dinner and rest the horses. Lia lay in the dark wagon, listening to the hushed sounds of Mark and Ben's conversation. They were, no doubt, talking about her, and she felt her tears start afresh. Ben's embrace had been comforting, but she wanted her mother more than anything. Her mother would know what to say even more than Ben, and Lia choked on the lump in her throat.

Her anger towards Mark had faded, leaving a bitter taste in her mouth. She knew he had been right; she was selfish. At the same time, though, he had no right to tell her that he understood what she had been through. She sighed and closed her eyes. Now she wished she had kept her temper, and she couldn't help feeling naked and exposed as she remembered the way she had described her feelings. Both Mark and Ben now knew more about the details of her experiences than she wanted them to, and her skin crawled as she shuddered with embarrassment. Depressed and feeling alone, when Ben told her dinner was ready she refused, saying she wasn't hungry. Surprisingly, he didn't press the issue.

"Get some rest, Lia," he told her, cradling her cheek in his hand before leaving her alone again. "Things will be brighter when we get to Tannenbury, you'll see." Lia hoped he was right.

The next morning, Mark and Ben were bright and cheerful despite their long, sleepless night, encouraged by the knowledge that they would soon arrive at their destination. They stopped to cook, and Lia could hear their quiet, excited chatter as they cooked.

She had remained in the wagon, silent and brooding, throughout the night, stirring only when the men slowed for rest stops. She hadn't gotten much sleep; she had lain awake for hours before finally dozing off, and she was exhausted when Ben told her it was time for breakfast. After she refused to eat again, Mark came to the wagon.

"You didn't eat," he told her, and Lia glared at him, her eyes filled with hurt. She glanced away.

"I know," she said, forcing an even tone. He gave her a look and shrugged.

"You're going to be hungry soon," he sang knowingly, his eyes sparkling with amusement at her stubbornness. Lia ignored him, pretending to focus entirely on the baby, and after a long moment she heard him walk away. Her chest heaved with the memory of her tumultuous emotions from the night before, but she managed to keep her tears in check. A moment later Mark reappeared, and she looked up with misty-eyed surprise.

"Here," he said, handing her a plate of food. "Just in case you get hungry." She mournfully met his gaze, and he sighed. "I'm sorry, Lia," he soothed gently. "I'm sorry I got mad yesterday. You're right, I can never understand what you went through, and I never should have said I did. I'm sorry." She took a deep breath, grateful for his apology.

"It's okay," Lia answered. She smiled slightly, feeling a little better. "I'm sorry, too. I've been thinking about what you said, and you're right. I can be selfish, and I'm sorry if I've been a burden to you." Mark's eyes snapped forward, and his gaze was unwavering.

"No, Lia," he told her firmly. "I was just tired and worried. I'm glad I can be here for you. I was just a bit overwhelmed, that's all. You're not a burden, Lia. Please, just forget everything I said yesterday, I mean it."

"Well, I'm sorry anyway," Lia answered, studying his face. Mark smiled warmly, and she shrugged, glancing at the plate of food he had brought her. "Maybe I am a little hungry," she said, reaching for a biscuit.

"Are you two getting along again?" Ben asked, walking up to the wagon. Mark and Lia exchanged a look before nodding.

"Good!" Ben exclaimed, grinning broadly and slapping Mark on the back as he winked at Lia. "I knew a good whipping would do the trick!"

"Ha!" Mark scoffed, rolling his eyes as he chuckled. "You haven't whipped me since I was knee-high, old man!" Ben's face straightened, and he raised a brow.

"Maybe you need a quick reminder of what a good lashing feels like," he warned, his voice low and his expression serious. Mark laughed nervously at his father's look.

"He wouldn't really whip me," Mark told Lia, seeming as though he was trying to convince himself rather than her. He and his father stared at each other for a moment.

"Don't tempt me, boy," Ben said, raising a finger of caution. "I promise you one thing, if you make my Lia cry again you'll get more than a whipping from this 'old man' of yours!" His face broke into relaxed grin. "You remember those words, son, you hear? Now, let's pack up and get going, now, shall we?" He motioned towards the breakfast dishes.

"Yes, sir," Mark answered quickly, moving in the direction of the campfire, and Lia giggled with amusement. She was a little unsure if the exchange she had just witnessed was a joke or not, but she could almost picture Ben Samuels giving his grown son a lashing.

"And cut me a green switch to bring along, just in case," Ben called playfully. Laughing to himself, he turned to Lia, his eyes sparkling. "He's a good boy, he is," Ben told her, pride in his voice. "Don't hold yesterday against him, love, he didn't mean what he said."

"I won't, Ben," Lia promised, her spirits lifted. "And thank you for...for..." Her voice trailed off, and Ben shushed her.

"No thanks needed, child," he told her, leaning into the wagon and kissing her forehead. "You should know that I got used to the idea of having you as a daughter a long time ago, when Mark first told me he wanted to marry you, and I don't think of you as anything less, no matter what happened between you two. You're family, Lia, and we're going to stick close together, you hear?" She nodded, surprised at how deeply comforting his words were. "Eat your breakfast, now, we don't want you losing your strength. We'll be in Tannenbury by nightfall." Lia happily obeyed.

• • •

Chapter Thirty-Three

When they arrived in Tannenbury, Mark and Ben were overjoyed to find that the blacksmith's position was still open, and that a medium-sized, two-bedroom house next to the shop was included with the job. The men unpacked quickly, then they set out to get their bearings, leaving Lia and the baby at home. When they returned, Mark told Lia about the town.

The town was smaller than Blackmoor, but it was still bigger than Brunbury, and there would be more than enough work to provide for their needs. It was a farming community, and Lia was excited when she learned that expansive fields surrounded the town, thinking of how she missed wandering as she had back home. The townspeople were pleasant, a refreshing change from the sour faces of the people in Blackmoor, and Mark was convinced they would be happy there.

The house was musty smelling but solidly built, and there was a large yard dotted with full grown shade trees. Apples and pears were ripening on the branches of a line of fruit trees along the edge of the property, and there would be plenty to harvest and store in the cellar for the coming winter. Before he had moved away, the previous blacksmith had cleared a huge area for a garden, and when spring came there would be room for a large crop of vegetables.

Lia busied herself straightening the house while Mark and Ben cleaned up the blacksmith's shop. She threw all the windows open to air out the mustiness, then focused on sweeping what looked like years of dust from the floors and shelves. When she was done, she unpacked their belongings and began organizing the house. After almost three days of feverish bustling about, she was finally satisfied with the somewhat clean appearance of the house, and she made her way to the shop to get some money from Mark to buy food for the evening's dinner.

The blacksmith's shop was more of a small barn, and the large, wooden, double doors were thrown open in the heat of the afternoon. As she approached, she could hear Mark and Ben arguing.

"I can't tell her!" Mark exclaimed, exasperated.

"The longer you wait, the worse it'll be," Ben answered, his voice strained as he tried to persuade his son to listen to him. "Believe me, I know."

"You don't understand Lia the way I do," Mark told him knowingly. "It's not going to matter if I tell her today or a hundred years from today!"

As Lia listened, her blood pounding in her ears, she wasn't sure if she should be afraid or enraged at their secretiveness.

"Do you want me to do it?" Ben asked. "I know you're afraid, son, but she needs to know, and soon."

"I'm not afraid!" Mark retorted, his voice growing angry. "I just don't want to hurt her like that, especially after that fight we had the other day!"

"You're being a selfish coward, Mark," Ben said. "You're more worried about how you'll feel than you are about her. I won't tell her," he promised, caution in his voice. "But you need to be a man and do it. Soon."

The conversation seemed over, and Lia couldn't contain herself any longer. Stepping into the shop, her face dark with fear, she glanced back and forth between the two startled men in front of her.

"Lia!" Ben stammered, his eyes darting towards Mark. "How long have you been standing there?"

"Long enough," she answered quietly, staring at Mark. "What don't you want to tell me?" Mark looked trapped, and his eyes begged his father for help.

"Is the baby sleeping?" Ben asked quickly, ignoring his son's silent plea. Lia nodded stiffly, and he almost ran to the door. "I think I'll go check on him, maybe sit with him for a while." He left, and Mark and Lia were alone.

She waited for him to speak, but he turned his back, moving towards a box of tools and absorbing himself in putting them away. Tapping her foot impatiently, she realized he wasn't going to start talking, and she stepped forward.

"Mark?" she prodded, reaching out and touching him arm. He froze, glancing down at her hand, and she heard his breath catch in his throat. Still, he remained silent, and she tried not to scream. "Tell me, Mark, I'll be fine. I promise." He turned suddenly and looked at her, and the pain in his eyes frightened her even more than his silence.

"I'm sorry, Lia," he whispered, his voice barely making a sound. She felt herself growing increasingly terrified, but she swallowed hard, waiting for him to go on.

"Mark, you're scaring me," she told him, her voice breaking. She forced a dismissive chuckle. "Come, now, it can't be that bad!"

"But it *is*," Mark said, averting his eyes. He sighed. "Lia," he began, taking her hands in his. Her heart anxiously leaped into her throat as she waited on bated breath for him to speak. "Your parents are dead." Her eyes grew wide at his words, and she stood there, motionless, as she tried to process what he had said.

"What do you mean?" Lia choked out, her mind reeling. "What are you saying?"

"They're dead," he repeated, his face full of dread as he searched her face. Yanking out of his grasp, Lia staggered back.

"I don't believe you!" she hissed, her eyes stinging. She shook her head in disbelief. "No, that's wrong. Your father said they told him to send me their love! That means they were alive when he left! No one's been back to Brunbury since, so how could you possibly know?" She felt faint, and she leaned back for something to rest against. There was nothing behind her, and she lost her balance. Mark moved forward to catch her.

"They would have sent you their love," he told her gently, and Lia felt her legs give out. Sinking to the ground, she stared at him blankly. "My father told you what he knew they would have wanted him to say." She felt as though she were dreaming. Her eyes were dry and empty, and she couldn't grasp what he was saying. Feeling her chest begin to hurt with the pain that rose up within her, she tried to speak.

"How?" she whispered finally, and Mark's face was hesitant.

"Thomas killed them, Lia," he answered after a long pause. "He hanged them. They wouldn't tell him where you'd gone, and he killed them." Lia thought she had known guilt when Belle had died, but that feeling was nothing compared to the emotions that surged through her when she heard what Mark said. They were dead because of her, because she had scorned Thomas. If she hadn't rejected him, if she hadn't taken his eye, maybe he wouldn't have wanted her bad enough to kill them.

Lia couldn't hold her cries back any longer, and she dissolved into wails of sorrow. Mark knelt down next to her, taking her in his arms and holding her quivering body tightly against him. Her stomach hurt as she screamed, and she began to kick and thrash in anguish. She wanted her mother to hold her, to tell her it was nothing but a filthy lie, and her body ached with longing.

Her tears ran out, and she sat on the ground, her chest heaving and her body shuddering with the dry sobs that wracked her being. Mark gently kissed the top of her head as he held her, but she didn't feel it, numb to everything but her heartbreak. It wasn't until she heard the cries of her son ring out in the late afternoon air that she finally moved, stiffly standing to her feet with Mark's help and staggering towards the house.

The news of her parents' deaths was more than Lia felt she could bear, and she spent her days in anguished misery, unable to eat or sleep. She could see their dangling, strangled bodies every time she closed her eyes, and she was tormented by the image of their faces, the same ones she had known and loved her entire life, swelling with decay as they lay in their graves. She felt as if her body and soul had been crushed, as if she was being suffocated every moment of every day.

Finally, after almost two weeks, Mark sent for the doctor, worried when Lia didn't show any signs of improvement.

"You need to sleep, Lia," Mark coaxed, trying to get her to drink the tea he had made from the powdered herbs the doctor had provided. She wrinkled her nose, refusing.

"I'm afraid to sleep," she told him, her eyes bloodshot with exhaustion. "Every time I close my eyes I can hear them choking." Her voice broke, and Mark reached out a comforting hand.

"But you need rest," he insisted, again trying to make her drink. "Think of the baby, Lia! How are you going to take care of him if you're not healthy?" His words rang in her ears, and she knew he was right.

Lia eyed the cup of steaming liquid, then took it from him and swallowed it down. She coughed, trying not to gag, and Mark moved a cup of fresh water to her lips to wash the foul taste from her mouth.

"My father is playing with John," Mark told her, sitting down on a chair next to the bed. "I'll stay with you for a bit."

The moments ticked by. The doctor had promised that the tea would work within a few minutes, but after almost an hour Lia was still awake. She could see Mark watching her with worried eyes, nervous as he counted each passing second, and she hoped he would stay by her side if she fell asleep.

A heaviness slowly began to settle onto her eyelids, and she sighed as she felt the tea begin to take effect. She was leaning against the wall at the head of the bed, her eyes unblinking, when Mark stood to his feet. He moved her onto her pillow, then he covered her with a blanket.

"Go to sleep, love," he whispered, leaning down and kissing her forehead.

Lia opened her eyes, blinking in confusion as she sat up and looked around. Everything was exactly as she remembered, but the colors were brighter, as if the room itself was alive and breathing, and the intense, sharp, clarity of her surroundings almost hurt her eyes. The sun was shining brightly, pouring through her window and filling the very air with warmth.

"I must be dreaming," she muttered under her breath, falling back onto her bed and pulling her quilt over her face in disappointment. She peeked out from under the blanket only a moment later, gazing at her room a second time, and she couldn't contain her giggle of breathless excitement. She didn't care if it wasn't real. She was home.

Leaping to her feet, she moved quickly to her window, throwing it open. A tiny pair of wrought-iron turtles was sitting on her windowsill, a gift from Mark, and she laughed with giddy happiness as she clutched them to her chest, unable to believe her eyes. She darted around her room, joyfully touching all of the childhood belongings she had left behind.

The gentle sound of a woman humming drifted up from the kitchen, and Lia's heart stopped when she recognized the voice. Now she knew she was dreaming, and longing ached in her chest. She held her breath, afraid to descend down the ladder for fear that she would wake up before she reached the bottom.

The humming grew slightly louder, calling to her, and she couldn't stand it any longer. She stepped towards the opening in her floor, glancing down into the sunshine-filled kitchen. Summoning her courage amid the anguish that threatened to spill from within her, she gingerly put her foot on the top rung of the ladder.

When she reached the floor, she turned and inhaled sharply, her throat growing sore as she gasped back a sob. She stared, terrified that if she blinked the thin, familiar figure would vanish.

Her mother was facing away, her shoulders rising and falling as she kneaded bread dough on the rough, wooden table, her voice ringing out clear as a bell as she cheerfully sang. Her hair was thrown up in a messy knot atop her head, the dark, auburn strands wisping out in all directions, each thin piece vividly illuminated by the sunlight pouring through the open windows. The worn, green calico work dress hung from her slender frame just as it always had, and Lia's face crumpled as tears rolled down her cheeks.

Lia moved across the floor, her feet silent, and she slowly reached out. Her fingers brushed against her mother's back, and Rachel turned quickly, startled.

"Lia!" she exclaimed, throwing her hands up in surprise. "I didn't know you were awake!" Small clouds of flour rose from her skin, filling the air with shimmering particles of sunlit gold. The gentle breeze that wafted over the sweet-smelling flowers outside flowed into the room and carried the glittery dust away in tiny, dancing swirls, leaving in its wake the warm smell of spring.

Lia gazed at her mother's soft brown eyes and beautiful features, memorizing what she saw and locking the image away in her mind. She extended her hand again, feeling the smooth skin under her fingers as she touched her mother's cheek.

Rachel's eyes searched her daughter's face, a sad smile playing on her lips, and she opened her arms wide. With a quiet, mournful cry, Lia let herself fall into her mother's embrace, burying her face in the familiar comfort. She breathed deep of her mother's scent, closing her eyes as she promised herself to always remember.

"It's all right, Lia," Rachel soothed, stroking Lia's hair. "Come, now, it's all right." The pain in her chest was more than she could bear, and she clung to her mother as she felt her legs grow weak with anguish.

"But it's not," Lia sobbed, sinking to the floor and hiding her face in her mother's skirt. "I can't bear the thought of never seeing you again!" Rachel shushed her, kneeling down to cradle her face.

"None of that, child," she said, gently scolding her. Lia tried to catch her breath, whimpering and gasping as she choked back her sobs, but she couldn't force the tears to stop.

"I want to come home," Lia whispered, her body quivering as she cried. "Please, Mum, just let me come home."

"Lia," Rachel breathed, lifting her daughter's face. "My beautiful Lia." Taking the corner of her skirt, she gently wiped the tears from Lia's eyes. "You'll make it through this," she said, her voice strong with confidence. "No matter what you may think." She leaned forward and kissed Lia's forehead, the warmth of her touch washing over Lia's face and travelling down into the tips of her fingers and toes.

She grew quiet as she held Lia close, rocking her back and forth and murmuring comfortingly into her ear. "My love," she breathed. "My beautiful, strong Lia." Lia savored every moment through her sorrow, her heart burning with the knowledge that she would never again seek comfort on her mother's lap.

"It's not your fault, child," Rachel whispered. Her words struck Lia deep inside, resonating throughout her soul. "I still love you, just as I always have." No sound came from Lia's throat as she

opened her mouth to scream, the guilt that had filled her rising up in her belly and escaping out into the air where it disappeared.

"Now," her mother said, reaching down to wipe Lia's face again. "Why don't you help me finish this bread?" Lia nodded quickly, sniffling as she stood to her feet.

As she took her place across from her mother, Lia fell silent, watching Rachel's small, strong hands as they beat and pummeled the dough. She remembered standing in the very same place as a child, watching her mother knead bread every morning. Now, the only thing that had changed was that Lia was no longer small, and her eyes stung as she desperately wished she was a little girl again.

Rachel looked up, her face glowing as she worked, and she smiled.

"Tell me about him," she said, her eyes bright with excitement, and somehow Lia knew exactly who she meant. "Tell me what he's like."

"He's a beautiful baby," Lia answered, her lip trembling as she tried to keep from crying. "He's a little angel. I named him after Papa." Her mother smiled dreamily.

"He'll be a good boy," Rachel said proudly, her voice firm. "Mark will teach him how to be a man."

Stepping back from the table and moving to Lia's side, Rachel held her daughter at arm's length, giving her a long look.

"You're a beautiful, strong woman, Lia," she smiled. "I am so proud of you." Lia felt a sudden panic rise up within her, and she glanced towards the window. She could see that the sun was setting, the sky bursting into flame with vibrant, majestic hues of orange and pink and deep red, the fiery colors beginning to cool and darken as the night slowly stole their warmth. The fading light washed over the *proud, waving flowers and grasses of the fields outside, turning everything it touched into gold.*

"No," Lia choked, frantically reaching up and taking hold of her mother. "I don't want to go!" Rachel's face was beaming with happiness as she kissed her daughter's cheek. The bronze light from the final rays of the sun lingered on her expectant smile, her eyes shining as she glanced towards the front door. Lia followed her gaze, her heart leaping into her throat as another wave of longing washed over her.

"Where's my Lia!" her father called out, his booming voice filling the room as he threw the door open and stomped inside.

"Papa!" Lia cried, her voice breaking as she ran towards him. Her father squeezed her tightly in his arms, his grip suffocating her for a moment, then he released her and held her shoulders tightly in his grasp. His face looked much younger than she remembered, and his gray eyes crinkled at the corners as he beamed at her proudly. His skin was smeared with dirt from the fields, and his clothes smelled of earth. She remembered how much she had hated the scent of dirt, but now she wanted to carry it with her forever.

"I love you, daughter," he said, his voice strong and clear. "And I'm proud of you. I wouldn't trade you for all the sons or gold in the world." He hugged her again, holding her close. "Take care of that little boy, my beautiful Lia," he whispered in her ear. "He'll be a strong young man, if he's anything like his mother."

The room was almost dark now, and her father and mother stood side by side, their arms around each other as they smiled happily at her. She felt helpless as she watched their faces fade in the dim of the oncoming night, and she stretched her hands out to them one last time. Suddenly remembering, she screamed after them, hoping they would hear her.

"I love you, Mum!" she cried, straining her ears for a sign that they had heard her. "Papa! I love you!"

"Lia?" Mark whispered in the darkness, slowly cracking her door open. "Are you all right?"

As the sleep left her, Lia felt suddenly weightless, and she realized that the heaviness in her chest was gone. Squeezing her eyes shut, she tried to picture her parents again, and tears streamed silently down her face. This time they were tears of relief, and her parents' words rang in her ears. They still loved her.

Mark moved towards her, and she could see his shadow standing over the bed. Her arms ached with sudden longing, and, without thinking, she reached up and took his hand. He was surprised.

"I just wanted to check on you," he stammered quietly, but she didn't answer, pulling him into the bed beside her. Resting her head on his chest, she wept soundlessly as he held her. He stayed by her side for the rest of the night, squeezing her tightly in his arms while she slept.

• • •

Chapter Thirty-Four

TWO MORE WEEKS PASSED, and August neared its end. Lia had accepted her parents' death for the most part, and the crippling sorrow she had felt was replaced by rage. Part of her almost hoped that Thomas would come find her, that way she could kill him like she should have in the barn that night in Brunbury.

According to Mark and Ben, however, that hope would never become reality. As it turned out, Tannenbury was surrounded by the lands of the Tierney family, and the Tierneys hated the Greenes. Apparently, many years ago, Thomas' uncle had carried off Lord Tierney's daughter, and when she managed to escape she had returned home beaten and bruised, rendered childless from the abuse she had suffered at the hands of the Greenes. The Tierneys had never forgotten, and they vowed to take revenge on any member of the Greene family they could get their hands on. It was common knowledge among the townspeople that any member of the Greene family who set foot on Tierney property was marked for death, and a reward of two hundred gold tokens would be paid to anyone bearing a Greene's head.

Although saddened by the thought that she would never repay Thomas for his savagery, Lia was also relieved to know that they were safe. There was more than enough work for Mark and Ben, and they made a good living. For the most part, Lia was content.

Ben and Mark took turns spending their afternoon breaks sitting with John while he napped, allowing Lia to spend time in the fields. She knew they felt bad for her, and that they were trying to give her a chance to recover from the emotional turmoil of the past weeks. She appreciated the opportunity to be alone, and while she never wandered past the field in front of her home it seemed that the short distance was more than enough for her to breathe and try to gather her thoughts.

In mid-September, crop harvest started in Tannenbury. The women in town had discovered that Lia knew how to put up preserves, and she was soon recruited to take part in the massive canning parties they held in their rush to get perishable fruits and vegetables jarred for storage. Lia hated canning, and she had refused the invitation to join in at first, but Mark had convinced her to go, telling her that it might do her some good to get to know the other women. As she prepared to head home after a long day spent trapped in the company of the gossiping ladies, she cursed herself for being stupid enough to listen to Mark's opinion on the matter.

Lia waved goodbye to the women and stepped out into the dark, moonless night, John's sleeping form cradled in her arms. Her home wasn't far, maybe fifteen minutes or so from town, but she began to feel on edge as she slowly and carefully placed her feet to keep from losing the path in the pitch blackness. Gripping John's sleeping form tightly against her chest, she nervously peered into the distance, trying to catch a glimpse of the lighted windows of her house. She couldn't see anything.

A stone skittered away in the darkness behind her. Lia paused and listened for a moment, straining her ears to hear over the sound of her racing heart. The noise came again, and she froze, unable to move, whimpers of terror instantly rising in her throat. Her muscles tensed as her skin began to crawl, and she sank to her knees.

"Who's there?" she wailed in a breathless whisper, her blood pounding in her ears. She wasn't sure which was worse: the thought of receiving an answer from somewhere in the blackness or the thought of no one responding. The night was silent now, save for the gentle wind blowing through the trees.

"Is that you, Lia?" Mark called, and she let out a quiet scream. He was standing in front of her within a moment, and the relief she felt made her entire body hurt.

"Calm down, it's just me," he said, pulling her to her feet. "I knew you girls had a lot of work to do, and I thought now would be about the right time to start heading over to walk you home." She swallowed hard.

"You were just in time," she managed to say, her voice wavering. "Thank you."

Lia skipped dinner, going to bed immediately after arriving home. The fear she had felt in the darkness lingered in her mind as she tried to sleep, and every time she closed her eyes the face of her attacker vividly appeared before her. She couldn't remember how long it had been since she'd last felt this terror as deeply as she now did.

The memory of the man's weight on her chest stole her breath, and her stomach turned at the thought of his touch. John stirred next to her, and for the first time since he had been born Lia felt revulsion well up inside of her. The baby was *his,* and in that moment she couldn't stand the thought of having a living, breathing piece of the bastard right there in her bed.

She hated herself for feeling that way, and the guilt that burned in her heart tried, desperately, to devour the loathing she felt for her sweet, beautiful son. The flame wasn't strong enough, though, and she leaped from the bed after only a moment, picking up the sleeping baby and depositing him in his cradle.

Weeping, Lia sank onto the floor in a corner of the room, burying her face in her knees. The bedroom door creaked open, and she glanced up to see Mark's shadow enter the room. He sat down next to her, gathering her into his arms. She didn't speak, too overcome by her cries, and he held her tightly against him as she sobbed.

"I can't stand him right now!" she wailed between halting breaths, tearing at her hair as she stared at the cradle that held her sleeping son. "I can't stand to look at him! My poor John, my sweet baby, and I hate him!" Her words dissolved into incoherence, and Mark shushed her.

"It's okay, love," he whispered.

"No, it's not!" she cried, shaking her head. "He's my child! I shouldn't hate him!"

"You don't, Lia," Mark told her firmly. "I know you still love him. You hate what happened to you, not him."

"I want this to go away! I don't ever want to feel this again!"

"I know, love, I know," Mark soothed, kissing the top of her head.

"I don't want to be afraid of the dark anymore!" Lia wept. "I don't want to be afraid anymore!"

When Lia awoke the next morning, Mark was gone, and she was lying in her bed with John resting beside her. The memory of the night before weighed heavily on her, and as she gazed at her son's sleeping face she couldn't believe she had thought, even for a moment, that she hated him.

"Lia?" Ben called through her door, knocking gently.

"Come in," she answered, and he quietly walked into the room. He pulled the chair in the corner close to the edge of her bed, concern furrowing his brow.

"Mark told me what happened," he began, reaching for her hand. He gently stroked her fingers, his worried eyes searching her face. "Are you okay?" Lia sighed, nodding slightly. Ben seemed to relax a bit before continuing.

"You know, I heard what you said that day in the wagon, when you and Mark were arguing," he told her quietly, his voice soft. "But I didn't realize the full meaning of it until Mark talked to me last night." She lifted her gaze to meet his, and she understood immediately what he was talking about. His eyes drifted towards the sleeping baby, and he smiled.

"It doesn't matter," Ben told her, pride in his voice. "He's *Mark's* son, not that bastard's. And that means he's my grandson just the same as he was the first time I laid eyes on him." Lia was overwhelmed by his words. She opened her mouth to speak, but Ben shushed her.

"I love you, child," he told her, squeezing her hand. "You've been through more than most people could ever imagine, and you can feel however you need to. Mark and I both know how much you love your John, and you don't need to feel guilty just because the memory of that dead pig still hurts you."

"Ben," Lia said, her voice breaking. "Why aren't you ashamed of me? How can you be so understanding of something so terrible?"

"I told you before, child," he answered, smiling at her. "I got used to the idea of having you as a daughter a long time ago, and I love you as if you were my own. How could I be ashamed of you?" She knew, now, where Mark had gotten his kindness, and her heart swelled.

"How is it that you always say just the right thing?" she asked gratefully. Ben chuckled, shrugging.

"Old age, Lia," he said, his face bright. "Everything else is giving out on me, but at least I've got a little wisdom to share before my mind goes, too." He stood to his feet. "Mark went into town to tell the ladies that you aren't feeling well and won't be back to help them finish their work," he told her, winking. "I know you must be disappointed, but I'm sure you'll survive." Lia rolled her eyes, laughing quietly.

"I don't think I could stand another moment listening to their babbling!" she said, making a face.

"I thought you might feel that way," Ben smiled. "You don't seem like the kind to enjoy the nonsense of gossip."

"You're right about that!" she chuckled. She glanced out the window, and she could see that the morning was growing late. "I'll start lunch," she said, moving to stand to her feet.

"I'll give you a hand," he told her. John opened his eyes, stirred from sleep by Lia's movements, and Ben reached for him.

"Better yet, I'll let you cook while I play with this handsome little man!" The baby yawned, then smiled up at Ben's face. Lia wrinkled her nose.

"You can change him while you're at it!" she chuckled, ignoring Ben's protests as she made her way to the kitchen.

October came, turning the leaves of the trees orange and red in its wake. Just a week after John turned five months old, Mark and Ben knocked on Lia's bedroom door with some news.

"We've gotten word of a job in Pryham," Ben told her. "It's a big job that pays well, and we do need the money, but we'll be gone for four days." Lia shrugged.

"It's not hot out anymore," she replied. "I'll survive in the back of the wagon for a few days." Mark pursed his lips, shaking his head.

"We need the wagon for tools and supplies," he said, his brow creased with worry. "You would have to stay here." Surprised, Lia thought for a moment. Part of her was relieved to hear that she couldn't go, and she gave the men a confident smile to counter their anxious expressions.

"You do realize I survived for months in absolute hell without either of you, right?" she asked laughingly, brushing off their concern. "I think I can make it a few days." Neither of them looked convinced, but it seemed that there was no other choice.

The next morning, Ben and Mark left at daybreak. The men kissed John goodbye as he slept, then Lia followed the two outside. Ben hugged her tightly, bidding her farewell as he fussed with worry, and she gave him a peck on the cheek, reassuring him that she would be fine. Mark finished loading the wagon, then stepped back onto the porch to say goodbye.

"I'll be fine, you two," she promised them again, and they reluctantly climbed into the wagon to leave.

The house was much quieter with Ben and Mark gone, and Lia missed them both, but she did her best to force herself to believe she didn't mind. It was worse at night than during the day, when she was alone in the dark with her thoughts, and she found herself counting the hours until they would return. She cursed herself for her weakness; she remembered when she loved being alone, and now, after only two short days, she was nearly reduced to tears at the feeling of loneliness that settled over her.

On the third night, in the midst of her light sleep, something startled her, and she slowly opened her eyes in the darkness, unsure of what had caught her attention. She held her breath as she strained her ears, listening intently for whatever had woken her.

Only a moment later, Lia heard a slight noise coming from outside, and she sat up in bed. She stood to her feet, careful not to wake John, then made her way into the kitchen. She glanced out the window, and she was surprised to see a light on in the shop.

"They're back early," she muttered to herself, unbolting the front door. She lit a lantern and stepped out into the cool October night, briskly walking towards the shop.

The double doors were thrown open, and Lia peeked inside. A lantern was burning brightly on a hook next to the door, but a quick search revealed that no one was there. She felt a cold finger of fear crawl up her spine as she thought of John, asleep in the empty house. After extinguishing the mysteriously burning lantern, she spun around and quickly began to walk back.

368

As she approached the house, Lia picked up her pace. She was almost there, and the unknown terror that had gripped her was disappearing with each step she took. Bursting through the front door and locking it behind her, she breathed heavily with relief as she stood in the kitchen, mockingly laughing at herself for her fear.

Lia gently cracked her bedroom door open and moved towards her bed. She blinked, disbelief filling her, then panic sank its cold talons into her heart. Her son wasn't there. Searching the room with her eyes, a frantic scream rising in her throat, her gaze rested on a dark, shadowed figure standing in the corner of the room.

"Hello, love," the simpering voice sang out. Her stomach turned when she recognized him, and fear rendered her immobile when she saw her sleeping son cradled in his arms. "I've been looking for you."

• • •

Chapter Thirty-Five

Thomas' face flashed with excitement as he moved towards Lia, a patch covering the eye she had ripped from his skull that day in the barn. Mark had said the Greenes couldn't set foot in Tannenbury, and she couldn't understand how Thomas was now standing before her.

"How did you find me?" she stammered, her eyes wide with confusion as she stared at him.

"I've been looking for you," Thomas repeated. "You and I have some unfinished business." He was right about that, and in her mind's eye she could almost see his hands dripping with her parents' blood. She felt her body begin to tremble with hatred, but she steeled herself, shaking her head to clear her thoughts.

"Give him to me," Lia whispered, holding her arms out for the baby. Thomas raised an eyebrow, relishing his control over her, and the only thing that kept her from flying at him to tear out his throat was the thought of her child getting hurt in the process.

"Is it Mark's?" Thomas curled his lip with disdain as he looked down at John. The loathing on his face told her that her baby wasn't safe, and she shook her head, her heart pounding with fear.

"I was attacked," she quickly explained, her eyes wide with the panic she was trying not to show. "Back home, before I met you." Thomas scoffed.

"Do you really think me a fool?" he snarled. She wanted to answer yes with all of her being, to tell him what she really thought of him, but she held her tongue.

"It's true," Lia answered hollowly. "I was taken in the alley next to the tavern, just a short time before I met you." Thomas furrowed his brow, considering her explanation, then his face darkened.

"You were pregnant when I met you?" he hissed, anger rising in his voice. "And yet you made me beg for even a kiss?"

"Give me my son!" she demanded, ignoring his question. Her voice became pleading, and she slowly moved towards him, her eyes filling with tears of defeat. "Please, Thomas," she begged. Inside, she was fuming, and she swore to herself that he would pay for her groveling.

After enjoying her humiliation for a long moment, Thomas scoffed arrogantly. Turning up his nose, he finally held the child out to her with a gracious, superior air. Lia held her breath, almost expecting him to pull back, but as the weight of her son settled into her arms she gasped with relief.

"Now," Thomas sneered, stepping closer to her. "On to our business." She swallowed hard against the vomit rising in her throat, knowing full well what his intentions were and that she was helpless against him.

"I won't fight you," she promised, gagging on the words as she spoke. "But only if you leave my son alone." Thomas narrowed his eye, momentarily confused, then he threw his head back in quiet laughter.

"Not here, love!" he told her, grinning maliciously as he studied her dread-filled face. "No, I've been waiting for too long to waste my first time with you *here*." Lia was too confused to feel relieved. She couldn't make sense of why he would search for her so fervently only to choose to bide his time after finally finding her.

Footsteps sounded in the hall, and she glanced up to see a man appear in the doorway. He walked into the darkened room and addressed Thomas.

"Someone will take notice of us," the man said quietly, his head bowed meekly. "Remember, Master Thomas, your family swore that no one will come for you if Lord Tierney finds you here." Understanding filled her as she listened, and suddenly Thomas' reluctance to take her made sense. He was too worried about being found by Lord Tierney to even think of satisfying his wants.

Thomas gave the man a poisonous stare, crossing the floor in a single step and hitting him in the face.

"Do I need a worthless nothing of a peasant to remind me of what my family said?" he snarled. Nervousness mingled with the anger in Thomas' voice, and Lia felt a twinge of satisfaction at the underlying fear she heard in his words. The man cowered, and Thomas decided to take the advice. "Let's go back to camp before we're found," he spat bitterly. Turning to Lia, he smirked at her furious glare.

"I'll not have you draw attention to us," he warned her coldly. "You keep yourself and that child silent or I'll break its filthy neck, do you understand?" She nodded.

Afraid for her son, she allowed herself to be gagged and led away from the house into the night air. As they disappeared into the woods, they were joined by several large, burly men, their massive shapes materializing out of the darkness just outside of town. Thomas ordered two of them to stay behind and keep watch over the house, while Lia was forced to follow the rest of them deep into the thick woods. The group was deathly silent; even their breathing was almost completely inaudible, and the slightest noise elicited a dangerous glare from Thomas.

After an hour of walking, they finally stopped, and Lia was shoved into a wooden cage near several tents that had been pitched between the dense trees. The cage had been crudely constructed from thin saplings, but it was large, and the dirt floor was soft.

In return for allowing her hands to remain untied so she could hold her son, she had promised not to remove the dirty cloth that had been tied around her mouth, and she bitterly kept her word. John had stirred only slightly during the entire ordeal, and now she sat in a corner of her makeshift prison, cradling him as she huddled under the thick, woolen blanket she had been given.

By her count, there were eight men altogether, not including Thomas and the two men keeping watch over her house, and they appeared to have brought nothing but horses and a few supplies with them. There were several small tree stumps protruding from the ground nearby, the remnants of what had been used to fabricate the cage, and she realized that Thomas must have been lying in wait for at least a full day before coming to get her. The idea infuriated her, and her skin crawled at the thought of him silently, secretly watching her.

As she watched the men sitting near their tiny campfire, Lia strained her ears to hear what they were saying. Apparently they felt safe, because, although still hushed, they spoke loud enough for her to catch most of their conversation.

"You have the girl, now," one of the men said, speaking to Thomas from under a heavy shock of brown, stringy hair. "Let's leave before we're discovered!" His broad, dirty face was fearful. Thomas was turned away from her, and while she couldn't see his expression she could hear the venom in his voice.

"Not until I get that bastard blacksmith!" he cursed. "I want them both, and I won't leave until I have him! I won't hear another word from you otherwise, Henry, or from anyone else for that matter!"

"That's unwise, Master Thomas," another man softly reasoned from behind a thick, unkempt beard and mustache. "You'll not survive if Lord Tierney finds you here!"

Thomas lurched forward in the blink of an eye, grabbing the man who dared to speak by the throat and tackling him to the ground.

"I decide what's wise, Nathan!" he hissed, and in the meager light of the fire Lia could see Thomas' shoulders shake with rage. "I won't take the advice of a worthless peasant!" She could hear Nathan choking and gagging as Thomas pinned him down, strangling him.

"Please, Master Thomas!" the man named Henry cried, jumping to his feet. He moved forward, obviously wanting to save the suffocating man from death, but he was too afraid to pull Thomas away. "Not a one of us wants to see you dead! Nathan spoke only out of concern for you, nothing more!" The man's voice was sincere, but Lia could see in his face that he was lying. His words had some effect, though, and Thomas released Nathan from his grip, turning his anger towards Henry.

"You try to save your brother with a lie?" Thomas hissed, standing on his toes as he confronted the man. Even stretched to his full height, Thomas' head barely reached the top of Henry's broad shoulders. "Do you think me such a fool that I would believe that? None of you would be here if your families' lives didn't depend on it!" As Lia watched the argument, she couldn't help thinking that Henry could break Thomas in half with a single sweep of his thick arms.

Still fuming, Thomas sat back down. The other men had fallen silent, all of them averting their eyes and ignoring the fight, but now that it was over they resumed their quiet chatter as though nothing had happened. Nathan picked himself up off the ground, gingerly rubbing his throat and rejoining the circle of men. Thomas glared at him as he sat, then turned his attention to other matters.

"Take her gag off and feed her something," he said to Henry, jerking his head towards Lia's cage. "We're far enough outside the town to stop worrying about someone hearing her if she decides to raise a fuss."

Henry leaped to his feet, instantly obeying Thomas' command. The men had been eating a few blackened, fire-roasted rabbits, and now he moved towards the chewed carcasses, his dirty hands plucking at the overcooked flesh to fill a plate for Lia.

"I want at least three of you on watch at all times," Thomas instructed, standing to his feet and yawning. "And one of you stays near her, you understand? She's not to be let out of your sight!" With that, he stomped towards his tent, disappearing from view.

It took almost an hour for Henry to glean enough flesh from the rabbit bones to form even a handful of meat, and Lia wished she could speak so she could tell him his efforts were wasted. She wasn't hungry, and even if she were she wouldn't eat after the filthy men. When he was finally satisfied with the amount of food he had managed to get for her, Henry approached the cage.

Lia glared at him, but he smiled warmly at her in return. He eyed her cautiously as he bent down to peer at her, and he held the plate out to her, sliding it through a gap between the rough, wooden bars.

"You can take it off now," Henry said quietly, gesturing at the gag. His voice was kind, which surprised her. "I've brought you something to eat." Working her jaw to relieve the cramps that had set in from the tight cloth, Lia turned up her nose in disgust when he offered her the plate.

"I'm not hungry!" she hissed, baring her teeth in a snarl. His eyes opened wide with fear.

"You must eat it!" Henry told her urgently, glancing behind him towards Thomas' tent. "He'll be angry with me if you don't! Master Thomas doesn't want anything happening to you!"

"You mean unless he's the one doing it," Lia corrected, her eyes flashing with anger. "I won't eat that filth!" Henry paused, thinking, and from the look on his face she could tell he was considering forcing the food down her throat.

"Don't even think about it," she warned, setting her jaw defiantly. "I swear, I'll tell Thomas you tried to take me if you so much as raise a finger!" Henry's face filled with panic as he processed her threat. He didn't know what to do, and Lia felt a stab of compassion. From what she had seen and heard, all of them hated

Thomas, and she knew Henry was only there because he had to be. She sighed, gesturing towards the plate.

"You eat it," she whispered. "I won't say a word. I'm not hungry, I ate dinner before you bastards broke into my house." Her voice was edged with bitterness, and she cursed under her breath. John sighed in his sleep, and she rocked him gently, covering him with the blanket as she held him tightly against her. Henry brightened at her suggestion, and he quickly gathered the scraps into his meaty fist and swallowed them down in one quick bite. He smiled at her, relieved, then sat down a short distance away from the cage.

"Master Thomas said you were a lively one," Henry mused, chuckling. "He's talked of nothing but you for months now."

"I'm sure," Lia scoffed sarcastically, making a face. "And did his other wives try to comfort him?" Henry raised a brow and shook his heavy head.

"He sent them all away to work the fields," he told her, his eyes sparkling as he remembered. "It was a sad day at the Greene estate, that's for sure. All those women screaming and wailing and begging him to reconsider. But he's had no time for other women, he only burns for you." Lia ground her teeth together with rage.

"That's my luck," she lamented, cursing again. "The bastard." She paused, giving Henry a sideways glance. "Why are you all so afraid of being found?"

"Lord Tierney will kill us!" Henry breathed, his face instantly growing dark with fear. "He won't abide a Greene stepping foot on his lands!"

"Won't Thomas' family come for him if he's found?" Lia prodded, remembering the bit of conversation she had overheard. "Surely his parents will come for their son!"

"No," Henry told her, his voice full of bitterness. "This was a fool's journey from the start. Master Thomas' parents and uncles warned him to give up this damn pursuit when they heard you and the blacksmith had been seen travelling here. They warned him that he was on his own, and that if he met his fate they would not avenge him." He grimaced. "And yet here we sit, only a half day east from the very home of Lord Tierney himself!" Lia's mind raced, and she was grateful for the man's loose tongue. If she could escape and find her way to Lord Tierney, all her problems would be solved.

"Aren't you afraid for your own safety?" she asked, cocking her head. "Aren't you and the others in danger, too?" Henry nodded grimly.

"Yes," he answered. "But Thomas has promised us each a full year's wage as a reward when we return. Our families will starve without the money, so here we are." Lia nodded slowly, and she almost pitied the man. She remembered the poverty she had seen in the town Thomas' uncle owned, and she could understand why the men would risk the danger of being caught by Lord Tierney.

Satisfied with the information she had been given, Lia yawned dramatically and turned away, hoping Henry would take her hint. He did, and he fell silent, allowing her time to think as she pretended to sleep.

Lord Tierney was close, and she knew he was her only hope. But Thomas had already threatened her son, and she didn't want to think about what he would do if he caught her before she reached the Tierneys. Still, the thought of what lay in store for both her and her son if she stayed with Thomas was even more terrifying, and she knew she had to try.

Henry kept watch for a few hours, then another man took his place. Lia stole a peek at her new guard, seeing him shifting as he tried to make himself comfortable on the ground a few feet away. His eyes were heavy with sleep, and she was almost afraid to hope that he wouldn't be able to stay awake.

The man leaned back against a tree, crossing his arms and shivering. He got up for a moment to retrieve a blanket, then he resumed his place, wrapping himself up tightly and sighing. As she watched, she could see his lids begin to close, and, before long, his breathing slowed. There were two other men a short distance away, but they both had their backs towards her, and her skin flushed hot with nervousness. She couldn't have asked for a more perfect opportunity.

Lia quietly inched her way towards the door of the cage. John made a tiny sound and stretched in her arms, and she held her breath, fear racing through her. The seconds ticked by, but he didn't move again, and she relaxed slightly.

She tried to reach the knotted rope that held the cage door shut. There wasn't much space between the wooden bars, and she couldn't get her hand far enough through. She clenched her jaw in frustration, screaming in her mind for the bars to give so she could get to the knot that prevented her escape, when she realized that the rope was loose enough to turn.

She managed to pull the knot to the inside of the cage, and she tore at the rope with her fingers. The knot was tied too tightly, and her hand began to ache as she fought to loosen it. The sleeping guard stirred, and she froze, her eyes wide as she stared at him. He rolled to the side, his sleeping face pointed directly at her, and she swallowed hard against the panic rising in her belly.

She couldn't untie the rope with only one hand. Pulling her knees forward and resting them against the side of the cage, Lia gently set John on her lap, begging him to stay quiet. Both of her hands now free, she struggled to loosen the knot. Her blood pounded in her head; she could feel herself running out of time.

Finally, the knot came free, and relief momentarily washed over her. Lia glanced at the sleeping man again, then she looked at the other two guards. They were still facing away, talking quietly as they warmed their hands over their small fire. Slowly, she gathered John into her arms and pushed the cage door open.

She silently stepped out of the cage, convinced that the men would take notice of her any second. Her chest was tight, and she felt like she couldn't breathe as she crept away in the darkness. She tiptoed through the woods, trying to put as much distance as she could between herself and the camp. Finally, unable to stand it any longer, Lia began to run, the beams of moonlight that shone through the trees providing barely enough light to see.

She reached a clearing and paused, staring up at the stars as she tried to get her bearings. Henry had said that the camp was only a half day east of the Tierney estate, and she whispered a prayer that she would make it there before Thomas came after her.

She made good time despite the darkness and rough terrain of the woods. John remained asleep, somehow undisturbed by her steps as she held him tightly against her, and she couldn't help the cautious optimism she felt at morning's first light.

Her confidence was short lived. As the sun began to rise up over the treetops, Lia heard the sound of horses, and cold fingers of terror instantly gripped her heart. She cursed and began to run faster, her feet flying over the dead leaves that layered the forest floor. John started to cry, his voice ringing out in the morning, and what little hope she had drained from within her as exhaustion burned her legs.

Lia panted as she ran, frantic as the pounding hoofbeats of the horses came closer. She clawed her way through the low-hanging branches of the trees, numb to the hot streaks they cut across her face. She could hear the men shouting now as they closed in, and she cast a fearful glance behind her.

She didn't see the cliff face looming up in front of her, and she ran face-first into the sheer rock. She was stunned, the jolt knocking her senseless for a moment. Gathering her wits, she gazed at the vine-covered wall barring her path, and she kicked it, screaming with rage. She was trapped, and she sank to the ground in defeat as the first rider came into sight. John was bawling uncontrollably, and tears stung her eyes as she stared down at him, rocking him in a half-hearted attempt at soothing his cries.

"We've got her!" the man shouted. She glared at him, and she didn't bother fighting back as she was pulled up onto his horse.

Thomas was waiting for her when the men brought her back.

"Stupid wench!" he screamed, his face red with anger. Lia's eyes burned with hatred as she was thrown into the cage. The body of the man who had fallen asleep while guarding her was lying on the ground a short distance away, his dead face drawn and pale in the mid-morning sun, but she didn't feel even the slightest bit guilty.

"Try that again!" Thomas warned, his body shaking as he clenched his fists. "I'll make you regret the very day you were born!" She scowled, turning her body away as she began to nurse John. His cries quieted, and she bit her tongue to keep herself from lashing back at Thomas with every filthy curse she could think of.

"Master Thomas," one of the men called, approaching. "Shall we prepare to leave?" Thomas turned, forgetting about Lia as he focused his attention on the man.

"Is there any sign of the Tierneys?" he asked. The man shook his head, and Lia frowned with disappointment. Apparently she hadn't gotten far enough for the Tierneys to take notice of Thomas' men.

"Then we'll stay," Thomas said, walking towards the campfire where the rest of the men were grouped. "Start cooking lunch."

Lia's eyes were bloodshot and tired from her sleepless night, and she seethed as she watched Thomas' every move. He ignored her until he was done eating, then he stood, burped loudly, and approached her with a bowl of soggy porridge.

"Eat," he commanded, sliding the bowl through the bars of the cage. Lia didn't respond.

"You're going to eat," he told her, his voice dangerous. She lifted her gaze, unable to hide her contempt.

"I won't," she told him coldly. "Just leave me alone." His face darkened, then he relaxed and walked away. He returned with three of his men.

"Take the bastard," Thomas commanded, pointing to the baby. Lia gritted her teeth as the men began to open the door to the cage.

"Do I get a spoon?" she spat, reaching out and grabbing the bowl.

"Sorry, love," Thomas answered, smiling triumphantly. "I know you too well for that." Cursing, she began to scoop at the porridge with her fingers, doing her best to spill as much as possible in the dirt.

"You must care for that little bastard of yours," Thomas mused, his face growing thoughtful as he leaned against the cage. "Interesting how you're so quick and willing to obey for fear of that *thing's* safety. Your parents did the same, they preferred to die rather than give up their beloved Lia."

Her eyes grew wide as rage blinded her. She wanted to fly at him, to reach through the bars and choke him. Satisfied with the furious expression on her face, Thomas turned away, chuckling to himself.

• • •

Chapter Thirty-Six

"IT'S ALMOST DARK," Thomas said loudly, addressing his men. "The blacksmith isn't back, and I won't risk waiting any longer. We leave tonight."

Lia was dragged out of the cage once the sun went down. Thomas stood over her, a lantern clutched in his fist. Shining the light on her face, he sneered.

"Hand him the child," he commanded, gesturing towards one of his men. Lia set her jaw, glaring at Thomas as she clutched John in her arms. Thomas rolled his eye. "You'll get *it* back," he snapped, gesturing again. "Or we can rip it from your arms if you'd prefer." Weighing her options, she scowled as she gently handed her son to the waiting man.

"Wise choice," Thomas sang. As Lia watched, the man who was holding John began to walk away, and her heart faltered.

"Where is he going?" she asked, fear rising in her voice. Thomas jerked his head, and another man took hold of her arms.

"To a gentle and painless sleep," Thomas answered, grinning at her. "I don't want a bastard infant, just you."

A new horror filled her as the glow of lanternlight jogged her memory. She remembered something, an image from her dreams, and in her mind's eye she could see her baby's broken body as it had appeared in her nightmares. She couldn't breathe.

"NO!" she shrieked, breaking free from the man holding her. She threw herself at Thomas, frantically clawing at his face.

"Get her off me!" Thomas howled, trying to get away. Lia managed to grab hold of his throat with her teeth, tearing at his flesh as she bit down hard. Blood filled her mouth, and her teeth slipped on his now-slick skin. Repositioning herself quickly, she snapped at the air, finding his ear and tearing at the thin tissue. A large chunk came free, and Thomas screamed like a dying animal.

Strong hands pulled her off of his writhing form only a moment later, and Thomas clutched at his throat and ear, cursing and thrashing on the ground. When he calmed down enough to stand to his feet, and after staunching the flow of blood from the wounds she had inflicted upon him, he lunged at her, punching her in the face. Lia's head snapped back; her vision went white from the force of the blow, and she could feel the warm trickle of blood that leaked from her nose. Her heart sank when she realized she hadn't done any serious damage to Thomas, and she began to sob with helplessness as someone tightly bound her hands in front of her.

"I've changed my mind!" Thomas snarled, taking hold of Lia's blood-soaked face. "We're leaving in the morning, after this filthy whore watches her bastard child die!" He let go of her face and hit her again, the back of his hand splitting her lip open.

"No, Thomas, please!" Lia wailed, her body numb with fear. "Please, I won't fight you again! I won't, just don't hurt him!"

"Let's go!" Thomas shouted, ignoring her. He began to walk, beckoning to the men to follow. Lia felt a hard kick in her back, and she stumbled forward.

"Stop, please!" she begged, collapsing to the ground. "Thomas, no!" He wouldn't listen, and the men began dragging her.

They walked for almost half an hour, stopping when they reached a small field at the edge of the woods. Lia was left in a heap on the ground, and she wept as she watched the men string a rope from the branches of a large tree. She caught sight of the man who had taken John standing near the tree, and she leaped to her feet, running towards her crying baby. No one stopped her until she drew close, then a rough hand caught her shoulder, knocking her to the ground.

"It's okay, love," she whimpered, crawling forward and calling to John. "Hush, love, don't cry!" Even as she tried to soothe her child, her own tears poured down her face, and she looked up as Thomas approached, bloody cloths wrapped around his head and neck as makeshift bandages.

"What are you doing?" Lia cried through halting breaths. Thomas sneered, drinking in her anguish as she was dragged to her feet.

Her hands were lifted above her head, and the rope that dangled from the tree branch was looped around the ropes that bound her wrists.

"Put the child over there!" Thomas commanded, pointing to the clearing. The man who held John obeyed, quickly moving to the middle of the deer-ravaged field and leaving the infant on the ground before rejoining the group.

"No!" Lia screamed, her voice echoing through the trees. "Give me my son! Let me go!" Thomas laughed as he addressed the men.

"Lift her up!" he gleefully yelled. One of the men pulled at the rope, lifting her. The weight of her body strained against the ropes on her wrists, and her arms and shoulders were instantly set ablaze with burning agony from the pressure.

Everything faded from her senses as she stared at her son, his arms reaching towards the sky as he cried. She knew it was hopeless.

"Please," Lia begged. "Please don't let him die!" Ignoring her, Thomas beckoned for his men to follow as he turned to leave.

"Listen for the wolves, love," he cackled as he walked away. "I expect you to tell me all about it in the morning!"

Her tears rained down as she fought against the ropes, shrieking with desperation. She could hear nothing but the sound of John's cries, and with each of his tiny wails she could just barely see the puff of vapor from his breath rise up in the light of the moon. Her body shuddered, and she felt the blood pulsing in her head as she strained to break free.

The hours passed, and Lia felt her eyes grow heavy with exhaustion. Her efforts to free herself had been useless and her strength was spent, but she did her best to persist, struggling weakly every few minutes. The rope had cut into her wrists, and blood dripped from her raw skin, running down her arms and congealing in thick, sticky streaks.

She had been afraid that her son's cries would draw the attention of the wolves, but when the baby fell silent, she became worried that the cold had already taken him. She didn't want to call out and prompt him to start crying again, but as the moments ticked by she couldn't bear it any longer.

"John?" she rasped, her mouth dry. Clearing her throat, she tried again, her voice hoarse and quiet. "Baby, are you all right?" She was comforted immediately by his waving arms as he reached towards the clear, star-filled sky, but the reassurance meant nothing at the thought of what was coming when the wolves would arrive.

The pain in her body had given way to tingling, then total numbness, and she felt lightheaded and faint as another hour passed. Through her daze, Lia heard a hollow, lonely howl rise over the trees, and the cold fear that the sound elicited jolted her back to her senses, instantly renewing her fight.

Too afraid to make a sound, she struggled silently, jerking and pulling as she twisted against the ropes, hoping they would give and let her fall to the ground. Her eyes frantically searched the dark for any sign of the wolves' approach, and she fought to keep from screaming from both the pain and the terror that gripped her.

Her body violently swung back and forth as she kicked and fought; then, stars filled her vision in a sudden burst of sickening light as she slammed against the tree. A loud pop filled her ears, and blinding, excruciating pain shattered her being as she let out a shriek of agony. She knew that her arms had been wrenched from their sockets. Her body twitched and convulsed as she swayed on the rope, each movement sending another wave of horrible, tearing pain through her.

The sound of the wolves drew closer, and Lia couldn't force her eyes to focus anymore.

"Baby," she moaned, her eyes rolling back into her head as she tried to soothe her child. He had been startled by her scream, and now his cries pierced the night, mingling with those of the wolves. "It's okay, love, don't cry!" Her heart burned with sorrow; she knew she was lying, and she couldn't stand the sound of her words. It wouldn't be okay, and within moments her child would be ripped apart under the ravenous teeth of the dogs. The howls came again, even closer this time, and, unable to bear the thought of what was coming, she finally succumbed to the nothingness.

"Cut her down!" a muddy voice rang out. Lia could hear the sound of the men moving around below her, and she tried to open her eyes. She felt herself drop, and she landed on the ground in a heap, crying out in pain.

She rolled onto her side, blankly gazing out into the field where her baby had once been. The bright, morning sunlight revealed nothing, and there was no sign of the violence she was sure had taken place. From what she could see, not even a single scrap of the linens John's tiny body had been wrapped in remained.

"Did you watch as the dogs lapped his blood from the ground?" Thomas laughed, standing over her. She didn't move.

He stepped a safe distance away and motioned to one of his men. The man braced his foot against her ribs, and, taking hold of her arms one at a time, he gave them a quick yank. Lia cried out again, feeling her arms move back into place, but she didn't make another sound.

She was pulled to her feet, only to lifelessly fall back to the ground.

"Carry her," Thomas commanded, and Lia was picked up and thrown over the shoulder of one of the men. She stared at the place near the woods where her son had spent his final moments until it moved out of view, then she closed her eyes against the brokenness of her heart.

"Baby," she whispered. "Sweet, little John."

She was carried back to the camp, where she was again deposited in the cage. She dragged herself upright, sitting as she leaned against one of the walls for support. Her breasts were full, ready for her son to nurse, and her eyes vacantly stared off into space as she felt the cold, bare place on her chest where John's warmth had always rested. She could hear her son's tiny screams in her mind, and she felt guilty for not, at the very least, witnessing his final demise. She had abandoned him.

Thomas was standing near the horses, talking with his men as they packed up camp and prepared to leave. Their voices drifted towards her, and something she heard caught her attention.

"She's practically dead," one of the men said, addressing Thomas as he nodded towards Lia. "She's got no fight left in her, that's for sure."

"For now," Thomas answered, his voice full of gleeful pride. "But give her a few days, and I'm sure she'll perk right back up. She'll be ready for me when I get her back to my estate." Lia's blood ran cold in her veins at his words.

Thomas thought he had conquered her, and now he was bragging of a victory won through the blood he had spilled. She clenched her teeth as a cold, calculated rage washed over her, warming her bones with its venom while at the same time freezing her heart with the resolve it gave her. The bastard wasn't going to win. No matter what.

Lia extinguished the fire that had begun to burn in her eyes, forcing herself to relax as Thomas walked towards her.

"Did he scream?" he taunted her, curling his lip with contempt. "Did your son cry for you?" He watched her, expecting a reaction of some sort, but she didn't even blink at his words. He cursed with dismay at her unresponsiveness, kicking the cage in frustration. The wood flexed and cracked under the force of his blow, but he didn't notice, spinning around and storming off.

Lia slowly shifted her gaze, looking at the part of the cage Thomas had kicked. The piece of wood he had struck was thin, only the diameter of her thumb, and it was now splintered in the middle. Her heart began to pound.

Her hand flashed out and she grabbed the splintered wood, giving it a quick pull. There was a quiet snap, and a moment later it was as though nothing had happened save for the sharp skewer that was now hidden under her skirts. Now all she needed was one tiny opportunity.

She didn't have to wait long.

The men spent the morning packing up camp and readying to leave, hurriedly gathering their things while Thomas barked out orders.

"Where's Henry and Nathan?" Lia heard Thomas shout, cursing. None of the men seemed to know, and one of them offered to go look for the two missing men.

"You have a half-hour!" Thomas agreed, cursing again. "If you've not found them by then, we leave without them!" The man obeyed, quickly disappearing into the woods.

"Get this packed up!" Thomas commanded, pointing at his tent. "Be quick about it!" He strode towards the horses and picked up his saddle, preparing to heft it onto the back of his mount.

A loud crashing sounded in the woods, and Lia stole a glance towards the trees. The man who had gone in search of Henry and Nathan burst back into camp, running as fast as his legs could carry him.

"Lord Tierney!" the man screamed, his eyes wide with fear. "He's coming this way!" Lia looked over at Thomas, and she watched his face turn white.

"Where?" Thomas screeched, his voice cracking with terror as he dropped the saddle.

"Little more than a mile!" the wide-eyed man bellowed. "I saw them from the ridge! They're on horseback!" He didn't need to say anything more, and the campsite erupted into panicked chaos as the men abandoned their things and rushed to finish saddling their horses.

"Get her!" Thomas shrieked, pointing at Lia, and she felt her body begin to tingle and ache with anticipation. One of the men tore open the cage.

"Let's go!" he commanded, gesturing, but she ignored him, remaining lifeless and limp on the ground. He turned to Thomas.

"She won't move!" he cried.

"Then pull her out!" Thomas screamed, giving him a furious glare, and the man reached in to drag Lia out of the cage. He began to carry her towards the horses, then he realized that the horse she would be riding had not yet been saddled. He dropped her on the ground in a heap, running forward to ready the chestnut mare, and she gave a quick look around.

No one was watching her; all of the men were completely absorbed in the rushed departure. Her eyes locked on Thomas' wildly-gesturing form, his back towards her as he shouted orders at his men, and she slowly stood to her feet.

Time seemed to stand still as she silently stepped forward, and her ears grew deaf to the frenzied pandemonium surrounding her. The day was chilly, but the goosebumps on her skin weren't from the cold, and a slight shiver of excitement raced up her spine. A shower of golden, autumn leaves rained down on her as she walked, the wind blowing the orange and red foliage in swirling gusts across her path. She was only a few steps away, and she could almost taste the pain he would feel.

As if dreaming, Lia watched her left hand reach out to touch Thomas' shoulder, her makeshift spear clutched tightly in her other fist. He felt her touch, and he spun around to angrily confront the person who had the gall to lay a finger on him. His face went pale when he saw her, and she could see a different kind of fear in his single, emerald-green eye.

Lia's face began to turn scarlet with wrath, and her eyes burned. She drew her hand back, feeling her muscles tense, then, with a furious roar, she plunged the wooden rod deep into his abdomen.

The sickening crunch of grating bone filled the air, and Thomas staggered back, staring down at his belly in bewildered shock. He gingerly touched the thin shaft protruding from just beneath his ribcage, then he looked up, dazed.

"BASTARD!" Lia roared, launching herself at him and tackling him to the ground.

"Help!" Thomas gasped, fighting her off. "Help me!" The other men took notice of her, and they froze, watching her straddle Thomas' body.

"Let's go!" someone shouted, jolting the men from their shock. "The bastard's as good as dead!" They leaped onto their horses, and Lia could feel the earth rumble underneath her as they raced off.

Thomas managed to struggle out from under her, and he clawed at the dirt, trying to get away. She stood, baring her teeth as she slowly stepped towards him.

"You killed my parents."

A breadknife lay on the ground, its silver blade glinting brightly in the golden rays of the afternoon sun, and Lia bent down to pick it up.

"You killed my son."

Thomas whimpered, the bandages that had been wrapped around his head and neck falling loose and trailing behind him as he crawled.

"Stop, Lia!" he cried. "Please, don't do this!" She sneered incredulously, leaping forward and pouncing on him. He screamed, but he was too weak to push her away.

"Beg, Thomas," she whispered, her knees pinning his flailing arms to the ground. "Beg me! Beg this worthless peasant for mercy!"

"Anything, Lia, anything!" he wailed.

"Anything?" she mocked, resting the blunt tip of the knife against his throat. She leaned down, her lips brushing against his chewed ear. "Give me back my son."

Lia stabbed him, burying the knife deep into his chest. He howled with pain, and she stabbed him again, and again, her throat burning with the force of her screams.

His cries had stopped, choked off by the blood filling his throat. Lia stared down at him, silently watching as his life gurgled out from between his lips. Red bubbles poured over his tongue to spill onto his chin, frothing and settling into the creased skin of his throat, overflowing and staining the front of his white, linen shirt.

His eyepatch had been knocked askew, and she could see the withered, loose skin of his eyelid covering the void where his left eye had once been.

Lia saw the light begin to fade from his eye, and a vile taste filled her mouth at the thought that his suffering was almost over. She held her breath, watching him with unblinking eyes, then she felt the sticky handle of the knife in her clenched fist. He would not have the privilege of dying from his wounds on his own.

Thomas could still see her, and his eye grew wide with horror as he watched her raise the knife above her head. His mouth moved in frantic soundlessness in an effort to speak, and Lia hoped he was trying to beg for his life. With a cry, she plunged the knife down into the center of his eye with all her strength, feeling the soft tissue give easily as the blade passed into his skull.

His body jerked and twitched beneath her, and she could feel every moment of his final throes of death. His muscles relaxed, and a rasping hiss rose from his throat as the last of the breath was expelled from his lungs. Overcome with disgust, she stood to her feet and stomped on his face, driving the knife deeper through his head until the handle disappeared into the oozing, broken membrane that had once been his right eye.

Finally satisfied that he was dead, Lia collapsed to the ground and began to weep. She had killed the bastard; she had avenged her parents and her son, but nothing would bring them back. She wished she could revive Thomas' dead body and kill him again, prolonging his suffering until the end of time.

As she sobbed, she heard the sound of thundering hooves, and she glanced up with bloodshot eyes to see a black horse appear before her. Its tall, heavyset rider was followed by a dozen more men, but Lia was too exhausted and heartbroken to care.

"Is that him?" a gruff, strong voice called. The man dismounted his onyx steed, marching to Thomas' body and kneeling beside it. "It's him!" he shouted, his eyes full of delight as he turned his attention to Lia.

He reached out, lifting her chin and meeting her mournful gaze.

"Did you do this, girl?" he asked gently, awe creasing his forehead. She nodded absently, and the man cradled her cheek, his mouth dropping open with shock. "Amazing," he breathed in disbelief. As Lia stared into his kind, brown eyes, she felt her mind begin to shut down, and everything went black as she fainted.

• • •

Chapter Thirty-Seven

WHEN LIA CAME TO, she was lying on her bed inside her room. There was a man sitting in the chair beside her, and he jumped to his feet when he saw her stir.

"I'm Lord Tierney's servant," he told her quickly, tucking the blanket in tightly around her. "He'll be back tomorrow morning, and he's left me to keep watch. Just rest, you're safe now."

Lia didn't hear the man; his words were murky and distorted in her deafened ears. Her mind was plagued with the image of baby John's sweet face, and her sore, swollen breasts reminded her again of her empty arms. She began to weep, and her sorrow and misery, coupled with her exhaustion, took her down into a fitful, tormented sleep.

Lia awoke at dawn, her pillow soaked with the tears she had cried while sleeping. Now, her eyes were dry, and she felt as though her body would never again have the strength to move. The man who had kept watch over her was still awake, his eyes red-rimmed with fatigue from his vigilance throughout the night, and he paced the floor quietly, trying to keep himself alert.

"I'll make you breakfast," he volunteered quickly, noticing her blinking eyes. "I'll be right back." Lia let him go, unable to speak to tell him that she didn't want food. She wanted nothing except to die.

A few moments after he left, she heard the front door of the house burst open, and pounding footsteps sounded in the hall. Lia didn't move, uninterested, and even the sound of a crowd entering her bedroom didn't faze her.

But in the midst of her paralyzing numbness, a tiny sound ripped through her mind, and her heart stopped in her chest as she squeezed her eyes shut. Someone stepped towards her bed, and she felt something lightly settle onto the mattress beside her.

Lia froze, certain that she was trapped in a horrible nightmare, a haunting dream whose purpose was only to torture her. Her face was creased with agony, refusing to entertain the hope surging through her being, but when she felt the soft, gentle touch she couldn't contain herself any longer.

"He's hungry, love," Mark whispered, stroking her face. Fearfully, Lia opened her eyes, and before her lay her son, his little hands waving and reaching towards her as his mouth opened to cry.

She took her child into her arms, and her body was wracked with gut-wrenching wails. The bed shook violently from the power of her cries, and John began to scream with her, suddenly afraid. Lia didn't care, unable to stop the flood of relief and confusion that poured from within her, and she didn't notice when her room emptied, leaving her alone with her baby.

He nuzzled at her hungrily, and Lia couldn't tear her eyes away from his beautiful face. He was fine; there wasn't a thing wrong with him, and her mind almost couldn't grasp that he was real much less question how he could have survived the wolves. She would wake up in a moment, she was sure, and her arms would be empty again. But as the hours passed, and she kissed and held her child, she realized that she wasn't dreaming. He was really there, he was really alive.

Lia slept all day, the sudden peace of John's presence revealing the depth of her exhaustion. No one disturbed her until dinnertime that night, when Ben knocked on her door, quietly entering. He carried a tray of food, and he tiptoed across the room towards her bed.

"Are you awake?" he whispered, and Lia nodded. Smiling, Ben set the tray down and stepped to her side, sitting on the bed next to her.

"How?" she managed to gasp, her thoughts impossible to sort through. "I saw him...the wolves...how?" He grimaced, reaching over to brush a wayward strand of hair out of her eyes.

"One of the horses threw a shoe," Ben began, his voice hushed. "We were late getting home. But just a few miles outside of town, two of Thomas' men found us. One of them was carrying the baby, running as fast as he could." He shuddered, his eyes growing distant as he remembered. "They're lucky Mark didn't kill them! They told us what had happened, that Thomas had left the baby to the wolves, and that you were strung up from a tree less than a mile from the road. Mark wanted to go after you," Ben told her regretfully. "But we knew Thomas wouldn't kill you, and we had to get the baby out of there."

"Who were they?" Lia whispered. "Which men?"

"Two brothers," Ben answered. "Nathan, and the one carrying John was named Henry. He said that Thomas had caused his own child's death, and he couldn't abide seeing it happen again."

"Where is he?" she asked, her mind reeling.

"He's gone," Ben told her. "He said that he and his brother needed to get back home." Lia frowned, disappointed that she wouldn't have the chance to thank him. She remembered what he had told her about his family starving without the money Thomas had promised, and her eyes snapped forward.

"The reward!" she exclaimed suddenly. "Don't I get a reward for killing Thomas? They can't be too far, can someone ride after them? I want them to have it!"

"Just calm down," Ben told her. "Mark thought you would, and he already gave it to them." She relaxed, happy that Mark had known what she would want, then she gestured for Ben to continue.

"We raced to Lord Tierney's and told him what had happened. I swear, I've never ridden faster in my life!" His face glowed as he spoke, and Lia smiled at his excitement. "Lord Tierney set out before we even finished speaking, and we stayed at his estate until he came back to tell us it was done. And this little one," Ben sang proudly, resting his hand on John's cheek. "While Mark and I paced up and down, sick with worry, he was busy romancing the Tierney women!" Lia gazed at her son's sleeping face, then Ben let out a stifled shout.

"You did it, Lia!" he quietly exclaimed, his voice crackling with uncontainable glee as he reached out and gripped her face in his hands. "The bastard's dead and rotting, and you did it without a bit of help!" His smiling face grew soft with sadness, and he stared into her eyes. "Your parents would be proud, rest their souls," he whispered, leaning over and kissing her forehead. "None of us expected any less from you." Lia's eyes stung, and she took a quivering breath. Thomas was dead, nothing more than a bad memory.

"Mark's with Lord Tierney," Ben informed her. "He told me to tell you that he's seeing to Thomas' final end. He said something about wanting to tell you for sure that the bastard's dead." Lia's eyes brightened and she giggled, remembering her fears about the man in the alley coming back for her. Mark wouldn't have had to stay and watch Lord Tierney dispose of Thomas' body for her sake; she had felt the breath leave his filthy corpse, and there was no doubt in her mind that he was dead.

"When will he be back?" she asked. Ben shrugged.

"Sometime tomorrow, I think," he told her, standing to his feet. "Or the next morning. But enough about that," he said quickly, reaching for her hand to help her out of bed. He gestured to the plate of food he had brought her. "You need to eat."

Mark didn't return the next day, and as evening fell, and after putting John down for the night, Lia went outside to sit on the porch. Ben was dozing on a rocking chair in the living room, and she was alone with her thoughts.

She moved onto the grass in the front yard and leaned back to stare up at the clear, night sky. The twinkling stars framed the full moon with their silvery light, and the trees and grasses around her rustled as the breeze gently moved them. The icy smell of snow lingered on her skin and in her hair, the promise of the cold nights to come, and if she closed her eyes, she could almost pretend that she was lying beside the creek back home without a care in the world.

Lia sat up and gazed out at the field just a short distance away, her heart aching with longing. She didn't miss Brunbury, but she did miss the memories she had of her childhood there. It hurt to think that she would never see her home again, nor would she spend her nights listening to the familiar trickle of her creek sing her to sleep. She thought of her mother, and tears stung her eyes.

So little time had passed since that night in the alley, barely more than a year, yet it seemed like a lifetime ago. The strong, fearless girl she used to be was gone, replaced by an emptiness inside of her where that girl's shadow had once lived. That girl was dead now, nothing but a memory.

Dead, just like her mother and father and Belle. Just like Thomas and the man who had taken her in the alley. A hot flash of anger coursed through her, and she clenched her teeth, cursing under her breath.

Thomas.

Lia smiled mockingly. The bastard had thought she was nothing but a weak little girl, but she had ended him.

A sudden realization dawned on her, and her heart skipped a beat.

She had proven him wrong. She had survived. Despite everything she had been through during the past year, she had survived. Her strength had been proven in the midst of all she had suffered, and any weakness she may have had belonged to who she had once been, not the person she now was. There were horrors in the dark, but she had faced them all and prevailed. There was nothing to be afraid of anymore.

"No more fear, Lia," she said firmly, speaking aloud to the sleeping birds that rested in the branches of the trees above her. She stood to her feet, determination burning in her eyes.

Purposefully, she stepped out into the night and began to make her way towards the nearby field. For a moment, she felt her heart falter, suddenly aware of each and every sound and shadow that lay hidden beyond the reach of the shining moonlight. Throwing her shoulders back, she set her jaw.

"No, Lia," she reminded herself, steeling her nerves with each step she took.

She reached the center of the field, her stark silhouette floating in the midst of the waist-high, autumn grasses surrounding her. The cool, blue light of the night sky bathed her in its pristine glow, and she closed her eyes.

Reaching her hands out, she began to move, slowly spinning as her fingers brushed against the tips of the grasses, the cool breeze running its fingers through her hair as she slowly danced.

"Lia?"

She opened her eyes to see Mark's shadowed figure approaching her, and she smiled to herself. Of course. She could never escape him, no matter where she went.

Turning, Lia put her hands on her hips, feigning dismay as she scowled at him.

"Is there nowhere I can go to be rid of you?" she huffed, fighting a giggle as she remembered her reaction the last time Mark had found her in the fields. She had been angry and upset back then, but now she was glad to see him. Confusion and disappointment filled Mark's face.

"I suppose you're going to tell me to leave now, aren't you?" he asked quietly. His voice was mournful, and Lia's heart began to race, instantly worried that she had hurt his feelings.

"No, Mark!" she exclaimed, quickly shaking her head. "Of course not! I wasn't serious, I was just...remembering." He gave her a puzzled look, but she shrugged off his questioning gaze and beckoned for him to come closer. "I don't want you to go, Mark, I promise."

Lia sat down on the grass, patting the ground beside her.

"I didn't expect to see you out here," Mark said as he sat down next to her. "I thought you were afraid to be out in the dark like this."

"I was," Lia replied, sighing. "But I thought I'd try to work on that." She eyed Mark, studying him out of the corner of her eye.

He was relaxed as he leaned back to stare at the sky, but his countenance held a strength that she had never noticed before. She found herself mesmerized by the sight of him, and, for the first time, she couldn't help noticing just how handsome he was.

Mark glanced at her, catching her staring at him.

"What?" he asked, smiling as she quickly looked away. She could feel her face grow hot with embarrassment as a thrill of nervous excitement raced up her spine.

"Nothing," Lia replied lightly, trying to appear disinterested. Mark reached out and took her hands in his, his fingers gently touching the scabbed wounds that had been cut into her wrists from the rope Thomas had tied her with. His face was pained, and he cursed under his breath.

"The bastard," he whispered, moving his hands to touch her swollen lips and bruised nose. "I'm glad he's finally dead." Lia smiled at him.

"I haven't thanked you yet," she said, changing the subject.

"Why would you have to thank me?" Mark asked, giving her a sideways glance. There were hundreds of reasons she could give him, but she couldn't seem to put them into words.

"Because of everything you've done," Lia finally answered, her voice cracking. "You've done so much for me, and I can't ever hope to repay you." Mark laughed.

"You don't need to thank me or repay me for anything, Lia," he told her. "I'm glad I can be there for you." The honest sincerity with which he spoke struck her deeply, and she looked away.

"Mark," Lia whispered, staring down at her hands. "Why on earth do you love me?" He was surprised by her question.

"You already know," he answered after a long moment. "I told the story at the midwife's house, remember?" She shook her head, unwilling to meet his questioning gaze.

"But that was why you fell in love with me," she said quietly. "Not why you kept loving me."

"I told you that, too," Mark reminded her. "That day in the fields, when you called me crazy and tried stabbing me." He forced a grin, then shrugged. "It doesn't matter, Lia," he said, trying to dismiss her question as he shifted uncomfortably. She glanced up at him, and she could see the anguish in his eyes.

"I don't understand, Mark," she told him, searching his face. "You said you loved me because I threatened you. I treated you as though you were nothing, I hated you, but you love me?" Mark swallowed hard. There was a moment of silence, then he reached into his pocket. He withdrew his hand, and Lia could see a small, silvery object clutched between his fingers.

"What's that?" she asked, pointing. He stared at the object a moment.

"Do you remember it?" Mark asked quietly, reaching out to drop it into her waiting palm. She gazed at the little trinket, squinting at the shape in the moonlight, then her eyes widened with recognition. She *did* remember it.

It was a small butterfly, the very first gift Mark had ever left for her on her windowsill. She had been enraged, upset at the thought that he had been lurking outside her bedroom, and she had tried to destroy it. Taking it into the barn, she had hammered at it, smashing and chipping the little wings in her fury. When she discovered that she couldn't break it apart, she had angrily tossed it into the ditch on her way to work, thus beginning her morning tradition and the demise of all the gifts Mark left for her.

"I threw this away!" Lia exclaimed, running her fingers over the dented wings in amazement. "How did you get it?" Mark chuckled.

"I was excited that morning," he told her, his eyes distant as he remembered. "I wanted to see your face when you found it on your windowsill." He shook his head ruefully. "I wasn't sure how you'd react, but I didn't think you'd throw it away." Laughing at himself mockingly, he smiled. "Somehow I got the idea in my head that if I kept leaving them for you, one day you'd start keeping them. I've never been more wrong." He glanced up at her, his eyes full of longing.

"You knew all along?" she asked, again gazing down at the little butterfly. "You knew I threw them all away?" Mark nodded.

"And I fished every single one of them out of that ditch," he told her, almost as if he didn't believe it himself. "I had a whole box of them at the shop back home."

"But you kept making them!" she gasped in disbelief.

"Yes, I did," he answered. "I don't really know why. Maybe I hoped that you would like one of them enough to keep it, that you would see all the work I put into them…that you would…I don't know." He sighed, unable to think of anything else to say, then he shook his head.

"Look at it, Lia," he continued, gesturing towards the trinket. "It's beautiful, and after I left Brunbury I couldn't make enough of them to keep up with the demands of those who wanted to buy them. Almost an entire year, hundreds of these little things, yet you were too stubborn to keep even a single one just because *I* made them. Even when the other girls at home went on and on about how much they liked them, you refused to change your mind." Mark's voice grew husky, and his eyes bored holes into hers as he tried to make her understand.

"Maybe I *am* crazy," he muttered, more to himself than to her. "But I love you for that. I love you for not letting anyone else decide what you think or who you are." He gave her a half-smile. "Even when your decisions are just plain stupid," he added, cringing as if expecting her to hit him. "I love you for all of you, not just the parts that I like. If I didn't, I don't suppose I'd be worth much."

"But I still don't understand, Mark," Lia breathed, her eyes filling with tears. "I was terrible towards you."

"I don't think I really understand it, either," he admitted, pulling at the grass with his hands. "All I know is that you took my heart, and you've had it ever since."

A strange, unfamiliar feeling crept into Lia's heart, bursting in her chest and leaving in its path a burning fire that ebbed into her soul. In that moment, she understood exactly what she felt, and the name of what was rising up within her stole her breath away.

"Do you remember when you wanted to know why I didn't love you?" Lia asked, her words sticky and dry with nervousness.

"Yes," Mark answered, giving her a strange look.

"I know why I couldn't give you a reason," she told him. "It's because there is no reason, except for how blind and stubborn and foolish I've been. I was too stupid to realize how much you mean to me." She reached out and gently brushed her fingers against his cheek. "You're the reason I'm still here, Mark. All the strength I have is because you've been by my side. Even when we weren't together, I carried you with me in my heart, and you gave me courage when I needed it most. You believed in me even when I didn't, and you never gave up on me."

Mark was silent, searching her eyes. Her body flushed with heat, and she felt herself begin to suffocate and drown in his slate-blue gaze. She could taste the words on her tongue, and a thousand butterflies took flight in her belly as she tried to draw a breath.

"I love you, Mark."

He froze, and Lia could almost feel his heart stop. He acted as though he wanted to look away, but she took his face in her hands.

She pressed her lips to his, feeling his body tremble as she kissed him. His arms moved to encircle her, his touch gentle, then his grasp tightened as though he were trying to pull her very being into his. Tears began to pour down his face, and Lia's heart ached with regret and longing.

"I've waited so long to hear you say that," he managed to whisper, his voice shaking. "I'm almost afraid to believe it." She lifted her hand and touched his face, gazing into his eyes.

"You have my heart, Mark," she breathed. "It was always yours, even when I refused to see it." He held her close and kissed her again, and her chest swelled with sudden, overwhelming happiness. She began to giggle, then she stood to her feet as Mark sniffled and wiped his eyes.

"Come here," she said, a smile playing on her lips. She reached for Mark's hands.

"What are you doing?" he asked, amused and bewildered as he stood. Lia stepped forward and placed her hands on his shoulders.

"You've waited long enough, Mark."

She began to sway, and Mark smiled as he wrapped her in his arms and moved with her.

They danced together, there in the fields beneath the autumn moonlight, and Lia closed her eyes as she rested her head against his chest, listening to his heartbeat.

She savored the warmth of his skin and the peace she felt in his arms, and she knew she was going to stay there forever.

THE END

Please Leave a Review!

Thank you for taking the time to read this book, I hope you enjoyed it! This is my first published work, and I would sincerely appreciate a review from you.

To review this title on Amazon.com, go to the book listing, click "Reviews", then click "Write a Customer Review".

To review on Goodreads, please visit Goodreads.com and search "August Shadow".

To review on Facebook, please visit my page:

@CHRISTINAJTHOMPSON.CJT.

I would love to hear from you! You can contact me via my Facebook page or by email at:

CHRISTINAJTHOMPSON@YAHOO.COM.

AUTHOR'S NOTE

Before delving into what will comprise this "Author's Note", I must first warn the reader that there are spoilers to come. So, if the reader has not yet finished the story, and would prefer to discover certain plot details throughout the course of actually reading the story itself, please do not read any further. Otherwise, consider yourself duly warned, and read on as I address a few things I felt needed further clarification.

While writing *August Shadow*, a concern of mine was that the reader may seek to place the setting in an actual, real-life time period or location. This attempt would be futile, however, as the setting is entirely fictional. Although there may be some unintentional similarities between the world Lia Grey lives in and the history of the real world, the truth of the matter is that I had no interest in the extensive research it would have required to choose a historically-accurate setting. Call it laziness, if you will, but I prefer to believe that doing such research would have stunted my creativity and detracted from the story.

As an avid reader, there is nothing more frustrating to me than when a book ends sooner than I expect it to. After finally reaching that last sentence, I can't help hoping that there will be an epilogue, a few more words that continue the story and prevent it from ending sooner than I believe it should. I sincerely hope that my book is involving enough to elicit such a similar response in my readers, and, just in case it has, I would like to take a moment to explain why I am guilty of the same thing I've hated other writers for.

I began writing an epilogue many times, only to realize, after several attempted drafts, that it just wasn't flowing. It didn't seem right. Perhaps, if I choose to continue the story with a sequel, the portions I tried to put into an epilogue will find their way into the beginning of a new work. Until then, and as a final detail, please rest assured that Lia and Mark do get married, and that their love is lasting.

Although I didn't write this story to make a statement regarding the abuse and sexual mistreatment of women, I feel that any work that touches on such abuse must, in some way, serve as one. The ordeals that Lia experiences throughout the story DO have a real-world comparison: even in this day and age, women are mistreated and vilified while perpetrators of violence – especially sexual violence – are ignored. Although Lia's experiences may seem unbelievable to some, the fact is that they are not. Her story is fictional, but the abuse, ostracization, and suffering she endures are very real to many women. I would like to believe that my story may help to open even a few minds to how wrong it is to judge people and, more importantly, how doing so may ultimately negatively affect them.

I truly hope that my readers have enjoyed *August Shadow*, and that it has been a memorable story. It is here, in these last few words, that I would like to offer thanks to those who have taken the time to read this work. Until now, I didn't fully understand why many authors choose to thank their readers above everyone else, but I can now say that I echo that sentiment. Without readers, a story, no matter how great, is nothing; just like almost everything else in this world, sharing with other people is the true meaning of fulfillment. I sincerely appreciate the opportunity to share this work – from the bottom of my heart: thank you for allowing me the honor of doing so.

55805698R00250

Made in the USA
Columbia, SC
20 April 2019